Down below, she caught a flash of movement. Her attackers were catching up.

"Where are you taking me?"

"Someplace safe where we can call for help. Trust me, I know this part of the forest."

What choice did she have? She'd prayed for God to send help and He had. Of all the people in the world, He'd sent Bryan.

"Come on." He held his hand out to her. The August sun beat down on them, the air thick with heat. Down below, the two thugs were weaving their way up the mountain.

"Where are we going anyway?"

"We need to get help, call the sheriff," he said.

She stared up at the rocky terrain. "Isn't there an easier way?"

"Sarah, would you trust me? I know where I'm going. Those guys won't be able to follow us. They'll give up."

It was the first time he'd said her name. The warmth in his voice only reminded her of ten-year-old wounds. "I really don't have a choice here. I'll do what you say." She wasn't so sure about the men giving up, though.

MONTANA MOUNTAIN DEADLOCK

SHARON DUNN

USA TODAY BESTSELLING AUTHOR

Previously published as *Montana Standoff* and *Big Sky Showdown*

LOVE INSPIRED
INSPIRATIONAL ROMANCE

LOVE INSPIRED®

INSPIRATIONAL ROMANCE

Recycling programs
for this product may
not exist in your area.

ISBN-13: 978-1-335-23088-1

Montana Mountain Deadlock

Copyright © 2020 by Harlequin Books S.A.

Montana Standoff
First published in 2013. This edition published in 2020.
Copyright © 2013 by Sharon Dunn

Big Sky Showdown
First published in 2017. This edition published in 2020.
Copyright © 2017 by Sharon Dunn

This edition published by arrangement with Harlequin Books S.A.

For questions and comments about the quality of this book,
please contact us at CustomerService@Harlequin.com.

Love Inspired
22 Adelaide St. West, 40th Floor
Toronto, Ontario M5H 4E3, Canada
www.Harlequin.com

Printed in U.S.A.

CONTENTS

Ever since she found the Nancy Drew books with the pink covers in her country school library, **Sharon Dunn** has loved mystery and suspense. Most of her books take place in Montana, where she lives with three nearly grown children and a hyper border collie. She lost her beloved husband of twenty-seven years to cancer in 2014. When she isn't writing, she loves to hike surrounded by God's beauty.

Books by Sharon Dunn

Love Inspired Suspense

Visit the Author Profile page at Harlequin.com for more titles.

MONTANA STANDOFF

For you know that it was not with the perishable things such as silver or gold that you were redeemed from the empty way of life handed down to you from your ancestors, but with the precious blood of Christ, a lamb without blemish or defect.
—*1 Peter* 1:18–19

I have set before you life and death, blessings and curses. Now choose life, so that you and your children may live and that you may love the Lord your God, listen to his voice, and hold fast to him.
—*Deuteronomy* 30:19–20

For my husband, Michael, whose encouragement and unconditional love have allowed me to grow both as a writer and as a daughter of the king. We are the evidence that where you came from does not determine where you're going.

ONE

Sarah Langston winced as the barrel of the gun jabbed her stomach. The knit cap, turned backward on her head, made it impossible to see. She could feel the motion of the SUV, but she had no idea where her captors were taking her. Fear permeated every cell of her body.

The man with the gun leaned close and whispered in her ear. "Tell you what. We'll give you one more chance. You let us know where your brother is and we'll let you go."

He'd asked that question fifty times before. Always, her answer was the same. Why wouldn't they believe her?

Her voice trembled. "I told you. I don't know where Crew is. He's homeless. He contacts me when he wants to talk."

Her pulse drummed in her ears as her muscles tensed.

The second man, the driver, hadn't spoken for a long time. The tires made a different sound when they'd switched from paved roads to gravel. They'd left the city. Where were they going? What did they intend to do with her?

Both of them had been wearing masks when they'd grabbed her outside her home. They must have been waiting for the opportunity to catch her alone. More than once in the last day, she'd felt the invisible press of a gaze on her only to turn and see no one. Yesterday, she noticed the same Chevy Suburban parked outside the grocery store and at a friend's house. She'd dismissed it as coincidence.

In an attempt at escape, she'd managed to pull the mask off of one of the thugs, the skinny one with the bulging eyes. After that, they put the blindfold on her and drove without saying anything other than that same question, over and over again.

She could only guess at why they were looking for Crew. Her big brother was in and out of addiction, jobs and her life. Maybe he owed them money.

The sound of the tires rolling along changed. They were on a dirt road. Tension filled the silent car. Why were they driving so far out of town?

She knew then that the man had lied. They had no intention of letting her go.

The car rumbled to a stop but her thoughts continued racing. When she'd pulled the skinny one's mask off, he'd gone ballistic. The men had not wanted to be identified. They were taking her out of town to kill her, some place where her body wouldn't be found.

Sarah's mind moved at the speed of light. She had seconds to plan her escape. She'd been working to loosen the ties around her wrists.

Her car keys with the pepper spray attached were in her pocket. She coughed and turned her body slightly while she slipped her hand into her jacket pocket.

The man next to her jabbed her stomach with the gun. "Get out and don't try any funny business."

The front door opened. She heard footsteps and then the door closest to her squeaked open.

The driver spoke. "Come on, sweetheart."

Sarah scooted along the seat toward the open door. She tried to picture where the two men were. Judging from his voice, the driver had stepped away from her door.

The gun pressed against her back as she scooted along the seat. Her fingers wrapped around the pepper spray slowly, carefully pulling it out of her pocket. Then in one quick movement, she turned and pressed the release button.

The groaning told her she'd hit her target. She tore off the knit hat and leapt out of the car.

An arm suctioned around her waist, and a hand slapped over her mouth. Her keys flew out of her hand, but she wasn't done fighting. She'd just have to use a different weapon. She bit down hard on the man's hand and felt a rush of triumph when he yelped and pulled his hand away. She scratched fingernails across the arm that held her waist. He didn't let go.

She elbowed him in the stomach, a hard swift jab.

His grip on her let up enough for her to angle away from him. Heart racing with fear and urgency, she ran toward the trees. Branches, sky and undergrowth were all a blur in front of her. Her sharp, rasping breathing enveloped her. Feet pounding, jumping over logs, pushing through the trees.

Please, God, help me get away.

The men behind her shouted, breaking branches, charging toward her. Their noise growing louder, closer, pressing on her.

Sarah pushed forward, willing her feet to move

faster. Fighting off the terror that rose inside her, she stumbled into the clearing that bordered Bridger Lake. She only had a second to survey her surroundings before the men burst from the trees.

On instinct, she turned and ran toward the other part of the forest and the mountain beyond that. If she could make it up the mountain without being caught, maybe someone in the fire tower at the top of it could help her.

She prayed she'd make it that far.

From the high metal tower where he watched for forest fires, Bryan Keyes drew the binoculars up to his eyes and scanned the forest and the lake below. He studied the tree-covered mountains in the distance, searching for wisps of smoke. As dry as the summer had been, the tiniest fire could rage out of control within minutes. Anything out of the ordinary would draw his attention. In the few weeks that he had been here, he'd memorized every patch of trees, every cluster of rocks. The solitude and monotony of fire spotting was a far cry from his usual job as a police detective recently relocated to Discovery, Montana.

His stomach coiled into a tight knot. He didn't want to think about his work as a cop. He'd taken a leave of absence when doubt had crept in, and he'd started wondering if he could ever really make a difference. After months of work gathering the evidence that Tyler Mason was using his temp work agency for human trafficking and illegal labor, Mason had avoided going to trial.

Bryan stepped away from the windows that wrapped around the tower's octagonal structure. Even thinking about Tyler Mason put his nerves on edge. He wanted justice. Though he'd grown up in Discovery, Bryan had been a detective in Spokane for years. Tyler Mason lured unsuspecting immigrants and sentenced them to lives of hard labor and imprisonment all over the United States. When Bryan uncovered a slave labor factory in Spokane, his investigation led him to Tyler Mason who owned a home and a business in Discovery. In an effort to take down Mason, he'd requested a transfer five months ago.

But then a key witness had disappeared, and the case had fallen apart. And now, the department didn't want to expend any more time or manpower on what seemed like a battle they couldn't win.

Gritting his teeth, he studied the landscape. A dust cloud on the road below indicated that a vehicle was headed toward Bridger Lake. Unusual to see people out here, considering how high the fire danger was. The metal of the car glinted in the late afternoon sun.

Bryan drew the binoculars back up to his face, watching as a man got out of the driver's side and opened the back door. A moment later, a woman jumped out. Bryan's back stiffened. The man grabbed the woman from behind, but she twisted away, running into the forest. The driver and a second man chased after her.

Bryan's heart pounded as he scanned the area, trying to get a clear view of what was going on. At this distance, it was hard to tell, but nothing about the interaction seemed friendly.

Finally, he spotted all three of them in the clearing by the lake.

He watched the man push the woman forward. The binoculars shook as Bryan focused in on the action.

He was too far away to see clearly and the angle was all wrong, but it looked like the woman's hands were tied behind her back. He couldn't be sure.

He adjusted the focus hoping to see more. No luck. The woman's long brown hair hid her face as she trudged forward with her head down. Then just before the three of them disappeared into the trees, one of the men reached into the back of his waistband. Sunshine shone against the metal of the gun.

His breath hitched. They were going to shoot her.

Bryan dropped the binoculars as adrenaline surged through his body. The most direct route to the woman was straight down the nearly ninety-degree mountain, a hard five-to seven-minute run on rocky terrain to the lake where the armed men had parked. It was the only chance he had of getting there on time. Hiking out to his truck and then taking the circuitous route on logging roads would take an hour or more.

He regretted having turned in his police issue Glock, but the forest service provided a rifle in case of bear attacks. He grabbed it and bolted out the door and down the narrow metal stairs of the tower.

Holding the rifle with both hands, he scrambled down the mountainside. Rocks rolled in the wake of his hurried footsteps. No clear trail came into view. He'd grown up camping in these mountains and had developed pretty accurate radar for finding his way. He knew where the road connected to the lake, but would he get there in time?

As he ran, he listened for the crack of a gun being fired breaking through the thick August air. Silence surrounded him. Did that mean the woman was still alive?

He jumped over a boulder. The terrain became steeper, and he dug his heels in. His foot caught on a root and flung him forward. The rifle flew from his hands, clattering to a stop on a sheer cliff some twenty feet down. He could maneuver around the cliff, but there was no time to climb down and retrieve the rifle.

He forged ahead, praying that he'd be in time. He worked his way through the thick trees seeking an open path.

Bryan stopped, blood freezing in his veins when a gunshot shattered the serenity of the forest.

TWO

From the moment she'd pulled the mask off one of her abductors, Sarah had sensed that the hours of her life were numbered. Now as they dragged her deeper into the forest, she knew she was nearing the end. The men were not bothering with the masks anymore. Clear evidence that she wasn't coming out of this forest alive.

One of the men—the muscular one with the deep voice—pushed hard on her back. "Where is he?"

They still hadn't given up their line of questioning. Some sort of last-ditch effort to get the information they'd kidnapped her for in the first place. Their desperation and rage had escalated since her second escape attempt.

She spoke between gasps. "I...don't...know...where my brother is." Her wrists hurt from where the rope cut into her skin. This time they'd made sure her bindings were tight.

Deep Voice grabbed her hair, pulled her close and hissed in her ear. "You're his sister." He shoved her forward. "You should know."

Sarah stumbled from the force of the push. "He doesn't have a phone. He lives all over the place."

Though she and her brother had been raised in foster care together, their lives had gone in very different directions. The last time she'd seen Crew, he had not been in good shape. He was sober, but rail-thin and shaking, probably from withdrawal.

"He talks about you," said the second kidnapper, a skinny man with acne scars whose eyes were still red from his dose of pepper spray. His words made Sarah frown. How well did Crew know these men? How had he gotten mixed up with people who were so clearly dangerous?

"I'm telling you, I haven't seen him in a month, and I don't know how to get in touch with him."

"You're lying." Deep Voice grabbed her arm at the elbow and swung her around, which made the rope dig even deeper into her wrist. "Where have you hidden him?"

She lowered her head and angled away from the criminal. "I'm not hiding him. Why won't you believe me?"

"You've got thirty seconds to tell me." She heard the slide on a gun click back. Even under the threat of death, she couldn't tell them. Why wouldn't they believe her?

"Yeah, stop protecting him." Acne Scars grabbed her shoulder and pushed her to the ground. She landed on her knees.

"Twenty seconds," said Deep Voice.

The menacing tone in his voice told her that he would have no qualms about shooting her.

Sarah closed her eyes. *Oh, God, please take me quickly.*

"Ten seconds."

Her whole body shook and she tasted bile. "I don't know where he is." Her voice was barely above a whisper. "I'm telling you the truth."

Please, God, send help. I don't want to die.

"Ten. Nine."

"You got anything to say?" said Acne Scars.

She shook her head. A cry rose up in her throat. "No, I can't tell you where he is because I don't know." Her stomach somersaulted. She couldn't contain her anguish. "Please believe me."

"Six. Five. Four."

As she leaned forward, every muscle in her body tensed. Tears formed. "Please."

"Three. Two. One."

She lurched at the boom of the gunshot as her body went rigid. No pain came. She took in a ragged breath.

She heard Deep Voice's harsh laughter. "That was a warning shot." Cold hard metal touched her temple. "Next time, it's for real. Put the blindfold back on her so she can't see it coming."

The hood went back over her head. A cold hand touched the back of her neck. The low voice was seductive. "Where is Crew Langston? Did you put him on a bus, help him get out of town?"

She shook her head, unable to form the words. Her heart pounded. She couldn't stop shaking.

"All right, lady, this is it." The hard gun barrel pressed against her temple.

Braced for another gunshot, she startled when she heard a thwacking sound, like a hard object making contact with flesh. One of the men groaned, and the gun was no longer pressed against her head. Flesh smacked against flesh. Men grunted. A body hit the ground close to her. Sarah struggled to get to her feet. Strong hands wrapped around her upper arm, warming her skin.

"Let's get you out of here and to a safe place." The voice sounded vaguely familiar. A hand grazed her forehead, lifting the hood off.

Her rescuer's eyes grew wide with recognition as her breath caught. Bryan Keyes. The man she thought she'd never see again. The man who had broken her heart into a thousand pieces.

The larger of the two assailants, curled up on the ground, stirred.

"Come on, we've gotta move. I'll cut you loose as soon as I can." Bryan glanced around. He was probably looking for the gun or the best direction to run.

Acne Scars lay facedown, not moving. A log not too far from him must have been used to knock him out. But Deep Voice had started opening his eyes. They couldn't wait any longer—they needed to move.

Bryan must have reached the same conclusion because he shook his head and then pulled Sarah toward the trees. She ran, hindered by her hands still tied behind her back. Bryan held her arm to steady her.

He pulled her deeper into the trees until they came to a steep incline.

"No way can I climb that with my hands tied," she protested.

He glanced over his shoulder, pulled a pocketknife out of his worn jeans and cut the ropes that bound her wrists together.

"Better?" His fingers brushed over her wrist where the rope had dug in. Even after ten years, his touch had the power to make her heart flutter.

She stepped away. "Wait, what if we tried to get to the car they parked by the lake?" The shouts of Deep Voice barking orders to Acne Scars reached her ears.

"We'd run right into them." He scrambled partway up the rock and turned back, holding his hand out to her. She took his help. They climbed until they came to a steep rock face.

"I'll boost you up and then you can pull me up," he said.

Down below, she caught a flash of movement. Deep Voice was wearing a bright yellow shirt, easy to see amongst the evergreens. And easy to realize that he was catching up. "Where are you taking me?"

"Some place safe where we can call for help." He glanced down the mountain.

She hesitated.

"Trust me, I know this part of the forest," he said. "Come on, we can't stop." He laced his fingers together, indicating that she should put her foot in them.

What choice did she have? She'd prayed for God to send help and He had. Now it was up to her to make the most of it. Sarah put her foot in Bryan's hands. He pushed upward as she reached out for a handhold. God must have a sense of humor. Of all the people in the world, He'd sent Bryan. Ten years was a long time. She'd been a sophomore in high school and he a senior when they'd fallen in love. Or what passes for love in a sixteen-year-old's heart. She couldn't say now if she had loved him or had just been desperate to be loved. But at the time, it sure had felt real.

With Bryan pushing her up from below, she reached for a gnarled tree sprouting up close to the rock. She pulled herself up, gripping the tree with both hands.

Bryan gave her a final push. She turned and reached down for him.

"I think I can get a foothold." He grabbed her hand, their eyes meeting momentarily.

The love between them had shattered when she became pregnant. They had agreed that the best thing for their little girl was adoption. But Bryan had been so angry afterward, had blamed her as though the decision hadn't been made together.

Bryan strained to get up the cliff face. "Other hand," he groaned.

She held both his hands and pulled as he struggled to get some traction with his feet. The muscles in her arms strained. "Almost there."

She pulled with all her strength, dragging him to the flat top of the cliff face. She leaned back, breathless from the exertion. Bryan scrambled to his feet.

"Come on." He held his hand out to her. The August sun beat down on them, the air thick with heat. Down below, the two thugs were weaving their way up the mountain, choosing an easier but less direct path.

"Where are we going, anyway?" Sarah still hadn't caught her breath.

"We need to get help, call the sheriff," he said.

She stared up at the rocky terrain. "Isn't there an easier way?"

"Sarah, would you trust me? I work here—I know where I'm going. Those guys won't be able to follow us. They'll give up."

It was the first time he'd said her name. The warmth in his voice only reminded her of ten-year-old wounds. "I really don't have a choice here. I'll do what you say." She wasn't so sure about the men giving up, though.

They crawled over rocks and through thick brush. A branch flicked across her forehead. She kept moving despite the stinging pain and the warm ooze of blood. The fire tower came into sight. So, he was some kind of forest ranger? By the time he'd left town to go to college, he hadn't spoken to her in months.

He led her up the narrow metal stairs into the tower, then stepped over to a small stand that contained the radio. He keyed the radio explaining that he needed a replacement and then said something about notifying the sheriff. He gave a brief but accurate description of the two thugs and their car.

While he talked, Sarah wandered around the sparse room. A double burner for cooking rested on a counter. Canned goods and gallons of water were stacked against the wall. An instrument of some sort with a map was in the dead center of the circular room. There was a desk and a chair in one corner, a cot in another. She sat down on the chair. A stack of books rested by the bed. He must stay up here weeks at a time. Yet, the place was utterly impersonal. Why had Bryan chosen such a solitary life? What had happened in the ten years since she'd seen him?

Bryan signed off and placed the radio back on the hook. He turned to face her. Those same warm brown eyes looked out at her, though they were edged with crow's-feet and worry lines now, and there was a hint of weariness in his expression that hadn't been there ten years ago. They had both been so naive and full of hope back then.

"What now?" She leaned forward, resting her elbows on her knees.

He walked over to the windows, picked up the binoculars and peered down the mountain. "We catch our breath."

"We wait?" Fear returned, sending a shock through her system. Those men meant to kill her.

"The forest service will notify the sheriff's department. They'll get those guys."

The memory of the gun pressed against her temple returned. Her throat constricted and her heart raced. "Do you think it's a good idea to just sit here?"

"We're not just sitting here." He handed her the binoculars. "Look, they've already left. I figured they would give up."

She walked over to the windows and peered through the binoculars at the shimmering water below. No car. She focused on the road where she saw the light-colored SUV heading away from the lake. So he was right. "Can they drive up here?"

"It will take them over an hour. And if they don't know these roads, they'll never find us." His voice was filled with reassurance.

Sarah let out a breath, relaxing a little.

He leaned close to her and touched her forehead where the tree branch had cut the skin. "I've got something for that. Go sit down." He pointed toward the cot.

Sarah put the binoculars down and wandered to the cot. She tried to take in a deep breath. Those men had meant to kill her. Would they give up that easily? After grabbing the first-aid kit from a storage box, Bryan walked across the room and sat close to her. She could feel his body heat.

He handed her a piece of leather. "Tie your hair back, so it's out of the way."

She gathered her hair into a ponytail.

He pulled disinfectant out of the first-aid kit and touched the end of the tube lightly to her forehead. "It's going to be okay, but we should get moving. After I deal with this cut, we'll hike over to my truck."

She closed her eyes as he gently pressed the bandage against her forehead. Memories of his touch all those years ago awakened old feelings. The power of the attraction made her forget the pain of how everything had ended…for a moment.

"There's a little country store eight miles up the road. You can call for a friend to come and get you." He wadded up the packaging the bandage had come in. "By that time, the sheriff will catch those guys."

The warm feelings evaporated. So he meant to ditch her as quickly as he could, just like old times. He'd only been doing his duty. It was the kind of person he was. But now that his duty was finished, he wanted nothing more to do with her. "I suppose I should go to the police." She hoped her voice didn't give away the hurt she felt.

"Yeah, you'll want to report this." His voice was tainted with a bitterness she didn't understand. "But not to the city police. This happened in the county. You'll want to talk to the sheriff."

"But they grabbed me at my house…in town."

He rose to his feet and ran his fingers through his wavy brown hair. He spoke without turning back to look at her. "If you don't mind my asking, why were those guys trying to kill you? What did you do?"

His tone was disconcerting. Did he actually think she was mixed up with something illegal? It had been a sore spot with them when they dated. His parents had never thought she was good enough for their football star son. His lawyer mother and business-owner father viewed her as the girl from the wrong side of the tracks. By that time, Crew was already having problems, too.

It didn't matter that she had been a good student and never been in trouble. She didn't have the wrong pedigree. She had no pedigree.

She took a deep breath and idly picked up one of the books in his stack. "They were looking for Crew."

Bryan's face brightened. "How is Crew?"

"I wish I could tell you. He has a drug and alcohol habit. Sometimes he has a place to live, sometimes not." Now she was the one who sounded bitter. Crew, two years older than her, had been her protector when they were kids. But years of having to be an adult too soon had worn him down. He'd started out a petty thief and picked up a drug habit along the way.

Bryan stroked his chin. "I always liked Crew. I liked the way he looked out for you."

Sarah felt a stab to her heart. Crew had made bad choices; she knew that. But the image that burned in her mind of her brother was of him offering her his last morsel of bread when they'd run away from an abusive foster home and hidden in the forest. Her heart warmed toward Bryan that he could remember the most positive thing about Crew, the reason she still loved her brother.

"I keep hoping he'll turn things around." And she wouldn't give up that hope no matter how bad things looked.

Bryan stepped away from the window. "Sometimes people do, you know. Get their lives together." He rested his gaze on her long enough to make her feel self-conscious. His look could still send an electric charge through her.

Sarah glanced down at the book she had picked up. C. S. Lewis, one of her favorite authors. But what was Bryan doing with a book like this? He'd never been interested in books with faith messages when she'd known him. Maybe his comment about people getting their lives together had been as much about himself as her brother. She hoped so. She'd found faith at the home where she stayed while she was pregnant. She'd gotten her life back on track at Naomi's Place. Maybe somewhere along the road Bryan had had a similar transformation. She'd never stopped praying for him.

She put the book back on the stack. "We should get going."

"Yeah, it's a little bit of a hike to get to the truck." Bryan walked across the room. "Do you want a drink of water before we go?"

She rose to her feet and stared out the windows that provided a panoramic view of the forest. "My throat is dry." She still couldn't figure out why Bryan would choose such a lonely job. He'd always been so outgoing. "How long do you stay up here at a time?"

Bryan lifted one of the gallon containers of water to the desk and retrieved a cup. "Three weeks on and one week off."

She crossed her arms and stared down at the rocks and forest they had climbed through to get here. She saw a flash of yellow and then Deep Voice stepped free of the thick forest. His gaze traveled up toward the tower. Panic pulsed through her. "Bryan, I think we have a problem."

THREE

Adrenaline flooded through Bryan's body. The thug charged straight for them at a steady and intense pace. He was the bigger of the two men, muscular to an excess. The short, thin man must have taken off in the vehicle, maybe planning on taking the winding road that would eventually bring him to the other side of the fire-lookout tower in case his friend didn't make it up the mountainside. It was a rookie mistake for Bryan to assume they'd both left in the SUV. He'd been too distracted by Sarah to think straight—and he was paying for that now.

"What do we do?" The fear in Sarah's voice intensified.

His mind catapulted from one possibility to another. She was the prime target. He had to get her out of here.

Bryan flipped open the glass door that led to the catwalk, grabbed a length of rope and tied it off on the central post in the tower. "He'll come up the stairs. You slip off this side of the tower. Go due east, and you'll see a trail that leads to an open area. My truck is there."

"But what about you?"

The look in her eyes was wild. She was so afraid.

He longed to take her in his arms, but after all they had been through ten years ago, would she even accept his comfort? "I'll hold him off." He walked over to a box and pulled out a set of keys which he handed to her. "Go to town and get help. I'll be all right."

She shook her head. "We should stay together."

"Go, Sarah. I can handle this guy." He pushed her toward the door. They didn't have time for a discussion.

She grabbed the rope, stepped out on the catwalk and moved to the edge of the tower. Her gaze locked on to him, longing filling her eyes. He'd seen that look before. She'd been a strong, resourceful young woman when he'd met her. But there was a vulnerable side to Sarah that stayed hidden from most people.

He pressed his hands against her face, kissed her forehead. "Go. You'll be fine."

The look of fear and doubt remained as she shook her head.

"And I'll be okay, too," he added.

She nodded, though the worry lines in her forehead intensified. She slipped off the side of the tower and disappeared from view.

He raced over to the radio. Where was his replacement? Had the sheriff made it out to the road by the lake and stopped the thug in the car? He had to let the authorities know what was happening. Before he could reach anyone, he heard the sound of footsteps on the stairs.

The fire tower door had no lock. He could buy Sarah precious minutes by holding this guy off. He'd taken down him and his cohort once before. This time it was only one man.

The footsteps intensified, grew louder.

Bryan grabbed a steak knife. There was no closet, no place to hide and try to get the jump on the guy…or was there? He crawled out on the catwalk and pulled himself to the roof just as the door burst open.

He pressed flat against the roof, angling his head so he could see through the skylight. Maybe the assailant would look around, figure they hadn't come to the fire tower and leave. That would be the best case scenario. He'd be able to catch up with Sarah and make sure she got safely into town.

From this angle he could see the top of the man's head. There was a pistol in his hand. So, he had found the gun.

The thug surveyed the room. Then he noticed the open door where Sarah had escaped. Bryan cringed. In his haste, he'd forgotten to close it.

The assailant stomped through the open door that led to the catwalk. He studied the rope where Sarah had descended.

With his belly pressed against the roof, Bryan swung around, head facing downward on the slanted roof. Sarah should be emerging into an open section of the forest. If the thug looked in that direction, he would see her and know where she'd gone.

Bryan slid down the roof. The man looked up but had no time to brace himself before Bryan leapt on top of him, knocking him to the ground and breaking a section of the railing around the catwalk. Both men recovered and rose to their feet. Bryan was relieved to notice that the assailant had dropped his gun in the struggle. The narrow catwalk provided little room to maneuver. Bryan struck the man across the face, hoping to throw him off balance.

The man had a square jaw and eyes like slits. His lip curled back, revealing large teeth. He lunged toward Bryan. If he could get an upper hand, find a way to subdue him and restrain him, the sheriff could question him and find out why they were after Sarah's brother.

"Where is the Langston woman?" The man barreled toward him.

Bryan dodged, but slipped off the edge of the catwalk where the railing had broken free. He fell to the rocky ground below. It took him a moment to recover. When he looked up, he couldn't see the man.

On hands and knees he scrambled to the base of the tower. The overhang of the catwalk shielded him from view. He worked his way around the tower back to the stairs.

Grabbing a thick branch for a weapon, he crept up the stairs. The door was slightly ajar. Peeking around it, he was rewarded with a quick image of the thug staring at the floor. He was looking for the gun. Bryan watched until the man's back was turned. He pushed the door open and landed a blow across the man's shoulders.

The thug groaned in pain, turned and swung for Bryan. Bryan hit him a second time on the arm with the log before the man wrenched it free. The two men wrestled. The assailant was twice his size, but Bryan refused to back down. Slowing this man down was the only chance Sarah would have to escape. They exchanged blows, drawing nearer to the open door.

Bryan lifted his arm, hand curled into a fist, ready to land a hit. The solid surface beneath his feet evaporated. He tumbled backward down the stairs. Like being smacked over and over, he could feel the hits to his body on the way down. He stopped at the bottom, still conscious, but disoriented. The assailant hadn't come after him. He heard the sound of things being moved around inside the fire tower. He was still looking for the gun and probably assumed Bryan was unconscious or dead.

Bryan wasn't sure if he could move. Had he broken any bones? Every muscle felt like it had been cut or bruised. He sat up. Pain shot through his body. It hurt to breathe. He needed to hide. He couldn't fight in his current state. But no, he couldn't back down, either. The assailant wouldn't give up until he found out where Sarah was. Bryan tried to push himself to his feet.

The noise inside stopped. The thug came to the top of the stairs. He lifted the gun, taking aim. "Where is she?"

By force of will, Bryan scrambled to his feet. He stumbled toward the shelter of the trees. He was pretty beat up. He probably couldn't outrun the thug, but he could hide, maybe draw the man into chasing after him instead of Sarah. He stepped into the trees and onto the trail.

Sarah appeared. A look of shock flashed across her features when she saw him. He had bruises on his arms. She grabbed him. "I couldn't leave without you." She wrapped her arm around his waist. The first shot from the thug's gun pierced the air. "We'd better hurry."

As she held on to him, he could feel his strength returning. Nothing was broken. He may have bruised a rib. He was in shock and badly beat up, but not to the point where he couldn't move quickly. They ran along the trail. A second shot broke off a tree branch in front of them.

They came to the clearing where the truck sat. "I can drive," Bryan said.

Sarah hesitated, drawing the keys close to her chest.

"It's not as bad as it looks," said Bryan.

She handed him the keys and sprinted around the truck to the passenger-side door. He climbed into the cab, started the engine and closed the door just as the assailant came into the clearing. Bryan hit the gas doing a tight turn to get out of the parking area. The back tires spat out gravel as a bullet collided with metal.

Sarah craned her neck. "I think he hit the side of the truck."

He'd probably been aiming for the tires. Bryan pressed the accelerator to the floor. He didn't want to give this guy a second chance. The truck jolted and lumbered down the mountain road.

Sarah leaned back against the seat, tilting her head. Her curly brown hair had worked free of the ponytail. Her face was covered with sweat and dirt. She turned her head, soft blue eyes resting on him. She'd come back for him, risked her life. "He won't be able to catch us now. Not on foot."

"Yeah." He didn't want to worry her about the second hit man. Had the sheriff made it to the car or had the thug gotten away?

"How far is it to this country store?"

"I'll take you all the way into town…and to the police station." He didn't like the idea of leaving her anywhere until he could be assured she was safe, though he dreaded the thought of returning to the police station. His departure had not been a quiet one. Incensed at the lack of justice over Tyler Mason, he'd let his chief know how he felt.

"Thank you for doing that." Sarah leaned back and closed her eyes.

He reached over and patted her leg without thinking. It was a gesture he'd done a thousand times when they were dating. She sat up straight, and her eyes popped open.

He bit the inside of his cheek. What a stupid move. Of course, he didn't think he could go back to where they had been ten years ago. Too much had changed, even before they parted ways.

He cleared his throat. "We do need to stop at the country store and make some phone calls. My cell phone is back at the fire tower. I need to find out if my replacement made it." He hated abandoning his post and worried that he'd sent his replacement into a dangerous situation if the guy was still skulking around the woods with a gun. Though he doubted the thug would hurt anyone else and risk having another person who could identify him.

The road evened out, decreasing the bouncing in the truck. Sarah folded her hands in her lap as a tense silence fell between them.

What did they talk about now? What *could* they talk about that wouldn't open old wounds? Even thinking about how their relationship had ended made his chest tight. No, he couldn't go there again.

Sarah leaned toward him and pointed through the windshield. "That must be it, huh?"

A hundred yards ahead was a concrete building with a parking lot full of trailers. As they neared the store, signs advertising raft and boat rentals and bait for sale came into view. A campground a mile up the road was the main source of business for the store along with the abundance of fishermen who came for the freshwater fishing. Bryan pulled into the dirt lot.

"It'll take me just a minute to make these calls," Bryan said.

Sarah nodded. The bandage above her eye had come lose. He reached over and pressed it against her forehead.

She lifted her chin as a show of resolve. She'd always been a strong person emotionally. She had had to be. But what she had been through today would have made anyone fall apart. He touched her cheek with his knuckles. "It's going to be okay. I'll get you into town." She nodded and tried to smile. Bryan resisted the urge to pull her into a comforting hug. It wasn't his place to do that for her anymore.

Bryan got out of the truck and ambled toward the store entrance.

Alone in the truck, Sarah glanced out the back window. A hard, cold mass of fear had settled in her chest. These men were not going to give up easily. What could Crew have done for this kind of wrath to come down on him? He must have gone into hiding or the men wouldn't have sought her out. Wherever he was, she hoped he was safe.

She looked out Bryan's window. Mixed in with all the trailers, there was only one car parked off to the side that must belong to the owner or store clerk. No one wandered around outside. Through the store window, she could see Bryan step up to the counter while the clerk rang up his purchases.

She would have been dead by now if it hadn't been for Bryan. How had a forest ranger learned to fight like that? She placed her fingers on the bandage on her forehead. His gentle touch had caused memories of being held by him to rise to the surface. All those years ago, she'd rested her head on his chest surrounded by his heartbeat while strong arms enveloped her. Back then, she had felt safe for the first time in her life when she was with him. But it didn't last.

Bryan emerged from the store holding two large cans. She leaned over and opened the door for him. He handed her one of the cans, an iced tea. "That drink I meant to get for you earlier."

Moved by such a small act of consideration, she opened the can and took a sip. The cool liquid traveled smoothly down her parched throat. She took several more gulps. "That tastes really good, thanks."

Bryan sat behind the wheel, popped the tab on his tea and placed it in the cup holder. "My replacement made it to the tower. No sign of the guy with the gun. I checked in with the sheriff and called the city police, too. They might be willing to get involved since the kidnapping took place in town. You can make your statement to them."

"Did the sheriff say if they caught the other guy?" She shivered despite the heat, not wanting to think about those men being on the loose.

Bryan started the truck. "The dispatcher hadn't heard anything. She's gonna send the deputy up to the tower to make sure the area is clear."

For a forest ranger, Bryan seemed to know a lot about how the police worked. She had to know what he'd been doing for the past ten years. "So did you go to college like you planned?"

Bryan's head jerked back and he laughed. He pulled

out of the dirt parking lot. "Boy, that question came out of nowhere."

"I was just curious." It was the first mention either of them had made of the past.

Bryan's truck came to a crossroads. He turned onto a paved two-lane. "I...ah...started out that semester, but it was a little too much for me to handle." Each word was wrought with tension.

Sarah crossed her arms and stared out the window. His discomfort made it clear that even such a benign question was off limits. She wondered, too, how and why he had ended up back in Discovery, but now she didn't dare ask. She longed to have a normal conversation with him, but that wasn't going to happen. It would be best if he just dropped her off at the police station. He could go back out to his lonely fire tower. If they ran into each other in town, they could keep the conversation to hello and the weather.

Bryan glanced at the rearview mirror. "What's this guy's problem?"

Sarah turned around to look at the SUV following too closely. Shock spread through her. "Bryan, that's the vehicle."

He glanced a second time just as the Suburban tapped their bumper.

"He must have been waiting for us." Bryan pressed the gas. "Knowing this was the only road that led into town."

"How could he know this was your truck?"

"I don't know. Maybe he was watching the store. Maybe he has a way to communicate with the other guy." Bryan pulled away from the Suburban only to have it catch up with them again. The car bumped the back of the truck again, causing it to lurch.

"Hold on." Bryan executed a sudden turn onto a dirt road.

The other car overshot the turn, but spun around and charged up the road toward them. Bryan turned off into a grassy field and veered back to the main road, but in the wrong direction—away from town.

The car caught up to them. Bryan gripped the steering wheel as the Suburban came alongside them and smashed against his truck. Metal crunched. The truck wobbled, but Bryan kept it on the road.

The second hit was harder. The Suburban seemed to be attached to the passenger side of the truck as it pushed them closer to the edge of the road.

Sarah looked through her window at the leering, maniacal face of Acne Scars, as their truck was pushed off the road toward the rocky incline below.

FOUR

Their truck flew off the road at a high speed, sailed through the air and landed in the river at the bottom of the rocky incline. Sarah gasped for air as the truck settled and water rose up around it. She felt as if every muscle in her body had been stretched, and her thoughts seemed to move in slow motion.

Sarah turned toward Bryan whose head was tilted at an unnatural angle. Panicked, she fumbled with her seat belt and reached over to shake him. "Bryan!" She wrapped her hand around his muscular upper arm. "Bryan, please."

He stirred, shaking his head and moaning in pain. She let out a breath. He was alive.

Bryan glanced from side to side as though trying to fathom what had happened. She reached across his stomach and unbuckled his seat belt.

The current propelled the car downriver. The metal frame creaked as the water pushed against it.

"We need to get out of here, right?"

He looked at her, blinking several times. "Yeah… yeah." His eyes were void of comprehension.

"Or would it be better to drift with the current?" The truck picked up speed and turned sideways.

He looked around. "No." His gaze became more focused. "The water gets deeper, more rapids."

"I think we are closer to the bank on my side." She glanced out the back window. Acne Scars's Suburban must have pushed with so much force that it too had sailed off the road and landed upside-down on the rocky shore.

She rolled down her window. Water seeped into the cab of the truck.

"Hurry," said Bryan. "Swim as hard as you can to shore. The current is pretty strong. I'll be right behind you."

She pushed herself through the window into the cold river. Rushing, swirling water suctioned around her. The cold of it shocked her into stillness for a moment as the force of the current pulled her under. She swallowed water and panic surged. She fought against it, struggling to the surface. She pierced the water with her hand, keeping her eyes on the bank which seemed to be slipping farther away.

She caught a quick glimpse of Bryan as he drifted downriver. He was pretty banged up from his fight, and he'd lost consciousness in the wreck. Was he in any condition to make a swim like this? His head went under as an awful sense of dread filled her.

I can't lose him.

She crashed into a submerged log. She was able to catch her breath by grabbing on to one of the larger branches that stuck out of the water. Holding her position, she desperately scanned the water for a glimpse of Bryan, breathing a sigh of relief when his head bobbed

to the surface as he stroked toward the shore, his movement steady and strong.

She pulled herself along the top of the log and then
pushed off, aiming for the shore. Up ahead she could
see the rapids—foaming, intense waves cresting and
swirling. Terror spread through her. No way did she
have the strength to swim through those. She needed
to get to land. She jabbed her arm through the water,
though her muscles had grown weak from the struggle.
Her legs felt heavy.

Rivers, just like oceans, had an undertow. The closer
she got to the rapids the bigger the risk of being pulled
under and drowned.

The shore grew nearer inch by inch. The water
calmed as she struggled toward an eddy. This time,
when she put her feet down, she touched bottom. *Thank
You, God.* Sarah dragged herself to the shore and crumpled onto a sandbar.

She heard footsteps and turned her head sideways.
Bryan had gotten ashore farther upriver. He ran toward her, looking over his shoulder and then increas-
ing his pace. The look of fear on his face fueled her
panic. Sarah sat up.

He reached down and grabbed her arm. "We've got
company. Come on."

Acne Scars must have gotten out of the SUV. Sarah
had barely caught her breath when Bryan lifted her to
her feet and pulled her toward the thick brush. Both
of them were soaking wet. Their shoes squished as
they ran. Her wet clothes, which weighed an extra five
pounds, slapped against her body. She was grateful for
the warmth of the sun. They'd dry off quick enough.

Bryan led her through the thickness of the forest.

The canopy reduced the light by half, and the temperature dropped ten degrees.

"Where…are…we…going?" Sarah spoke as she ran, taking a breath after each word.

"Back to the store. We can call for help from there. The sheriff will have to meet us and escort us back to town."

The forest thinned. They came to the steep incline that led back up to the road. Only prairie grass grew on this side of the hill. Bryan scanned the area above them. "This is the only way to get to the road. We'll be exposed as we go."

Sarah took in a breath to push down the rising fear. "If it's the only way."

"Stay behind me." Bryan made the steep trek with ease, continually glancing side to side and up above.

Sarah scrambled to keep up with him. She could see the road not more than twenty yards above them. How much farther to the store after that?

Bryan stopped suddenly, his eyes growing wide. He turned and pulled her to the ground, placing a protective arm across her back. A zinging sound followed by an explosive echo shattered the silence of the forest.

Panic made her voice shake. "He has a rifle. Where did he get a rifle?"

"He probably had it with him in that car." From the ground where they lay, he turned to face her, reached out a hand and smoothed her wet hair back from her face. "It's going to be okay."

The tenderness of his voice was a soothing balm to her anxious, fear-filled thoughts.

"We'll get to that store," he assured her. "Stay low. The high grass will provide some cover."

They crawled the remaining distance to the road taking an indirect path. Still lying on his belly, Bryan lifted his head and peered over the asphalt then back down the hill.

He tugged on her wet shirt. "Follow the road but use the slope of the bank for cover. We should be safe."

Sarah took in a breath to calm her nerves. Her heart still hadn't stopped racing.

Why was this happening? What kind of trouble had Crew gotten himself into? This had to be something more serious than an unpaid debt.

Bryan must have picked up on her fear. He grabbed her hand and pressed it between his. "We're almost there."

She nodded. They ran, crouched over until the store came into view. At that point, Bryan straightened, grabbed her hand and sprinted the remaining distance. Sarah glanced over her shoulder at the forest beyond the road.

As they neared the store, the windows looked dark. The car that had been parked on the side of the building earlier was gone. Sarah slowed her pace. The store was closed.

"Now what?"

Bryan surveyed the parking lot. "We've got to break in. We can leave a note, letting them know what happened. Maybe they have an alarm system that will bring help out here."

He trotted around to the side of the building, picked up a rock and smashed the glass on the side door. No alarm sounded. Bryan reached through the broken glass and unlatched the door. "Not exactly high security."

They stepped into what looked like a combination storage and break room. All it held was a Formica table with mismatched chairs, a coffeemaker and a shelf lined with canned goods, paper towels and boxes of fishing lures. They secured the door behind them as best they could, then with Bryan taking the lead, they walked into the darkened main part of the store.

Sarah reached for the light switch. Bryan grabbed her hand and shook his head. Sarah's gaze traveled to the large window at the front of the store.

A percussive boom shattered the air as the glass in the window splintered into a thousand pieces spraying everywhere. Sarah screamed and dove to the floor.

Bryan dragged her toward the protection of the checkout area. He kept one arm around her while he reached up to the top of the counter and pulled the phone down. "We can't wait for the sheriff." The beeps from him pressing the numbers seemed to come on top of each other. "Jake, how fast can you get to the bait store on River Road? I'm in some serious trouble here. Armed man on the perimeter. Bring extra firepower if you've got it....Good."

Sarah pressed her back against a cupboard. "Who was that?"

"A friend. He lives close. He'll get here faster than the cops."

"Why didn't you call the police?"

Bryan's expression hardened. "They've got a pretty lousy track record so far today."

She grabbed Bryan's shirt and glanced toward the broken window. "That guy knows we're in here. We don't have much time."

"Which is why we're not staying in here." Bryan

opened and closed the drawers and cupboards on the checkout counter, clearly searching for something. "Sometimes they have a gun for protection." He opened one more drawer before giving up. He looked at her. "Make a run for the back door. Open it as little as possible. I'll be right behind you."

Questions raced through Sarah's head—How would the friend find them if they left the store? Wasn't there a risk that the friend would be shot, too?—but she knew it wasn't the time to ask them.

Sarah crawled toward the back door, reaching up to work the latch. She glanced back at the shattered window. The shooter wasn't in view, but that didn't mean he couldn't see them leaving the store. He had to be hiding in the trees across the road. She eased the door open to a narrow slit and squeezed through. Bryan pressed close to her back as they made their way along the outside wall of the store.

"Over there," he whispered, pointing to one of the boats for rent. He scrambled toward it and lifted a corner of the canvas cover. "Get in."

When she came to the end of the boat, she saw that a shed concealed it from view of the trees where Acne Scars likely hid. Sarah crawled through and lay down on the bottom of the boat, positioning her feet underneath the seat. Bryan crawled in beside her, reaching up to move the canvas cover back into place.

Lying on his side, he turned toward her and whispered, "Stay quiet. Jake's car has a loud engine. We'll hear it coming. We need to jump out and be ready to get in when he arrives."

She nodded, wondering when her heart rate would return to normal. She knew it wouldn't be any time soon when he lay close enough for her to feel his breath on her cheek. She inhaled his faint musk scent and looked into his deep brown eyes. The minutes ticked by. She dared not move.

A door slammed. She gasped. Bryan placed a calming hand on her shoulder. Footsteps crunched on gravel, growing closer. Every muscle in her body remained frozen. Her heartbeat drummed in her ears. Warmth radiated from her shoulder where Bryan's hand remained.

The footsteps passed by the boat and then stopped. She dared not take a breath. If Acne Scars tore the cover off the boat, they'd both be dead in an instant. A century went by before the footsteps resumed.

Bryan squeezed her shoulder. She turned her head to see him better. For a long moment, they lay in silence facing each other. She used to think she could drown in the deep brown of his eyes.

He motioned with his eyes. At first, she didn't know what he was trying to say. Then she heard it, the distant rumble of an engine.

This plan was fraught with risk. Was the killer lying in wait in the store? Had he returned to his post in the trees or had he assumed they'd run back into the forest and left altogether? There was no way to know.

The engine noise became more distinct. Bryan reached up to flip back the cover. He lifted his head above the rim of the boat and then pulled himself out. She rolled toward the edge of the boat and sat up.

"Hurry, we don't have much time."

She jumped to the ground and followed him as he raced toward the shed, pressing his back against it. She leaned close to him, holding on to his muscular arm. The car engine sounded like it was on top of them.

"Now, now." He pulled her toward the parking lot. The car was still twenty yards away. The first rifle shot kicked up rocks in front of them. The car zoomed into the lot at a high speed, turning a hundred and eighty degrees. The second rifle shot hit the side view mirror.

Bryan yanked open the back door, pulling Sarah ahead of him so she could get in first. A bullet hit the door as Bryan crawled inside. He slammed the door shut. The car stirred up gravel, swerved and sped down the road.

FIVE

By the time they had reached the outskirts of Discovery, Sarah's heart rate had mostly returned to normal. Though she kept glancing over her shoulder expecting to be fired at, she could manage a deep breath.

Bryan hadn't said anything on the ride into town other than to ask her if she was okay and introduce her to Jake. They sat close together in the backseat, their shoulders touching. What they had been through left them both speechless though she found some comfort in having him close. Bryan seemed to take his own comfort from the handgun that rested on his thigh.

As soon as they had gotten into the car, Jake had tossed it back to Bryan. Another gun sat on the front seat of the Dodge Charger. Bryan kept up a steady vigil of checking all the windows at intervals. From his actions, he too worried they would be attacked again. Even though she knew both of the men who had come after them were now on foot, the fear settled in her belly like a heavy rock.

She'd almost died today. And all because of something Crew had done. Sarah closed her eyes and tried to make sense of it all, but nothing seemed to fit. Yes, her brother had been in trouble before, but she knew he had a good heart. How had he gotten mixed up with those thugs? She'd seen the level of violence these men were capable of. Her heart squeezed tight. What if the sheriff didn't catch those men? What would they do to her brother when they found him? She had to get to Crew before those thugs did.

Jake slowed the car as he came within the city limits. He was a burly man with salt-and-pepper hair. He dressed in army surplus fatigues and smelled like cigars. She guessed he might be in his mid-fifties.

What kind of life did Bryan lead that he knew men who had access to guns at a moment's notice?

Bryan tensed as they drew nearer to the police station. Jake pulled into the parking lot, and they all exited the car.

Bryan slapped Jake on the back as they gripped hands. "Thanks, you saved my life."

"That makes us about even," said Jake. "You can take it from here?"

Bryan raised a leery eye toward the police station. "I'll be all right."

Jake got back into his car as Bryan escorted Sarah up the sidewalk. Sarah glanced back at the rough-looking man getting into his car. "So how do you know Jake?"

"We worked together on a case when I came here. Then he took early retirement."

A case? She wanted to ask what case he'd have worked on as a forest ranger, but the bitterness embedded in Bryan's words indicated he didn't want to tell her anything else.

Inside the station, only a few officers sat at computers. A series of cupboards, some of them locked, took up one wall of the police station. At the far end of the long, narrow room was an office with a window. The sign on the door read Chief Sandoval. Radios and scanners buzzed on and off throughout the station.

All of the men and the one woman working at their computers raised their head when Bryan stepped inside.

The officer closest to the door said, "Hey, Bryan."

The greeting was neither friendly nor hostile.

Bryan looked at one officer and then another. "Have you guys heard anything about what happened on Fire Mountain today?"

"I picked some things up on the scanner," said the female officer. "Don't think County ever caught up with those guys."

Sarah cringed. That meant they were still out there. At least it was a long walk into town.

Bryan rested a hand on her shoulder. "This is Sarah Langston. She's the woman who was abducted and almost killed today. She needs to make a statement, and we'll have her look at mug shots. She can identify her attackers and so can I."

"I'll get right on that. Just give me a second to set things up." The female officer scooted back her chair and disappeared around a corner.

From the familiarity that Bryan had with the other officers, it was clear he had some sort of connection to the police. "So how does a guy in a fire tower have such a cozy relationship with the city police?"

"I used to work here." Bryan angled his head, not making eye contact. He shifted his weight from one foot to the other.

Sarah stepped a little closer to him. "Used to?"

His expression turned hard as granite. "It's a long story." His voice became thick with emotion. "And not one I want to tell."

Even though she knew his anger was over whatever had happened on the job, his retort stung—a reminder of a much more personal anger that he had directed at her ten years ago. When she'd found out she was pregnant, they'd gone to a pregnancy counseling center. Naomi's Place had been warm and filled with love, a safe place for teens to live while they were pregnant. They both had agreed that giving up their little girl was the best choice for everyone. But after Bryan signed away his parental rights, he became sullen. His silent rage had made her feel like he blamed her for not wanting to keep their child. It didn't make sense. They had made the decision together. They didn't get a chance to talk things out. Instead, he left. His parents moved away shortly after.

In the two years after Bryan left, she had been adopted by a loving family. The adoption had come too late for Crew, who was past eighteen and already descending into his life of crime, but it had helped cement Sarah's resolve to take her life in a different direction. She too had left for college to get a degree in social work. She'd returned because she loved Discovery, because Crew and her adoptive parents were here, and maybe somewhere in the back of her mind she hoped Bryan would come back, as well.

Now he *was* back. But whatever he'd been doing, the years had not been kind to Bryan Keyes. The vulnerable teenager she had known was lost to a man with an eight-foot wall around his heart. And she had no desire to try to climb over it.

The female officer returned. "Why don't you come this way? I've set up an interview room for you. It'll be easier to concentrate in there." She held out her hand. "I'm Officer O'Connor, but you can call me Bridget."

Sarah stepped toward Bridget. Fear rose up. She didn't want to think about those two men. She glanced back at Bryan. "Can Bryan come with me?"

The officer spoke gently. "I have to take your statements separately."

"It'll be all right." He reached out and squeezed her upper arm. "Bridget has a very gentle bedside interrogation technique."

His joke made her smile.

Bridget opened a door labeled Interview Room One. "Right in here."

Sarah took in a deep breath. Tension wove around her chest at the prospect of having to relive the terror of the last few hours.

And worst of all was her certainty that it still wasn't over.

The look of vulnerability Bryan saw in Sarah's eyes as she turned the corner nearly tore his heart out. She was still shaken, still afraid. If he could just hold her. He remembered the softness of her skin and the light floral scent of her hair. Heat rose up his neck. Even after ten years, the memory held a power over him.

All the more reason for him to keep some distance between them now. He wouldn't do her any favors if he got distracted by the past. Only by staying focused on the danger could he truly help her.

He couldn't make the interview any easier for her, but maybe he could make sure those guys didn't come after her again. Once the thugs got back into town, Sarah would still be in danger unless Crew came forward.

Bryan looked through the window where Chief Sandoval sat hunched over his desk. Overwhelmed with frustration as the case against Tyler Mason dissolved, his parting words to his boss weeks ago had been harsh.

He understood why Sandoval had no desire to waste manpower and resources trying to find a new angle on the investigation. Mason did such a good job of playing the part of a fine upstanding businessman that most people fell for his act. Unless they could get another eyewitness to Mason's human trafficking ring who could put the finger on Mason, they really didn't have a case.

A tightness embedded in Bryan's chest as he walked toward Sandoval's glass office. The older man raised his head and peered through the window, giving away nothing in his expression.

Bryan tapped on the door.

"Come in."

"Sir?"

Sandoval leaned back in his chair. "Have you decided to put that badge back on, Officer Keyes?"

Bryan shook his head. If his job wasn't about getting justice, he wasn't so sure it was a job he wanted.

Sandoval's chair creaked as he leaned forward and rested his elbows on his desk. "Too bad, you're a good officer."

The compliment warmed him. Whatever conflict

they had had, Sandoval was a competent chief. "I need to talk to you about another matter."

Sandoval nodded. "Go ahead."

"There's a woman in the interview room with Bridget right now. I witnessed two men try to kill her earlier today. I think her life is still in danger. She can identify them."

Sandoval straightened the papers on his desk. "So you think they will come for her again?"

"They were pretty relentless up on the mountain. Can we set her up with some protection?"

"Why were these men after her?" Not showing a high level of interest, Sandoval glanced at his computer monitor. "What does this relate to?"

"They wanted to know the whereabouts of her brother."

"Is the brother a criminal?"

Bryan was uncomfortable with the classification—the Crew he knew had been a good person, just on a bad path. "He has a history of drug use," Bryan admitted.

"So this might be about a bad debt or stolen drugs." Sandoval seemed distracted as he rose from his chair and opened a file cabinet drawer.

"We don't know. My gut says it's more serious than that. These guys were pretty persistent. Sarah's not involved in drug culture—if they were going to kill her to send a message to her brother then it seems like more is at stake here than a simple debt."

"I can't spare an officer to provide 24/7 protection, but I can send an extra patrol through her neighborhood at night. The dispatcher can be made aware if a call does come from her home." He slammed the file drawer shut.

That wouldn't be enough to keep Sarah safe, but pressuring Sandoval would not be effective. "I appreciate that, sir." He turned to go. If the department couldn't protect Sarah, maybe he'd have to.

He wandered back through the station. The female officer who had been with Sarah walked toward him holding a computer printout. "Thought you might want to look at this. These are the two men she identified."

Bryan studied the photographs. "Yeah. Those are the guys." Something clicked in his brain, and he examined the picture of the short, skinny man a little closer. Earlier, they'd been a bit preoccupied with running for their lives. He hadn't had time to think about who these men might be.

"Smoke is coming out of your ears," said Bridget.

Bryan tapped the piece of paper. "Something about this guy is ringing a bell." He looked up from the paper. "Where is Sarah, anyway?"

"She's reading through her statement so she can sign it." Bridget poked him in the chest. "I'll need to do a sit-down with you, too."

He stared at the printout. "Can we do it later?"

"Sure, but I don't want to wait too long." She returned to her desk.

Bryan gripped the corners of the computer-generated photograph. The skinny thug was connected to a previous case he'd worked. That had to be why the guy looked familiar. He'd seen him in another photograph. His brain clicked through the possibilities. Only one case had been the focus of his attention since he'd come back to Discovery.

He peered around one of the carrels where a young officer with a buzz cut and thick eyebrows sat with a stack of papers in front of him.

Bryan waved the printout. "Grant, do you know what they did with my old case files?"

"They're right where you left them. You only took a leave of absence—no one was going to pack away your stuff."

Bryan worked his way to the back of the station. A six-foot-high divider separated the detectives' work area from the patrol officers' desks. His desk had been swept clean of anything personal, but it looked like someone had bothered to keep the dust from collecting. After retrieving his work phone from a drawer and placing it on the charger, he opened a file drawer and pulled out three thick manila files. How much surveillance and how many thousands of photographs had he taken?

He flipped open the first folder, shuffling through the photographs, and then the second as his heart pounded in his chest with anticipation. Was he so obsessed with Mason that he had imagined a connection? One after another, he looked at the photos and laid them aside.

Finally, he found the photograph he'd been looking for. Tyler Mason dressed in his usual expensive suit outside of a hotel in Mexico flanked by two men who were obviously acting as his bodyguards.

One of them was the same guy who had run his truck off the road.

Bryan swallowed. His fingers curled into a fist. If these guys were connected to Tyler Mason, this thing was way bigger than a couple of low-level drug dealers looking to get paid. Could this be the break he needed to blow the Mason case wide open?

"Keyes, I need to get your statement." Bridget's head peered around the divider, pulling him out of deep thought.

"Yes, of course. Is Sarah still in the interview room?"

"She was done. She said something about going to find her brother," Bridget said.

He let go of the photo as it drifted down to the desk. "She's out there by herself?" A sense of urgency girded his words.

Bridget shrugged. "She called a friend to come get her. What's the big deal?"

"I'm concerned those guys she tangled with aren't going to give up that easily."

"Don't you think they are still tromping through the woods or sitting in the back of a sheriff's car by now?"

"I'm pretty sure they have friends in town." His heart pounded from the sense of urgency he felt. "What was her home address?"

Bridget tilted her head. "I don't know if I can disclose that."

He grabbed her forearm. "You heard from the report how determined these guys were. I have a feeling they're not working alone."

Bridget let out a breath. "Okay. It was on Madison Street...." She thought for a moment and then looked down at the stack of papers she held in the crook of her elbow, flipping through several pages. "Three twenty-one Madison Street, that subdivision on the edge of town."

After grabbing his phone off the charger, he stalked toward the front of the station, his mind racing as he walked. His truck was floating down the Jefferson River. His car was parked at his house. He stopped in front of the young officer he'd talked to earlier. "Grant, loan me the keys to your car."

Grant raised his eyebrows. "Because…?"

"Because you're my friend and you can come out to my place and get them when you get off shift."

Maybe Grant picked up on the desperation in his voice, but he tossed the keys without further questions. "You owe me, buddy. I'm going to have to get a ride from my wife to go out there and get the car."

"Yeah, yeah. Thanks, man." Bryan pushed through the doors of the station and skirted around to the side parking lot where the officers kept their private cars.

His thoughts sparked at lightning speed as he sat behind the wheel and shoved the key in the ignition. It couldn't be just coincidence that the same man who worked for Tyler Mason had been after Sarah. Maybe he'd cut short his fire-tower hiatus and come back on the police force if Sandoval would let him pursue the connection.

He'd talk to the chief later. Right now he needed to make sure Sarah was not in any immediate danger.

SIX

"Thanks for the ride, Cindy." Sarah shut the passenger-side door of the compact car and made her way up her sidewalk.

Cindy leaned out of her open window. "You've been through a lot. Take a hot bath and try to forget about it. Don't worry about coming in to work tomorrow."

Cindy was not only her friend but also her supervisor at the adoption agency. Still, Sarah shook her head. "Work is the best thing for me. I'll be there tomorrow."

Cindy waved and sped off down the gravel road. Sarah crossed her arms. Though it was past dinner time, the sky was still a cloudless blue. At this point in the summer, it didn't get dark until nine o'clock. The temperatures had soared to the high nineties in the middle of the day and were only just starting to drop. Still, between her river-drenched clothes and the edge of fear she couldn't shake, Sarah was shivering. It was past time to get inside where she could get warm, and maybe start to feel safe again.

Sarah turned back toward her house. She lived on the edge of town on a two-acre plot. Her nearest neighbor was not visible around a bend in the road. Across the road, there was only a cornfield.

A chill ran down her back when she saw her purse and tote lying on the grass. She'd dropped them when the kidnappers grabbed her. She placed her palm on her chest where her heart pounded erratically with fear. Was she even safe here anymore? Would they come back for her? Or would they give up now that it was clear she didn't have the information they wanted? Probably not. Though finding her brother seemed to be their priority, eliminating her was now a concern, as well. She was a loose end. She knew what they looked like.

Sarah gathered up her purse and tote. Her cell phone had fallen out. She picked it up and put it in her jacket pocket. She retrieved her extra set of keys from the hide-a-key. After putting her keys in her pocket as well, she turned the doorknob and stepped inside. Shadows shrouded the living room in gray light. She'd drawn the shades to keep the place cool during the day.

The house was completely silent. She couldn't recall if she had let her cat, Mr. Tiddlywinks, out before when she'd come home for lunch. She took in a sharp breath as anxiety threaded through her chest. Maybe it was a mistake to come home.

Had the sheriff caught up with the men in the forest or had they found a way back into town? Even if the sheriff didn't catch them, it would take them hours to walk to a road where they could hitch a ride. She had some time to come up with a plan. She could stay with Cindy for a while, but she didn't want to bring danger to her friend.

Her thoughts turned to Bryan. She wouldn't have to

worry about his safety—he could clearly take care of himself. She'd been anxious to leave the station without saying goodbye to him. Dormant feelings of hurt and confusion came alive in his presence. Still, she felt the assurance of protection when she was around him. Part of her wished she hadn't been so hasty in leaving.

The rest of her realized that there was no time to waste. She was exhausted and bruised. Cindy's suggestion of a nice hot bath sounded wonderful, but she knew she couldn't. Finding Crew was her priority. The window she had to warn Crew before those men found their way back to town could be closing.

Sarah retrieved a comb from the bathroom and got the glass out of her hair. She set out a change of clothes.

Her stomach growled. She needed to eat something quick. Sarah walked over to the refrigerator and pulled out a yogurt. While she ate, she'd come up with a strategy for locating Crew.

Discovery was only a town of about fifty thousand people, but locating a homeless person was never easy. Still, she knew some of their hangouts. She'd start with the shelter where her friend Julia worked.

A squeaking sound alerted her to a fat yellow cat running his paws up and down the glass of the patio door. "Mr. Tiddlywinks. Did you miss me?" She slid the glass door open, allowing the cat to meander in. He rubbed against her leg. She lifted up the fat cat who weighed at least ten pounds. He purred in her arms.

The silence of her house unnerved her. Logically, she knew those men couldn't come after her so quickly. Still, she couldn't shake the fear that embedded itself in every muscle in her body. She shuddered as images of the kidnapping washed over her like a wall of water.

Only the memory of Bryan's steady voice, of his hand grabbing hers calmed her.

Sarah sat the cat back down on the floor. She reached over and rested her hand on the countertop for support. While the cat ate his food, she checked to make sure the patio door was locked.

She took her yogurt and stood in the living room staring out across the road at the ditch and the open field beyond that. A car rolled slowly past, crunching gravel beneath its tires. The hair on the back of Sarah's neck electrified. That wasn't one of her neighbors' cars.

She turned back toward the kitchen. A man wearing a mask stood at the patio door, raising the butt of a rifle to smash it against the glass.

Dropping her yogurt, Sarah turned and flung open the front door. The car that had gone by moments before was turned around and waiting ten yards away.

Sarah turned and sprinted up the road. The car rumbled toward her. The masked man with the rifle came around the side of the house. The car drew closer. She struggled for breath, willing her legs to pump. The rumble of the car engine surrounded her.

She dove into the ditch. If she cut across the field, there was a house on the other side. But she had to get there first. And now, in addition to the attacker with the rifle, the man in the car had gotten out and was chasing her.

Sarah stumbled and fell. She rolled over on her back. The man from the car was the first to close the distance between them. He dropped to his knees and grabbed her. She screamed, kicking and flailing her arms. She tore off his ski mask. Car Man was a stranger—he definitely wasn't Deep Voice or Acne Scars. *How many of them are there?* she wondered. *How many will come after me?*

She managed a blow to his nose, and he reeled backward. She crawled through the tall grass. He grabbed her ankle and yanked her backward. Rocks and hard dirt grazed her stomach.

She rolled over on her back, kicking, trying to break free. He lunged toward her, squeezing her biceps and shaking her. "You're coming with me." He was all teeth and bloodshot eyes. His fingers tightened around her arms.

Footsteps pounded. She saw an elbow and an arm suction around the man's neck. He was jerked backward, his eyes wild with surprise.

The man let go of Sarah. She fell to the ground and scrambled away, eyes wide as she looked at…

Bryan!

He had Car Man in a choke hold that he didn't release until the man had gone still. He let go, and the man fell to the ground, not moving. Bryan glanced toward the road where Rifle Man still jogged toward them.

He reached out for Sarah's hand. "This way."

He pulled her toward the field of corn.

Sarah glanced over her shoulder. Rifle Man was taking aim. A red dot appeared on Bryan's shoulder blade. Sarah pushed Bryan to the ground.

"What're you doing?" Bryan protested.

She gestured to where the red laser dot was now skimming over the grass.

She caught the look of stunned gratitude on Bryan's face. They crawled the short distance to the high corn ready for harvest.

A rifle shot zinged through the air, slicing a corn-stalk above them. Bryan angled sideways, altering the direction he crawled but still moving toward the shelter of the corn. Sarah scrambled behind him. Once shielded by the rows of corn, they half crouched, half ran.

Another rifle shot popped behind them.

Bryan grabbed her hand. "My car is a ways from your house. I saw what was going on and jumped out. If we can get to it, we can escape."

He parted the stalks of corn. Crouching low, they moved perpendicular to the rows. He stopped, turned toward her and placed a finger over his lips.

Sarah held her breath and listened. She detected a swishing sound. One of the men was moving through the cornfield.

Bryan lifted his head above the corn and then dove back down. He pulled on Sarah's sleeve. They wove through the rows, zigzagging and backtracking to try to throw off their pursuer. Again, Bryan tilted his head to get a read on where the man was. Wind rushed over the top of the corn.

A rifle shot hit right in front of them. Sarah stifled a scream but her heart pounded so hard she thought it would break her rib cage. Bryan grabbed her hand and pulled her along the furrows between rows. They ran as fast as they could while still bending at the waist until they came to the edge of the field.

Both of them lay on their stomachs while Bryan separated the stalks so they could look out. Her house was about a quarter mile up the road. She could see the assailants' car and Car Man not far from her house. He patrolled up and down the road, watching the cornfield. Midway between the cornfield and her house was Bryan's car, parked at an angle on the gravel road with the driver's-side door flung open.

Bryan whispered in her ear. "We'll use the ditch for shelter and then swing around the side of the car so they don't notice us until the last second."

Sarah nodded. They waited for the moment when the guard on the road turned his back and then slipped out of the cornfield and crawled up the ditch, soldier-style. Once they were close to the car, they waited until Car Man turned his back again before racing to the back bumper and around to the passenger-side door. Bryan crawled in first and slipped over to the driver's seat. He slid down low in the seat to avoid detection.

Sarah crawled in, leaning forward—careful not to be seen above the dashboard.

Bryan's face went pale. His mouth hung open.

Panic spread through her like wildfire. "What?"

Still crouched low in the seat, he padded his pockets and then touched the steering wheel. "They took the keys."

Sarah's throat went dry as a shiver ran down her back. She lifted her head a few inches above the dashboard. Car Man had spotted them and was now making a beeline for them.

"He's seen us."

Bryan reached under the dash. "Old car like this. I can hot-wire it."

Rifle Man raced toward them from the cornfield as well, holding his rifle with both hands.

Bryan sorted through the wires he had pulled out.

They were sitting ducks—and both assailants were closing in. "Hurry." Fear paralyzed Sarah.

The car sparked to life. Bryan reached over and closed the driver's-side door while shifting out of Park.

"Stay down." Bryan pressed his hand softly on her head. He hit the gas and sped toward Car Man.

Bryan's arm rested over her back as she leaned forward, the warmth of his touch seeping through her cotton shirt. She lifted her head just above the dashboard. They whizzed past the man on the road.

Sarah looked out the back window as Bryan gained speed, creating a dust cloud behind them. Both men ran for their car. Her house grew smaller as they sped away.

One thing was clear. She wouldn't be able to stay in her own home until they found Crew and got to the bottom of this.

The assailants' car gained on them.

Bryan gripped the steering wheel. "What's the fastest way back to civilization from here?"

Sarah glanced out the side windows and then through the windshield trying to get her bearings. "Take a left at the next crossroads."

"If we can get into some traffic, they're not likely to try to come at us." Bryan leaned forward, hyperfocused on the landscape in front of him.

The pursuers' car was within twenty feet of them.

They drew close to the crossroads. The other car edged toward their back bumper. Bryan pressed harder on the gas.

Sarah dug her fingers into the dashboard. "Not too fast. The gravel acts like marbles and you'll flip the car."

Every muscle in Bryan's arm tensed as he spoke through clenched teeth. "We're all right."

He stared straight ahead, his gaze locked in place

until he made an abrupt left turn at the crossroads, not slowing down and spitting gravel with his back tires. Sarah pressed her back against the seat and dug into the armrest as the back end of the car lifted into the air.

The car landed on the paved road with a bump. Bryan pressed the accelerator to the floor.

The pursuers' car overshot the turn and veered over to the other side of the road, fishtailing.

The distance between the two cars lengthened. Several cars going in the opposite direction whizzed past them.

Sarah took in a breath. "The highway that leads back into town intersects with this road. We'll be there in a few minutes."

Bryan sat back in his seat, relaxing his grip on the wheel. "Good. Do you have a friend you can stay with?"

"Yes, but that's not where I want to go right away. I need to find Crew. I have to warn him and find out what this is all about and get him to a safe place, too."

Bryan glanced over at her. "Let's get the police to take care of that. I'll help them."

"He's my brother. This is my problem," Sarah said.

Bryan approached the stop sign where the country road intersected with the multilane highway. "Does your friend know how to use a gun or have a husband who does?"

Sarah looked behind her. The other car was gaining on them again. "You're not hearing me. I'm not going to my friend's house until I find Crew. He's my brother. I will deal with this."

"Those thugs couldn't find your brother. What makes you think you can?"

"My determination." She didn't want to have to take any more help from Bryan.

"They seem pretty determined to me. You're not safe, Sarah. Do you understand that?"

"I can handle this."

He pulled out onto the highway. "Look, I don't know exactly what is going on here, but this is way bigger than Crew owing a couple of low-level dealers money. Whoever is behind this has resources. You've had two sets of thugs come after you."

Sarah laced her fingers together and bit her lip. Bryan was right. They knew where she lived. They might even know where she worked and who her friends were.

"The only way to end this is to find Crew. I'm going to start by asking around at the homeless shelter. I have a friend who works there."

Bryan let out an exasperated sigh. "Then I'm coming with you."

"Fine, if that is what you want to do." Her tone was defiant, but Sarah found herself secretly grateful for his help and protection, however stirred up he made her feel.

They came to the mall on the edge of town. "Where is this homeless shelter anyway?"

"On Division Street. I guess a lot of this is new since you were last here."

Bryan nodded. "I've only been back for five months."

She took in a breath, trying to calm down. "What made you come back here?"

"An investigation I had been working on in Spokane for more than a year. Turns out Discovery is ground zero for the whole operation." Bryan slowed down as they entered the heart of town.

"Oh." So it was his work that had brought him back here. She couldn't hide her disappointment. Why had she even hoped that he'd come back to see her?

"The last I heard of you, you had left for college. I assumed you were never coming back," he said.

Her spirits lifted. "You kept tabs on me?"

"I stayed in touch with some of the people even if I didn't come back," he said.

"When I left, I didn't intend to come back. But then, Crew was here and my adoptive parents were here." She turned to look at him. "I guess Discovery will always be home for me."

He held her in his gaze for a long moment. She thought she saw affection in his eyes. What was running through his head? Did Discovery only hold bad memories for him?

The evening sky turned gray as they approached the dead-end street where the homeless shelter was. Sarah checked her watch. They had maybe an hour of daylight left.

Once it turned dark, the chances of finding Crew would be close to zero. The homeless shelter came into view.

Sarah craned her neck to look out the back window. How long did they have before this new group of men caught up with them?

SEVEN

Bryan glanced in his rearview mirror. Nobody was behind them, yet he couldn't shake the feeling of being watched. He parked the car beside the shelter and looked over at Sarah. She still had the same clothes that had gotten soaked in the river earlier. The ruffled button-down shirt she wore might have been white at some point but he doubted it ever would be again. He hadn't changed either since getting back to town. His T-shirt was ripped, his worn jeans sported mud stains and he had bruises on his arms. "We look like homeless people."

Sarah laughed, a soft, easy laugh that had always been music to his ears. "We'll blend right in."

As they approached the shelter, they saw two men seated on the steps while a third used a bucket as a chair. One of the men on the steps stared at the ground and hugged himself, but the other man met Bryan's gaze.

Sarah stepped forward. "I'm looking for Crew Langston. Have you guys seen him?"

The man who refused to make eye contact shot up

abruptly from the steps and wandered away, shuffling his feet.

The man on the bucket squinted and tilted his head toward the darkening sky. "Crew Langston?"

Sarah directed her comment toward the man on the bucket. "He's a tall, thin guy with dark hair. Likes to wear denim shirts and a bandanna around his neck."

The man on the steps let out a heavy breath and said, "I don't know the guy."

"I heard he got clean and got himself a place on Sixteenth Street." The man on the bucket touched his matted gray hair.

"I didn't hear anything like that," the man on the steps replied.

"You don't even know the guy."

The other man lifted his chin in the air and crossed his arms. "I know his name...."

The two men had descended into one of the illogical discussions common to people with mental illness. They probably weren't going to get any more information out of them. Could they trust the information they'd been given?

Although he doubted he'd get much of an answer, Bryan gave it one more try. "Do you know the address on Sixteenth Street where Crew is living? Or even what the house looks like?"

The man on the bucket shook his head. "Didn't see it for myself. Just what I heard."

"You ask too many questions," said the man on the steps, cutting a suspicious glance toward Bryan. He closed his eyes and turned his head, indicating that the conversation was over.

Bryan tugged on Sarah's shirt so she stepped away

from the two men. "Sixteenth Street runs most of the length of town."

Sarah crossed her arms and stared up at the sky. "That would be wonderful though if my brother had a place of his own. If it's true." Her voice held a note of hope. "It'll be dark soon. I suppose we could drive up and down the street and hope we see him."

Bryan pulled out his cell phone. "There has to be a faster way." Who did he know who could connect him to that kind of information? "Even if Crew does have a place, I doubt he's staying there right now. I'm sure word has gotten to him that those thugs are looking for him."

"They might not know Crew has a place. It was news to me and I'm his sister."

She could be right. His training as a detective told him to follow whatever lead, no matter how thin. "Give me a minute to make some calls." He'd start with one of the officers whose patrol took him on that street.

"I'm going inside to talk with my friend Julia. She might know something." Sarah trotted up the stairs and disappeared.

Sarah's voice floated out from an open window. He felt a tug at his heart when he heard her ask a question and then laugh. He had to admit that he still cared for her after all this time, but after the way he'd been so immature and let her down all those years ago, she'd probably want nothing to do with him once they found Crew. Sarah's voice faded and Bryan turned his attention to figuring out where Crew might be living.

After talking to a couple of officers, Bryan managed to narrow a probable location down to a two-block area where someone matching Crew's description had been seen in the last few weeks. It was something, any-way. He glanced up from his phone at the warm glow coming from the homeless shelter. Maybe Sarah had had better luck.

"Hey, Sarah."

Sarah looked up in the direction of the voice. A man dressed in a long coat and knit hat offered her a gap-toothed grin.

She couldn't find Julia in the shelter and had wandered out the back door to see if anyone else knew anything about Crew.

She turned toward the man who called her name.

"Eddie?" Eddie was one of Crew's friends. They'd eaten lunch together months ago when Crew called her and asked if they could meet. Eddie was not an addict, but a man prone to wandering when he went off his schizophrenia medication. Though he looked closer to forty, Eddie was in his mid-twenties. His parents, an older couple, had gotten used to a pattern of their son coming in and out of their lives. They supplied Eddie with a cell phone so he could call them when he wanted to come home.

From the light she saw in his eyes, she was catching him on a good day.

Eddie edged toward her. "I heard you asking around. You're looking for Crew?"

She nodded as hope fluttered in her heart. "Do you know where he is?"

"I saw him less than half an hour ago. I can take you to him. It's just over by the fairgrounds."

Sarah turned in the direction Eddie indicated. The high chain-link fence and labyrinth of buildings that

made up the fairgrounds were visible from the homeless shelter. Because the buildings were underutilized,
the fairgrounds were a known hangout for homeless
people when events weren't being held there.

"Can I get my friend to come with us?" She pointed
in the general direction Bryan might be.

"No, only you. That guy's a cop. I can tell." He
sounded afraid. "We should hurry. Some guys were
after Crew. He might not be there much longer."

Sarah steeled herself. Eddie had huge trust issues.
It wasn't really surprising that Bryan made him nervous. She didn't want to scare him away. She had to
find Crew. "You'll stay with me, Eddie?"

Eddie looked at the ground, shifted his weight. "It's
not far."

He led her through an opening in the fence that surrounded the fairgrounds, past several buildings and
corrals. Four homeless people huddled in a tight circle craned their necks as Sarah and Eddie passed by.

"In here." Eddie pushed open a door that had a
broken padlock. They stepped inside a long, narrow
exhibit building. Sarah squinted. The building had a
series of low-walled stalls where kids showed their
4-H animals. Shadows covered most of the building.

"Where is he?"

A tiny light came on at the other end of the building.

"Crew?" Sarah walked toward the light. She heard a
scuffling sound behind her and when she turned back
around, she saw that Eddie had disappeared.

Sensing danger, Sarah stopped. Had Eddie been
spooked? Was that why he'd left her behind? A man
at the other end of the building stalked toward her. She
squinted. "Crew, is that you?"

"Sarah Langston." The man came closer, holding a flashlight. He was dressed in a suit. As he drew near, she saw that he was clean-shaven. "I have a message for you."

"Is it from my brother?"

In the distance, she heard Bryan shouting her name. His voice grew louder.

The man seemed on edge, glancing from side to side.

"Please tell me. What is the message?"

"Sarah." Bryan stood in the doorway.

When Sarah spun back around, the man was gone.

Bryan approached her. "What were you doing here?"

"There was a man who might know something about my brother."

"A homeless man?"

"No—well, yes and no. The man who was waiting here for me wasn't homeless. He was wearing a suit. But it was one of Crew's friends who led me here." Sarah tried to sort through what had just happened. "He lied to me." Eddie must have been paid to be the courier and bring her to the other man. That's why he'd claimed to have seen Crew. He knew she wouldn't come unless she thought she'd be meeting her brother.

"What did the man say?"

"You scared him away." Sarah walked the length of the dark building with Bryan following her. "He said he had a message for me."

"He didn't say specifically he had a message about Crew?"

"No, but what else would it be about?" She stood beside the half-open door the man must have slipped out of. She stepped outside into the darkness. The man had clearly been nervous and was probably long gone by now. Eddie would be much easier to track down. "We have to find Eddie. He must know something."

They searched the fairgrounds, the shelter and an area by the river where homeless people often slept. No sign of Eddie.

Bryan placed a supportive hand on Sarah's shoulder as they headed back toward the car. "I've narrowed down the possibilities for where Crew's place might be. Let's go see if we can find it before we call it a night."

Bryan's car rolled slowly down Sixteenth Street. Most of the houses looked like single-family dwellings. Nothing Crew could afford even with assistance.

"There, maybe." Sarah pointed to a three-story building that had a number of apartment units. A man stood outside, tossing a garbage bag into a Dumpster. Sarah jumped out of the car and approached the man who looked to be about college-age.

"I'm looking for someone." She pulled out her phone and clicked through her photos until she found a picture of Crew. "This man."

The young man looked at the photograph. "Yeah, I've seen that guy."

Sarah's spirits lifted. "Really?"

"I've talked to him when he was on his way home from work. He lives in the basement apartment over there." The man pointed across the street. "Haven't seen him around for a couple of days, but he's got a roommate."

"Thank you." Sarah headed across the street.

They descended a concrete stairway and Sarah tapped on the door. "I know he's not going to be here. But maybe the roommate knows something."

"It's a place to start." Bryan sounded encouraged, too.

They waited. Sarah rocked heel to toe. "It's kind of late. Do you think the roommate is sleeping?"

Bryan leaned forward and tapped on the door a second time—louder this time. "The clock is ticking for your brother. We can get somebody out of bed if we have to."

Sarah smiled. Glad she didn't have to do this alone even though it was Bryan who was helping her.

They heard footsteps and then the door swung open to reveal a man dressed in a brown uniform. He was a few years younger than Crew, clean-shaven with a narrow face and thin nose.

"We're sorry to bother you so late at night," Sarah said.

The man shrugged. "Actually, I was just getting ready for work. Graveyard shift, security."

Bryan leaned in the doorway. "We wanted to talk to you about your roommate, Crew Langston."

"Crew hasn't been around for like three days. Which is really weird because the guy has been hyperresponsible since he got clean."

"I'm his sister. Do you know where he might have gone?"

The young man's face brightened. "You're Sarah? Why don't you come in?" He stood to one side so they could enter. "I'm Nick Sheridan, by the way."

They stepped inside. The apartment was clean and sparse.

"Like I said, I don't know where he's gone. They called from his work. He didn't show up for his shift there. That old beater car he bought is gone, too."

So Crew had saved enough to buy a car. How long

had he been clean? Why hadn't he told her? "You have no idea where he went? He didn't say anything to you?" Sarah fought off a rising sense of desperation as she struggled to find the right question to ask.

Nick shook his head.

She asked the question she was dreading the answer to. "Do you think he started using drugs again?"

"He was pretty serious about his recovery. He wanted to give it a full six months before he told you to make sure he was going to make it this time."

"He said that?" Sarah's throat went tight from joy. Tears formed at the corner of her eyes.

"Yeah, your opinion of him means a lot to him." Nick buttoned up the shirt of his uniform. "If you don't mind, I'll be late for work if I don't get going."

"Oh, sorry." They still didn't have any information that would give them a clue as to why Crew would disappear or why the men were after him.

The man picked up his keys and headed toward the door.

Bryan spoke up. "Was there anything unusual in the days before he left?"

Bryan's question seemed to spark something. "Come to think of it, a blonde woman came to see him about a week ago. She wasn't someone I had ever seen him with before." The man moved toward the door and Sarah and Bryan followed him.

"Do you know what they talked about?"

He stepped outside. "They went for a walk. When she arrived, she seemed upset or scared." He shrugged. "I only saw her that one time. Crew disappeared a few days after that." He placed his key in the door and locked it.

Bryan pulled a card from his wallet. "Let us know if you hear anything more from him or remember anything else."

Sarah dug through her pockets for a card of her own. "I really need to talk to my brother."

The man examined both cards. "Sure, I'll let you know if I hear anything."

They stepped up into the dark night and headed toward the car. Sarah slipped into the passenger seat and the heaviness of fatigue set in.

"So tell me where your friend lives and I'll drop you off," Bryan said.

Sarah gave him directions to Cindy's house. "And for your information, she does have a husband, but I have no idea if he owns a gun."

"She lives in town?"

Sarah nodded.

Bryan cruised through the quiet residential streets. A warm glow came from some of the house windows. Others were dark.

Sarah's life had flipped completely upside-down from where she had been this afternoon when she thought she would leave her house after lunch and finish a day of work. She'd found out that her brother had gotten his life together and had fallen off the face of the earth all in a few short hours. And now Bryan was back in her life. She wasn't sure how she felt about that. His police training was invaluable and had already saved her life. For that, she was grateful. Dormant feelings of attraction had been stirred up by his return. But every time she thought about how he had abandoned her when she'd needed him most, a shield went over her heart.

Thinking about what Bryan meant to her after all these years would make her fall apart. She preferred to focus her energy on finding Crew.

She voiced the thought that teased the corners of her mind. "If it's not drugs or a debt, what is it? What's happened to my brother?"

Bryan shook his head. "Hard to say. I wonder who this woman is who came to his place…if she's the reason he's gone underground."

"I doubt he had much money. He couldn't get far." Sarah felt a rising frustration at the lack of answers. She watched the houses clip by through the subdivision. "That's it. Cindy's house is on the cul-de-sac."

Bryan slowed and checked his rearview mirror. He sat up a little straighter. "Is there another friend you might want to stay with?"

Sarah looked around. "Why?"

Bryan looped around the cul-de-sac past Cindy's house. He turned back out onto the street. A moment later, he tilted his head back. "That's why."

Through the back window, Sarah saw a car pull away from the curb and slip in behind them. Anxiety coiled through her. Not again. "They aren't going to give up, are they?"

"I thought maybe they were just headed in the same direction as us. But when they pulled in at the edge of the cul-de-sac and didn't get out to go into a house, I knew something was up."

"How did they find us?" Weariness and fear wrestled within her.

"They probably had Crew's place staked out."

The car hung about twenty feet behind them. They weren't exactly being stealthy.

"Now they're trying to intimidate us." Sarah's voice held a tremble.

Bryan adjusted his hands on the steering wheel. His voice remained steady. "Or they are just waiting for an opportunity."

Sarah wiggled in her seat. "So what do we do?"

"I can't just dump you at a friend's house."

"I agree. That would put them in danger, too."

"We'll stay close to civilization, try and shake them off. They're not going to try anything if there's a risk of being caught."

"Where do we find civilization at this hour?"

Bryan sped up. "I'll think of something."

Sarah turned around again. The menacing glow of the headlights behind them fed her fear.

EIGHT

Bryan drove through town. They needed to hole up somewhere for a while. So many of the businesses were new to him—and he was sure that a lot of the places he remembered had closed over the years he'd been gone. "Is Martin's still open twenty-four hours?"

"I think so." Her voice sounded strained.

He pushed toward the edge of town and up a hill. When he checked the rearview mirror, there was no one behind them. But he knew that didn't mean they were in the clear.

These guys had to be working for Mason. They were organized and professional, which would make them very hard to shake. But if he could *prove* the connection to Mason, then this could be the link he needed. His instinct told him that this could reopen the case he wanted so badly to see brought to trial, but what he needed was more evidence, a tighter connection than a thug who had been photographed with Mason and had come after Sarah.

Martin's was an all-night diner and truck stop best known for its milk shakes. Bryan pulled into the lot, relieved to see it was still open. Several semitrucks were parked in the far corner of the lot. Inside, three patrons hunched over their food in booths. All three were men, all three sat by themselves.

Bryan studied the décor…or lack of it. "This place brings back some memories."

They had had more than one date here. Sometimes after football games, half the school would come here to celebrate or commiserate.

"Yeah…some memories." Sarah's voice laced with pain.

"Sorry, maybe it wasn't the best choice," Bryan said.

"No, it's one of the few places that are open at this hour…and ten years is a long time, right? We should be over it by now."

He stared at her for a long moment, wondering what she meant. Over the pain they had caused each other? Or over the love they had felt?

A fifty-something waitress with candy-apple red hair and purple eye shadow set two menus on the table. "Still got a pot of coffee going. Grill's been closed down for an hour. I can do sandwiches or reheat some lasagna."

"Actually, just a pot of tea and maybe a couple of slices of that blueberry pie I saw on the way in," Bryan said.

Sarah settled in the booth opposite Bryan. A soft smile graced her lips. "You remembered blueberry was my favorite."

The waitress brought the tea and pie. Bryan sipped his tea and watched Sarah dig into her pie. He liked the way she closed her eyes after each bite, relishing the sweetness and flavor. Her curly brown hair fell in layers around her face and her cheeks had a natural glow.

She'd always had a prettiness that was unassuming, not created from makeup and endless beauty routines.

She wiped a dab of blueberry from her lips and smiled at him. Her gaze shifted over his shoulder and her smile faded away. She laid her fork on the table and continued to stare.

"That's him."

Bryan craned his neck to see what she was looking at—a television screen running a local commercial for a used car dealership.

She pointed to the man on the screen who called himself Crazy Ray. "That's the guy I saw in that building Eddie led me to."

"Are you sure?"

Sarah slipped out of the booth and walked closer to the television, nodding her head. "That's him. I'm sure of it." She turned and sat back down in the booth.

Bryan shook his head. This didn't make any sense. There was a part of him that thought maybe the well-dressed guy at the fairgrounds had been Mason. Was he so desperate to nail Mason that he was trying to make connections that didn't exist?

Sarah poured another cup of tea. She took several sips and then yawned. "I'm really tired. I want to sleep in my own bed."

"It's just not safe to do that, Sarah."

She rolled her eyes. "I know that's how it has to be. I don't have to like it, though."

He thought for a moment. "The female officer you spoke to, Bridget, gets off duty in an hour or so. You'd be safe with her. We can call her, see if that will work."

Sarah rested her head against the back of the booth. "Okay, if that's what we have to do...." She closed her eyes. "I drank a lot of tea. I need to use the little girls' room."

"I'll call Bridget." Bryan pulled out his phone.

Sarah rose from her seat and walked toward the counter where the waitress was filling salt and pepper shakers. The waitress pointed off to one side and Sarah disappeared around a corner.

Bryan phoned Bridget. Once he explained the situation, she was glad to take Sarah in for the night.

"I've approached Sandoval about protection already, but that was before the attack at her house. Maybe he'll reconsider," Bryan said.

He talked for a few minutes more before hanging up and then he called Sandoval to let him know there was no need to do a patrol past Sarah's house, since she wouldn't be there. Sandoval said he'd look into what he could do for protection for Sarah now that there was clearly an ongoing threat. Bryan said goodbye and hung up.

One of the truckers got up and lumbered toward the door. Bryan watched the corner where Sarah had turned. She should have been back by now.

He rose to his feet and headed in the direction Sarah had gone. Around the corner, he found a room that had probably been a casino or bar at one time but now was empty. He spotted the restroom and walked over to it.

"Sarah?" He knocked. "Sarah." He scanned the room. His gaze rested on a glass door in the corner. Panic sparked inside of him. The thugs could have been watching through the windows, waiting for their chance, and grabbed Sarah when she headed to the restroom. He ran toward the door and flung it open, searching the dark landscape. The lights of downtown Discovery glowed two blocks away.

He ran outside, feet crunching the asphalt.

Then he heard a scream. He sprinted in the direction of the sound. He turned a corner to see lights on a pickup truck come on. The truck moved slowly through the lot. That had to be the one.

He stayed in the shadows for a moment and then sprinted toward the truck. He jumped into the truck bed just as it accelerated through the lot. There was a passenger in the cab. It had to be Sarah.

She turned her head slightly, eyes growing wide. Her mouth had duct tape over it. Bryan scanned the truck bed for a weapon. He picked up a jack, leaned out the side of the bed and smashed it against the driver's-side window.

The car swerved wildly, crossing the center line. A horn blared. Bryan tried to hold on and brace himself, but there was no time. The truck smashed into an oncoming car. Bryan flew backward. His body impacted with a hard object. He heard screaming just as he lost consciousness.

Sarah pressed her back against the truck door, trying not to hyperventilate. She hadn't been injured in the crash, but she'd seen Bryan go flying. Was he all right? Was he even still alive? There was no way to know.

Her kidnapper had glass in his hair and blood streamed down his face from various cuts, but he was still conscious. "You stay here. You don't move, do you hear me?" He leaned toward her, poking a meaty finger in her chest. His eyes were wild with rage.

Sarah nodded, wishing she could push him away,

but her hands were bound together in front of her with duct tape.

Though it was dark, a single working headlight on the other car revealed that the man behind the wheel of the other car was slumped forward. She craned her neck. Bryan had been thrown clear of the truck close to the edge of the road.

Her kidnapper walked over to the other car and peered inside. Satisfied that the other driver wasn't going to move, he skirted around the back of the truck and headed toward where Bryan lay facedown.

Sarah twisted at the waist and fumbled with the door handle. How far could she get running with her hands tied in front of her? She wouldn't have a chance to find out if she couldn't get the door unlocked.

She prayed for another car to come along. Her hand pressed against the door lock and got it released. Now for the handle. But before she could tackle that, the thug rolled Bryan down the bank out of view and returned to the truck.

He came to the driver's side, got in and turned the key. The engine chugalugged but didn't turn over. He tried several more times. He grimaced. He beat the dashboard with his fist.

Sarah recoiled at his anger. All she had to do was push the door open. Downtown Discovery was only a few blocks away. Martin's was just up the hill. If she got away, she could get help—send someone to Bryan to make sure he was all right. Someone would see her. If someone was out at this hour and if the kidnapper didn't catch her first.

The thug took out his phone and dialed. He waited for a moment and then spoke in a rapid-fire manner.

"Listen, I'm outside Discovery just past Martin's. You better get over here quick. I got the package, but I'm in a world of hurt. Hurry."

He looked over at Sarah. "Get away from that door." He leaned forward and yanked on her shirt.

Sarah struggled to clear her head. This man hadn't killed her on the spot. Just like before, he must have intended to take her somewhere remote before killing her. The choice bought her a chance at escape, but how would she get away?

The thug leaned toward her. "Don't even think about running."

Sarah froze, knowing that now he'd be watching her like a hawk. But with his eyes on her, he didn't see the figure approaching the truck....

Bryan appeared in the driver's-side window with the jack in his hand. He hit the assailant on the back of the head. The beefy man slumped into Sarah's lap. She scooted toward the door. Bryan ran around the front of the truck, opened the passenger-side door and pulled Sarah out.

She turned to face him.

He touched the duct tape on her mouth. "One swift movement. It's gonna hurt."

She nodded.

He yanked. Her face stung. She sucked in air.

"He has help coming," she said.

Bryan pulled a pocketknife out of his jeans pocket and cut the duct tape on her hands. "Let's get going then." He glanced over at the other driver. "We can phone for help as soon as we're in the clear."

He pulled her away from the road into the darkness of the tangled brush. They headed up the hill toward

Martin's and their car. Another truck whizzed by on the road, stopping at the accident, probably the kidnapper's backup.

Their feet pounded the hard earth until they came to the edge of Martin's parking lot where the lights didn't reach. They hid behind a line of Dumpsters. Bryan peered out. A man stood beside their car scanning the parking lot.

Sarah leaned close to him. "What is it?"

He watched the man a moment longer. "Could just be a guy waiting for a ride, but it's too risky. We can't go back to the car."

Bryan sat down beside her and pulled out his phone. "This is Bryan Keyes. There's an accident on the west end of town. Send an ambulance. We're being pursued. We need to be picked up. We're headed toward downtown."

Headlights shone toward the Dumpsters. Tires rolled slowly over asphalt.

"They found us." Fear saturated her voice as she grabbed his arm.

Bryan tugged on her sleeve. She followed him farther into the darkness. The land beside Martin's was a fenced field. Two empty city lots separated them from downtown. Behind them, the truck had stopped by the Dumpsters. Doors slammed.

Sirens sounded in the distance. "There's our ride," said Bryan. "Hopefully that will scare them away."

The two men came toward the field. Bryan stretched the barbed wire fence so Sarah could crawl through.

"Stay low," Bryan whispered. They sprinted toward a clump of trees. The men came to the edge of the fence. One muttered something about a flashlight.

Two horses lying on the ground by the trees stirred to life as they approached. The sirens grew louder.

The horses whinnied and stomped. Sarah pressed close to one of them, so in the shadows it would look like she was part of the horse.

Light flashed across the field.

"Get on," said Bryan. "I'll boost you." He held his cupped hand toward her. Ride bareback? She hadn't done it in years. But Bryan wasn't giving her much of a choice as he hoisted her up onto the horse's back. "Ride to the edge of the field. Work your way toward downtown."

She didn't have time to ask him what he was going to do before he slapped the horse's flank. Sarah pressed against the horse's back and held on to its mane. Behind her, the flashlight bobbed up and down as the men raced across the field.

The horse's hooves pounded out a rhythm against the soft ground. A second set of hooves thundered behind her. She could just make out Bryan's silhouette. When her own horse came to an abrupt stop, Sarah slipped off and made her way toward the fence. Bryan was right behind her.

The flashlight no longer bobbed across the field.

Bryan leaned close to her and whispered, "It'll take them a minute to regroup."

They crawled through the fence and entered a residential part of town. Most of the houses were dark. From inside one of them a dog barked as they ran past. Lights came on.

Their escape through the field had caused them to veer away from downtown. Main Street was at least four blocks away. An ambulance went by. They slowed their pace, though Bryan continued to glance around.

The glow of the downtown lights came into view. A police car with its light flashing was parked in a parking lot. The officer got out as they approached.

"I was afraid you weren't going to make our date," the officer joked.

"We got a little hung up." Bryan slapped the other officer on the shoulder blade. "Sarah, this is Grant."

Sarah nodded.

Compassion colored Grant's features. They must look like they'd been put through the wringer. "Are you sure you don't want to go to the emergency room?"

"We need to get her to the station. I'm convinced that it's the only place she'll be safe right now."

Bryan opened the passenger-side door of the patrol car. "The back is kind of uncomfortable. I'll ride back there."

Sarah slipped into the front passenger seat. The officer's computer took up a lot of the seat space. Grant got behind the wheel and swung the car around.

"Oh, by the way." Bryan leaned forward. "Your car's parked up by Martin's."

"Thanks a lot, buddy," Grant said.

Bryan was probably joking around to forget about what they had just been through, but the camaraderie between the two men did nothing to lighten Sarah's spirits.

She rested her head against the seat. She rubbed her wrists where the duct tape had been. She touched the bandage on her forehead. Though she made no noise, tears formed at the corners of her eyes and flowed down her cheeks. She stared, not really seeing the view in front of her. Would this ever come to an end?

From behind, a gentle, warm hand touched her shoulder and squeezed.

NINE

Bryan flipped through the Mason file for the ump-teenth time. At least when he had been up in the fire tower, he'd been able to think of something other than this case. But here at the station, it seemed to meet him at every turn.

He checked his watch. It was nearly noon. Sarah had fallen asleep on a couch in the break room after fresh-ening up in the bathroom and changing into a brand-new shirt Bryan kept in his desk for court appearances.

Bryan got a few hours' sleep himself, and then brought the file with him so he could watch over Sarah. He didn't think those thugs would be so bold as to enter the police station, but he'd been foolish enough to think she was safe going to the bathroom in a truck stop. He wasn't taking any chances.

He tossed the folder to one side. He had one thin thread that connected Mason to what was happening to Sarah. Why couldn't he let it go? Sarah looked peace-ful as she slept. Without thinking, he reached over and touched her soft brown hair. Sarah stirred but didn't awaken.

Sandoval should be on shift soon. Though the chief

had seemed more open to providing protection when he'd talked to him on the phone, Bryan had started to have mixed feelings about it. After last night, he didn't feel totally comfortable turning her over to some rookie officer. He wanted to be the one to protect her.

He grabbed the investigation folder. He flipped through the pages of the file, reliving each step forward in the investigation. Growing angry each time he thought of the legal roadblock Mason's lawyer had put in the way. Mason was a business owner known for making large donations to various community causes. He had the air of respectability and way too much money to spend on an unscrupulous legal team.

The real blow to the case was the disappearance of their key witness, a young Mexican woman named Eva who had been promised citizenship and a job. Instead, she had been moved from one factory job to another, locked in a room with dozens of other people every night. She escaped once she was moved to Montana and had come forward to the authorities. Bryan was pretty sure that Eva was dead, though they hadn't found the body.

The thick file slid off his lap and fell on the floor. He kneeled and gathered the papers back into a pile. Sarah stirred on the couch. She rolled so her face was away from him.

One of the papers caught his eyes. In preparation for the trial, they had subpoenaed all of Mason's financial records. The page he held was a list of Mason's assets. Mason owned houses in other states. He traveled out of the country often. And he was a mostly silent partner in several different businesses. His eyes scanned the list, resting on the words *part owner, Crazy Ray's used car dealership.*

Still clutching the paper, Bryan sat down on the carpet. So there was a connection between Mason and the man who approached Sarah at the fairgrounds. Excited, he paged through a phone book until he found the number for the car dealership. When he dialed, a message machine informed him that Ray had closed the shop and left for vacation as of today. Bryan clenched his teeth. How convenient and suspicious.

Through two sets of glass doors, Chief Sandoval made his way into the station.

Sandoval stopped as he passed the break room, his gaze resting momentarily on Sarah. "I heard you had quite a night."

Bryan stood up from the floor. "That's not half of it." He stepped outside the break room. Feeling a rising sense of anticipation, he placed the papers from the messed up file on his desk. "I think her missing brother connects back to the Mason case."

The chief drew his eyebrows together. "Keyes, you've got to let that Mason case go."

"No, listen to me. One of the men who tried to abduct her in the forest worked for Mason." Bryan stepped toward Sandoval. "And last night, the guy who approached her, probably to threaten her, when we were out looking for Crew is one of Mason's business partners, a man named Ray Mitchell—he owns a used car place."

"Those are tenuous connections. Have you contacted this Ray Mitchell?"

"His message machine says that he left for a vacation." Bryan stepped closer to the chief. "Reinstate me."

The chief pressed his lips together. "I'm not so sure you can see clearly where this case is concerned."

"Give me seventy-two hours. I'll make the case against him." And he'd make sure Sarah was safe. As important as it was to Bryan to see Mason brought to justice, it was also crucial to make sure Mason and his thugs would leave Sarah and her brother alone once and for all.

"And if you can't, you'll come back and be the good detective you've always been." The chief leaned toward him and looked him square in the eye. "Don't let your life be defined by this investigation."

Bryan nodded. "Just three days, that's all I need."

Sandoval rubbed his chin. "I'll put the paperwork through for your reinstatement."

Bryan slumped back down in his chair. He stared at the pile of papers, the sum total of the case against Mason. He'd have to call the Ranger Station and let them know he couldn't go back up in the tower. Once again, this case would be his focus.

Now that he was seeing connections, he wondered if this woman Crew was with might be Eva. Eva had dark hair, but she might be wearing a wig to disguise her appearance. Maybe he'd been too hasty in assuming she'd been killed. It would definitely explain why Crew's roommate said she was scared. But how would she have met Crew?

Sarah stirred and rolled back over. She opened her eyes.

Bryan leaned against the doorway that separated his office from the break room. "Hey, did you get rested up?"

"Guess I was pretty worn out." She sat up and ran

her fingers through her curly hair. "So am I going to be able to go back to my house?"

She must have heard some of the conversation between him and Sandoval. "I don't know about that. I think it would be better if you stayed close to me."

"What about work? I'm supposed to go in today."

"Where do you work?"

"A place called Loving Hearts. It's a church-affiliated adoption service. Our office is downtown."

"Maybe you should ask for time off until we have assurance that we can keep you safe." Really the only guarantee she had for safety was if Mason was behind bars and his hired henchmen went with him.

"They need me at the office. I want to go in to work. I want my life back." She looked off to one side and let out a heavy breath.

"Sarah, you saw how serious these guys are."

She swiped a tear away from the corner of her eye. "I guess if that's how it has to be." She turned to face him. "So what do I do now?"

"You're safe in the station. I'll go with you if you need to go out."

"But you're going to be working on the case that has you so upset. This Tyler Mason guy." Her words carried traces of hurt.

"You heard what I said to Sandoval?"

"Is that the only reason you stayed with me? Because you thought there might be some connection between what Crew has gotten himself into and your big case?"

"Sarah, you have to know that that isn't true. After all we've been through in the last twenty hours you trust me more than that, don't you?"

Old insecurities plagued him. If she still saw their relationship in terms of what had happened ten years ago, the answer to that question would be no.

She stared at him, her eyes glazing. "I want to believe you."

Moved by her sadness, he leaned toward her, reaching out and covering her hand with his.

She pulled her hand away. "Your boss seems to think you don't see too clearly where this case is concerned, as if you're obsessed."

He felt the sting of her rejection. She couldn't receive the comfort he offered. "I just want Mason taken down. I don't like it when a bad guy gets away with acting like some sort of good citizen. If that makes me obsessed, then I guess I am."

"But that's your focus—arresting Mason. Not helping me, or finding Crew."

He could feel the wedge being driven between them. The unresolved pain that was always there would make it impossible for her to trust his motives. "I don't want to see you hurt."

She studied him for a long moment and then stared at the ceiling. "I'm hungry and I need to brush my teeth."

"I can have some takeout brought over. I've got a tube of toothpaste in my locker you can use. Problem solved."

Sarah smiled. "Like camping, right? You brush your teeth with your fingers."

He laughed. "I'll have one of the officers run across the street to the drugstore." He appreciated her sense of humor. This couldn't be easy for her. "Maybe we can get you back in your house before the day is over."

A take-out meal waited for Sarah when she returned from freshening up. Though a little big on her, the blue button-down shirt brought out the color in her eyes. The years had only enhanced her natural beauty.

He shuffled the papers he'd been poring over. "You look good."

Sarah blushed. "Thanks."

At least she could receive his compliment. Bryan worked through the afternoon while Sarah rested and read a book she borrowed from one of the other officers.

Her cell phone rang and she pulled it out. Her forehead wrinkled when she looked at the number. "Hello?"

The voice on the other end of the line sounded frantic.

Sarah leaned forward, her expression pensive. "Crew, is that you?"

Sarah could feel panic taking over, invading her mind and tensing her muscles as Crew spat out his words.

"I never meant for you to be hurt. I didn't know they would do something like this."

Anxiety built up inside her. Her brother was desperately afraid and not making much sense. "What's going on? Who are you in trouble with?"

"It's not me. I was only trying to do the right thing. I was only trying to help her."

Bryan stepped toward Sarah, leaning in so he could hear the conversation.

Sarah struggled to remain calm. "Who were you trying to help?"

"I wanted to do the right thing and it ended up getting you hurt. I'm so sorry."

"Crew, it's all right. Just tell me where you are. I can come and get you. The police will help protect you."

"I have to keep moving. There are spies everywhere."

Spies? What did Crew mean by that? "Tell me where you are now. Are you in town?" Sarah took in a breath. "I can be there in five minutes."

Sarah could hear Crew's breathing on the other end of the line.

"Crew, please. Where are you?"

"I can't stay here long." His voice trembled.

"Please tell me. I want to help."

"Lewis and Clark Park."

The line went dead.

Sarah pulled her phone away from her ear and turned to face Bryan. "He says he's at Lewis and Clark Park."

"I'll bring him in." Bryan headed toward the interior of the station. "I'll see if I can get some backup."

She grabbed his arm as he swept past. "I'm going with you."

"Sarah, I can't risk it."

She squeezed his arm. "He's my brother."

"I don't want you out in the open like that."

"I'm the one he trusts. If he sees a bunch of cops coming toward him, he might bolt."

Bryan studied Sarah for moment. "All right, you can come, but you stay close to me at all times."

Bryan led Sarah to the parking lot behind the station where the patrol cars were. They jumped in and sped through downtown and several residential neighborhoods. Bryan grabbed the radio. "This is Unit Fourteen. I'm headed toward Lewis and Clark and requesting backup in bringing in a witness who may be in danger."

The dispatcher responded. "Unit Fourteen, Unit Nine is on the corner of Eighteenth and Grand. ETA is about five minutes."

"No sirens," Bryan commanded. "The man is approximately thirty years of age, dark curly hair, six feet tall." He clicked off his radio and glanced toward Sarah. "How does he dress?"

"I haven't seen him in months, but he has this pair of red high-tops that I gave him. I replace them whenever his current pair wears out. Oh, and he usually has a bandanna around his neck."

Bryan relayed the information to the other officers through the dispatcher.

A second patrol car responded saying they could be there in seven minutes.

Bryan pulled into the lot that surrounded Lewis and Clark Park. Sarah jumped out and surveyed the area. The park spread over five acres. A playground and a pavilion were close to the road. Beyond the rolling hills where college students sat under trees and played Frisbee was a second access road. The park had a river flowing through it, a natural amphitheater, and it connected to hiking trails.

Not all the park was visible from this vantage point. To the south the park connected with a cemetery and at the base of the rolling hills to the west was the public library, a popular hangout for some of Discovery's homeless. Would Crew be there? She should have gotten him to give her a more specific answer.

Another patrol car rolled by on the other road that bordered the park.

Bryan scanned the park. "This is a lot of acreage to cover. He didn't say where he'd be?"

"He said he had to keep moving." Sarah's fast walk turned into a jog as she searched for her brother. The more she searched without seeing him, the harder it was to breathe, as if her torso was wrapped in a tight cloth.

The beautiful, sunny afternoon brought an abundance of people out to the park. A group picnicked in the pavilion. Several bunches of children ran through the park or played on the slides and swings.

"He may have gone to the cemetery. Plenty of places to hide up there," Bryan suggested.

The other two police officers got out of their car. They waved in Bryan's direction and then proceeded to split off.

"He could be hiding behind a tree or down by the creek bed." She let out a breath. "I think he'll come out if he sees me."

"Why don't you try calling the number he phoned from?"

"He doesn't have a cell. It was probably a pay phone or the free phone in the library." Anxiety settled in her stomach like a rock. What if Crew had gotten scared and run away already?

"Hey, those guys look familiar." Bryan pointed across the park to three men headed down the hill toward the library.

"Yeah, from the shelter." Sarah took off at a dead run. "Hey, Eddie."

Eddie turned at the sound of his name. His eyes

grew wide with recognition. The other two men continued on down the hill, giving nervous glances over their shoulders. Sarah's feet pounded across the lush grass of the park.

Sarah and Bryan were within twenty feet of Eddie when the sound of screeching tires on the road by the cemetery entrance drew their attention.

Two men, one of them Acne Scars, held a third man by his shoulders despite his attempts to struggle away. A van screeched to a halt. The sliding doors opened and the struggling man was tossed in. His abductors piled in behind him.

"That was Crew." Sarah took off running.

Bryan kept up with her as they sprinted up the hill. The van rolled toward the cemetery, not going fast enough to draw attention to itself.

They were out of breath by the time they made it to the top of the hill. The other two officers were not in sight and the third patrol car still had not arrived.

"They can't get out by way of the cemetery. They will have to circle around and come out another way. We might be able to cut them off at the park entrance."

They ran to the patrol car and jumped in. Bryan pulled away from the street.

Sarah scanned the landscape. Trees partially blocked her view of the entrance. "There it is."

The van rolled into view. It pulled out onto the street just as Bryan gained speed and slipped in behind it.

He grabbed the radio. "Our target has been taken in a dark van heading east on Babcock."

The van continued to move at a normal speed.

Sarah leaned close to the windshield. "Maybe we can sneak up on him."

"I wouldn't count on it. We're in a patrol car," said Bryan.

Traffic grew thicker the closer they got to the shopping district with four-lane through streets, fewer lights and big box stores.

The light up ahead turned yellow. The van sped up and raced through it.

Bryan hit the sirens. "He's on to us."

Cars pulled to the side of the street to get out of their way. Bryan pressed the accelerator and zigzagged around the vehicles that were slow in reacting. The van sped through a red light. Two cars crashed into each other. Bryan swerved to avoid them.

He looked up ahead. "Where did it go?"

Sarah leaned forward, peering through the windshield.

Please, God, don't say we've lost them.

Desperation settled in. She glanced up and down the street and at the side streets as they sped past. Sirens still flashing, Bryan slowed down.

She spotted the van rolling through the parking lot that connected with a home improvement store.

"There." She pointed.

The light turned green. Bryan zoomed toward the side street that connected with the parking lot. He radioed the other patrol cars advising them of his position. "You might want to get over here and see if we can block off the entrances."

Bryan rolled past the row of parked cars. None of them looked even remotely like the van. He turned and drove up the next row.

"Maybe we lost them," she whispered as a sense of

despair overtook her. What would those men do to her brother? "We have to find him."

Bryan turned down another row. He pressed the brakes. Four car lengths from them stood the dark van.

Bryan picked up the radio and explained where he was. "Be advised. I have located the vehicle. I will wait for your arrival as suspects are likely armed and dangerous." He clicked off the radio and turned to Sarah. "You stay in this car."

Bryan slipped out of the driver's seat, crouching behind his open door. He drew his gun.

The other patrol car came to a stop on the opposite side of the van. Two officers got out, weapons drawn. Bryan lifted his chin, pointed toward the van and then held up two fingers. One officer remained behind his car door while the other moved forward to assist Bryan, who ran toward the van from the opposite direction.

With his gun drawn, he approached the driver's-side window. His arms slackened. He moved to the back of the vehicle when the officer appeared, shaking his head.

Fear twisted through Sarah. The men weren't in the front seat. What if they had gotten away? Bryan held up his gun. The other officer knocked on the van doors. He backed up without taking his eyes off the doors.

They waited a moment, both of them ready to shoot. Seconds ticked by. Sarah tensed. She brushed away images of Crew being harmed.

At Bryan's signal, the second officer strode forward and opened the van doors.

The interior was empty.

TEN

Sarah's footsteps pounded behind Bryan. Her voice was drenched with anguish. "Where is he? What happened?"

"They must have pulled into the lot here to switch vehicles." Bryan holstered his gun. Whether they'd planned it ahead of time or got the car into place when they realized they were being pursued, it was a clear indication that a mastermind was behind the whole operation.

"What do we do now? They're going to hurt him... or worse."

"We'll impound this vehicle for evidence," said the other officer. "I can take care of that."

"That won't help my brother." Sarah rested her palms on Bryan's chest, her eyes pleading. "We need to find those people now."

"We don't even know what kind of car they got away in." He could feel Sarah's desperation in every word she spoke. It was his desperation, too. This wasn't just about Mason. The clock was ticking for Crew. "We go to the source." Bryan stalked back toward the police car.

Sarah followed behind him. "What are you talking about?"

Once they were inside the car, Bryan gripped the steering wheel until his knuckles turned white. "I know Tyler Mason is behind this. I'm going to go to him and get some answers now."

Sarah buckled her seat belt as Bryan sped through the parking lot.

"I'll take you back to the station," Bryan said.

"We don't have time for that."

Bryan tapped the steering wheel. Sending his business partner on a vacation was a good indication that Mason knew the spotlight was back on him. He doubted his appearance would come as a surprise to Mason. Sarah's appearance, on the other hand…who knew how the man would react to the arrival of the woman his thugs had been trying to capture for the past day? "No, it's not safe for you to come with me."

"I can't sit in that police station thinking about what my brother might be going through. I have to do something."

They were wasting precious time arguing. "All right, come with me, but stay in the reception area, where there are other people around. Mason wouldn't try anything, even on his home turf, if there's a chance he might be seen. He'll do everything to keep his hands clean."

"I want to meet this man who you think is behind all this."

"Sarah, I don't think you want to look into his eyes." They were the eyes of pure evil.

The force of his voice took any argument out of her. "All right, I'll do what you say."

He took several side streets into a business district. With each passing block, the rage inside him simmered to a boil.

"Do you think they were looking for Crew because of the woman his roommate saw him with, the woman he's trying to help?"

Bryan nodded as he watched the street addresses. "I suspect that they want information from him…probably about this woman." The idea that the woman might be Eva, his missing witness, still tickled his brain. Why else would Mason work so hard to get at her?

He arrived at a building with doors marked for a bookkeeping business and a massage studio. He parked in front of the office that said Workforhire.

Sarah rested her hand on his. "Are you sure you want to do this?"

Her touch soothed his ragged nerves. "We're out of options. We have to find your brother before it's too late. We need to stir things up. See if Mason blinks."

"Let's do this," Sarah said.

They swung open the door and stepped into a reception area done in rich browns and tans. A man and a woman both dressed in suits sat on the high-end leather couches. Bryan's investigation revealed that Mason had a number of legitimate clients. But the math didn't work out for the kind of assets Mason owned compared to the number of people who openly found work through his agency. Most of the other businesses Mason owned barely broke even.

Sarah took a seat on the couch. Bryan stalked over to the receptionist, a twenty-something blonde with short, spiky hair. She adjusted her headset as Bryan approached. Her eyes grew wide with recognition. He'd come to this office several times when he'd been running the investigation.

No doubt, Mason had trained her in the latest diversion and stall tactics if he were to show up. He skirted past her without even making eye contact.

"Sir, where are you going?"

Bryan strode toward an ornate wooden door. He pushed it open.

Mason looked up from his keyboard. His mouth formed a perfect O shape. His cold gray eyes gave away nothing.

The receptionist scurried up behind Bryan, directing her comments to Mason. "I tried to stop him."

"It's all right, Cassandra. It seems Officer Keyes is quite adamant about talking to me. Close the door on your way out." His voice was icy, his words clipped.

Cassandra backed out, easing the door shut.

Mason laced his fingers together. His skin was tanning-booth orange and his dark eyebrows stood in sharp contrast to his brassy blond hair. "I guess I can't call you Officer Keyes. The last I heard, you were babysitting a forest."

Mason's condescending tone was calculated to get a rise out of him. The man wanted him to lose control. Despite the rage that smoldered inside, Bryan wasn't about to take the bait. "Well, I'm back on the force."

Mason made a clicking noise with his tongue. "Oh, good, back to writing tickets for the jaywalkers."

Bryan planted his feet. "I know that you're responsible for Crew Langston being kidnapped."

Mason raised his eyebrows. "I've never heard of the man." The nervous tapping of his fingers on the desk gave him away. He was lying.

Bryan lunged toward Mason's desk. "What have you done with him?"

Mason stood up. "Officer Keyes, why must you persist in this line of questioning?" Despite the plastic smile, his voice had a waver to it. Mason was behind all of this. He was sure of it now.

Bryan gritted his teeth. "If anything happens to him, I'll see to it that it's hung around your neck."

Mason skirted around his desk and sat on the corner. "And I told you I've never heard of the man." He lifted his chin in a show of superiority.

Bryan's rage threatened to explode.

Keep your cool. The last thing you want is for him to file assault charges.

Bryan leaned toward him. "What has he done? Did a high school dropout junkie actually manage to get one over on you?"

Mason blinked and looked away. Bryan detected a flicker of emotion. Mason was good at hiding his true motives. But the mask had fallen away for a second, revealing fear. Somehow, Crew had managed to outsmart the mighty Tyler Mason.

"This is a business, Mr. Keyes. I don't appreciate your threatening attitude. Unless you have need of some temporary labor or would like to sign up for our service, I suggest you leave."

The nerve. Mason's holier-than-thou posturing made his blood boil. He had to get out before he took a swing at Mason. "If a hair on Crew Langston's head is harmed, I will come after you and nail you to the wall."

"You tried that once, Officer Keyes." His words dripped with sarcasm. "It's hard to send an innocent man to jail. And that's what I am—an innocent man. So I suggest you quit harassing me."

Bryan's hand curled into a fist. His voice turned low and husky. "I'll see myself out."

Sarah rose to her feet when he came to the reception area. She waited until they were outside before she spoke.

"Did he say anything about Crew?"

"It's what he didn't say. I'm more convinced than ever that he's behind this," Bryan said.

"Where do we go now? How does this help us find Crew?"

Bryan mulled through the possibilities. "I stirred up Mason. Let's watch this place and see if he leaves… sends someone out to check on things. My guess is he'll use the receptionist."

"They'd want to take him somewhere they could question him and not be disturbed." Sarah opened the passenger-side door. She rested her elbow on the hood of the car, a note of urgency laced through her words. "We don't have much time. I doubt their methods of questioning are humane."

"I know, but what are we going to do? Search every building in town?" Frustration formed a tight knot at the base of his neck. "Our best bet is to see how Mason reacts. He has to lead us to them."

Sarah pressed her lips together and hung her head. He understood the sense of helplessness she must be wrestling with.

She looked off into the distance. "I guess they won't kill him as long as he doesn't tell them what he knows. He'll hold out. My brother is more stubborn than me." She slipped into the car.

After he sat behind the wheel, Bryan turned the key in the ignition and pulled the patrol car into an out-of-the-way spot. "I'm going to call the station, have them bring over something less conspicuous."

Within ten minutes, an officer had shown up with an unmarked car, a white sedan. Bryan and Sarah waited through the early evening. The sun was low in the sky when Cassandra emerged through the front doors. They tailed Cassandra around town while she stopped at several businesses and an office supply place. None of the buildings she entered were likely candidates for holding Crew.

Bryan wondered if he'd made a bad call when the police radio sparked to life.

"Unit Nine, I've got a report of a disturbance. Car dealership on Nineteenth and Main. Neighbor saw lights flash on and off. Place is supposed to be closed."

Bryan grabbed the radio. "This is Unit Fourteen. I'm taking that call. We're en route."

"Affirmative," dispatch responded. "Are you in the neighborhood?"

"Close enough. Send backup. No sirens." Bryan sped up the car. "This is more than a disturbance." He hung up the radio.

Sarah looked at him, her eyes questioning.

"The dealership on the corner of Main and Nineteenth is Crazy Ray's. That's got to be where they took him."

ELEVEN

Sarah gripped the armrest as Bryan sped down Nineteenth Street. The businesses on this end of town were all on one-and two-acre lots, mostly RV and motorcycle dealerships and home repair stores. They passed two lots that had buildings with For Sale signs. He pressed the brakes as they rolled into Crazy Ray's, past rows and rows of cars. Bryan killed the headlights and slowed to a snail's pace. He stopped. "Let's not park too close. You stay here. My backup should be here any second."

"Okay." She wasn't about to wait this out in the car. Crew was her brother. But they didn't have time for arguments. She'd do exactly what he'd said—she would stay there...right up until she got up and left. He hadn't specified how *long* she should stay there, after all.

She waited until Bryan was twenty feet from the building before pushing open her own door. She sprinted with a light step, came up behind Bryan and placed her hand on his back.

"I should have guessed you weren't going to stay in the car," he whispered.

She stared out into the lot. Where was that backup?

Bryan drew his gun. The dealership was dark. A note on the door indicated the store was closed while the owner was on vacation.

Another car with lights turned off rolled through the lot. That must be their backup. Two officers, barely shadows in the twilight, exited the car. Responding to Bryan's hand signals, they disappeared around the side of the building.

Bryan pushed on the front door. It opened. A place like this probably had all kinds of security and an alarm system—which had been turned off. A clear sign that somebody was here.

Bryan slipped inside, Sarah pressed close behind him. Darkness covered the showroom floor. Cars appeared in silhouette.

Bryan raced over to a room marked Office. "Stand back and to the side." His whisper was forceful.

Sarah pressed against the wall.

He tried the doorknob. "Locked."

Sarah turned her head. To her side was a white door, slightly ajar. She tugged on Bryan's sleeve and pointed.

He tiptoed across the floor. Resting his back against the wall, he pushed the door open, revealing a repair shop connected to the dealership. She could discern only the outlines of cars and equipment. No movement, no light. Only silence.

Yet, the pathway of unlocked doors suggested this was the way the perpetrators had come. Could they have left already?

Her heart drummed wildly, sweat snaked down her back.

A muffled thud emanated from a corner of the room.

A single word boomed through the space. "Police."

More noise, banging, louder this time.

Bryan hit the lights. The main area contained only an elevated car.

"There!" said Sarah, pointing at the door across the room. Bryan took the lead, kicking the door in. An officer lay on the floor by the door that led outside, not moving.

She gasped. There was blood everywhere. Not just on the floor by the downed police officer. She saw blood on a tan leather chair. Duct tape around the arms of the chair.

The second officer burst through the outside door.

Tires screeched in the parking lot.

"I got this," the officer said, leaning over his partner. "You go catch those guys."

Bryan pulled her through the door and dragged her to the car. She'd gone numb.

That was Crew's blood in there.

Though she had no clear memory of her actions, she must have gotten in the car. She shook herself free of emotional paralysis at the moment Bryan pulled out of the lot onto the street. Red taillights burned in front of them.

Bryan stayed close to the brown car as it sped through the streets up until a delivery truck pulled out from a side road, slipping in between them right before they came to a stop at a red light.

Bryan angled his head. "I can't see him."

Though the delivery truck blocked their view, the light must have turned green. The row of cars eased forward.

Bryan rolled down the window and leaned out. "He switched lanes. He's turning." Bryan cranked the wheel, pulling out of the line of stopped traffic. Several cars honked as he headed up the street where a green arrow indicated cars could make a left turn.

Sarah scanned the street. Though traffic was light at this hour, it was hard to find the other car. Then she caught sight of a brown vehicle turning off onto a side street, traveling faster than the flow of traffic. Bryan closed the distance between them. He radioed his position and the direction the car was going. Sirens sounded in the distance. The car doubled back toward Crazy Ray's but abruptly turned into one of the for-sale lots, a former car repair place. Taillights disappeared around the empty building.

Bryan followed as the sirens grew louder. They sped around the corner. Her vision filled with taillights. The thugs had stopped for some reason, but now they were trying to get up to speed again.

Sarah searched the dark lot. "Stop, I think they dumped him."

Bryan didn't slow down. An engine roared as the assailants' car rolled back out onto the road. "Why would they push him out?"

She searched the dark lot. "Maybe because they knew they were going to be caught. I saw them come to a full stop." She discerned a lump toward the edge of the lot. Her heart squeezed tight.

Bryan stopped the car and radioed the patrol unit to continue up the road after the car. "We were the ones with the best chance of catching them. Those guys will get into the flow of traffic and be lost. I hope you're right about them dumping Crew."

Sarah pushed the door open.

In the dim light, it was hard to see anything. Frantic, Sarah sprinted toward the motionless shadow at the edge of the lot.

They had taken a gamble by not following the car. She could only hope—and pray—that it would pay off.

Please, God, let it be Crew.

As she drew closer, she was able to see the outline of a man lying on the ground, still not moving. Her heart stopped. Time seemed to slow down as she took the remaining steps toward the body.

"Crew? It's me." No response. She dropped to her knees.

With trembling fingers, she touched his neck. A faint pulse pushed back. The coppery scent of blood filled her nostrils. "Hang in there. We'll get you help."

Behind her, she could hear Bryan already calling for an ambulance.

Bryan approached and kneeled beside her. Leaning closer to Crew, he placed his palm on Crew's chest, examined the blood on his clothes and then took his hand and squeezed it. "He's pretty beat up." His voice was filled with indignation.

Sarah released a cry. "I know."

In the distance, the sirens cut through the stillness of the night.

Moments later, the flashing light turned into the lot. Bryan ran out to meet the ambulance and direct them to where Sarah waited with Crew.

Two EMTs, a man and a woman, carried a stretcher over to them. When the man shone a flashlight on Crew's face, the amount of crusted dried blood shocked her.

Crew was lifted onto the stretcher.

"I'll ride in the ambulance." Her voice came out monotone. Shock had settled in. She felt only numbness.

Bryan rested a hand on her shoulder. "I'll be right behind you."

She draped her hand over his. "Thank you."

They trotted across the broken concrete to where the ambulance waited. She squinted at the bright lights as she climbed in and sat beside Crew. He'd been hooked up to an IV, but remained motionless, with his eyes closed.

She touched his thick, dark hair.

Please, God, don't let him die.

She studied Crew. His shirt was bloody, his face bruised. A thousand memories scrolled through her head. She'd been five and Crew had been seven when their parents died. Their grandmother had taken them in until she died. After that, it had been a series of foster homes. Some good, some not so good. Crew had been the one constant in her life.

They pulled up to the emergency room doors. Sarah stepped out and watched as they unloaded the stretcher. She glanced around the lot and at the entrances. No sign of Bryan.

Sarah entered through the doors where they'd taken her brother.

The woman at the check-in desk stood up. "Ma'am, it would be best if you waited until the doctor came out to talk to you."

"But I want to be with my brother."

"They have to determine the extent of his injuries and what needs to be done." The woman handed her a clipboard. "In the meantime, why don't you fill out this information about your brother."

With a heavy heart, Sarah sat down in the waiting room. She stared at the form on the clipboard. Health Insurance, Address, Place of Employment—all normal things that most people took for granted. She tossed the form aside. She didn't want to think about this right now.

She paced. She found a vending machine with snacks and a soda. She paced some more.

She slumped down in the chair and stared out at the dark night. Bryan should be here by now.

What had delayed him?

The taillight of the ambulance had no sooner slipped out of view over a hill when Bryan's phone buzzed with a new text. He pulled over, expecting it to be from Sarah.

I suggest you stop your investigation right now.

No need to sign that one. Mason was up to his old tricks. Of course, it would be from a number that couldn't be traced back to him. The guy was good at covering his tracks.

The text didn't scare him. It fueled his anger and indignation. He'd been running away from Mason's thugs when he'd climbed up into that fire tower with Sarah, and it seemed like he'd been running in one way or another ever since. No more.

If it was the last thing he ever did and the hardest thing he did, he would see to it that Mason went to jail so that no one would have to fear him or his cohorts ever again.

And he was starting to think he was getting pretty

close. Mason was becoming either sloppy or desperate. Setting Crazy Ray's up as a torture chamber wasn't too smart. Mason had to know they'd linked the dealership to him or he wouldn't have sent Ray on *vacation* where he couldn't talk.

He turned his steering wheel and entered the flow of traffic. Mason's thugs hadn't killed Crew, but they had dumped him and left him for dead. Had Crew finally given them the information they wanted? Or had they given up? They knew they were being tailed. Maybe they'd decided Crew's information wasn't worth getting caught over.

The road curved as he headed uphill. The hospital was built next to the hiking trails that connected with Lewis and Clark Park. He pulled into the hospital parking lot. Though the lot wasn't as full as it would have been during the day, he had to park a ways from the emergency room doors.

As he approached the emergency room, a man in scrubs came through the hospital's sliding doors. "Are you Bryan Keyes?"

"Yeah." How did this guy know his name?

"Sarah Langston asked me to keep an eye out for you. She misplaced her phone. They've taken her brother to surgery on the third floor. There's a waiting room up there right through the main entrance. She wanted you to know that you'll find her there."

Nodding his understanding, Bryan passed through the sliding doors. A woman with her head bent over a book sat at the registration desk. He walked over to the elevator, stepped in and pushed the button for the third floor.

Moments later, the doors slid open. The second he

stepped out on the carpet, Bryan knew something was wrong.

At this time of night, he didn't expect a huge staff, but no one occupied the nurses' station. Bryan strode toward the hallway. Empty. A huge piece of plastic had been stapled across an opening at the end of the hallway along with a sign that read Closed For Construction.

He'd been set up.

Bryan turned and bolted for the elevator.

Why the misdirection? Had they come back to finish Crew off and didn't want him interfering? Or... oh, no, were they after Sarah again and wanted him out of the way?

Glancing side to side, he waited for the elevator doors to open.

Footsteps pounded behind him. He whirled around, ready to land a blow. The assailant, his old buddy Deep Voice, grabbed his arm. A second man came up from behind.

He had only a moment to register the needle sinking into his biceps before he collapsed to the floor.

TWELVE

"Miss Langston?"

Someone shook her shoulder. She opened her eyes. Predawn light streamed through the window. She'd been asleep on the waiting room couch for hours.

She looked up at the woman who had awakened her. Dressed as a nurse, she was middle-aged with kind eyes.

"Your brother is stabilized. He's got some fractured ribs and lacerations. The thing we are most concerned about is his brain. He received severe blows to the head. We'll have to watch him for several days to determine the extent of the damage."

"Is he conscious?"

The nurse shook her head. "You're welcome to go in and sit with him. Room 117."

Sarah stood up. Her head still hadn't cleared from the fog of sleep. Bryan wasn't in the waiting room. As she made her way down the hall, she tried his cell phone. No answer. Sarah pushed open the door of 117.

Crew looked peaceful. The blood had been cleaned off him and replaced with clean white bandages around his head and on his hand. A nurse checked an IV and pulled the blankets up higher on his chest. Beside the bed on a tray sat a wallet, a watch and a creased picture of her and Crew. They must have tossed out the bloody bandanna.

The nurse pulled a chair from a corner of the room. "Sometimes it helps if you talk to them. The jury is still out on how much someone in a coma can hear."

Sarah winced at the word *coma*.

"I'm sure the talking won't be in vain. I've seen amazing recoveries in my time." The nurse patted Crew's head and left, her soft-soled shoes barely making any noise as she crossed the room.

Sarah leaned over the bed and took Crew's hand in her own. "Hey, big brother." His fingers were as cold to the touch as porcelain. She spoke some more to him about shared childhood memories. Overcome with sorrow, she stepped away from the hospital bed. She had to do something or the sadness and fear for Crew's future would consume her.

Finding Bryan seemed like the easiest task. But when she tried calling again, he still wasn't picking up. Maybe he'd been called to another job?

Sarah cleared her throat and dialed the police station. "Hello, I'm trying to locate Officer Bryan Keyes. Has he come by there or called in?"

"Not that I noticed, and he's not on the roster yet," said the desk sergeant.

"Can you have him call me if he does come in?" Sarah gave her name and number and hung up.

A chill that had nothing to do with the room permeated her skin. What had happened to Bryan?

She studied her phone. With two phone calls she had exhausted the possibilities of who she could contact.

She didn't know anything about Bryan anymore—who his friends were, who was important in his life. Ten years ago, he had been her whole world.

Her gaze traveled over to the tray that contained all of Crew's worldly possessions. A revelation crept into her head. No phone.

Crew had called her when she was at the station, but he had no cell phone in his possession. He could have used a pay phone or the free one at the library, but…what if he'd simply borrowed a phone from someone? It was worth checking. She clicked through her phone until the number she was looking for came up. She dialed it.

"Hello?"

She recognized the voice. "Eddie, is that you?"

The line went dead.

She wandered the room. No use calling back; he'd check the number. Eddie had been leaving the park when Crew was taken, and he was the one who had lured her into the fairgrounds building. Why didn't he want to talk to her? She remembered what Crew had said about there being spies everywhere. At the time it had seemed paranoid, but now…

She stared out the window. The tall street lamp glowed in the early morning light. She stepped a little closer to the window. Down below, Bryan's white sedan stood out. Panic flooded through her. Bryan had made it to the hospital. So where was he?

Sarah stroked Crew's cheek and kissed his forehead. "Hang in there."

She ran out into the hallway and back to the emergency room check-in desk. The admin woman was the same one who had been on duty when Crew was brought in.

"Did a man come through here looking for me, Sarah Langston? He's tall, broad shoulders, dark brown hair. He had on a black T-shirt."

The woman shook her head. "Sorry. We had an abundance of senior citizens and teenagers last night but no one who looked like that."

Sarah ran out to the white sedan. Locked. Empty.

Her hands were shaking when she dialed directly into the police station.

"Discovery Police Station." The same desk sergeant she had talked to earlier.

Sarah struggled to speak in a calm voice. "I think Bryan Keyes is missing. He was supposed to meet me at the hospital, but something must have happened to him. His car is here, but he never came into the E.R. That was hours ago."

"I'll send a unit over."

Sarah hung up and searched the lot. Where else would he have gone? The pharmacy and doctors' offices were all closed at night. Her gaze rested on the general registration and admittance area, separate from the E.R.

She hurried over to the sliding glass doors and stepped onto the carpet.

A lone woman sat behind her computer. "Can I help you?"

"Were you working about five or six hours ago?"

"Yes, I was. I get off shift in about forty-five minutes."

"Did a man about my age come through here?"

She thought for a moment. "Tall guy, dark shirt? Sort of messy handsome look?"

Sarah nodded.

"We don't get that much traffic. I thought it was odd that he didn't ask me for directions. He went straight for the elevator like he knew where he was going."

"Where could he have gone?"

"The third floor on this wing is under construction, so he probably went up to the second floor."

"There's no one on the third floor?" Realization spread through her.

The admin lady furled her forehead. "Not at night. The construction guys show up around nine."

Sarah darted over to the elevator. Bryan hadn't gone to the second floor. He'd been lured to the third floor; she was sure of it. As the elevator rose, she realized she probably should have waited for the police to show up. But she couldn't just sit around, not knowing if Bryan was up there. If he was hurt. If he needed her help.

She pulled her key ring from her purse and adjusted the pepper spray in her hand. The door slid open. Sarah stepped onto the carpet. Treading lightly, she walked over to the nurses' station.

A door whooshed open down the hall. The crinkle of thick plastic pressed on her ears. Sarah ducked behind the high counter of the nurses' station and peeked around to watch as a man stalked past, his footfall heavy on the floor.

She lifted her head a few inches above the counter. She saw the man from the back as he stared at the elevator—muscular, thick neck…it was Deep Voice, the guy who had taken her into the forest to kill her.

Bryan had to be around here somewhere. She scampered on all fours toward the wall of plastic. Carefully lifting the plastic at the corner, she cringed at each noise as she scooted through.

Sarah came out into an expansive open area where the walls had been gutted, the floors torn up and building materials occupied most of the floor space. She ran around a stack of drywall. Bryan slumped in a corner of the room. His chin resting on his chest, his shirt torn, hands tied in front of him.

"Bryan."

He lifted his head, but it wobbled on his neck. His eyes were unfocused. His breathing labored.

"Let's get you out of here."

She had only minutes before the guard came back.

"Knife in my pocket." Bryan bent his head, indicating the pocket of his jeans.

She dug out the pocketknife and cut him free. She angled underneath his shoulder and helped him stand. They couldn't go back to the elevator. With Bryan limping along, she searched the room. There had to be a stairwell around here somewhere.

She spotted it just as she heard the crinkling of plastic. No way could they outrun the guard. Sarah flung open the door of the stairwell. She let go of Bryan, allowing him to slump to the floor.

Then she waited, holding the pepper spray in her trembling hand.

Pounding footsteps. The stairwell door swung open. She aimed and pressed the button. Deep Voice shrieked, groaned in pain. Stepping over him, she pressed the door shut and helped Bryan get to his feet.

He was coming around, more able to walk though still dizzy. They had just made it to the second floor landing when the door above them swung open. Deep Voice shouted down at them, his voice bouncing off the tight walls. The time between footsteps indicated he couldn't see clearly.

Sarah pushed open the door and stepped out onto a floor that appeared abandoned, as well. The signs on the doors indicated that these were specialists' offices. The elevator was at the end of the hall. She pushed the button for the first floor. Bryan leaned against the wall for support.

Behind them, the stairwell door burst open. Deep Voice stumbled toward them, swaying a bit and stopping to rub his eyes.

The elevator doors remained shut.

The thug loomed closer to them.

Sarah pushed the button again.

He was within twenty feet. His reddened face stood in sharp contrast to his snarling mouth that revealed yellow teeth.

The doors swung open. Bryan stumbled inside, but when she moved to follow, Deep Voice grabbed her shirttail and held her back. Bryan leapt toward her, gathering her in his arms. He pulled her free and pushed the man. Caught off guard, the thug stumbled backward and the elevator doors slid closed.

The elevator descended and Bryan held her while he leaned against the wall, strong arms surrounding her. She rested her palm on his chest where she could feel his heart racing. She tilted her head and looked into his eyes. "What happened to you?" Her voice came out in a breathless whisper.

Still not totally free from whatever they had drugged him with, Bryan blinked several times. "They *encour-*

aged me to drop the investigation. And I think they wanted me out of commission. When I got to the hospital, someone was waiting outside, dressed in scrubs, to tell me you were waiting for me on the third floor. Once I showed up, they drugged me."

"But they didn't try to kill you."

"I'm sure they would have eventually, but not before I could be used to somehow get them access to you or Crew." The elevator doors opened. Bryan pushed away from the wall. "Is Crew still…?"

She pulled free of his embrace. "Yes, he's alive— but not conscious."

Strength returned to Bryan's voice. "We better get over there. I don't think he's safe."

THIRTEEN

Bryan's head still felt fuzzy from the drugs that had left him incapacitated but conscious. He tried as best he could to scan for any signs of danger.

Sarah squeezed his hand and pulled him down a hallway. "His room is up here." Her voice filled with urgency.

From inside the room, a woman screamed. A man in scrubs emerged. The same man who had misdirected Bryan before. His eyes grew wide at the sight of Bryan. He turned and bolted. Bryan ran after him, but in his weakened state he knew he wouldn't be able to keep up. The man disappeared around a corner.

Bryan braced his hand against a wall, gasping for breath. He returned to the room where a nurse and Sarah both leaned over Crew.

"Is he…?"

"When I came in here…" The nurse put a trembling hand to her mouth. "That man was holding Mr. Langston by the collar and slapping him."

Bryan approached the hospital bed. Crew lay with his eyes closed, still unconscious. "Do you know who he is?"

"He's not anyone I've ever seen on shift," said the nurse.

Bryan pulled Sarah aside while the nurse continued to fuss over Crew. "I don't think Crew told those guys what they wanted to know. That's why they came back here. You heard what the nurse said. That guy could have used the opportunity to kill Crew, but he didn't. Instead, he tried to wake him up."

"So they didn't toss him out of the car because they were finished with him."

"They must have panicked because we were closing in on them," Bryan said. "I'm sure Mason encouraged them to finish their mission."

The nurse left the room.

"Staff watched him pretty close through the night. This was probably the first chance they had to find him alone." Sarah clutched Bryan's shirt and gazed up into his eyes. "What are we going to do?"

"I'll make sure there's an armed guard outside Crew's door."

Sarah glanced out a window. "I called into the station when I couldn't find you. They should be here by now."

"We'll go find them and post one outside Crew's door until we line up something more permanent," Bryan said. "I'm not sure what our next move should be."

"I think we need to find Eddie. He loaned Crew his phone to call me. He's the one who lured me into that building. I think he knows something."

Bryan rushed out to the nurses' station and told them to send the policemen to Crew's room when they showed up.

They stayed in Crew's room while they waited for the officers to arrive.

Sarah stood up. "Are you hungry? I can grab you a snack out of the vending machine."

"Anything to fill the hole in my stomach." His throat was parched. "Mostly, I could use some water."

Sarah left and returned a moment later with a container of bottled water and several bags of chips. He gulped the water.

She scooted the second chair toward him, leaned in and touched a bump on his head he'd gotten courtesy of Mason's thugs.

"What exactly did they do to you?" Her fingers were softer than rose petals.

"I didn't get the impression they wanted to beat any information out of me. They wanted to incapacitate me. I'm a little foggy on the details. One of them grabbed my chin and said something about me going back to the fire tower and leaving the police force, about how any investigation I was pursuing would only lead to trouble."

"But he didn't use Tyler Mason's name."

"Of course not. It was intended as a veiled threat." Bryan clenched his teeth. "Mason won't tie himself to any of this."

The officers arrived. Bryan gave them instructions as well as a description of the man who had impersonated medical personnel.

In the parking lot, morning sun lightened up the sky and warmed the air. Bryan rubbed his eyes.

Sarah offered him a sympathetic glance. "You must be tired."

"Believe it or not, I slept some up on that hospital

floor." He climbed into the car and started it. "Where can we find this Eddie guy?"

"It's still early. Lots of homeless people sleep down by the river in the summer. Some of them hang out at the library later in the day."

"We'll try the river first." Bryan drove for several blocks. He checked his rearview mirror. "We have a friend."

Sarah craned her neck. "How long has he been on us?"

"Since we left the hospital. He disappears and then shows up a couple of blocks later. He thinks he's being sneaky." Bryan turned away from the direction of the river. "Let's lose him for good."

He took the first on-ramp that led out to the highway. Bryan pressed the gas and wove through traffic.

"I can still see him back there." Her words were saturated with tension.

He increased his speed, then slowed and took the exit leading back into town without signaling first. The dark car switched lanes and followed.

Bryan's frustration grew. "When are these guys going to give up?"

"Can you lose him?" Sarah asked.

"Sure, but I don't know what good it will do. Even when we manage to lose them for a little while, they always seem to have a good idea of where we're going next, so they can track us from there."

Sarah touched his forearm. "I have an idea where we could go that they wouldn't expect—Naomi's Place."

Bryan's back stiffened at the name of the pregnancy counseling center they'd gone to when Sarah had become pregnant. His throat clamped shut. He couldn't respond to her suggestion.

She squeezed his arm. "The director will help us. We can hide out there until we're in the clear."

He felt tightness in his chest. Going back there would only remind him of how he had failed Sarah ten years ago. "You're in touch with her, are you?"

"Yes, I work for an adoption agency, remember?"

Bryan clenched his teeth. There must be other places they could go to escape the endless cycle of being tailed.

"We've got to go someplace they're not expecting us to go. Naomi might be able to loan us a different car. We could slip out the back," Sarah said.

Bryan expelled a breath. Sarah had a point. They needed to do something unexpected. Something Mason couldn't anticipate. "Is he behind us now?"

She glanced out the back window. "Not that I can see. Now is our chance."

Bryan turned up a side street. "If he catches up with us, the plan is off." He wove through several more residential streets.

Naomi's Place was an old school that had been converted into a residence. Hedges and trees concealed much of the building from view. Bryan pulled around to the back.

Sarah took the lead, knocking on the door. A young girl, obviously pregnant, answered the door.

"We need to talk to Naomi. Tell her Sarah Langston is here."

The girl eyed Bryan suspiciously. "I'll go get her. You can wait in the living room."

They walked past an industrial-sized kitchen where

several girls laughed and joked with an older woman while they did dishes.

The girl led them into a huge room filled with what looked like secondhand furniture. The long, narrow room with several seating areas had probably been a classroom at one time. Bryan sat down on a plush couch as a knot of anxiety formed in his stomach. This was a trip down memory lane he did not want to take.

Though Sarah had lived here until their baby had been born, he had come only twice for counseling. Memories flooded his mind. He recalled the pressure his parents had put on him. They had never liked Sarah. They wanted the whole thing washed away as though it had never happened. He'd been too young to stand up for himself and then he'd taken his frustration out on Sarah, giving her the silent treatment when she needed his support.

He shifted in his chair, crossing and uncrossing his legs. Then he bolted up to his feet.

Sarah gazed up at him. "This place might not have good memories for you. But it does for me. I found kindness and God's love here."

"Let's get this over with."

She rose to her feet and met his gaze. "We never could have given her the life she deserved, Bryan. We were just kids."

He slumped down in the chair, ran his hands through his hair. He studied her for a moment. The soft angles of her face, her creamy skin and bright eyes. "I know that now. I didn't know it when I was seventeen. I guess I had this dumb idea that we could have been some sort of happy family, but Mom and Day were just so…"

"Your parents were right."

Her answer shocked him.

"They were not nice to me. But they were right. The adoption gave all three of us a chance at a good life."

He looked into Sarah's clear, bright eyes. She seemed to have made peace with the past, even if he couldn't.

A tall woman with dark hair streaked with gray stood in the entryway. "Sarah, how good to see you and…" She studied Bryan for a moment. "Oh, my, the name escapes me, but I remember you." She looked again at Sarah, a faint smile forming on her face.

Sarah put her hands up. "Naomi, it's not what you think. We're not…" Color rose up in her cheeks.

Bryan stood up. "We need your help with a police matter." Bryan flashed his badge. "It's a long story, but if we could borrow your car and leave ours here, we'd really appreciate it."

Naomi drew her eyebrows together and studied Bryan for a moment.

"Sarah's in some danger," Bryan said.

Naomi slowly nodded. "Sure, Sarah, if that's all you need. I'll go get my key from my office." She left the room and returned a moment later, holding the key and a photograph. "What's so strange about you coming by is that I was just thinking about you. I've been sending out invitations for a reunion. You girls who were here that winter ten years ago had such a wonderful bond, I thought it might be nice for you to get together again. You remember these girls."

She handed Sarah the photograph. Bryan peered over her shoulder. Sixteen-year-old Sarah with two other girls sitting in front of a Christmas tree.

"I didn't have any trouble finding Rochelle. She still

lives here in town, but we have no way of contacting Clarissa. The three of you were so close. I don't suppose she stayed in touch with you?"

Sarah shook her head. "I got a postcard from her about a year after she left. She had a job in California. After that, nothing."

She looked at Sarah. "I do hope to see you here for the get-together." She handed the keys to Bryan. "It's the little blue car. Maybe we'll see you here, too."

He shrugged noncommittally to avoid being rude. After all, she was helping them, and she seemed to be very important to Sarah. But at the same time he knew he didn't want to come back here. The place was a reminder of the hole inside him over the life that might have been. The family he could have had if they hadn't rushed things.

Bryan took his house key off the key ring and then handed the rest over to Naomi. "In case you need to go anywhere. We'll make arrangements to get the car back to you."

They walked out to the gravel lot where the car was parked. Neither of them said anything for several blocks. He still felt stirred up, unable to shake the regret that plagued him.

"Should we try the river first?" asked Sarah. "Eddie hung up when I called him. He might not be anxious to see us."

"Or maybe he's dying to tell us what he knows," Bryan said. "Get that burden off his chest."

"Let's hope that's what it is." Sarah looked at the pedestrians on the street. "Eddie isn't a bad person. I'm not sure what's going on with him."

Bryan parked some distance from the river. He got

out of the car and waited for Sarah. At this hour, most of the homeless had wandered toward the center of town to sit in the park or the library. They walked past smoldering fires from the evening before. A man with a thick beard and tangled white hair slipped deeper into the trees when he saw them.

"Maybe we're too late, huh?"

"No, I think we're just in time." Bryan pointed to a man sleeping beneath a piece of cardboard. His distinctive dress shoes stuck out from under the edge of the cardboard.

Sarah stopped. Her eyes filled with fear. "He's not moving," she said in a harsh whisper.

Mason couldn't have gotten to him first. Or could he? Bryan stalked toward the prone figure. He lifted the cardboard, searching for signs of life. Eddie lay still with his eyes closed, hands at his side.

Sarah released a sharp half breath.

Bryan leaned closer to the prone man. He detected the slight up and down motion of Eddie's chest. He poked him in the shoulder. Eddie sat bolt upright, his eyes growing round at the sight of them.

He angled away from Bryan, intending to get to his feet.

Bryan grabbed his arm and pulled him down. "Oh, no, you don't."

Eddie yelped with exaggerated pain, massaging his arm where Bryan had touched him.

"Eddie, we need to talk to you about Crew. I already know you loaned him your phone when you two were in the park yesterday." Sarah got down on her knees, so she could look Eddie in the eye.

Eddie spat out his words. "He wanted to talk to you.

I didn't have anything to do with those men taking him. That wasn't me. No." Eddie grimaced, becoming more agitated. "Somebody else did that."

"Is that what Crew meant when he said there were spies?" Sarah's soft voice seemed to calm Eddie a little.

"For maybe five days now, there's been guys around the river and down at the shelter trying to find Crew, offering money to anyone who knew anything and was willing to talk." Eddie wrung his hands. "Not me, I wouldn't take it."

So anybody who saw Crew in the park could have tipped off Mason's men.

"But you dragged me to the fairgrounds when you knew full well Crew wasn't there." Sarah's voice held no judgment.

Eddie hung his head. "The guy gave me fifty bucks. He said he wasn't going to hurt you." Eddie fidgeted and wiggled. "Can I go now?"

Sarah draped her hand over Eddie's. "We know you wanted to help Crew. You're his friend."

Eddie clawed at his hair. "I heard they messed him up bad."

Bryan sat on the other side of Eddie. "Do you know why?" He fought to keep his voice calm and gentle, like Sarah's, so he wouldn't spook the man. "What were those men after?"

Eddie gnawed on a fingernail. "Crew wouldn't say. He just disappeared like five days ago. I didn't know if he was coming back, but then he showed up. He'd heard they came after you 'cause of him disappearing."

"Did he say anything else to you?"

Eddie stopped wiggling and pulling at his hair.

"Only one thing. He said 'if something happens to me, tell Sarah to go to the safe place.'"

Bryan glanced over at Sarah, who had gone completely white. "Eddie, you don't say a word of this to anyone."

Eddie put his finger to his lips. "It'll be our secret."

Bryan patted Eddie's shoulder. "That's right." He helped Sarah to her feet.

Concern etched across Sarah's face. "Eddie, why don't you use that phone to call your parents? Spend some time at home."

Eddie nodded and scratched his head.

As they walked back to the car, Sarah still had a stunned look on her face.

"You know what he's talking about, right?"

"The safe place is a cabin in the backwoods." Sarah opened the car door. "Crew and I ran away there when we were in a foster home that was less than wonderful. That must be where he took this woman." She climbed into the passenger seat.

Once behind the wheel, Bryan turned to face her. "You remember how to get there?"

She nodded. "I think I can find it. You can't access it by car. We'll have to drive up to the lake and then hike in four or five hours. I have some daypacks at my place and a hiking map."

"I don't know if it's safe to go back to your place."

"Who's to say he doesn't have men watching your place, too? Besides, you don't have a truck anymore that would make it up that mountain. My car is all-wheel drive." She crossed her arms. "And I need to check on my cat."

"Oh, yes, the cat." The level of care she showed for everything in her life made her even more endearing.

"Mr. Tiddlywinks is pretty independent, but he's been by himself for almost two days."

Bryan couldn't hide his amusement. "We'll go back to your place for supplies, and to make sure your cat is okay. I don't want to waste much time. We need to get to that cabin to see if the woman is up there."

"You have an idea who the woman might be, right?"

Bryan let out a heavy breath. "We had a key witness disappear right before we were ready to take Mason to trial. Eva was the one person who could link Mason to the abuses that were happening."

Sarah sat back in the car seat. "You think it's her."

"Why else would Mason be so gung ho to get to her? He's overplayed his hand in a lot of ways. Sending his business partner to talk to you was kind of desperate."

Bryan drove Naomi's car across town, turning on the country road where Sarah lived. He saw no sign of a tail as he drove. Sarah's plan to switch out cars had worked.

"How is Naomi going to get her car back?"

"I'll call her," Sarah said. "She can bring your car out here and make the trade. I'll leave the keys in a place she can find them."

Her house came into view. Bryan pulled up into the driveway. The area around Sarah's house was flat and open. Not many places to hide. No cars were parked along the road.

"Looks okay," she said.

Bryan pushed open the car door. "All the same, we better check it out." His voice threaded with tension as his hand hovered over his gun.

FOURTEEN

They circled the entire house. The front door was unlocked just as she had left it on the day she'd run out of here. She pushed the door open and stepped inside.

Bryan peered over her shoulder.

Clearly the men had come back here after chasing them away.

Though the house wasn't in complete chaos, cupboards and drawers in the kitchen were open. Desk drawers, file cabinets, even her bookshelves with the photographs on it, had been disturbed.

She shuddered, unable to let go of the sense of violation. "Why?"

Bryan pressed close to her, placing a calming hand on her back. "They were on a mission to get Crew. Maybe they thought they could find some information that would help them."

A mournful meow came from the back of the house and a fat yellow cat appeared from around the corner. She swept the cat up and held him close. "Did you miss me?" She closed her eyes as he purred in her arms. "I know we don't have time to deal with this mess, but I have to at least make sure he has food and water."

Bryan nodded. "I understand."

After feeding the cat, Sarah grabbed two backpacks from the closet, changed her clothes and found hiking boots. "These are daypacks. There's food and water, supplies for extreme weather conditions and a first-aid kit."

"We'd better get moving." His voice filled with a sense of urgency.

Once they were out of town, it took only minutes before they were on a forest road headed toward the lake. Bryan checked the rearview mirror several times, though he was fairly confident they hadn't been followed.

"So how old were you when you and Crew ran away to this place?"

She liked that he was curious. "I was twelve and Crew was fourteen. He stole a car. Things had gotten so bad with our foster care family at that time. We decided we would run somewhere nobody could find us."

"And so you came upon this forest service cabin?"

"We stayed up there for a couple of weeks. There were some canned goods already there and Crew was pretty good at catching rabbits and fish. We had a campfire every night, and we took turns reading from our favorite books. We called it the safe place because it felt like nothing in the world could hurt us there."

"So what happened?"

"A ranger found us. Crew wanted to run, but I knew we had to go back." Sarah bent her head. "They put us in a better foster home after that, but I think by then Crew figured he couldn't trust anyone but me."

"You know, the whole time we were dating you never told me any of that."

Sarah lifted her head. Was Bryan finally ready to talk about the past? "When you're sixteen, there's a lot of shame attached to not having a family. It was embarrassing enough that I was in foster care. I didn't share details with anyone. I wanted everyone to see me as a normal kid. I don't think your parents were very happy about their golden boy son dating the orphan even without me bringing up the unpleasant details."

His expression grew serious. "I wasn't very golden to you. I was kind of a jerk."

"It was a hard time for both of us." She looked away, not sure of what else to say, but feeling as though his admission had torn away at the protection around her heart. She toyed with the idea that there might be something between them again. How did he feel about her? Would he walk away after his case against Mason was wrapped up? The thought of being abandoned by him again doused the warm feelings she had for him. She had to know that he would stay with her no matter what.

The mountain road became more treacherous. Bryan focused on his driving.

Sarah studied the narrow, bumpy road. "There's no real parking lot. We're close enough now. You can pull off anyplace the road widens."

Bryan drove for a while longer until the trees to the side of the road thinned. Angling around the trees, he steered the car away from the road.

"I don't think we've been followed, but just in case, I don't want to take a chance that they find the car and disable it. Let's camouflage it, so it's not visible from the road."

They cut branches and picked some up from the

forest floor. Satisfied, they headed through the forest after Sarah checked her compass.

"So this place must be hard to find," Bryan commented as they trekked up a steady incline.

"Forest rangers know about it. Crew and I stumbled on it."

"Have you been back there since that first time?"

"Couple Easters ago, Crew was doing pretty good. We went up there together."

They came out on the opposite side of the lake from where the thugs had initially brought Sarah. The fire tower, high on the mountain, was still visible.

The sun had sunk low in the sky when the cabin, nestled in a valley and surrounded by trees, came into view. A creek flowed not too far from the cabin, silvery in the waning light.

As they approached the cabin, Sarah saw no signs that anyone occupied it. Maybe that had been intentional on Crew's part.

"She's not going to be expecting us. She might be afraid," Bryan said.

"I think I know how to handle this." Sarah knocked on the door. "Hello, my name is Sarah. I'm Crew's sister. I've come to help you."

Bryan leaned toward the door. "Eva, if you're in there, this is Bryan Keyes. The policeman you talked to about Tyler Mason. We can protect you."

No response.

Sarah touched the door with her hand. "I know you're afraid."

The soft padding of careful footsteps reached her ears. Hope rising, Sarah glanced over at Bryan, who looked equally excited.

Without any warning, the door burst open, swinging outward and knocking Sarah to the ground. A woman with a tangle of wild blond hair ran out and bolted for the trees.

Sarah lay on her back with the wind knocked out of her. Bryan took off running after the woman. Still fighting for air, Sarah rolled over on her stomach and watched as Bryan caught the woman. He held her wrists while she screamed and kicked.

"We're not going to hurt you." He spoke in a soothing voice, but it didn't do any good.

She wrenched one hand free and slapped him across the face. Sarah stumbled to her feet and ran toward them. "I'm Crew's sister." As Sarah drew closer, the woman gradually relented in her wrestling with Bryan. Clearly the woman was not the dark-haired Eva Bryan had described, but she looked familiar to Sarah.

"I'm going to let go of you. All right?" Bryan waited until the woman nodded. He released her wrists.

Breathless from her struggle, her shoulders moved up and down. She lifted the tangle of blond hair out of her face. Though she was rail-thin, intense blue eyes, high cheekbones and angular features made her a beautiful woman despite the malnutrition.

"I know you," said Sarah.

The woman nodded, relaxing a little.

"You came into my office six or seven months ago. You had a baby girl whom we helped you put up for adoption."

Understanding spread across the woman's face. "Crew said you help me. You did good for my baby." She spoke with a strong Russian accent.

"Nadia." Sarah touched the woman's cheek. "Your name is Nadia. I remember."

The woman glanced around nervously. "We go inside, please?"

They entered the cabin. A rolled-up sleeping bag with a pillow on top of it rested in a corner of the room beside a propane camp stove.

Nadia rubbed her stomach. "Crew supposed to bring me food days ago."

Sarah dug through her pack and pulled out a protein bar. She handed the food to Nadia. "Crew's in the hospital." She couldn't purge her voice of the emotion that statement brought up. "He's in critical condition."

Nadia's eyes widened. "Crew will be all right?"

"We think so," Bryan replied.

"Crew is a true friend." Nadia's entire body trembled as she brought her hand up to her mouth. "He going help me get away for good, save some money. I need leave town." Desperation colored every word she spoke.

Bryan stepped toward her. "Maybe we can help—"

The boom of a rifle shot interrupted the conversation. The window by the cabin door shattered. Bryan pulled Nadia to the floor.

"Looks like they found us," Bryan said. His voice filled with indignation. "But how? I'm sure we weren't tailed."

Sarah hit the deck only a second after Bryan. She scrambled on all fours across the wooden planks. She waved Bryan and Nadia forward. "There's a back window in the other room."

A second shot tore through the thin wood of the

door. Nadia screamed and covered her head with her hands.

Bryan tugged on her shirt. "We have to get out of here."

Nadia cried and murmured something in Russian as she shook her head.

Crouching below window level, Sarah returned. "Come on, Nadia, we have to go or they'll kill us for sure." Sarah grabbed the frightened woman's hand.

Still hysterical, Nadia complied.

"Stay low," Bryan commanded.

The window in the second room faced the back of the cabin. Nadia climbed through, then Sarah and Bryan.

The cabin door swung open on its hinges and banged against the wall just as Bryan's feet hit the ground.

It would take the shooter only seconds to figure out where they'd gone. They had to get out of the line of sight.

"This way." Bryan led them around to the side of the cabin and then toward the forest that would provide some cover. They were exposed for about twenty seconds.

Sarah hesitated, taking a moment to slip into her backpack. Bryan pulled Nadia toward the trees. Sarah ran twenty paces behind them. The first shot landed only a few feet behind her. Heart pounding, Sarah winced and then responded by running harder.

Bryan and Nadia reached the trees first. "Run," he shouted at Nadia and let go of her arm.

He sprinted back to Sarah and pulled her toward the trees, as well. The shooter stood in the open field a hundred yards away, lining up another shot.

Nadia ran about twenty yards into the trees and then stopped.

"Keep moving," Bryan shouted.

Nadia complied though she looked over her shoulder several times. They sprinted, jumping over logs, pushing branches out of the way. When ten minutes passed with no sign that the shooter had followed them, they slowed their pace.

Out of breath, Sarah studied the trees around her. "I'm all turned around. If we can get back to the lake, I can navigate from there."

"Not a chance. They'll be expecting us to do that. They'll be watching. I'm sure it's not only one guy after us." Bryan stuck his hands in his hair and stared at the sky. "What I can't figure out is how they found us. I'm sure no one followed us up here."

Sarah rolled her eyes. "So how do we get back to the car?"

Bryan turned one way and then the other. "We keep moving south. If we can find the road, we can find the car."

Sarah couldn't let go of the fear gripping her heart. Were they going to get out of here alive? "That could take hours."

"Going the obvious route could get us killed." His brisk walk turned into a jog. "Let's keep going."

Sarah increased her speed, as well. Nadia lagged behind. Her run turned into a walk and then she trudged. Sarah stopped and waited. "Do you want some water?"

Nadia nodded. She took the bottle and gulped. "Sorry, I not so healthy. I have addiction problem for very long time. Just now getting strong."

"But you kicked it," said Sarah.

"I get away from my boyfriend, but he find me and he not so nice. He the reason I addicted in first place. Crew trying to help me get out of town."

Bryan, who had been listening from a distance, asked, "Nadia, what is your boyfriend's name?"

At first, Nadia took a step back. Her posture stiffened. Fear flashed in her eyes.

Bryan persisted, his voice growing softer. "Is his name Tyler Mason?"

She nodded.

A look of hard resolve materialized on Bryan's face. "So you got away, cleaned yourself up and found a place to live, but then he found you." Nadia nodded again.

The crackling of a branch caused them all to jump. Bryan put his finger over his mouth in a "be quiet" motion. Another breaking branch, this one closer. Bryan lowered himself to the ground and the two women followed.

Twigs and dried pine needles poked at Sarah's skin.

Nadia gulped and gasped. She squeezed her eyes shut. She wasn't handling this well, but who could blame her? The thought of Mason finding her obviously had her terrified. Nadia, more than Sarah or even Bryan, knew exactly what Mason was capable of.

Footsteps grew more distinctive as their pursuer crunched over the undergrowth.

Sarah reached over and placed a hand on Nadia's mouth. Her whole body vibrated with terror. *Please, God, don't let her scream and give all of us away.*

A fallen log shielded them on one side, but they would be exposed if the shooter passed by them to the west.

The footsteps continued. Judging from the sound, the man was maybe twenty feet from them. Sarah held her breath. The footsteps stopped.

Nadia continued to shake as tears ran down her face. This was a woman who had been abused in her life. She gripped Sarah's hand and Sarah squeezed back, her heart going out to the woman.

Sarah had only visited with her briefly when she brought three-month-old April in for adoption. Nadia hadn't wavered at all in her decision to give the little girl up. Her determination to give her daughter a better life was admirable. Sarah understood that desire. She'd been through the same thing.

The footsteps, the crunching and breaking of undergrowth, resumed. After what felt like a century, the sound of the shooter stalking through the woods faded altogether.

Bryan was the first to push himself up off his stomach. Still crouching, he turned a slow half circle, his hand wavering over his gun. He whispered, "Let's get going. Be as quiet as you can. Move as fast as you can."

Sarah helped Nadia to her feet. She wrapped an arm around her. "It's going to be all right. We'll get you to a safe place."

Nadia shook her head. "He will always find me. He found me here in the forest." Sarah picked up on the despair in Nadia's voice.

"Don't give up hope," Sarah said.

Nadia responded with a quivering smile.

They traversed down the hillside, being careful where they stepped, stopping to listen and watch. Bands of sunlight filtered through trees as the afternoon transitioned to evening.

After a while, without any disruption or indication that their pursuers were close, Bryan asked, "Why is Tyler so bent on finding you?"

Sarah could imagine the disappointment Bryan wrestled with. He had thought they were making their way toward the woman who could tie up his investigation. Instead they had found fragile, wounded Nadia.

"He say it because he love me." A pained expression crossed Nadia's gaunt features. "But I don't think that is love. When I first came to America, he said I too pretty to work with the others who came with me. I thought I going to have the life, be a rich man's girlfriend."

Bryan slowed his pace and glanced over at Nadia. "You were one of the people he brought over here. And you know about the others?"

Nadia stuttered in her step. Her face went pale. She nodded for a long time before speaking. "I see some things."

"You've seen how he treats those people."

Again, the frightened young woman nodded.

Bryan stopped walking and turned to face her. "Nadia, I think there is a way to guarantee that he will never hurt you or anybody again."

"I do not believe it."

"He should go to jail for the things he's done."

"I wish that," said Nadia, her voice growing stronger, filling with bitterness.

"I think we can make it happen." Bryan touched her thin forearm. "First we have to get you in protective custody."

Heading downhill, they continued to walk through the forest.

Sarah's thoughts went back to the adoption she had arranged for the woman. Though she did not remember who Nadia had listed as the father of the baby, she did remember that there had been no objection from him. The adoption had been smooth in that way. The father had signed away rights easily. "Tyler made you give up the baby?"

Nadia shook her head. "He didn't love the baby. I knew I couldn't get away if I had April and I want her have something better. After adoption, it take months for me to find a way to escape. I have no money, no way to leave town." The whole time she talked, Nadia's voice trembled.

They heard the rumble of a car on the road long before a road came into view. Bryan lowered to a crouch and sought out a tree for cover. Sarah grabbed Nadia's hand and pulled her toward a tree not too far from Bryan. Nadia braced her back against the tree and stared at the sky.

Sarah peered around the tree to where a section of the rutty dirt road was visible.

"Looks like they're running patrols," Bryan whispered.

Sarah stared down the hill and at the surrounding landscape, none of which looked familiar. "How are we going to find the car?"

"I think if we stay this far back and walk parallel to the road, we'll run into it without getting caught."

Nadia glanced back up the hillside from where they had just come. She looked scared.

Fear danced across Sarah's nerves, as well. The shooter was still up there somewhere.

How many of Mason's men had followed them up

here? Three? Four? At least one stalked through the forest behind them. And another drove a truck up and down the mountain road looking for them. They were being squeezed from both sides.

She wasn't sure if Bryan's plan would work. He probably had his own doubts. What other choice did they have though?

Bryan signaled for them to get moving. Sarah helped Nadia to her feet. The unfocused look in Nadia's eyes worried her. The young woman was fading away emotionally.

They walked parallel to the road, using the trees for cover.

Uphill, Sarah caught the glint of gunmetal in the fading light.

"Down." Bryan had seen it, too.

Now Nadia displayed a look of utter terror. She bolted free of Sarah's grip and out through the trees, running in a zigzag pattern. The first shot tore through a branch only inches from her .

Nadia let out a cry and kept running.

Did the shooter have a clear view or had Nadia's movement cued him in? Sarah resisted the urge to shout for Nadia to stop. It would only alert all their pursuers of their position. But it was too late for that caution now. She ran with Bryan at her heels.

Shortly afterward, Nadia stopped running and collapsed to the ground.

Up the hill, the shooter emerged from the trees, making a beeline toward Nadia.

"I'll hold him off." Bryan drew his gun.

The boom of the gunshot sounded behind Sarah. She dared not look back. She focused on getting to Nadia.

She couldn't see the sniper anywhere. Had Bryan managed to drive him back?

Another shot shattered the silence. This one clearly from a rifle.

The gunshot caused Nadia to leap to her feet once more. Sarah grabbed at her shirttails. "Nadia, calm down. You have to be still."

Nadia flailed her arms. She cried with loud jerking sobs. Sarah wrapped her arms completely around her. "It's okay."

Gradually, Nadia's breathing slowed.

Bryan's footsteps pounded behind her.

His hand touched Sarah's back. "Let's keep moving."

"How? Where? We're sitting ducks here."

Bryan holstered his gun and pushed them toward a large tree that provided a degree of cover. He pointed downhill.

She could just make out the metal of the car beneath the camouflage of branches.

Bryan leaned close to her. "I say we make a run for it."

FIFTEEN

Though he could not see the shooter above them, Bryan assumed the man was making his way downhill and looking for an opportunity to line up a clean shot. They'd have about a hundred yards with no trees for cover. It was a risk, but they had no other choice.

They darted from tree to tree. Sarah took Nadia's hand and pulled her forward. At least Nadia wasn't crying or screaming anymore. He could not imagine what sort of trauma and abuse Mason had put the young woman through. He didn't want to imagine it.

In all his investigation, he'd never learned of Mason having a girlfriend, which meant that Nadia must have been a virtual prisoner. Would Bryan be able to set her free or would they all be captured?

They rushed toward the open grassy area. Bryan took up the rear. He faced uphill with his weapon drawn. A rifle shot rang out, stripping the bark off a tree not too far from him.

He glanced over his shoulder. Sarah and Nadia were feet away from the car. Now that he knew where the shooter was, he watched the trees and brush for movement. He saw a flash of white, fired off a shot and dashed behind a tree. He peered out, studying the forest. That should hold the shooter off and buy him the time he needed to get down the hill.

Down below, Sarah tore the last branch off the car. Bryan zigzagged down the hill, looking over his shoulder. When he no longer had tree cover, he bolted the remaining distance to the car.

Sarah left the driver's-side door open as she directed Nadia to the backseat.

A rifle shot sounded behind him, and when Bryan looked back, he saw the shooter barreling down the hill. Bryan increased his stride, leg muscles pumping. His hand reached out for the car door. His gaze traveled to his shoulder where a tiny red dot rested.

He ducked. The window in the driver's-side door shattered. Bryan crawled behind the steering wheel where Sarah had already put the key in the ignition.

Nadia screamed and cried from the backseat while Sarah sought to comfort her. Bryan turned the key in the ignition, shifted into Reverse and pressed the accelerator. He cranked the steering wheel and turned out onto the road. A Jeep appeared around a bend, heading straight toward them.

"Is it them?" Sarah asked from the backseat.

"We'll assume," said Bryan as he gritted his teeth.

The Jeep didn't stop or pull over. Bryan accelerated to a dangerous speed. His bumper collided with the bumper of the Jeep as he nudged it down the hill. At first, the driver pushed against the force of Bryan's car.

Bryan shifted into Reverse and backed up. The Jeep remained on the road, its engine rumbling.

They couldn't get around it. Not on this narrow section of road.

Bryan shifted into First and zoomed toward the other car. He meant to crash into them. The other car reversed. The driver turned the wheel so the back end of the car slipped off the road.

Bryan squeezed past by directing his car partway up on the other side of the bank. It was working, but it was also a slow process, giving the shooter time to come after them from the woods. Several shots hit their back bumper.

Bryan increased his speed despite how hazardous the road was. The car shook and wobbled wildly.

"They must have shot out a tire." He gripped the steering wheel, willing the car to go further.

The car slowed and bumped along even though he pressed hard on the accelerator. He checked the rear-view mirror. A pair of armed men were chasing after them, and gaining ground.

"We're going to have to run for it." He pulled toward the shoulder of the road. Down below was a grassy hill that led to the river. "Maybe it's better this way. I think they must have slapped a tracking device on your car. How else could they have found us? They must have been close enough to spot us hiking. Get out now. Head toward the river."

Sarah pushed open the door and grabbed Nadia's sleeve. Bryan took cover behind the driver's-side door and glanced up the hill. He searched the grassy hill for the two armed men. He looked on the other side of the road. A steep bank met with forest. One of the shooters darted stealthily through the forest. He saw a flash of blue, probably part of the pursuer's shirt, but even as he watched, the man lost his footing and tumbled downhill. A groan of pain came from the trees. Bryan turned his attention to the grassy hill below. Nadia bobbed in and out of sight between the low-growing junipers as she headed toward the river. He couldn't see Sarah.

He tensed. The second shooter headed down the hill toward Nadia. Nadia disappeared behind some brush, as did the shooter. An agonized scream filled the forest.

Bryan raced down the hill, his muscles straining. He searched the cluster of junipers where he had last seen Nadia. Where was Sarah? Fear enveloped him. Had he missed the sound of the shot? Did she lie bleeding in the grass?

The juniper trees shook.

Bryan lifted his gun, aiming at the tree. "You don't want to do this!" he called out.

The shooter stepped out from behind the gnarled trees. His arm was wrapped around Nadia's neck and he held the gun to her head with his free hand. "Yes, I want to do this."

From all the men who had come at them over the last few days, he didn't recognize this man.

"All I want is this woman," the thug said next. "So back off and I won't hurt you."

Bryan shook his head. He didn't believe that, not after all the times his cohorts had tried to kill him and Sarah for days. He lifted his gun and the man reacted by pressing his own gun harder against Nadia's temple.

Nadia made tiny gasping noises filled with intense distress. Her face was red. Her eyes filled with terror.

He needed to buy time, weaken the man's resolve. "What are you, the new hired muscle? Do you have any idea what your boss does?"

A flicker of emotion passed over the man's face.

He opened his mouth to say something, but he didn't get a chance.

From behind the shooter, a large log rose up and slammed down on his head. Sarah appeared as the man crumpled to the ground.

"I hid when I saw him coming," Sarah explained. "Nadia wouldn't listen to me. She kept running."

On the hill above them, the man Bryan had watched fall paced the road, searching down below. He walked with a limp. The man on the ground in front of them moaned.

"We don't have much time." Bryan grabbed one of Nadia's hands and Sarah took the other one. They ran toward the cover of the cottonwoods that grew along the river. Nadia kept pace with them as they sprinted along the river.

Though it would be the fastest way back to civilization, following the river was too obvious. "Back into the trees," Bryan commanded.

The two women scrambled after him up the hillside. They jogged for some time until they came to a camp with a tent, a raft and fisherman's gear, but no person in sight.

Bryan searched the camp. "Hello?"

"I don't think anyone is here," said Sarah. She glanced nervously in the direction they had just run.

They both looked at the raft at the same time.

"We can get in touch with the owner via the forest service." He sprinted toward the raft. "Pay him back."

"Nadia, we need your help." Sarah grabbed a section of the rope that ran around the top of the raft. "Grab the paddles."

They ran for the river at a diagonal, putting more

distance between them and their pursuers. The trees thinned and they crossed the rocky shore to the river. The water gushed and murmured as it slipped over the rocks.

Bryan glanced up the shoreline, but didn't see the gunmen. The sky transitioned from light gray to charcoal.

"I'll help you push out." Sarah stepped into the water. "Nadia, get in. Hold on to the oars."

Cool river water whirled around his legs as they pushed the raft toward the center of the river. The water was up to his waist by the time the raft gained momentum. Sarah placed her foot on the edge of the raft and Nadia helped her in. She scooted to the back of the raft and lifted Bryan in. The raft picked up speed as the river pulled them forward.

Bryan handed Sarah a paddle. "Now." In unison their paddles sliced through the waves as the boat undulated over the top of the water.

"Let's work toward the opposite shore."

The water in this part of the river might be ten feet deep. Sarah touched Nadia's tangled blond hair. "Can you swim?"

Nadia shook her head.

They entered rougher water. The raft swayed more from the power of the rapids swirling around them. There was no sign of a gunman near them.

"We're losing air." Sarah's voice filled with panic.

They must have scraped against something sharp when they pushed it in the water.

Nadia let out a tiny gasp.

"Get to the shallow water," Bryan commanded as he paddled hard.

Water spilled over the collapsing side of the raft. It filled quickly. Sarah unzipped a pouch in her backpack and put something in her jacket pocket. She let go of the pack. Bryan had lost his when they'd abandoned the car.

Sarah grabbed Nadia's hand and wrapped it around the rope that bordered the rim of the collapsing raft.

"Hang on as long as you can. The shallow water isn't that far." She clutched both of Nadia's cheeks between her hands. "Can you do that for me?"

Nadia nodded.

"We'll stay as close as we can," Bryan said as he slipped into the water but held on to the raft rope. Sarah's backpack floated away. The rapids chugged and swirled them around.

The force of the undertow suctioned around Bryan's legs. He had to let go of the raft so he could stay above water. He stroked toward the shore and watched as Sarah and Nadia floated farther downstream. They drifted around a bend out of sight. He felt solid earth beneath his feet. He stood up, splashing through the shallow water.

He ran along the shore hoping to see the two women in the fading light. He prayed he could get to them in time.

Nadia thrashed and grabbed at Sarah, pulled her under. Sarah gulped for air.

She's going to drown us both.

Only part of the raft was visible as it bobbed away from them. Nadia grabbed Sarah's arm. Sarah spoke between plunging underwater and rising to the surface. "Let go."

Nadia was like an anchor around her arm.

"Float, Nadia."

The weight lifted, but not because Nadia was floating. No, it was because she had let go. Nadia disappeared beneath the current. Sarah swam hard toward her. Her head bobbed to the surface and then she was sucked under again.

Oh, dear God, please no. Save her.

Sarah swam downstream, her muscles growing heavy and tired. Then in the light of the setting sun, Nadia's head surfaced.

She was too far away. She'd never get to her. Sarah dragged her arms through the water as hope sank. She had to at least try.

Water splashed downriver and off to the side. Bryan dove into the water and swam toward Nadia. She watched as he caught her and dragged her to shore.

Sarah swam to the bank and trudged toward the sound of the coughing and sputtering. She found Bryan kneeling next to Nadia, who lay on her side gasping for air and spitting up water.

"We made it." Sarah shivered. Aware now that the dropping temperature and being soaked to the bone was making her cold. "We have to build a fire."

"With what?" Bryan sat back, crossing his arms over his chest, probably trying to keep warm.

Sarah unzipped her coat pocket. "I grabbed the waterproof matches out of the pack before I let it float away."

Nadia sat up as well, her voice a little strained. "I'm cold."

Bryan craned his neck at his surroundings. "They might be searching the shoreline. A fire would make us an easy target."

"Let's hike back away from the river, see if we can locate a place that shelters us from view where we can make camp." Her voice vibrated from being chilled.

Bryan shook his head. "No camp. We have to find a way out of here before they catch up with us." He placed his hands on his hips, studying the darkening landscape.

"We can't move very fast if we don't get warmed up," Sarah countered.

Brian spoke slowly as though he were mulling over their choices. "Mason wants her back under his control…or worse. They've already shown that they're not going to give up easily."

Nadia's voice trembled. "Can't feel end of fingers."

Her comments brought home the gravity of what they were up against. "Twenty minutes by a fire sheltered from view and we'll be able to get out of here faster," Sarah pleaded.

Bryan didn't answer right away. His gaze fell on Nadia, who crossed her arms over her body and rocked back and forth. "Nadia, you stay here." He spoke to Sarah. "Move a hundred paces up the hill. I'll do the same downriver. If we don't find any place that would work to build a fire, we keep moving."

Sarah bolted up the hill. She and Bryan might be okay without stopping to sit by a fire, but Nadia wouldn't be. She'd been in rough shape physically and emotionally when they'd found her. She couldn't handle much more. She needed a break, and a few minutes to pull herself together. Unfortunately, Sarah wasn't doing very well finding a place suitable for that. The hillside was mostly brush and grass, nothing that could hide a fire from view.

She wondered, too, what the extent of Mason's manpower was. Once he'd been alerted to their location would he send more men besides the three they'd encountered?

A single word drifted across the night air. "Here."

She ran toward the sound of Bryan's voice. He emerged from the darkness. "Over there, rocks and a small cave. You start the fire. I'll get Nadia."

Sarah jogged up the hillside. An outcropping of boulders came into view. The flat rock jutted out from the side of the hill providing an overhang. The boulder in front of it blocked the view to the shoreline.

Sarah gathered kindling and a few larger logs from fallen trees and started the fire. Minutes later, she heard footsteps. Bryan slipped around the boulder, ushering Nadia forward. She gravitated to the fire.

"I kept it small," said Sarah. "Nadia, get as close as you can."

The tight space between the boulder and the overhang provided little room to move around as all three of them huddled close to the fire.

Nadia held her hand out toward the heat. Firelight flickered across her face. "Is it worth it?" she whispered.

"What do you mean?" Bryan squeezed in close beside Sarah, their shoulders touching.

"Maybe I go back to him. Give up." Despair colored her every word. "He will never stop." She let out a small cry. "And he hurt Crew."

"Nadia, don't say that. I know this is hard and hiding in that cabin was scary, but we'll get you out of here, and after that, the police will help you. They'll keep you safe," Sarah said.

Bryan shifted. "Nadia, you are the only one who

can put him behind bars. And after he goes to jail, you won't have to be scared anymore."

In the flickering firelight, a tear drifted down Nadia's cheek. "I wanted my baby to be safe. He threaten hurt her if I do not do what he says."

Sarah cupped a hand on Nadia's shoulder. "And he doesn't have that power over you anymore. April is safe and happy."

Despite the tears, Nadia's voice held a lilt of joy. "I did a good thing for her."

"Yes, you did. He can't find her and he can't hurt her. All those records are sealed." Sarah stamped down a rising anxiety. She hoped that what she said was true. The reach of Mason's power surprised even her.

Bryan tugged on his T-shirt. "I'm starting to dry out."

"I warmer now," said Nadia.

Sarah stood up, looking for some way to douse the fire. She froze. Twenty yards away a flashlight beam bobbed in the darkness. Sarah's heartbeat quickened. The light came straight toward them.

SIXTEEN

Bryan jerked to his feet. Kicking dirt on the fire, he grabbed Nadia's shirtsleeve at the shoulder. "Come on, let's go. Run."

"Hold it right there," a voice boomed out of the darkness.

The nighttime had grown so quiet, Bryan heard the hammer on the pursuer's revolver click back.

"Put your hands up and step out, please, where I can see you."

Bryan couldn't quite process what was going on. The guy with the flashlight wasn't acting like one of Mason's henchmen. He sounded too…polite.

Both Nadia and Sarah stepped out away from the rocks.

"Is that all of you?" asked the voice in the darkness.

Bryan stepped out as well, squinting as the intense light shone on them. He could make out only the outline of a man behind the light.

"Are the three of you aware that campfires are illegal because of the high fire danger this time of year?"

Bryan laughed, relief spreading through him.

"Do you think this is a joke, son?"

Obviously, the ranger thought that they were teenagers out having some fun.

Bryan dropped his hand. "Sir, you have no idea how delighted we are to be busted for fire violations."

The ranger aimed the light directly on each of their faces. "Just what is going on here?"

Bryan stepped forward. "Sir, I'm a police officer with the Discovery P.D., and we need to get this woman into protective custody."

Bryan's explanation didn't seem to assuage the ranger's suspicions, so he tried another angle.

"I worked several weeks fire spotting. I'm a friend of Michael Duhurst."

The name-dropping must have finally won over the ranger. The defensiveness of his body language—shoulders back, chest out, gun pointed at them—melted. "Well, then, I guess I better get you down to my car and back to town. It's up over the ridge."

"You saw the fire from above?" Sarah sounded anxious.

The ranger pointed with his flashlight. "I patrol a road that runs along that ridge."

If the ranger saw the fire, someone else might have seen it, too. "Let's get to that car," Bryan urged.

They hiked up to the road. The ranger swung open the driver's-side door. "Don't mind Angie, she's friendly enough."

After Nadia climbed into the backseat, Bryan grabbed Sarah's damp sleeve. He glanced around the dark landscape. "If anything happens, you watch out for her."

Sarah nodded.

Angie turned out to be a black-and-white border collie, who settled in between Nadia and Sarah, alternating between licking the two women's faces.

The ranger turned around and grinned. "She likes people."

Bryan climbed into the front passenger seat. In the light of the car, he could see that the ranger was an older man, his gray hair cropped close to his head. Leathery skin spoke of years spent outside in the sun.

Bryan held out his hand for the ranger to shake. "Bryan Keyes."

"Daniel Monforton. Everybody calls me Ranger Dan."

The headlights cut a swath of illumination down the road. Bryan leaned back in the seat, still not willing to give up the idea that Mason's thugs would make another run at them.

In the backseat, Nadia laughed when Angie licked her fingers. She rested her forehead against the dog's and said something affectionate in Russian.

Sarah locked gazes with Bryan. She was probably thinking the same thing. How nice it was to hear Nadia laugh for the first time.

The ranger glanced toward the backseat. "She took to you like a fish to—"

The honking of the horn interrupted Daniel's sentence as his head fell forward onto the steering wheel. A sea of red spread out from Daniel's shoulder. The shot had come through so cleanly it left only a tiny hole in the driver's-side window.

The SUV veered off the road, rumbling down the hill. Nadia screamed from the backseat and Angie let out three quick barks. Adrenaline kicked through his body as Bryan grabbed the steering wheel. His feet fumbled to find the brake. The car rolled down the hill, gaining speed.

He brought the car to a stop.

Sarah leaned over from the backseat, placing her hands on Dan's neck. "He's still alive."

"Help me pull him over to the other seat." Though his voice remained calm, Bryan's heart raced. "Nadia, stay put and stay down."

The dog whined when Nadia let out a cry, but she did as she was told.

Bryan opened his door. He leaned in and wrapped his hands underneath Dan's armpits and pulled while Sarah pushed his legs out of the way. Dan moaned—conscious, but barely.

He glanced up the hill, speculating on where the shot had come from. Sarah climbed into the backseat and positioned herself so she could prop Dan up from behind.

Bryan cranked the wheel, easing upward toward the road. He switched off the headlights. "We're an easy target with them on."

"But we'll have to go so slow," Sarah said. "We need to get him to a hospital."

In the dark, he couldn't assess how badly Dan had been hit. The terrain hardened, indicating that they were back on the road. Bryan pushed the accelerator as hard as he dared. He checked the rearview mirror. Nothing. He could feel if they veered from the road when the SUV slanted at an angle. On the other side, the high embankment brushed against the side of the vehicle. Bryan gritted his teeth. He could do this.

Daniel stirred, expelling a pain-filled breath.

Sarah touched his head and made soothing noises.

"He's still got a pulse," she whispered. "But it's getting weaker. I think he's lost a lot of blood."

Tension knotted through Bryan. The clock was ticking for Daniel, but if they all died, Daniel wouldn't have any chance of survival.

Angie let out a high-pitched whine. The sound of the tires rolling over the hard-packed dirt filled the car. Bryan stared out at the blackness in front of him.

He drove through the dark until he was satisfied that they were out of danger. He clicked on the headlights, increased his speed and headed out toward the main road. They encountered no other cars on the country road and only a few on the highway leading into town. Bryan zoomed up to the emergency entrance and pressed the brakes, stopping in front of the wide doors. Even before he came to a complete stop, Sarah pushed her door open and disappeared inside. She returned a few minutes later with two EMTs and a gurney. Dan's body was as lifeless as a rag doll when they loaded him onto the gurney.

"Nadia, come on, let's go inside."

Sarah ushered them into a waiting room while Bryan parked the car, then joined them inside. Bryan paced while Sarah stared down at the blood on her hands, Dan's blood. "I wonder if he has any family."

"I can call Michael, the guy who got me the fire spotting job. Dan seemed to know him." Bryan took out his phone.

Sarah stood, as well. "I'm going to go check to see how Crew is doing."

Nadia lifted her eyes. "Crew is here?"

"Yeah, he's...he wasn't conscious when we were

here earlier. I'll check and see how he's doing and come get you if he can have visitors," said Sarah.

"I like that very much," said Nadia.

Sarah trotted down the hallway and disappeared around a corner.

Bryan clicked through the contacts list on his phone until he found Michael's number. Once he got Michael on the line, he learned that Dan's wife had passed away and his only child lived out of state. Dan had a brother who lived in town, though.

"I think his name is Harry," said Michael. "I'll let the other rangers know. Dan is sort of the grandfather around here. He'll have lots of visitors tomorrow."

Bryan gripped the phone. *If he makes it.* "I'll see if his brother is listed in the phone book." Bryan said goodbye and hung up. He wandered through Admitting and another waiting area before he located a phone book. He found a listing for Harrison Monforton and made the call. Harry promised he'd be right up.

Bryan clicked off his phone and hurried back to see how Nadia was doing. When he entered the emergency room waiting area, Nadia was no longer in the chair where he had left her. Panic spread through him as he searched the area around the waiting room, still unable to find her.

The armed guard stood outside Crew's room as Sarah approached. When she walked up the hallway, a nurse raced into Crew's room. She was alone and she wasn't pushing a crash cart, but still, the drawn look on the nurse's face and her hurried step made Sarah's stomach do somersaults. Something wasn't right.

Sarah recognized the armed guard from the station.

"I'm Sarah Langston, Crew's sister. Do you remember me from the police station?"

He nodded. "Bryan's friend."

"Yeah." She glanced up and down the hall. "Have things been pretty quiet here?"

"No disruptions since they posted me."

In the room, Crew remained motionless and pale as the nurse bent over him.

"Has he woken up at all?" Sarah tensed, afraid of the answer.

The nurse shook her head and then glanced at the monitor by Crew's bed. "His heart rate and blood pressure have been dropping." She stood up straight, gripping the handrail and looking Sarah in the eye. "I have to be honest with you, none of this is a good sign."

"Can I sit with him for a moment?" Her throat tightened with emotion.

"Sure." The nurse left the room.

Sarah pulled a chair up. Crew's face could have been carved from stone...so lifeless.

She cleared her throat. "Hey, big brother, you have to pull out of this. 'Cause otherwise it just wouldn't be fair." She touched his cold cheek with the back of her hand. "You finally get your life together and then..." She sobbed. "And then it's taken from you because you tried to help Nadia, to do the right thing. You've gotta wake up," she whispered.

Sarah closed her eyes and prayed while she held Crew's ice-cold hand. When she was done, she stood up and slipped back into the hallway.

Bryan rounded the corner, his eyes wide with fear. "Did Nadia come this way?"

Sarah shook her head and then looked at the police officer. "Have you seen a blonde woman, pretty but thin?"

The officer shook his head.

Bryan balled his hands into fists. "I slipped around the corner to find a phone book. That was all." He turned back to the officer. "She's a material witness in a crucial case, and she's in a lot of danger. We've got to find her."

The officer pulled his radio off his utility belt. "I'll alert the other officer in the building. If she's in the area, we can find her."

"It's been five minutes, she's probably miles from here by now." Bryan's voice simmered with anger, threatening to explode.

"Let's not give up that easily. Some of the staff might have seen something through the glass, and I think Nadia would have put up a fight." Her words sounded upbeat, but Sarah feared they'd gone through so much only to lose Nadia to Mason.

As they ran through hospital corridors, Sarah wasn't sure if it would do any good to search. Bryan was right about Nadia likely being long gone by now. Both of them had let their guard down. She pushed through the waiting room. On the other side of the glass, a staff member stood hunched over a chart resting on the counter.

"Let's search the perimeter first and then question the staff, since time is everything now," Bryan suggested. They pushed the doors open; the cool night air surrounded them. She scanned the parking lot. A car wove through the rows looking for a parking space.

"I'll go this way," Sarah said. "We'll meet back here."

"Wait." He grabbed Sarah's sleeve and pointed. "Is that…"

The emergency room, hospital and doctors' offices formed a U-shape of connected buildings. On the opposite side of the U with the minimal light spilling from a distant lamppost, she could discern a person moving along the sidewalk.

Sarah squinted. Was that Nadia walking Angie on a leash?

Sarah took off running across the parking lot. "Nadia!"

Bryan ran behind her as the scene unfolded in slow motion. Nadia waved at them. The dog tugged her forward. The car she'd noticed earlier closed the distance on Nadia. Bryan ran faster, pushing past Sarah. Brakes squealed. A man jumped out from the passenger side, his hands reaching claw-like toward Nadia. Nadia screamed, pulling back as the man lunged at her on the sidewalk.

Sarah fought to keep up with Bryan as he sprinted across the lot.

Angie barked, jumping at the man. Nadia fell backward on the sidewalk. The assailant threw off the dog just as Bryan landed a hard punch against the man's jaw.

The car tires spun, burning rubber as it sped away. The assailant left behind fought back, raising his fist. Bryan blocked him and responded with a blow to the man's stomach, which bent him over. Behind him, the dog barked like a Gatling gun as Nadia held Angie's leash.

Bryan pulled his gun. "Stay right where you are. Hands behind your head."

"I'll call the police," Sarah said between breaths.

"Looks like your friend didn't want to stick around and help you out." Bryan jerked his head in the direction the car had sped away.

The man tightened his square jaw and sneered.

This was the first time they'd managed to detain one of Mason's hired thugs. Maybe after a couple of days in jail, Bryan could get him to share information about Tyler Mason.

"Nadia, why did you leave the hospital?" Sarah asked.

"I worry about dog." She wrapped her arms around the collie. "Can she stay with me? She protect me."

Sarah looked at Bryan.

Bryan shrugged. "I'm sure Dan's not going to be in any kind of shape to take care of her. If it's okay with his brother, it's fine with me."

The police sirens sounded in the distance.

Once the assailant was taken into custody, Sarah took Nadia in to see Crew while Bryan checked in on Dan.

Nadia's face fell when she saw Crew. She touched his forehead.

"Where did you two meet, anyway?"

"Rehab class. The only time Tyler not with me. He just friend, not romance." Nadia smoothed the blanket that covered Crew. "I want for him get better."

"Me, too." A lump formed in her throat. "I'll leave the two of you alone for a minute." She stepped out of the room and talked with the guard at the door for a few minutes.

Bryan stalked up the hallway. She ran up to meet him.

"Dan's going to be okay. He was even coherent enough to talk to me. He doesn't have a problem with the dog staying with Nadia. We need to get her out of here and into a safe house." He reached up and brushed Sarah's cheek lightly with the back of his hand. "Once we get something set up, you might want to think about staying there, too."

"How long? Until Mason goes to trial? Bryan, I have a job. I have a life."

"I can't keep you safe." Frustration was evident in his voice.

"I don't know if that's part of your job description." Sarah stared into his deep brown eyes. This was not the boy she had loved all those years ago. The kid who lost his sense of direction by trying to please everyone around him. Bryan had shown himself to be a man of integrity, willing to take on enormous responsibility. More than any man should have to carry on his own.

"It has nothing to do with the job." His fingers brushed over her cheeks and skimmed her lips.

If he kissed me now, I wouldn't pull away.

Bryan cleared his throat and looked behind him, aware of the officer in the hallway. The smolder in his eyes was enough to make her legs wobble.

"We better do what we need to do." His voice had a husky quality.

Nadia emerged from Crew's room, her eyes red from crying. They drove back to the police station. Bryan arranged for some food to be delivered and invited both women to rest on the couches in the police break room.

After they ate a meal of cheeseburgers and fries, Nadia settled down on a couch with Angie lying at her feet. Still a bit stirred up, Sarah closed her eyes but couldn't sleep. Bryan's desk was outside the break room; she could hear him making arrangements for a safe house for Nadia and for a lawyer to take her deposition. Slowly she drifted off to sleep. She awoke hours later with a blanket over her. Probably Bryan's doing.

She stretched, placing her bare feet on the cold linoleum floor. Nadia rested peacefully on her side. Angie had jumped up on the couch, snuggling between the back of the couch and Nadia's legs.

Sarah slipped into her shoes and peeked around the corner to where Bryan worked at a computer. He stopped when he heard her coming, lifting his fingers off the keyboard and turning to look at her.

"Hey." His eyes still held that same fiery essence she'd seen when they were at the hospital. "Sleep okay?"

She nodded.

He pushed a ziplock bag toward the edge of his desk. "One of the female officers put this together for you."

The bag contained a toothbrush and other toiletries. "Thank you."

"Oh, and these." He swung his chair around and picked up a pile of neatly folded clothing still with the price tags on them. "Officer O'Connor guessed at your size. There's a shower in the women's locker room."

Sarah stared down at the bag. For a moment, she felt a terrific rush of excitement at the thought of finally being clean, in fresh clothes. But then she caught herself. Was this her life now? She missed her own deep bathtub. She missed her cat and the quiet summer nights on her porch watching the sunset. She missed working at the adoption agency.

He must have picked up on her sadness. "We're hours away from setting up the safe house."

"Where is it?"

"In a little town about sixty miles from here. We've hired extra security. The background checks are still in progress. We want to make sure there's no way Mason can get to Nadia or to you. His network in Discovery is pretty extensive."

"I don't want to go." She looked into Bryan's rich brown eyes, realizing going to the safe house wasn't just about being cut off from her normal life. It also meant she wouldn't be with Bryan. The loss was like a hole blown through her heart.

"I know you don't want to stay locked away like this, but it might be our only option. It wouldn't be for all that long. Most of the legal case against Mason is already put together. Nadia's testimony is what we needed."

Sarah's throat went tight. Her heart pounded. She wanted to share her feelings, but the words wouldn't come. "Thank you for everything you've done...for Crew and for me."

He turned slightly away from her. "Family is everything."

She caught a tinge of bitterness in his voice. Was he thinking of the family he didn't have with her? Of the daughter they'd put up for adoption?

Sarah closed her eyes. She'd been foolish to think that they could take up where they'd left off. An unhealed wound would always exist between them, one that time couldn't fix. She couldn't bring their daughter back into their lives. Marie was with a family who loved her. They were her parents now. She couldn't reverse the events of ten years ago. If only they had gone slower, waited until they were married and settled. Things could have been so different.

"Guess I'll go take that shower."

Bryan focused on his computer screen. "Down the hall and to the right."

Sarah took a steaming hot shower, dried off and dressed. She combed out her wet hair and padded down the long hallway to the main part of the police station.

Bryan wasn't at his desk. Only two other officers worked at their computers. The clock said it was only 7:00 a.m. When she checked the break room, Nadia and Angie continued to doze.

Bryan came up behind her, touching her shoulder lightly. "Might want to wake her up."

"Where have you been?"

"In the interview room. That man who tried to grab Nadia at the hospital isn't giving up anything. He won't even admit that Mason hired him. It's entirely possible he's never met Mason. Second-or third-party associates could have hired him. Mason's really good at keeping his hands clean, but this has his fingerprints all over it."

Sarah gazed in at Nadia, who slept so peacefully. "Why do I need to wake her?"

"The safe house is ready."

Sarah's heart sank. "Guess this is it then."

She wouldn't be seeing Bryan Keyes anymore. She was out of excuses for being with him, and they couldn't seem to build a bridge over the chasm they had created ten years ago.

SEVENTEEN

Bryan deliberately didn't look at Sarah as she rode in the passenger seat while he drove the two women to the safe house. The sadness in her eyes stabbed at his heart. Over and over, his desire to hold her met him at every turn. The memory of the kisses they'd shared haunted him. But every time he looked in her eyes, all he felt was pain. The reality of them being separated drove the point home. As long as they were together, he could entertain the fantasy that they would be a couple again. The truth was the damage was too extensive. He'd failed his daughter. And then he had torn Sarah to pieces over that. He couldn't get past the self-condemnation. No matter how hard he tried or how much he wanted Sarah. He wanted to change the past and he couldn't do that.

"I think you will like the house," he said. They passed a sign indicating they had entered the small town of New Irish.

Sarah turned her head and stared out the window.

"The case against Mason can be assembled within a month. We'll be able to put him in jail even sooner.

There's a huge flight risk because of his connections in other countries. No judge is going to grant bail."

Sarah smoothed over her shirt. "That doesn't mean Mason won't stop giving orders to do us harm. I'm sure he'll find ways to get things done even from a jail cell."

He couldn't argue with her.

Nadia spoke from the backseat. "Will I be able to go outside with Angie?"

"There's a fenced backyard, and we have security people at the house all the time."

"But no running through the hills with the dog?" Disappointment colored her words.

"We don't want you to have too much exposure, and you can't go anywhere alone," Bryan explained. "The woman who lives at the house is a retired police officer. She'll provide your cover to the community, probably say you are her nieces or something."

"Not a lot of freedom," said Nadia. "But someday. I come to America for freedom. First I am Tyler's slave and then slave to drugs." Nadia's words sunk in deep, reminding him of why he wanted to take Tyler Mason down. He destroyed so many lives.

They pulled up to a blue house with a chain-link fence and blooming flower beds. A woman with silver hair cut in a bob walked down the steps to greet them. "Hello, I'm Evelyn." She ushered the women in. Angie stayed close to Nadia, wagging her plumagelike tail. "Why don't the three, or rather, four—" she smiled down at Angie "—of you come in and I'll show you around."

Bryan followed them inside to where a tall man with a buzz cut and high cheekbones sat at a table. The man stood up, revealing the gun on his belt. He held out his hand. "Jason Smith from Firelight Security."

Bryan shook his hand. He had a vague memory of looking over Jason's profile before sending it to another officer for a deeper background check. Firelight had a solid reputation for security. The department could not afford to lose officers for the 24/7 watch Nadia required.

Nadia's exclamations over features in the house floated in from another room. Sarah slipped out into the backyard. Bryan followed her. Her hair shone in the sunlight. How many times had he buried his face in that hair, enveloped by the soft floral scent? Her shoulders were slumped. All of her body language communicated sadness.

"I'll get one of the other officers to bring some things from your house if you want to make a list."

"We went there once to get the backpacks. Everything was okay. Why can't I get my own things?"

"Sarah, we need to think in terms of high security here. Not take any chances. We've come this far. You can have your stuff, just let us be the ones to get it for you."

"And my cat? Someone will bring Mr. Tiddlywinks?"

He smiled. "And your cat."

She turned to face him. "I know this has to happen. I see how badly Mason wants to take me out of the equation along with Crew and Nadia." She crossed her arms over her chest. "I just don't like it."

He descended the steps. "Wish it could be some other way." From the moment he'd climbed in the car to bring her here, an ache had entered his heart. Being away from her would be torture.

"I know you're doing the best you can." She touched his jaw with the softness of a feather and then leaned in and kissed his cheek.

He wrapped his arm around her waist and pulled her close. His lips covered hers. He kissed her for the beautiful memories they shared, not the ugly ones. He pressed harder, kissing her for what might have been. He rested his palm against her neck, holding her close, not wanting to let go. "I'm sorry." He kissed her again. "I'm so sorry."

She wrapped her arms around him and hugged him.

He pulled away. "I have to go." He turned, knowing that looking back at her would rip him to pieces. He said goodbye to Jason Smith, who still sat at the table. Bryan stepped across the threshold of the front door.

He climbed into the police vehicle and zoomed toward the road. What tore him up more than anything was that he wanted to be the one to stay with Sarah, to keep her safe rather than leaving her in the care of some stranger. He hadn't protected her heart all those years ago. Maybe if he could make up for it then the ache inside would go away.

His cell phone rang.

"Yeah." Bryan pulled over on a shoulder.

"Bryan." He recognized Officer Grant Pittman's voice. "I know we're done with the background checks for the safe house, but I found something when I did a little digging."

"What did you find?"

"It's not a big thing, but you said to flag anything that didn't feel right. I didn't catch it on the first pass 'cause it's not what you'd normally look for. But I read over the resumes of the guys we hired from Firelight and something caught my eye."

"One of them worked through Mason's temp agency?" Certainly they would have flagged something like that.

"No, not that tight a connection. I started doing some cross-referencing and turns out one of them used to live in Spokane and work for a restaurant Mason owned."

Bryan tensed. "Which guy are we talking about?"

Grant's reply was like a sword through Bryan's chest. "Jason Smith."

Angie's intense barking alerted Sarah to trouble inside the house. She ran up the stairs from the backyard, flinging the door open. The living room was empty. Persistent barking and scratching led her to the downstairs bathroom where Angie had been shut away.

The dog burst into the living room, sniffing the furniture frantically and darting back and forth. Sarah ran into the kitchen and peered out the window. Nobody was in the front yard. She sprinted halfway up the stairs. "Hello, Nadia? Jason? Evelyn?"

Silence.

She bolted the rest of the way up the stairs, searching the first bedroom and bathroom. In the second bedroom, Evelyn lay on the floor, unconscious but breathing. A heavy weight pressed on Sarah's chest, making it hard to breathe. What exactly was going on here?

Sarah fell to her knees as fear spread through every fiber of her being. "Evelyn, can you hear me?"

Evelyn's eyes fluttered open. "Hit from behind," she mumbled.

Evelyn didn't seem to be hurt anywhere else. No cuts, no bleeding. Sarah grabbed a pillow from the bed and placed it underneath Evelyn's head. "Just lie here, I'll figure out what's happened." She noticed Evelyn's gun in a holster and belt draped over a chair. She pulled the gun out and placed it in the older woman's hand. "Just in case."

Sarah hurried downstairs and out onto the front porch. She ran to the edge of the yard. A small compact car still sat in the driveway, as did the larger black truck. Nobody had left the house in a vehicle, anyway. She pulled her phone out of her pocket to call Bryan.

Bryan's car roared up the road. He braked and rolled down the window. "Where's Nadia?"

Sarah shook her head. "I'm not sure. I think—the cars are still here, but I don't see any sign of Nadia. Evelyn was knocked out. They must have got to Jason, too."

Bryan turned off the engine and jumped out of the car. He grabbed Sarah by the elbow and headed toward the front door, glancing in one direction and then the other. "They're not in the house?"

"Not that I can find."

He pulled her inside.

"Evelyn is upstairs," she whispered. "She'll be okay."

He pressed against the wall. "Stay close to me."

"What's going on here?"

"Jason is in on this," he said. He put his finger across his mouth, indicating she needed to be quiet. He raised his head to the second floor, listening. His hand wavered over his gun. Only silence.

Angie barked from a room off to the side. Bryan pulled Sarah in that direction. The room contained a washer and dryer and a wall where coats were hung. Angie scratched at the outside door.

Sarah shrugged. "They couldn't have gone out the back door. I was in the backyard. They didn't go out the front. I would have seen them going up the street. They had to have gone out this side door."

He eased the door open, peered outside and ducked back in. "There's a field out there and beyond that a barn."

"You think that's where they went? Why not just jump in the car and escape with Nadia?"

"Maybe you interrupted him when you came in from the backyard."

She clutched his shirtsleeve. "We need to call for help."

"We don't have that kind of time." His finger trailed over her cheek and across her lips. "You stay here. I'm going to see if I can sneak up on him."

"No, you can't go. That's too dangerous."

"Sometimes you don't have a choice." He kissed her full on the lips.

The intensity of his kiss burned her to the core as he pulled her back into the living room. "We'll get a better look at the barn from here." He pointed toward the window.

A shot boomed through the air, shattering the window. He jumped on top of her, taking her to the floor.

Stunned and trembling with terror, Sarah lay on her stomach. Angie barked and tugged on Sarah's shirt.

"That's where they are. Jason has sniper training. Maybe he gets a bonus if he takes us out, too." He crawled toward the front door. "Pull those drapes."

Avoiding the shards of glass, Sarah crouched and moved across the floor, shutting all the curtains. Bryan slipped out the front door. He'd have been a sitting duck if he'd gone out the back door where the sniper would've seen him coming.

She pulled herself up just above the windowsill and peeked out. Bryan had circled around to the back of the house. As she watched, he dove down and crawled through the tall grass toward the barn. No more shots were fired. The sniper hadn't seen him.

Sarah took in a deep breath that did nothing to calm her nerves. She felt helpless. She couldn't just sit here. Bryan could die. She needed to help him somehow.

Thudding noises came from the second floor. Sarah met Evelyn as she careened down the stairs. She held her gun. "I saw from the window. There's two of them. One is still up in the barn and the other is headed in this direction." Evelyn lifted up the gun. "Do you know how to use one of these?" Still unsteady on her feet, Evelyn swayed.

She'd gone hunting with Crew and with Bryan when they'd dated. She didn't really know if she could shoot at a person…but maybe the bad guys wouldn't realize that. "Yes, I think I can remember."

"Get the car." Evelyn handed her the gun. "Take the road that loops around to the back of the barn. They won't see you coming. I'll cover you and Bryan from the attic window with my husband's rifle."

Sarah sprinted out to the car, hopped in and drove. Instead of taking the fork that led back out of town, she turned onto a dirt road. The car was an electric one that didn't make much noise. She'd be able to get pretty close without being detected. Off to the side, she could see the top of the barn. A rolling hill shielded the rest of the structure from view.

She prayed for strength and courage.

Two shots in rapid succession boomed through the air. Sarah cringed and gripped the steering wheel tighter.

EIGHTEEN

Bryan ducked down in the tall grass. A shot whizzed past him and another traveled over his head toward the barn. He stared back at the house, unable to discern anything. Was Sarah shooting from a high window?

He lifted his head. In the exposed door of the barn loft, he caught a flash of motion. Then he heard it— the swishing sound of someone moving through the tall grass.

Two men? Bryan pressed his stomach hard against the ground and listened. Wind rustled through the grass.

He sensed eyes on him.

Heart raging in his chest, Bryan flipped over, scanning everywhere, aiming his gun—right, middle, left. Someone was here…close.

Still unable to shake the feeling of being watched, he dragged himself forward in the grass. His belly scraped over hard dirt and pebbles. Three feet from him, he spied drops of blood.

A hand grabbed the back of his collar, pulling him upward and choking him. Bryan flipped over and managed a boot to the man's knee. The assailant released only a small grunt of pain before he swiped Bryan hard against the jaw with the butt of a rifle.

The blow to his face stunned Bryan, made his eyes water. He rolled to one side as the man came after him again, realizing a moment later that he'd dropped his gun. When Bryan reached for it, the man crushed his fingers with his boot.

Bryan craned his neck. One of the man's hands was bloody, the fingers curled in at unnatural angles. Somebody had gotten off a good shot. With his hand still anchored to the ground by a boot, Bryan swung his legs and hit the man in the back of the knees. The assailant buckled to the ground. Bryan stood up, landing a hard blow to the man's head. A shot whizzed through the air. Bryan hit the deck. Another shot from the other direction stirred up dirt not too far from Bryan's head. He was in the middle of a firefight.

The man who had attacked him fell onto the ground face-first, not moving but not dead. The bullet hadn't hit him. The blow Bryan had given him knocked him out. Bryan grabbed the man's rifle and scampered through the grass. When he lifted his head, he detected no movement by the loft door. He'd be exposed the remaining distance to the barn, but he'd have to take his chances. He was running out of time before Jason Smith gave up and just took Nadia. He pushed himself to his feet and sprinted toward the barn.

A rifle shot exploded the air around him and then another.

From the back side of the barn, Sarah heard the volley of shots, cringing each time. She eased the car toward a small door, slipped out and pressed the barn door open. The door squeaked on its hinges. Sarah held back, her heart pounding in her chest.

After a moment, still in a crouch, she peeked into the building. Footsteps pounded across the loft. The scent of hay and manure hung in the air, though it looked like the barn hadn't been used in some time.

The lower half of the barn consisted of a series of stalls. She started checking them, but found no one. Nadia must be up in the loft with Jason Smith.

Sarah pressed against the rough wood of the stall. What could she do to get Nadia away from the shooter? Maybe she could create a distraction that would bring him to the edge of the loft so she could shoot him. Then she could climb the ladder and get Nadia. They'd have to jump from the loft to the ground outside to avoid Jason.

She looked around for something to make noise with. When her search brought her to the next stall, she stopped. Nadia sat hunched over in a corner, her hands and feet bound, a gag in her mouth.

Sarah ran over to her. She picked up a nail from the barn floor and cut Nadia free. "Quiet," she whispered. She grabbed Nadia's hand. Looking over her shoulder, she wove in and out of the stalls. The stomping of the shooter stopped. Had Bryan been able to disable him? They slipped through the door as a rifle shot splintered the wood above them.

She could hear Jason shouting expletives as she and Nadia raced back to the car. Sarah started the car. She glanced out at the road and then at the field that lay between the barn and the house. She had a choice to make. She knew she was supposed to get Nadia out of there, but she couldn't leave Bryan behind.

She hit the gas and zoomed out into the field. Bryan stood in the middle of the field aiming a rifle at the barn. She accelerated toward him. Without a moment's hesitation, he jumped into the backseat. "I think I got him when he ran around the side of the barn after you two."

The car slowed through the taller grass.

"This isn't an off-road vehicle." Bryan's voice held a note of humor.

"We'll make it." Sarah pressed harder on the accelerator.

Bryan glanced over his shoulder. Jason was halfway across the field. He favored his left leg. That must be where he'd hit him.

The car slowed to a crawl.

Bryan yanked open the door to tug Nadia out of the car. "Run," he commanded.

All three of them crouched low and sprinted toward the backyard. Angie burst out of the open door, meeting them at the gate.

Evelyn peeked her head out. "Hurry, get inside. Help is on the way from Discovery. We've only got one policeman in New Irish and I don't think he would be of much use."

Sarah and Nadia collapsed on the floor, exhausted and out of breath. Bryan darted over to a window, pulling a curtain back and peering out. He bent over, gripping his shoulder.

Sarah scrambled over to him. "You're hurt."

"Just a nick." He grimaced.

Evelyn stepped across the floor holding her rifle. "I can watch the field."

Bryan leaned against the wall. Sweat beaded his

forehead. Sarah peeled back his bloody shirt. She sucked air through her teeth. "That's quite a gouge." She touched the skin around the wound and he winced. "I don't think the bullet went in."

"First-aid kit in the bathroom," Evelyn said without taking her eyes off the window.

Nadia jumped to her feet and headed toward the bathroom. She returned a moment later and slid the kit across the floor to Sarah.

"I think our guy has given up," said Evelyn.

"They don't give up." Bryan spoke through gritted teeth.

Evelyn scooted along the window. "I can't see him anywhere."

Sarah placed disinfectant on Bryan's torn, bloody skin. She stared down at the kit. There wasn't a bandage big enough to cover the cut. She grabbed some gauze and placed it gently over the cut.

Gratitude shone in his eyes. He winked at her. "Thanks for saving my bacon."

She touched his cheek. "Thanks for saving mine."

Outside, sirens sounded in the distance.

The tightness of Bryan's expression told her he was still in pain. "Looks like the cavalry is here."

She put out a hand to help him to his feet. The four of them trudged toward the front door as the police sirens grew louder.

A single thudding noise came from the side entrance. Jason Smith appeared, the rifle aimed at Sarah as she stepped toward the front door. Bryan pushed her out of the way. The boom of a rifle blast contained within the four walls of a house echoed in her ears as Jason tumbled to the floor, still alive but in pain.

Evelyn let the arm that held the rifle she'd just fired fall limp at her side. "You said they don't give up, so I was ready."

Discovery police officers burst through the door ready to shoot. They escorted Nadia and Sarah out while Bryan briefed them on what had happened. After receiving first aid, Jason was taken into custody.

Sarah sat in the back of the police car with Nadia and Angie. She craned her neck to see Bryan coming out on the porch. As the police car pulled out of the driveway, Sarah wondered if there was any hiding place where Tyler Mason wouldn't find them.

NINETEEN

Bryan placed the phone in the cradle and studied the two weary women in front of him. They'd been brought directly to the police station from the safe house. "We've made arrangements for you to stay at a hotel for the night."

"Just for one night?" Dark circles had formed under Sarah's eyes. Nadia didn't look much better.

"We can't risk him finding out where you are. Our best option right now is to move you often." Bryan glanced around the police station. This time of day, most of the officers were out on patrol. The other detective had left to do an interview on another case. Only two other officers sat at their desks.

Bryan stood up and rested an arm on one of the walls of the carrels. He addressed his comment to Grant, who sat at his desk staring at his computer. "Quiet day, huh?"

"Compared to yours," said Grant, running his hands over his short buzz-cut hair. "We did have a break-in at the 2100 block on Oak Street."

"What business on Oak Street?" Sarah had come up behind him. Her voice sounded strained.

Grant sat up a little straighter in his chair and tilted his head. "That adoption agency downtown. Why?"

"That's where I work." When she turned to look at him, her face was whiter than porcelain. Fear danced across her eyes.

Bryan pieced a picture together. This wasn't a coincidence. "They searched your home. And now your workplace…."

Sarah thought for a moment. "There would have been pay stubs, letters in drawers." She turned away. "There's even a magnet on my refrigerator that says where I work."

"They put two and two together and figured out you might have something to do with April's adoption."

Nadia released an audible breath. "No." She jumped to her feet, shaking her head and pacing, her voice growing more and more frantic. "He will use the child to get my silence. He never loved the baby."

Sarah ran over to Nadia, grabbing her hands at the wrists. "He won't find what he's looking for. Those records are sealed in computer files. There are passwords and other security measures."

Tension melted from Nadia's body. "If you say." Sarah let go of her wrists.

Bryan walked over to Grant. "Can you keep an eye on those two? And I think the dog will need to go out for a walk. The women are not to leave the building."

"I'm stuck at my desk for at least two more hours. I can do that," said Grant.

Sarah ran over to Bryan. "Where are you going?"

"Out to see the extent of the damage at the robbery," he said.

"I'm going with you." Sarah touched his sleeve. He

saw the look of hard resolve in her eyes. "I'll be able to tell you if any information on the computers has been compromised."

The truth was he didn't want to leave her anywhere and risk losing her again. "All right, but don't get out of my sight." Bryan stalked over to Nadia. "You stay here. Don't even go outside to take a breath. Do you understand me?"

Nadia nodded.

"Officer Pittman will deal with the dog."

Nadia lifted her chin. "I stay here."

"We'll get you moved to that hotel in a couple of hours."

Nadia slumped back down, her expression indicating that she understood. "Don't let him get April." Fear and desperation clouded her eyes.

Bryan drove Sarah toward the robbery location.

Sarah laced her fingers together as the city streets passed by. "Would he really go after the baby?"

"Maybe," Bryan said. "He's getting desperate. He can't get at Nadia directly. He's tried."

Bryan slowed the car as they came to a large brick building that housed several offices. Patrol officers had already cordoned off the place.

"Let's go inside." He pushed open his door.

Sarah led the way up the sidewalk. Bryan stopped one of the techs working the scene. He placed his hand on the small of Sarah's back. "We need to go inside. She works here. She'll know what's been taken."

The tech wiped the sweat from his forehead. "Pretty obvious what they stole. After they rooted through a bunch of file cabinets, they pulled all the hard drives from the computers."

Sarah seemed to collapse, her shoulders slumped and her head bent. "He's trying to find out who April's adoptive parents are."

Adrenaline coursed through Bryan's body. The break-in had taken place hours ago. How long would it take Mason to find what he was looking for? With all the men he had on his payroll, there was bound to be a computer expert or two who could get past the security measures. "We can call the parents, warn them."

"I don't remember their phone number. All that information is private. It was on the hard drives. I doubt they are listed in the phone book. They only have cell phones. And I'm sure I deleted them from my contacts list ages ago."

"Can you disclose where the adoptive parents live… for April's safety? We can dispatch an officer to check on them."

"They live out in the country. I took April out to them for visits several times. It would be faster for us to go there," said Sarah. "Besides, I feel responsible here."

"Then let's go. I'll alert the station as to what is going on."

She grabbed his hand. "What if Nadia hears the radio? She does not need any more turmoil. We don't want her doing something crazy."

"I can't go maverick on this." He turned a half circle and looked up at the sky. "I can phone it to the chief, though. Nothing for Nadia to overhear." The concession was worth it for Sarah's grateful smile.

Once they were out of town, Sarah directed him along country roads. The car crested over a hill, and a cabin at the base of a heavily forested mountain came into view. A car stood in the driveway. Nothing appeared amiss. Bryan pulled up close to the front door.

Sarah led the way up the front porch stairs. She knocked on the door. "Her name is Mackenzie and his name is Christopher. They're a neat couple. April is the second child they've adopted. The other is a four-year-old autistic boy named Ethan." Her words held a warm glow.

"You like your work?"

She gazed at him, blue eyes shining. "It's rewarding."

"Did you do it because of Marie?" It was the first time he'd spoken their child's name. He'd feared that all the pain of their bad choices would come rushing back with that single word. Instead, he felt a sense of release. Something that had been in the darkness, that he had refused to think about, was brought into the light.

She studied him for a moment. "Not entirely. I wanted to do a job like this because Crew and I languished so long in the foster care system. Things might have turned out better for Crew if someone had cared a little more about finding us a permanent family. I didn't want another kid to have to go through that."

"I think what you do is a good thing, a noble thing."

Happiness at his admiration shone in her eyes. "Thanks."

Bryan leaned in and knocked on the door a second time.

"Someone must be here. There're two cars in the driveway." Her voice had a nervous edge to it.

Bryan walked around the house. No one was in the backyard. Sarah met him on his way back. "The door isn't locked. I think we should go inside and take a look."

He pushed the door open and stepped across the threshold. A fan whirred on the high ceiling of the cabin.

"Mackenzie?" Sarah took several steps into the living room. "Christopher?" She walked toward the kitchen. "Ethan?" With each name, her voice became more filled with anxiety.

Bryan's hand hovered over his gun. "I'll search upstairs." He didn't want to leave Sarah alone. They'd been blindsided too many times. "Why don't you come with me?"

They moved silently up the carpeted stairs and down the hallway.

"Mackenzie? It's Sarah from the Loving Hearts adoption agency."

They searched all the bedrooms. The house was empty, silent. Bryan stopped in front of what was probably a bathroom. His back stiffened. "This is the only door that is closed." He adjusted his grip on the gun.

Sarah pushed the door open. Bryan slipped inside, scanning the room. The shower curtain shook. Someone was in the bathtub. He kept his gun aimed at the trembling curtain and signaled to Sarah that she should pull it back.

A woman with a gag on her mouth and fear in her eyes reeled back from Bryan pointing the gun on her.

"Mackenzie." Sarah bent toward the woman and peeled off the gag.

Bryan holstered his gun.

Mackenzie let out a burst of air once the gag was off. "The children. They took the children."

Sarah worked to untie Mackenzie's hands. "We think they only came for April."

Fear clouded each word Mackenzie spoke. "Then where's Ethan?"

"He wasn't in the house that we could find." Bryan struggled to keep his voice steady. Would they hurt an innocent child?

"He may have hidden. When he hears a stranger's voice, it scares him." Mackenzie leaned forward to untie her feet. She grabbed Sarah's shirtsleeve. "Why do they want April? Do you think she's all right?"

Sarah patted Mackenzie's arm. "She will be. We'll find her. Right now, why don't you focus on figuring out where Ethan went?"

Bryan leaned toward the woman. "Can you tell us what the men looked like?"

"They were wearing masks. There were three of them." She stepped out of the bathtub and ran down the hall calling Ethan's name.

Bryan and Sarah chased after her down the stairs. She emerged from one of the side rooms on the first floor. "Ethan isn't in his usual hiding place." She ran one direction and then the other. "I have to call Chris."

Bryan understood Mackenzie's panic, but he needed information. "Can you tell us which way the men went?"

Mackenzie stopped. Her eyes glazed as a confused look came across her face. "We were upstairs and they came barging in. They took her from my arms. It happened so fast. The man knew April's name." A veil seemed to drop over her eyes as her voice grew cold. "He said 'come to Daddy' and he took her."

TWENTY

Sarah let what Mackenzie had said sink in. So Mason had felt this mission was so important, he'd taken care of it himself. Or maybe he was running out of hired guns to do his dirty work for him.

Bryan jumped into action. "We've got to get search parties out in every direction. They couldn't have gotten far." He turned back to face the frightened mom. "How long ago were they here?"

Mackenzie rubbed her temple and squeezed her eyes shut. "Ah… I was…tied up and left there maybe ten or fifteen minutes before you guys showed up."

Bryan nodded and pulled his phone out.

Sarah wrapped her arm around Mackenzie. "Let's focus on finding Ethan. Is there another place he would hide if he were afraid?"

"The thing is…he'd come out if he heard my voice," Mackenzie said.

Sarah fought hard to remain calm. Mackenzie didn't need to see the fear that pressed on her from all sides. "How about the backyard? He couldn't hear you from inside the house. Is there a place for him to hide outside?"

Realization spread across Mackenzie's face. Her voice had a haunted quality. "What if he ran after his sister? He's very protective of her."

The thought of a four-year-old boy lost in the forest, chasing after dangerous men, sent chills through Sarah. In the next room, Sarah could hear Bryan making frantic calls to get a search underway.

Mackenzie crossed her arms over her body. "I have to call Chris." She muttered something under her breath and stepped into another room.

Bryan emerged with his phone in his hand. "I've asked for law enforcement and search-and-rescue to find these guys…and the little boy."

Sarah felt numb all over as fog invaded her brain. "She thinks the boy may have gone after his sister."

Bryan kicked the leg of a chair. "This is bad. How could anyone put a kid in jeopardy like that?"

"As soon as Mackenzie calls her husband, we'll go out. We'll start calling for Ethan. He couldn't have gotten far." If something didn't get him first. The forest was crawling with bobcats and bears—and men like Tyler Mason.

Bryan's phone rang again. She watched his expression harden as he listened and then answered by saying, "Well, get her over there as fast as you can." He clicked the phone off.

Sarah stepped toward him. "What is it?"

Bryan's hands curled into a fist. He ran his fingers through his hair. His expression grew grimmer as he closed his eyes and tapped his forehead with his fingers. "Mason knows we're keeping Nadia at the station. One of his thugs got her on a phone and let her listen to April cry. Nadia fell apart and tried to leave the station. She'd do anything to make sure that baby is okay including trading herself for the baby's safety."

Sarah swallowed as her throat grew tight. Mason was pulling out all the stops. "I assume the other officers are watching her closely so she can't leave the station."

"They're taking her to the hotel room right now. We'll have two officers with her at all times. She'll be shielded from Mason's destructive influence for a while anyway." Bryan took in a heavy breath. "One good thing. We have a better idea of where Mason is. We can pinpoint which cell tower provided the signal for his phone call."

Mackenzie emerged from a side room, her eyes red from crying. "Chris is on his way here from work."

"There will be search teams all over here in less than thirty minutes. In the meantime, we can cover the area in a wider and wider circle calling out for Ethan. It won't do any good for me to go alone if he only responds to your voice," Bryan said.

Though she still looked like she was in shock, Mackenzie nodded.

"I'll go with you, too," said Sarah.

They circled the yard and then outside the yard. Mackenzie called Ethan's name over and over, her voice growing weaker. A helicopter soared overhead. Probably part of the search team.

"What was your son wearing?"

"A yellow shirt and orange shorts." Mackenzie rubbed her neck, her voice filled with anguish. "Those are his favorite colors."

Bryan glanced up and down the road "Did you hear a car pull up or the sound of one leaving?"

Mackenzie's hand fluttered to her chest. She bit her lower lip. "It all happened so fast." She stared up at the sky, probably trying to piece the horrible memory together. "Come to think of it, I didn't hear a car. It's quiet out here. The horses make a lot of noise when someone shows up."

With the two women following him, Bryan stalked around to the side of the house circling a corral confining two horses. "That means they parked some distance away so they wouldn't be noticed." He continued to survey the area surrounding the house, pointing to the forest that jutted up against the backyard. "What's on the other side of those trees?"

"There's an old logging road," Mackenzie said.

Bryan picked up his pace. "Let's look for your son through there."

Mackenzie trotted toward the forest. She ran in an erratic pattern, calling Ethan's name. Sarah and Bryan moved slower. Desperate, Sarah searched the lower levels of the forest for a flash of orange or yellow.

Mackenzie ran deeper into the forest shouting Ethan's name. Her voice grew hoarse. She stopped when they were completely surrounded by trees and the house could no longer be seen. She lifted her head toward the forest canopy. "Ethan," she whispered. A tear trailed down her cheek.

Sarah placed her hand in Mackenzie's. She closed her eyes. Silence descended like a shroud.

Please, God, please.

"Hey," Bryan spoke in a soft hush.

Sarah opened her eyes and followed the direction of Bryan's pointing. From beneath thick evergreen boughs slanted close to the ground, two feet with one yellow and one orange sock were visible.

Mackenzie gulped air. "Ethan." She darted toward the tree and reached in through the branches, pulling out a blond child who pressed his face against her chest, not saying a word as Mackenzie laughed and cried. "Oh, thank You. Thank You, God."

After both mother and child calmed down, Bryan approached them. "Will he talk to us? He might know something about the men who took April."

Ethan grunted in protest and gripped the neck of his mother's shirt. Mackenzie made a soothing noise and stroked the little boy's head. "He might give you yes and no answers."

"Ethan, did you see the men who took your sister?" No response.

Mackenzie repeated the question. Ethan nodded.

"Did you follow them?"

Again, Mackenzie had to repeat the question before Ethan responded in the affirmative.

"Which way did they go?"

With his face still pressed against his mother's chest, Ethan pulled his arm away from his body and pointed through the forest.

Bryan's gaze cut through the trees as he nodded slowly. "So they did take the old logging road." He turned to face Mackenzie. "We're going to get your daughter back." Bryan raced to the house. Several other police cars and a search-and-rescue unit with tracking dogs had arrived.

Bryan explained where he thought Mason and his men had gone and pointed out Mackenzie as she emerged from the forest carrying Ethan. "I'm going to get the jump on this." He looked over at Sarah. "You coming with me?"

He jogged toward the car, not giving Sarah time to respond. She raced after him. Once inside the car, he explained his urgency. "It'll take them twenty minutes to get this search organized and to get the dogs onto some kind of scent." He shifted gears. "That's twenty minutes we don't have."

Mackenzie ran toward them holding a canvas tote. Sarah rolled down her window.

"This is April's baby bag. If…when you find her, she'll be hungry and scared. She'll need these things."

"Thank you." Sarah draped her hand over the other woman's. "We're going to find her."

Mackenzie stepped away from the car.

Bryan sped up the road until he came to a spur road that must be the logging road Mackenzie had referenced.

"Why would they go this way? It'll take them forever to get back into town," Sarah said.

"I doubt their plan is to go into town just yet. They don't want to be caught. Mason's got Nadia suitably frightened."

"You really think he will just give up the baby so he can have Nadia?"

"Yes, I think April is a tool to him. But I have a feeling he won't be satisfied with just having Nadia back as his girlfriend. He's probably figured out we've been prepping her to testify. He's knows I'm back on the case. I think if Nadia goes back to him, she'll disappear…forever."

Judging from the frightened look on Sarah's face, Bryan feared he had said too much. He softened his tone. "Mason's only objective in life is to survive and to keep on doing whatever benefits him."

Sarah shook her head in stunned disbelief. "Certainly, he doesn't think he can stay in Discovery conducting business as usual."

"He'll probably tie up loose ends, disappear and reinvent himself in another part of the world." Bryan pounded the steering wheel as determination coursed through him. "We have to get this guy."

The car lumbered up the steep road and Bryan shifted down. He hoped his gamble would pay off. Trusting the testimony of a frightened four-year-old boy, who perceived the world differently than most, might not have come out of the police rulebook, but he had a gut feeling.

They'd lost precious time. He had to find a way to make up for it. The car laboriously climbed the hill. Once they reached the peak, Bryan turned the engine off. "Let's see if we can spot anything."

The mountain was a high point that provided a three-sixty-degree view of the surrounding area. The only higher spot was about two miles away as the crow flies, the mountaintop where the fire spotter tower stood. This part of the hill had very little vegetation. Thick forest occupied the lower elevations with barren areas that had been logged.

Bryan pulled the binoculars out of his glove box. "If they came this way, they took that road down there." He put the binoculars up to his eyes. The thick forest limited his view of the winding road. He turned in the opposite direction. Though the house wasn't visible from this angle, he spied the police and search-and-rescue vehicles moving out from a central point.

Sarah stared off in the distance at a plume of smoke rising up from the forest. Her hand fluttered to her mouth.

"That's a long ways away and it's a small area," he said.

"They wouldn't call off the search because of a fire, would they?" Anxiety laced through her words.

"That fire is miles from where these guys have probably gone," Bryan tried to assure her even as doubt crept in.

The fear in her eyes intensified.

Bryan studied the distant fire again. "Something that small will be contained quickly."

He examined the ant trails of dirt roads that crisscrossed through the hills, disappearing in patches of forest and emerging on the other side.

"There." Sarah pointed to the adjoining hill. Metal reflected the sunlight. A blue vehicle made its way down the mountain. "It's got to be them."

He assessed the direction the other police vehicles had gone. None of them headed the right way.

A revelation sparked in his mind. "That day Mason's men brought you out here, why did they take you all the way out here into the backcountry?"

"They intended to kill me." Sarah shuddered. "They probably thought no one would find the body out here."

"That's probably why they didn't kill you right away in town or me when they had me. The best way for Mason to stay clean is for the bodies never to be found." That had to have been what happened to Eva.

"Why are you being so morbid?"

"I'm not. What I'm asking is did you get the impression that either of those men who took you knew this area? People usually don't choose new and strange places like that for committing a crime."

Sarah seemed perplexed by the questions. "My eyes were covered for most of the journey."

He could tell by the tightness of her mouth and furled eyebrows that she really didn't want to relive any part of that day. He spoke gently. "Try to remember what they said. It's important."

She thought for a moment. "One of them did seem to know the area. He barked directions at the other man who was driving."

"So my bet is that same thug is with Mason now, guiding him through all these back roads so he's not likely to get caught. They're not going to take the obvious route. They want to avoid detection. And at least one of them knows where he's going."

They got back in the car and went down the other side of the mountain, entering a stretch of road that had thick forest on either side. The light diminished by half. They came to a place where the road forked in two directions. Bryan gave his best guess which way to turn based on the direction the other vehicle had been traveling. The road narrowed and turned into a washboard.

Though he kept his doubts to himself, he wondered if they had made the right choice. That vehicle they saw could have belonged to anyone.

The forest thinned. A helicopter flew overhead.

"Is that headed toward the fire we saw?"

Bryan peered up through the windshield. "Yeah, it might be."

The whop-whop-whop-whop of helicopter blades faded. Bryan made slow progress on the precarious road. He traveled at less than fifteen miles an hour as they rounded a bend. A creek flowed in front of them…

…and a blue truck just like the one they'd seen at a distance sat motionless in the middle of the creek.

Bryan tapped his hands on the steering wheel. "Looks like they tried to ford the creek and got stuck."

Judging from the amount of mud on the vehicle, they'd put substantial effort into trying to get it out. Sarah leaned her head out the window, listening. Only the creaking of the trees and a distant caw of a bird pressed on her ears. "I don't think they're close."

"Let's check it out, make sure the truck was really them." Bryan pressed on the handle and quietly eased the door open.

Sarah remained on high alert as she followed behind Bryan. The pounding of her feet on the dirt seemed exaggerated. The cool water swirled around her ankles as she stepped into the creek. The license plate was for Discovery's county and the frame around the plate was from Crazy Ray's, a tenuous connection. The tinted windows didn't allow her to see anything inside. At the center of the creek, where the vehicle bogged down, the water rose up past her knees. Her shoes sank into the mud. Sarah opened the passenger-side door. A toddler-sized windbreaker lay on the seat.

Bryan opened the driver's-side door. Sarah pointed to the windbreaker and he nodded.

"Check the registration," Bryan whispered.

She opened the glove compartment. The car was registered to a Richard Hart. She shrugged her shoulders, indicating that the information wasn't helpful. They both closed the doors at the same time.

Bryan met her at the front of the car. "I say we go up this road a ways. The windbreaker is enough for me to think it might be April."

They pushed through the muddy water and out onto the road. They'd gone only a hundred yards when the faint cry of a child reached their ears. Sarah's heart ached for the little girl. Bryan pointed in the direction the sound had come from and made a motion indicating they should separate and surround the area.

Sarah crept through the brush. The crying stopped. She heard men's muffled voices and then the crying started up again. Her foot snapped a twig. She cringed, but there was no interruption in the men's conversation. The voices grew louder, more distinct as she got closer. She crouched low and peered out from beneath the brush. There were two men, both of them armed with handguns. A rifle sat propped up against a rock. She recognized one of the men as Acne Scars, one of her kidnappers.

April stood at the center of the clearing. No one held her, no one comforted her. Her voice had grown hoarse from crying. She swiped at her eyes and plumped down in the dirt. A man she recognized from Bryan's files as Tyler Mason stood some distance away from the other men, talking on the phone. The conversation indicated that he was making arrangements for someone to come and get them. Mason hung up the phone and paced.

April, a little wobbly on her feet, dumped down to a crawling position and veered away from the two men.

"Get her," Mason commanded, still holding the phone to his ear.

One of the thugs grabbed April above the elbow and

dragged her toward him. April shook her head several times and let out a sputtering sob.

Sarah peered across the clearing, hoping to see Bryan. How were they going to rescue that little girl? They were outmanned and had only one gun.

Mason dialed another telephone number. "Hello, is this Discovery Police Station? I have a message for you to pass on to Nadia Akulov. Tell her she has five hours to meet at the rendezvous point. She'll know what I'm talking about. If she doesn't show or she brings police with her, no one will ever see April again. Can you manage that?"

Despite the midday heat, a chill coursed through Sarah's bones. A hand touched her back. She jumped but managed to stifle a scream. Bryan took her hand and pulled her deeper into the woods. He leaned close and whispered in her ear. "Go to the car, get it turned around and wait." He pressed the car keys into her hand. "It may be ten minutes, it may be an hour. Wait for me and be ready to go."

The plan seemed foolhardy at best, but she nodded. Right now, all they had was foolhardy. Sarah ran quietly but quickly back to the car. It took some maneuvering to get it turned around on the narrow road. Perspiring from her effort, she shifted the car into Park. Her pulse drummed in her ears as she watched the rearview mirror.

TWENTY-ONE

Bryan crept in close to the clearing. He watched. He waited. What he needed was an opportunity. Just a few seconds when all three of the men dropped their guard. None of them seemed to want to hold April, which was good. Mason strode away from the group, his back to the others as he talked on the phone to whoever was supposed to come and get them. This time his words were harsher, filled with anger and impatience.

One of the men rose from the flat rock where he'd been sitting. "I got to go water a tree."

April sat on the ground. Her head bobbed as she nodded off. Now all he needed was for the other man to be distracted. He picked up a rock and threw it so it hit a tree some distance away. The second hired gun ran toward the sound, leaving April unattended.

He wasn't going to get a better chance than this. He scrambled into the clearing, grabbed April and put his hand over her mouth to keep her from making a sound before slipping back into the thick brush.

The disrupting cries from the men pressed in on him.

Bryan clutched the child and slipped deeper into the forest. "I'm not going to hurt you, baby girl," he said in the most soothing voice he could manage while he tried to figure out what to do. He couldn't run right out to the road. They'd find him.

He hid behind a rock, gathering April close to his chest. She gazed up at him. Soft lashes framed her dark brown eyes. She clutched his shirt at the collar. She studied him, but did not cry out. His heart melted over her vulnerability.

One of the men ran by the rock. He could hear the other crashing through the trees, getting farther away. Mason screamed and cursed, every word filled with rage. Bryan peered out from behind the rock. No movement, no close sound. Now was the moment. Holding April tight, he sprinted from tree to tree to shield himself from view.

He worked his way back toward the creek, while the men shouted all around him. April clung to his collar. He held her close. Finally, the creek and the car came into view. Moving in spurts, he darted from a tree to a rock.

The men's voices grew louder behind him. He'd be fully exposed once he crossed the creek. He ran through the water, frustrated with the way the mud slowed him. Sarah had left the passenger-side door open, but would he get there in time? A rifle shot sounded behind him. April pressed harder against him.

Sarah started the car rolling even before he slid into the passenger seat. He leaned out, grabbed the door and slammed it shut as she sped up. April trembled against him.

He touched her silky hair. "It's all right." He circled his arms around her. She tilted her head and gazed at him. "You didn't make a peep, did you?"

She stuck a finger in her mouth. The thugs got off several rounds before Sarah slipped behind a bend. Each shot made April flinch. She looked at him, eyes filled with trust.

Sarah drove without slowing, checking behind her several times. Finally her grip on the wheel relaxed. She glanced over at Bryan and April. "She knows you won't hurt her. That's why she's so quiet."

Bryan chuckled. "Either that or she's so scared she's speechless." His heart swelled with affection for this helpless creature.

"The bag Mackenzie gave us is on the floor by your feet."

Bryan leaned forward and picked up the baby tote. He opened it, pulling out a cup with a lid that was half-full of amber liquid.

April made a "ba" sound and reached for the sippy cup. Bryan pulled out a stuffed cat. "You want this?"

She looked at him and then at the toy. He tucked it close to her armpit and she held on to it. April took several gulps of juice from her cup.

"They probably didn't think to feed her or give her water." Sarah's voice was filled with indignation.

Sarah increased her speed as the road evened out and the car rolled over the hills. She looked down at her instrument panel. "The gas gauge is going down really fast. They might have hit our tank when they shot at us."

"I think we might have bigger problems than that." Bryan pointed up the road at the approaching car. "I think that's Mason's ride out of here."

Sarah sucked air through her teeth. "Maybe they'll

slip past us and think we're just a family out enjoying the wilderness."

Still about two hundred yards away, the car edged toward them.

Bryan glanced out his window. His mind raced with possibilities for escape. "This is Mason we're talking about. He probably phoned ahead and alerted them about us."

"What do we do?" Sarah scanned the road, panic evident in her voice.

Bryan slumped down in his car seat and angled April so she was lying down and not visible through the window. "The road veers off up here. Hurry. See if you can get there before they pass us." Not much of a plan. For sure, the men had seen their car.

Sarah adjusted her hands on the steering wheel. "Are we hoping that Mason hasn't alerted them?"

"Yes, and we're hoping that these guys aren't even connected to Mason. We're hoping all sorts of unrealistic things."

Sarah pressed the accelerator. "The gas needle's on empty anyway. We're not going to get very far."

The car was within fifty yards of them. He couldn't see the driver or the passenger clearly. Sarah turned her head so the driver wouldn't have a clear view of her, either. She veered off on the spur Bryan had pointed out. The car eased past them just as their car lumbered up the side road.

Bryan craned his neck. "Can't see them anymore. Maybe we're safe."

"Should I try to get back on that road?"

Bryan leaned over and looked at the instrument board. "We'll run out of gas before then. Take this thing as far as it will go. Then we'll hike up the road. If Mason got cell reception, I should be able to also. One of the other searchers has to be close." Bryan gazed down at April, who had fallen asleep in his arms.

Sarah glanced over at him, her expression warming. "She seems really comfortable with you."

"Yeah. Weird, huh?"

The car chugged. Sarah pumped the gas. "That's all she wrote."

"Let's get to the top of that hill." Still holding a sleeping April, Bryan pushed the door open. He rested the little girl against one shoulder and hoisted the baby bag onto the other. "Phone Grant Pittman." He recited a number to her. "He's part of the search."

Sarah pressed the numbers. She waited. "He's not picking up."

Bryan adjusted the sleeping child in his arms. "She's getting heavy."

"I saw a sling in the bag." Sarah rooted through the tote and pulled out what looked like a long piece of fabric. "We can take turns carrying her."

"I'll go first. Once we contact someone, we'll have to walk out to where they can find us." Bryan glanced down the hill. The men in the car must have decided picking up Mason was their priority—but once Mason was in the car, Bryan was sure he'd start tracking them. "Mason and his men will be looking for us soon."

"I know. We'd better hurry." She flung the sling over Bryan's shoulder and fastened it.

"Here, let me take her for a second." April stirred but didn't wake when Sarah gathered her into her arms.

Bryan held the sling open so Sarah could place the toddler in it. He cut a glance through the trees toward the road. "I still don't see them." He looked down at April as she slept. It was his responsibility to get the three of them out of here unharmed.

"At least they won't be able to bring their car where we're going. We've got a head start on them." Sarah held up the phone. "Who do you want me to call now?

"Try Jake."

"Jake? The guy who picked us up when the men brought me to the lake?"

Bryan nodded and recited a number to her. "He lives close. He'll be able to get here fast."

They hiked the remaining distance to the ridge. Bryan continued to glance over his shoulder. He thought he saw the shimmer of a car through the trees, but couldn't be sure.

Sarah stood at the top of the ridge. Her spine went stiff.

"What's wrong?"

"I think we have more pressing issues than Mason."

Bryan walked up to where Sarah stood. He tensed at what he saw.

Patches of fire dotted the landscape below. Flames engulfed the mountain opposite them.

TWENTY-TWO

"Those fires are still pretty far away, right?" Even Sarah could hear that she sounded like she was trying to convince herself. Her gaze darted nervously toward him as fear took up residence in her knotted stomach.

"The problem is roads may be cut off. Help might not be able to get to us." Bryan's voice gave away no anxiety, though he must be in just as much turmoil as she was.

His calm fortified her own. "So how are we going to get out of here?"

Bryan resumed walking along the ridge, taking long strides. "We have to try to reach someone. Notify them of our position."

Sarah scrambled to keep up. "Okay, so give me a second and I'll keep trying to reach Jake."

"We don't have time to spare." Bryan walked even faster. April stirred in his arms. He patted her head, soothing her. "Maybe if we can get to an open area, a helicopter can reach us."

"We could try sneaking back down the road. We know the fires aren't in that direction."

"Too risky," Bryan said.

"So what are you saying?" Sarah spoke between breaths as she jogged beside Bryan.

He pointed toward the horizon. "We need to get to fire tower six. There's a helicopter landing pad not too far from there. We can call for help on the radio. Someone might even still be there."

Sarah stared down at the forest below. Plumes of smoke rose up in at least three places.

Bryan stopped. He leaned close to her, their shoulders touching. He traced a path down the mountain and up the other side. "That's where we'll go. I think we'll be able to avoid the worst part of the fires."

Sarah looked down the mountain in the direction they'd come. A man in a light-colored shirt moved along the tree line. He held a rifle. "Let's get down on the other side of this mountain."

They hiked across the barren part of the mountain into the forest. When Sarah glanced up at the ridgeline, three men stood watching the forest below. She picked up her pace. Despite having to carry April, Bryan stayed ahead of her.

Several deer ran by them and the faint smell of smoke lingered. They walked for at least twenty minutes before Bryan suddenly stopped. He tilted his head toward the sky. "I need to get my bearings. See where that tower is at. Hold her for a minute."

Sarah lifted April out of the sling, which woke her. Thankfully, she didn't seem to mind shifting over to Sarah. The baby nestled against her, her forehead glistening with sweat. Despite the tree canopy, the forest seemed to be getting hotter.

Bryan walked over to an evergreen with low branches and proceeded to climb it. Sarah rooted through the baby bag and found a package of crackers for April. With April settled chewing on her food, Sarah dialed Jake's phone number.

"Hello?"

"Jake. This is Sarah Langston. I'm the one who— I'm a friend of Bryan Keyes." Sarah explained their situation.

Jake said, "Bryan was right about road access. They're not letting anybody into that area at this point."

"We're going to try to make it to fire tower six." Sarah pressed the phone against her ear. "That's the closest place where a chopper might be able to land."

"I'll do everything I can to alert the authorities that you're trapped in there. I can let the police department know, too."

"Thanks, I'll try to stay in phone contact."

Sarah hung up the phone. April offered her a bite of her half-chewed cracker. Sarah touched the little girl's soft cheek. "Thanks, sweetie."

Bryan shouted from the tree. "I think I see our route."

The sound of branches breaking alerted Sarah to someone or something moving through the forest. She gathered April more tightly in her arms and slipped behind a tree. Any hope that it was some animal fleeing the fire faded when she heard human voices. Sarah peered out from behind the tree. Her breath caught. She'd left the brightly colored baby bag out in the open.

Mason's men moved through the forest, their voices growing louder. Sarah gazed up and over at Bryan, who had concealed himself in the thick boughs.

Sarah remained still. April made a "ba ba ba" sound and kicked her leg. Sarah placed her fingers gently over April's mouth, hoping she'd understand.

The men's voices quieted.

April pulled Sarah's hand away and shook her head.

Sarah squeezed her eyes shut.

Please, don't make any noise.

She heard what could have been a footstep. And then another. Her heart pounded in her rib cage. Sweat trickled past her temple. April played with her necklace, touched her earrings. Several minutes passed.

Bryan poked his head through the branches. "I think they went past."

"Was it them?"

He climbed out to the end of a thick branch and dropped down. "I heard them, but never saw them, so I can't be sure."

"What if they're out in front of us now?"

April held her hands up to Bryan. He gathered her into his arms. "That's a chance we're going to have to take. We're not that far from the tower."

Her sense of direction had gotten completely turned around. "Will we be going by the lake?"

"No, we'll come in on the other side. No high, steep mountain to climb." He started walking with April looking back over his shoulder. Sarah walked behind. April waved at her. At least the little girl had no idea what kind of danger she was in.

Before long, they hit a wall of heat. In the distance, she could hear trees crashing to the ground. The air filled with smoke. April coughed.

Bryan tore off a piece of his shirt. "Is there water in that bag?"

Sarah dropped the bag on the ground and rooted through it. "There's a juice box."

Bryan saturated the piece of cloth with the liquid

and then tore off two more pieces of fabric and wet them down, as well. "Put this over your mouth. Help me get April back in the sling."

All of them were sweating. The temperature had to be past a hundred. The air grew thicker and hazier with smoke. Bryan increased his pace. The trees thinned, and they stepped into a clearing.

Bryan pointed off in the distance. The dome-shaped roof of the tower rose above a rock formation.

Almost there.

Bryan raced up the tower stairs. By the time Sarah had entered the tower, he had set April on the floor. He ran around the tower closing all the windows.

Sarah glanced around. "Where's the fire spotter?"

"He must have left once he saw the fire down below. Fire should move downhill toward the lake. Smoke inhalation is our biggest worry," he said.

April picked up a cup and tried to drink. Sarah found bottled water and poured some into April's sippy cup.

Bryan picked up the radio. "This is fire tower six. I have an emergency situation here."

Dispatch came on the line. "Fire tower six was evacuated twenty minutes ago."

The smoke outside grew thicker.

"This is Bryan Keyes." Sweat trickled down his face. "I manned this tower up until a few days ago. I'm here with a woman and the missing nine-month-old child. Can you send in a chopper to get us?"

"Let me see what I can do. Out," said the dispatcher. She came back on the line minutes later. "Fire tower six. We have a bird that is approximately seven minutes away. Can you get to the landing pad by then?"

"We'll be there." Bryan clicked off the radio. His eyes darted around the room. He grabbed a blanket and one of the water bottles. "Wet this down. Your clothes, too."

They worked frantically and were out the door and down the stairs in less than three minutes. Bryan wrapped the damp blanket around April and held her close to his chest. The mechanical noise of the chopper grew louder as they ran. They zigzagged around a burning tree. April cried. Bryan held her tighter. Sarah grabbed hold of his shirt as the smoke thickened.

The helicopter sounded like it was on top of them though it was still some distance away. Smoke obscured their view. Sarah coughed. Finally the helicopter descended, creating an intense wind. April coughed and cried.

Bryan signaled Sarah to get into the helicopter first. He handed April to her and then climbed in himself.

The helicopter lifted off. Sarah belted into a seat, holding on tight to April. Bryan leaned forward and spoke to the pilot. "There are at least four other men stranded out there."

Whatever Mason and his men had done, they didn't deserve to die in this fire—no one did.

"Roger that, we can send another chopper to search the area," said the pilot.

As the helicopter gained elevation, Bryan stared out the window at the landscape below. The fire had jumped in some areas, creating patches of forest that were black or burning while others were untouched.

The pilot radioed ahead. The helicopter set down not too far from Mackenzie and Christopher's home. Mother and father stood outside their house along with little Ethan, but all three of them ran toward the chopper as it came down. Bryan climbed out first. Sarah handed over April.

The parents tearfully gathered April in their arms, thanking and hugging both Sarah and Bryan. They walked back to the house, mother holding baby, father carrying Ethan on his hip with his arm around mother. A happy family. Nadia emerged from the house and ran toward the family.

"What's that about?" Bryan grabbed Sarah's hand.

"I imagine Nadia just wanted to see that April was okay."

Two police officers stood behind the family, watching their surroundings and Nadia.

The family embraced Nadia.

"She gets to see April even after the adoption?"

"Limited contact. But Chris and Mackenzie agreed to send Nadia pictures and a letter every now and then letting her know how April is doing." She turned to face him. "It's the way I set up the adoption with Marie. You had already stopped speaking to me by then, once you signed away parental rights. I made those decisions on my own."

The pain in her voice stabbed at his heart. Bryan's throat tightened. He hadn't let himself think of these things for ten years. "You have pictures of Marie?"

Sarah nodded. "She was adopted by a couple in Wyoming. I got to meet them."

Bryan leaned close, kissing Sarah on the cheek. "I'm sorry I did that to you, left you like that."

Sarah turned toward him. Her eyes filled with love. "You're forgiven."

Warmth pooled around Bryan's heart. The sincerity of her words made him feel as though he'd been re-leased from the cage he'd been in for ten years.

Grant approached them. "Could you two use a ride back into town?"

Bryan nodded. Grant led them to his patrol car. Bryan and Sarah sat together in the backseat holding hands, but not speaking.

As they came to the outskirts of town, Grant spoke. "Chief wants to debrief you about what happened out there with Mason. He's got kidnapping charges against him now. That guy is going away for a long time.

If he gets out of the forest alive.

"Sarah, I think he's going to want a statement from you, too," added Grant.

They entered the quiet station. Sarah gave her state-ment and then wandered out into the break room where she settled on the couch that had become her home away from home. After he completed his statement, Bryan found her asleep there. He shook her shoulder.

"Hey, I borrowed a friend's car. I can take you home."

Sarah sat up, joy evident in her voice. "I can go home?"

"They managed to rescue one of Mason's men out of the forest. It looks like the others perished—Mason included."

Sarah let out a breath. "So there won't be a trial."

Bryan shook his head. "Nadia is staying one night at the hotel. It's all set up for her, and she doesn't have anywhere else to go."

"Can we swing by the hospital to see how Crew is doing?"

"Sure," Bryan said.

Bryan drove through town and found a parking spot close to the hospital entrance. Still holding hands, they entered the hospital. The woman at the nurses' station stood up when she saw them coming.

"Hey." The nurse studied them from head to toe.

They must be quite a sight. She'd rinsed her face off at the police station, but looking over at Sarah, Bryan registered that her clothes were torn, dirty and smelled like smoke.

"Crew regained consciousness about an hour ago," said the nurse.

Sarah rushed toward his room and flung open the door. Bryan followed behind. Crew was sitting up in his hospital bed. He looked pale and weak, but a light came into his eyes when she entered the room. "Hey, little sister."

She wrapped her arms around him. "I thought I'd lost you."

Sarah's joy was infectious.

"Haven't seen you in a while." Crew offered Bryan a weak salute.

"Took me ten years to get back," Bryan said.

"Well, you were the best thing for my sister." Crew ruffled Sarah's hair.

Sarah blushed. "That was a long time ago."

They visited for a few minutes more until Crew started to nod off. Sarah kissed his forehead and walked out with Bryan.

They drove in silence. The street light flashed by and then thinned out.

"Do you think what Crew said is true, about you being a good thing for me?" She turned in her seat. Her gaze weighed on him.

"I think he had it backward. You were easy to be with, easy to love." He adjusted his hands on the steering wheel as the familiar stab of pain shot through him. "We were so young. We made mistakes."

She reached over, draping her hand on his. Her touch eased his hurt.

"We'll always have regrets. When I said you were forgiven, I meant it. Now you just have to forgive yourself."

Her words were a soothing balm soaking through him, melting the hurt and the self-hate he'd lived with for so many years. They had made some wrong decisions as a couple, but they'd made the right decision for their little girl. Were they ready now to move on from the past, and have the future they'd tried to rush before?

Bryan turned onto the gravel road that led to Sarah's house. The tires crinkled over the road when he slowed down.

"I'm sure your cat will be glad to see you." His attempt at joviality had a ring of sadness to it. What were they to each other now that all this was over? Mason was dead. He had no more excuse to be with her.

"Mr. Tiddlywinks is pretty independent. Though I'm sure he'll have some choice words for the neglect he's suffered." When Bryan pulled into the driveway, she turned to face him. "Walk me to the door? I have something I want to show you."

Sarah stepped inside and turned on a single light over her desk. She opened a drawer and pulled out a photograph, taking it to Bryan where he waited by the door.

"It's Marie. She was in a dance recital recently." She

placed it in his hand and then wrapped her hand around his. "You can keep it. I have another copy."

A bright-eyed, smiling little girl stared back at him. He touched the picture with his finger. She had the same curly brown hair as Sarah, but the slightly crooked nose and round eyes were his. His throat tightened. He gazed up at Sarah.

He gathered her into his arms and kissed her. Her lips were warm and inviting. He rested his hand against her back and pulled her closer, deepening the kiss. He held her for a long moment, his forehead pressed against hers. He didn't want to go but his feelings jumbled up inside of him and he couldn't find the words. He pulled away from her, turned and walked toward the door.

Sarah stood stunned from the power of his kiss. Outside, she heard the car door slam and the engine roar to life. She turned on a kitchen light.

"Mr. Tiddlywinks. Here, kitty kitty." As she wandered through the house a pungent odor surrounded her. She couldn't quite place it.

She switched on the light in her bedroom, checking under the bed where Mr. Tiddlywinks liked to hide. No cat.

Sarah sniffed the air. Smoke. Did her clothes smell that bad? She took a hasty shower and put on fresh clothes, throwing the smelly ones in the outside garbage.

She returned to the living room. The acrid stench lingered. She opened several windows. Her cat was outside running his paws up and down the glass of the patio door.

Sarah's breath hitched. She'd left the cat inside the

last time she was here. Her pulse skyrocketed. Now she knew why the smell of smoke was still so strong. Mason was in her house.

Sarah ran toward the front door as fast as she could. Not fast enough.

TWENTY-THREE

Bryan made it to the end of the street. He pulled the car over and clicked on the dome light, staring down at the picture Sarah had given him. Bright eyes and a mass of curls. What a beautiful child. The hardness around his heart melted away.

He'd kissed Sarah wishing he could tell her he wanted to start over with a clean slate, but he couldn't manage to get the words out. Maybe tomorrow he'd give her a call when he wasn't so tongue-tied. He pulled out on the road that led back into town. Cars blipped by him. He was within a few blocks of his house when he realized his house wasn't where he wanted to be. Who was he kidding? This wasn't something that could wait another day. He loved her.

He scanned the road looking for a place to turn around. Hopefully, she hadn't already gone to bed.

Tyler Mason slammed Sarah's head against the wall. She slipped down to the floor.

"Where is she? Where's Nadia?"

Sarah's vision filled with dark spots as she turned around to face her attacker.

Mason grabbed her by her shirt, yanking upward and smashing her back against the wall. His face was close enough for her to feel his hot breath. "You'd better tell me now."

She shook her head. "She deserves a life, a chance to get away from you." Mason smelled so heavily of smoke, it made her nauseous. A streak of black marred his face. "How did you get out? They said you were dead."

He pushed her harder against the wall. "I have resources you couldn't begin to comprehend. What was one more helicopter flying around in the air?"

Mason's henchmen must have gotten separated. Mason had left the others to die.

His eyes bulged as he leaned close. "You'd better tell me in the next three minutes or it's curtains for you. And then for your brother. And then for your little boyfriend. And after I've disposed of all of you, I'll still find some other way to get to her."

Mason had lost everything. This wasn't about protecting his illegal business anymore. It was about revenge. He would kill Sarah either way. The least she could do was buy Nadia some time.

Mason grabbed her by the hair and dragged her into the kitchen. He pulled a kitchen knife out of the holder and then pushed her toward the back door.

"Open it," he said through clenched teeth.

She could hear the cat meowing as Mason pushed her down the stairs out into the field behind her house. She doubted he really cared all that much anymore about committing his crimes where no one would see them, but it had probably become such a habit that it didn't even occur to him to simply kill her inside, where her body would easily be found.

Bryan's face, the tenderness of his touch flashed in her mind. She loved him and now she would never see him again, never get to tell him how she felt.

Mason pushed her hard and she fell on her knees.

She closed her eyes. Her last thought was of Bryan and her prayer was that he would recover from losing her yet again.

When his knocking went unanswered, Bryan had let himself in. And from the moment he stepped across the threshold, he knew something was wrong. His gaze darted around and then he saw the open patio door. He rushed outside. Darkness covered the field.

Mason's voice, low and sinister, floated through the air. "Have it your way."

Bryan darted softly through the field, focusing on the direction Mason's voice had come from. He drew his weapon. He squinted. Was that a silhouette of a person, or a shadow? He lifted his gun and fired.

A scream filled the night air. Sarah's scream.

Bryan ran. Feet pounding. Heart racing. He gathered Sarah into his arms.

"He's dead," she whispered, pressing close against his chest.

His arms enveloped her.

"What made you come back? How did you know?"

He touched her soft hair. "I didn't know. I…wanted to tell you I love you."

She touched his cheek, kissed his lips and then pressed close against his chest. His heart pounded;

heat radiated and adrenaline coursed through him. He closed his eyes, nestling his cheek against her head.

"I love you, too," she whispered. "I don't think I ever stopped loving you."

EPILOGUE

Through the window of the bridal shop, Sarah spotted Bryan standing out on the sidewalk. She felt a rush of joy as she stepped out to meet him.

He gathered her in his arms.

"You didn't see me when I came out in that last wedding dress, did you?"

Bryan raised his hand. "Scout's honor. I just got here from the station." He hooked his arm through hers as they walked past the downtown shops. "I have some good news. The last of Mason's henchmen have been taken into custody."

Sarah took in a breath of crisp September air. "That makes me feel a lot safer."

Bryan stopped at a storefront that read Jefferson Expeditions. "I read something about this guy. He takes people out in the wilderness and teaches them survival skills."

Sarah shrugged. "What does that have to do with anything?"

"I was thinking maybe we could do that for our honeymoon. You know, go tromping around the woods."

She caught the twinkle in his eye and gave him a

friendly punch in the shoulder. "I think we've done enough of that."

Bryan slipped his hand into hers. They walked several more blocks to the café where they planned on eating. Bryan held the door for her and they found a quiet booth. Sarah rested her arms on the table and leaned toward Bryan. "I told you Crew said he'd give me away at the wedding, right?"

Bryan nodded.

"It seems he's bringing a date to the wedding." Sarah was buoyant with excitement.

The waitress arrived and set their menus in front of them.

"Oh, really, who is he bringing?"

"Me," said the waitress. Bryan registered surprise when he saw that their waitress was Nadia.

She had a warm glow to her cheeks and she had gained weight.

"You," said Bryan, shaking his head.

Nadia raised her head and squared her shoulders. "I give you folks few minutes think about what you want for your meals."

As Nadia walked away, Bryan continued to shake his head. "Some things come full circle, don't they?"

Feeling a surge of love for the man she wanted to spend her life with, Sarah grabbed Bryan's strong hands. "Yes, they do. And sometimes you get a second chance with your first love."

He squeezed her hand, love shining in his eyes. "Yes, indeed."

* * * * *

BIG SKY SHOWDOWN

How great is the love the Father has lavished on us that we should be called children of God.
—*1 John* 3:1

For Susan, Kathy and Jenny, my cheerleaders and fellow suffering artists. For the inspiration, the feedback and the accountability.

ONE

Fear skittered across Heather Jacobs's nerves as half a dozen birds fluttered into the morning sky. Something had spooked them. She gripped the firewood she'd gathered a little tighter. She was alone here. Her guide, Zane Scofield, had taken his rifle, binoculars and hostility and left muttering something about scouting for elk for the next bunch of hunters he would guide into the high country of Montana.

This trip was to take her up to fulfill the last request of the father she barely knew. Five days ago, a certified letter had come to her home in California. Her father's dying wish was that she spread his ashes in his favorite spot in the Montana mountains and that Zane, the outfitter who had worked for Stephan Jacobs, be the one to guide her to the spot on Angel Peak. Heather hadn't seen her father since she was five years old. Her memories of him were faint. Her mother, who had died over a year ago, had never had anything nice to say about her ex-husband.

A brushing sound behind her caused Heather to whirl around. The logs she held rolled from her arms. Her heartbeat revved up a notch. The hairs on the back of her neck stood at attention. She sensed another being nearby.

What kinds of wild animals lurked in the forest?

Now she really wished Zane was closer. He knew how to deal with wildlife. Even if they'd been on each other's nerves since they left Fort Madison two days ago, she at least felt physically safe when he was around.

She stood as still as a statue, listening to the sound of the creaking trees and the drumming of her pulse in her ears.

Taking in a breath, she leaned over to pick up the firewood she'd dropped. Again, she heard what sounded like something moving toward her. She straightened, her gaze darting everywhere. Adrenaline charged through her, commanding her to run.

The smart thing to do would be to head back to the safety of the fire and camp and maybe even find Zane. A flash of something neon yellow caught her eye. Not a color that occurred in nature. Her heart skipped a beat. Whatever was out there was human. For a moment, she found that reassuring. Better a human than a wild animal. But then apprehension returned. Just who was out here, and why did they seem to be following her?

She saw blond hair for a quick second. A yelp as though someone were in pain filled the forest. The cry sounded childlike. Concerned, she ran toward where she'd seen the movement. Crashing noises up ahead alerted her as another moan of pain filled the forest.

Was a child hurt? Afraid?

She sprinted in the general direction of the noises, running around the trees and ducking out of the way of low-hanging branches. She saw the flash of blond again, a boy. More than ten years old, she would guess—but not by much. Perhaps twelve or thirteen.

She caught only fleeting glimpses of the child in the early-morning light.

She came into a clearing as silence descended once again. Her heartbeat drummed in her ears. She pivoted one way and then the other, searching.

"Please come out. I won't hurt you." The thought of a child in distress made her chest tight. What if he was lost and separated from his family?

She caught movement and heard footsteps to the side of her. She turned, expecting to see the blond boy. Instead, an older, darker-haired teenager emerged from the trees with a knife raised above his head and teeth bared. Terror swept over her like a wave.

She turned and bolted away. She may not be used to this environment, but her work as a personal trainer meant she was in top athletic condition. She could outrun the violence that pursued her.

The blond boy emerged from the other side of the forest, also wielding a knife. He wasn't injured. She'd been tricked into going deeper into the forest by these two. But why? What did they want from her?

They gave her little choice as to what direction she could run. She turned sharply and sprinted, willing her legs to move faster. Her heart pounded against her rib cage as she increased her speed.

She glanced over her shoulder. The boys gained on her by only a few yards. She ran faster. She could run all day if she had to.

The trees thinned.

Her foot slipped as the ground beneath her gave way. She found herself twirling through space and colliding with the hard earth as she landed on her back. She stared up at the blue sky and swaying tree boughs. With the wind knocked out of her, it took her a moment to comprehend that she'd fallen in a deep hole that had been camouflaged with brush and evergreen branches.

Her eyes traced over the twenty feet of dirt wall on either side of her that held her prisoner. She tilted her head to where the sunlight sneaked through the trees.

A grinning face appeared overhead, blond hair wild and uncombed. The child looked almost feral. They'd forced her in this direction so she'd fall in the hole.

Fear snaked around her torso and caused her to shiver. Now that she was their prisoner, what did they intend to do to her?

The blond boy shook his head, still smiling, pleased with himself. He formed a gun with his fingers, aimed it at her and mimed pulling the trigger. She winced against such a dark action from someone so young.

The older, darker-haired boy popped his head over the edge of the hole. He high-fived the younger kid.

"Dude, we're so going to get extra rations for this," said the older boy.

The blond boy continued to grin as he gazed down at her. "Maybe even a promotion."

"You stay here and guard her," said the older boy. "I'll head up to the patrol station so they can radio it in to base camp."

Patrol? Base camp? That sounded like they were part of an organized group. That meant more were coming, and they probably weren't boys. A chill enveloped Heather that had nothing to do with the crisp fall morning. She wasn't rich or famous—they couldn't hope to hold her for ransom. But the other possibilities for why they would want to kidnap her made blood freeze in her veins.

The older boy disappeared as suddenly as he'd appeared. The blond boy wiped his knife on his pants and stepped away as well. She could hear him above her pacing back and forth, breaking twigs beneath his feet.

Heart racing, she stared up the slick, steep walls. If she could get out, she should be able to overtake or outrun the blond boy. She needed to hurry before the others got here. She positioned her foot in the side of the dirt wall and tried to climb. She slipped. There was nothing to hold on to but moist earth.

The boy popped his head over the edge of the hole again. "You can't get out, lady. Don't even try."

"Why are you doing this?"

He sneered at her in a sinister way. Her heart seized up.

She was trapped. Her only hope was that Zane would get back to camp soon, see that she wasn't there and come looking for her. That was a thin hope at best.

Zane Scofield stared through his high-powered binoculars, scanning the hills and mountains all around him. He did need to scout for elk for future trips, but he also had to get away from Heather before he lost it. Just the thought of her made him grit his teeth.

Most of what Heather knew about her father had come through the bitter lens of her mother who had left a drunk in Montana twenty years ago. That was not the Stephan Jacobs whom Zane had come to know seven years ago. The Stephan whom Zane had worked for and been a friend to had been sober and loved God with all his heart.

When Heather had shown up at Big Sky Outfitters, dressed simply in jeans and a sweater, he had wondered what such a beautiful woman was doing on his doorstep. Then of course, she'd ruined that good first impression by talking down the man who had saved Zane's life in more ways than one.

There was no reply Zane could make to her snide comments, wondering why Stephan had left Big Sky Outfitters to her when he'd supposedly "never cared" about her anyway. Zane was sure that wasn't the truth—but he couldn't contradict her when he didn't know the whole story. Men like Stephan were not in the habit of sharing their pain. Zane suspected that a twenty-year estrangement from a daughter was one of those wounds that never healed. Maybe that's why the older man had never mentioned her.

And to make things worse, she'd told him that she intended to sell the business to a competitor, who Zane knew cared more about making money than sharing the beauty of God's creation with people. Stephan's legacy would be marred by a man like Dennis Havre.

Zane wanted to honor Stephan's dying wishes to bring his daughter to the chosen spot to scatter the ashes because the man had meant so much to him, but being with Heather for three more days might be his undoing.

He'd also come up to this vantage point for another reason. For the last day or so, he'd had the strange sense that they were being watched. Bow-hunting season didn't open up for a couple more weeks, so only extreme backpackers and men on scouting expeditions were likely to be up in the high country this time of year. So who had been stalking them and why?

He saw movement through his binoculars and focused in. Several ATVs were headed down the mountain toward the campsite where he'd left Heather alone. The speed at which they moved, like they knew where the camp was, set alarm bells off for Zane. He zeroed in on one of the ATVs and saw the handmade flag flying on the back end of it. He knew that flag. His mind was sucked back in time seven years ago to when he had lived in these mountains as a scared seventeen-year-old. If this was who he thought it was, Heather was in danger.

He jumped up from his concealed position and bolted down the steep incline. A thunderstorm of emotion brewed inside him. If he hadn't met Stephan when he did, his life could have gone in a much different direction, and those ATVs reminded him of everything he'd left behind.

Seven years ago, Zane and his brother, Jordan, had escaped foster care and been taken in by a man named Willis Drake. Willis saw a conspiracy around every corner and thought being armed to the teeth and living in the forest would keep him and his followers safe.

At first, Willis had seemed like the father Zane had longed for, teaching him how to shoot and how to live in the wild. If he hadn't taken the job with Stephan, he would have continued to idolize Willis and buy into his crazy theories.

Once authorities tried to catch Willis doing something illegal, Willis and his followers left the area. That had been nearly seven years ago. Now it looked like he might be back. That was frightening enough on its own. But for Willis and his gang to be headed toward where Heather was… That was downright terrifying. He had to keep her safe from that lawless group.

He raced down from his high spot and rushed through the trees to the open area of camp. The fire was burned down to nothing more than hot coals. Both pack mules were still tethered to trees. Heather was gone. Pushing away the rising panic, he sprinted toward a different part of the forest where he had directed her to find firewood. He spotted several logs together as though they'd been dropped.

He could hear the ATVs drawing closer, but not coming directly into the camp. They were headed a little deeper into the forest. He ran toward the mechanical sound, pushing past the rising fear.

He called for Heather only once. He stopped to listen.

He heard her call back—faint and far away, repeating his name. He ran in the direction of the sound with his rifle still slung over his shoulder. When he came to the clearing, he saw a boy not yet in his teens throwing rocks into a hole and screaming, "Shut up. Be quiet."

Zane held his rifle up toward the boy. He could never shoot a child, but maybe the threat would be enough.

The kid grew wide-eyed and snarled at him. "More men are coming. So there." Then the boy darted into the forest, yelling behind him, "You won't get away."

Zane ran over to the hole. Heather gazed up at him, relief spreading across her face.

Voices now drifted through the trees, men on foot headed this way.

Zane grabbed an evergreen bough and stuck it in the hole for Heather to grip. She climbed agilely and quickly. He grabbed her hand and pulled her the rest of the way out. "We have to get out of here."

There was no time to explain the full situation to her, but he tasted bile every time he thought about what might be going on. His worst nightmare coming true, his past reaching out to grab him by the feet and pull him into a deep dark hole. The past he thought he'd escaped.

He led Heather through the trees back to the camp where the mules were tied up. They mounted and took off, bolting for the trail just as several men burst into the camp on foot. One of them lifted his handgun and aimed it at them but didn't fire. "Stop right there."

Zane spurred his mule into a trot and Heather fell in beside him.

He had no idea why Heather had been targeted by Willis. He only knew one thing. If Willis was back in the high country, no good could come of staying here. He needed to get Heather to safety and fast. He knew what Willis was capable of. Their lives depended on getting out of the high country.

TWO

Heather's thoughts raced a hundred miles an hour as the trail narrowed and grew steeper. Confusion and fear battled within her. What was going on? Who were those men? And where were they going? Zane had told her this morning that they were only half a day away from where she could spread her father's ashes, and now it looked like they were headed back into town, back to Fort Madison.

He dropped back and allowed Heather to go ahead of him on the trail as it became too narrow to ride side by side. Though they slowed down when the terrain became more dangerous, the mules traversed the steep inclines and switchbacks with ease. Above them was rocky mountainside. Below, the trail dropped off at nearly ninety degrees.

She tightened the reins to stop Clarence, her mule, and craned her neck looking past Zane at the trail behind them. The men had not followed them.

Zane drew his eyebrows together. "Keep moving, Heather." Panic tainted his words.

He seemed to know more than he was letting on.

"They didn't follow us," she said, but she turned

back to face the trail ahead of her and nudged Clarence to start moving again. It would be nuts to think of going to Angel Peak knowing that there were crazy men like that up here. Still, she felt a sense of defeat that they'd had to turn back when they were so close to their goal. She'd been on an emotional roller coaster since she'd learned of her father's dying wishes. On some level, she'd come to Montana looking for answers. If Stephan—she couldn't bring herself to call him Dad—had loved her enough to leave her everything, why hadn't he gotten in touch with her when he was alive? She wanted to be a good daughter even if he hadn't been a good father, but she wanted this trip to be over so she could sell Big Sky Outfitters and return to her life in California.

Clarence lumbered along.

"Make him go faster. Just because we don't see them doesn't mean they've given up," Zane said.

After she kicked Clarence with her heels to get him going, she shouted over her shoulder, "You seem to know who these men are." Maybe there had been local news stories she wasn't privy to?

"I'll explain later. Just go. Keep moving." The sense of urgency never left his voice.

Heather glanced up the rocky incline as a rumble turned into a roar. Rocks from above them cascaded down the mountain like a waterfall. An avalanche of rocks was coming straight toward her. She spurred Clarence to go faster. Her chest squeezed tight with terror and all the air left her lungs. Rocks crashed against each other. A tremendous thundering noise surrounded her.

Clarence backed up then bucked. She slid off, falling not just off the mule but off the path altogether, tumbling down the side of the mountain. The crashing was all around her as rocks pelted her legs and arms.

Finally, her body came to a stop. The dust settled. She stared up at blue sky, trying to take in what had just happened. The mules brayed on the trail above her but didn't run. A heavy weight pressed on her leg. The rest of her body felt sore and bruised.

Zane made his way down to her, pulling rocks off her leg where she was trapped. His voice was filled with concern when he asked, "Can you move it?"

Still stunned, she wiggled her foot. "I think I'm just a little beat up."

He reached out a hand for her. "They caused the avalanche to block the trail. I saw more men up there." He pulled her to her feet.

So the rockslide hadn't been an accident.

"There's no time to clear it. I'm sure they'll be coming down after us. We'll get back to Fort Madison another way." So Zane's plan *was* to take her back to town. He climbed up over the rocks then craned his neck back down at her.

Heather moved to follow him but the pain from the bruising slowed her.

"Hurry." He climbed back up to where the mules stood.

Still a little shaken, she followed. No way could the same men who had come for them in camp have gotten ahead of them on the trail. That meant there must be even more of them chasing Zane and her. She could not process what was happening.

Zane turned his mule around on the narrow trail and then helped her get Clarence faced downward, as well. The mules were calm again. She stared back down the trail. Were they headed into a trap? Those other men who had come after them in the camp must still be around.

Her gaze traveled up the steep incline where the rockslide had started, but she saw no movement or any sign of people. She and Zane hurried down the trail and through flatter open country. Every now and then, she glanced over her shoulder, expecting to see men behind her. Nothing. And yet, Zane pushed on.

They rode for several more hours, slowing down as the mules fatigued.

Then, for no reason Heather could tell, Zane sat up straighter in the saddle. His hand brushed over the holster that held his pistol.

The action sent a new wave of terror through her. What was he sensing that she didn't pick up on?

He spurred his mule, but the animal continued to plod along.

"They need to rest," she said.

A strange popping sound shattered the silence. Zane's mule's front legs buckled. Heather's heart filled with horror as the animal collapsed on the ground. The mule had been shot through the head.

"Dismount. You're an easy target," Zane shouted at her. He dragged his legs out from under the dead animal and pulled out his pistol. He needed to keep Heather safe, out of the gun battle that was about to take place.

Heather shook her head. She stayed mounted on a frightened Clarence, who stepped side to side jerking his head anxiously. Heather's gaze was fixed on the dead mule. Shock must be setting in for her. He had to pull her from the paralysis before she became unable to make life-saving decisions or follow his orders.

"Get down then. Get off of there." He turned in a half circle, watching the trees, using his skills to pick apart each section, probing for movement.

She slipped out of her saddle and pressed in close to him. "What's going on?" Her voice trembled.

Zane surveyed the landscape. "The shooter is probably getting into position to line up another shot. That gives us a minute." And a chance at escape. He glanced at Clarence, debating his options. They might be a target if they got back on him. But the mule would give them speed.

Another rifle shot penetrated the forest close to Clarence. The mule whinnied and took off at a gallop, crashing through the trees. At least he hadn't been killed, but the shooter had taken out their best chance to get away fast.

Another shot shattered the air around them. The percussive noise beat against his eardrums and made his heart pound. The bullet stirred up the ground around Heather. She gasped and moved closer to him.

Zane grabbed Heather's hand and pulled her toward the brush for cover. "Run," he ordered her.

Though he saw nothing when he looked over his shoulder, he could detect the human noises behind them, heavy footfalls and the rustle of tree boughs being pushed out of the way. The shooter was on the move, coming after them.

He let go of her hand so they could both run faster. His feet pounded over the pine-needle-laden ground.

They ran for a long time without stopping. Heather

kept up a steady pace. He had to hand it to her. Even after the bruising she'd suffered in the rockslide, the woman could run.

He lagged behind then slowed his pace to catch his breath. "I think we lost him."

She stopped to listen, tilting her head. Then her gaze fell on him. "Who are these men?" Her eyes seemed to look right through him. "You know who they are, don't you?"

A heaviness pressed on his shoulders and chest. How could he begin to explain? He narrowed his eyes at Heather. He barely knew her. What if they were after Heather for some reason? She was the one they'd tried to take captive.

Some distance away, a human voice yelped as though the man had run into something. Zane's muscles tensed as he peered over his shoulder.

He saw Heather's eyes grow wide with fear, and then she started sprinting down the trail, with Zane following on her heels. She jumped over a tree that had fallen across the path. Zane hurried to catch up with her.

He heard a noise to the side of him. Two muscular young men jumped out of the trees. One grabbed Zane's hands before he could react. The other placed a hood over his head and pulled Zane's pistol out of the holster. Zane twisted from side to side trying to get away.

The last noise he heard was Heather's scream.

THREE

Stunned and afraid, Heather watched as the men dragged Zane deeper into the forest. She rushed to get back over the log, determined to free him.

A third man appeared from out of the trees and came charging toward her. She had no choice but to run the other way.

The horror of seeing Zane taken captive plagued her as she sprinted off the trail and into the forest. Running hard, she pushed through the tangle of trees. Despite her speed, her feet hit the ground with precision as she chose her steps over the varied terrain. Her pursuer stayed within yards of her but never gained on her. She looped back around to the trail where it would be easier to put some distance between herself and the man.

She bolted up the trail, running for at least twenty minutes before she looked over her shoulder and saw no one. The man had given up. She slowed to a jog. Now that she was safe, her only thought was to help Zane.

Aware that another pursuer might be lying in wait, she stumbled toward where she'd seen the young men drag Zane. There were at least three men, two that had taken Zane and one who had come after her. Even if one of them had been the shooter, what about the other men and boys they'd seen? Just how many people were after them? With each turn in the trail, she feared she'd be caught in another violent encounter.

But after wandering for what seemed like ages, she was less worried about a confrontation and more worried about never finding anyone at all. All the trees along the trail looked the same. If she could find the log that had fallen across the trail, she might be able to figure out where Zane had been taken. But she did not know these woods. Zane was the navigator.

A heaviness descended on her. Zane could be miles from here by now, or worse…he could be dead. Her stomach knotted at the thought. She wiped it from her mind. Giving in to fear would only make things harder.

She pushed off the tree and jogged out to the path. If she worked her way back to the clearing where Zane's mule was shot, she might be able to retrace her steps to where Zane had been taken.

As she followed the trail, she fought against the images that threatened to make her shut down. Pictures of Zane shot and left for dead played through her mind.

She stumbled into the clearing where the dead mule still lay. Her stomach roiled at the sight, and she thought she might vomit. She whirled away, but not before she noticed that the saddlebags and Zane's rifle had been taken.

Turning in a half circle, she wondered if she was being watched. Her own intense heartbeat drummed in her ears.

At least from here, she thought she could find her way back to the fallen log. The memory of fleeing after the shots were fired was blurred by trauma. All the same, she took off in the general direction she remembered going. She'd gone only a short distance when she heard a crashing noise to the side of her. Scrambling to find cover, she slipped behind a tree. Heather pressed her back against the rough bark as her heart thudded at breakneck pace.

She held her breath. The noise of someone moving toward her intensified. Her muscles tensed. The forest fell silent. She waited. Then she heard a familiar *clomp clomp clomp*.

Heather almost laughed as she raised her head. Clarence stood on the path. He jerked his head at her. The metal on his bridle jangled.

"Hello, old friend." She rose to her feet. The saddlebags were askew, but still intact. She opened one and took out the little wooden box that contained her father's ashes. She placed it in the inside pocket of her coat where it pressed against her stomach so she could feel that it was safe. She had been only a short time away from closing this chapter of her life. So much had changed so quickly. Tears welled up. Why had her father wanted her to come back to Montana anyway? She wiped her eyes.

Come on, Heather, pull it together.

Her eyes were drawn to a bloody gash on Clarence's neck. The mule sidestepped when she placed her hand near the injury. She couldn't discern the cause of the wound. It could be a bullet had grazed him, or maybe he'd scraped it on some brush. She straightened the saddlebags and placed her foot in the stirrup. Heather rode a short way when she saw smoke rising off in the distance. A camp.

She spurred Clarence to go faster.

Once they'd gotten close, she slipped off Clarence's back. It could be another hunters' camp doing some scouting or it could be where Zane was being held. Or the men who had been after them might be there without Zane. It could be a chance for help or she could be stepping into danger. Either way, she had to find out.

She let the reins fall to the ground, opting not to tie Clarence up. At least if she did not come back, the mule would be able to find his way back to civilization. And not coming back was a high probability.

She pressed her boots lightly on the crunchy snow, moving toward the rising smoke. Before she even arrived at the camp, she heard voices. Though she couldn't discern the words, it was clear a heated discussion was taking place. She slowed her pace even more, choosing where she stepped carefully. The scent of wood smoke filled the air. The argument stopped and the voices fell silent.

Flashes of color and movement caught her attention. She sank to the ground to take in the scene. Though the trees obscured some of her view, she caught a glimpse of a young man pacing, the hue of his greasy light blue coat distinctive enough to separate him from the forest colors.

Her throat constricted with fear. She recognized him as one of the men who had taken Zane. And there was another boy there, too, though she couldn't see him— she just heard the sound of his voice, mingled with the static of a radio transmitting.

The young man in the blue coat was clearly distressed, hunched, moving in an erratic pattern and slapping his forehead with his hands. She shifted her position, hoping to spot Zane.

Bluecoat tossed another log on the fire and stood close to it. At first, she thought the man had on red gloves, but then she saw that his hands were red from the cold. His tennis shoes probably didn't do much to keep the autumn chill out either.

Bluecoat turned and spoke to a spot that was just outside of Heather's field of vision. "What did he say?"

The other boy replied. "He doesn't trust us to bring him in. He's sending Mason and Long to come and get him. He's mad we didn't get the girl."

Heather breathed a sigh of relief. They had to be talking about Zane. And from what they'd said, it sounded as if Zane was still alive. And even better, it looked like there were only two young men guarding him for now. The third one, the one who had chased her, must have taken off.

Bluecoat threw up his hands. "Oh, sure, and then they get all the credit. While we have to go back out on patrol."

"You know what Willis says. You gotta earn it." The second kid stepped closer to the fire. He was taller than Bluecoat, though just as ragged looking in a tattered brown parka and worn combat boots. At least he had some gloves. Heather guessed he might be eighteen or nineteen years old. "They'll be down here in seven to ten minutes."

Heather moved in a little closer. Her foot cracked a twig. Both boys stiffened, stepped away from the fire and glanced around nervously.

Though she was in an uncomfortable position, she tucked her arms close to her body and didn't move. Her heart beat so loudly, she was afraid it would give her away. Her front foot strained to maintain balance.

Both boys skirted the camp, searching the area before returning to the fire.

Heather exhaled. She waited until they started talking again before she crept in a circle around their camp trying to find Zane. She hurried from tree to tree to remain hidden.

"How long before they get here?" Bluecoat stepped even closer to the fire.

"A few minutes. I told you that. They're coming on the ATVs to haul him up," said Browncoat.

Both young men had handguns in holsters fastened to their belts. She recognized Zane's pistol on the second man. She edged a little closer, finally spotting Zane far from the fire. The pillowcase was still on his head. His hands were tied behind his back. He wasn't slumped over, which she hoped meant that he was conscious.

She moved farther away from the center of the camp and then circled around to where Zane was. The rumble of the ATVs filled the air. Still some distance away, but she knew she didn't have much time.

She scooted through the evergreens until she was lined up with the tree where Zane was tied. Each time she took a step forward, she waited until the conversation intensified to cover the sound of her movement.

Her eyes fixated on Zane's hands where they were bound behind the narrow trunk of a lodgepole pine. Crouching, she positioned herself so most of her body was hidden behind Zane.

Zane must have sensed something was up because his head jerked. The action was enough to cause the conversation between the two men to trail off. She pressed her belly against the ground, shielding herself behind Zane.

She squeezed her eyes shut as the footsteps came toward them. Her heart pounded out a wild rhythm. The footsteps stopped several feet away. She assumed the guard was scanning the area, though she wasn't bold enough to sit up and check. After a few moments he walked away, and then the conversation resumed.

She brushed her hand over Zane's, hoping he would understand. He gave her a thumbs-up. She pulled her pocketknife from her jeans' pocket and cut him free.

The roar of the ATVs pressed on her ears. More voices carried through the trees after the engines died. Two more men entered the camp. All the men were facing away from Zane. Now was their chance for escape.

Zane reached up and tore off the hood, taking no more than an instant to orient himself before he turned and slipped into the trees with Heather.

He breathed a prayer of thanks that Heather had been so smart and brave in breaking him free.

Adrenaline kicked into high gear as he jumped to his feet and sprinted alongside her. Behind him, shouting and protest rose up. Then a single wild gunshot echoed through the trees.

"Don't kill them!" one of the men ordered. "Willis wants them alive."

Zane caught up with her as they raced toward an open area. The ATVs roared to life. They needed to get to terrain where the machines couldn't follow them. She glanced around.

He pointed toward a rocky incline. She hurried after him just as one of the ATVs burst through the trees.

Another bullet whizzed past his ear. They slipped behind a rock and pressed low to the ground. Killing them might not be an option, but wounding them must still be on the table. Zane and Heather pushed themselves upward, using the larger rocks for cover.

They rushed toward the top of the incline. When he glanced down over his shoulder, he saw that one of the men had a high-powered rifle. It was pointed right at him—but before the sniper could take the shot, they reached the ridgeline and headed down the other side.

They sprinted down the grassy side of the hill until they entered a cluster of trees.

Both of them gasped for breath.

Zane ran his hand through his hair and paced as adrenaline coursed through him. "We need to get out of here. It's just a matter of minutes before they catch up with us."

"Who are those guys and why did they kidnap you?"

Her question felt like a weight on his chest. She'd saved his life. He owed her an explanation, but there was no time for that now. "The trail on up the mountain is blocked by the rockslide, so we'll have to go by way of the river."

He didn't wait for her to respond. Instead, he turned and bolted through the trees. If she wanted to stay alive, she'd follow him. She'd already proven she had good survival skills.

The landscape bounced in front of him as he kept pace with Heather.

The sound of the ATVs grew louder then died out and then intensified again. Heather and Zane entered a wide meadow. An ATV emerged from the opposite side of the meadow. Its rider came to a stop and yanked a rifle from a holder attached to the ATV.

Zane grabbed her and pulled her toward the thick evergreens. The first rifle shot stirred the ground up in front of her feet. She jumped back. Zane tugged on her sleeve. Both of them dived toward the shelter of the heavy brush as the sound of more ATV engines filled the forest. The mechanical roar pressed on him from every side. He wasn't sure which way to go to get away. Were they being surrounded?

Zane hesitated for only a moment before choosing a path. They scrambled downward through the trees. The steep path they were on couldn't be called a trail, which would make it that much harder to be followed. The noise of the ATVs died out again. Though he doubted the pursuers had given up.

They jogged until they were both out of breath and needed to stop.

A sense of urgency pressed in on Zane as he pointed off in the distance. "We need to go to the river and get across that bridge. We don't have much time before they catch up with us."

Looking over to the side, he saw where the ATVs snaked down a distant hill. Far enough away for now—but closing in, faster than he and Heather could possibly move on foot.

"How are you going to get to the river? We can't outrun them." Her voice trembled with panic.

As if on cue, a braying noise alerted both of them as Clarence entered the flat area where they stood.

"Looks like our ride's here." Heather hurried over and patted Clarence's neck. "I found him earlier. I'm starting to really like this old mule."

"They always find their way back," Zane said. "Let's drop some of this weight." He reached for the saddlebags.

He pulled a few essential items out and stuffed them into his pockets before yanking the bags off the mule and tossing them on the ground. "We'd better hurry."

A moment later, the sound of the ATVs engines clanging filled the forest around them growing louder and closer. He mounted Clarence and reached out a hand for her to get on behind him. Zane spurred Clarence into a trot. The animal was surefooted enough on the rough terrain that he was able to keep a steady pace. But would be fast enough for them to get away?

Heather wrapped her arms around Zane's waist and pressed close to him. She buried her face in his shoulder-length hair, melting into the warmth of his back. The solid shape of the box that held her father's ashes pushed against her stomach. Until that moment, she'd almost forgotten it was there. Saying goodbye to the father she never knew and finding some closure seemed like the furthest thing from her mind.

They needed to get off this mountain alive. Judging from how ragged and dirty the men and boys all looked, they must live up in the mountains for extended periods. That meant they knew how to survive in the harshness of the high country.

The rushing roar of the river greeted her ears even before she saw the cold gray water and the bridge.

Zane turned his head slightly. "Dismount. We'll lead Clarence across. You go in front of me."

She slid off the mule. The bridge was primitive; the railings were made of narrow but strong cording. The bottom was fashioned from logs bound together with the same cording, stretching across the wide rushing water, connected at either end to sturdy trees. It swayed when she stepped on it. She steadied herself by grabbing the rope railing. Zane fell in behind her, leading Clarence, who hesitated only a moment before he stepped on the unsteady structure.

The ATV noises stopped nearby. The shouts and cries of men out for violence filled the forest. Before long, two of the men emerged through the trees. One of them drew a handgun and shot. The shot went wild. All the same, the gunfire made her stutter in her step.

"Keep going," Zane urged, and he peered over his shoulder.

They were halfway across the bridge.

She couldn't see around him or the mule on the narrow bridge but the look on his face when he turned back around indicated that something had alarmed him.

"What is it?"

"Hurry! The men started to cross and backed up."

Then she heard it—an awful creaking. The bridge swayed. It was unstable and about to break.

They couldn't go back.

She lost her balance and buckled to one knee. Heart racing, she pulled herself to her feet and stepped as fast as she dared across the uneven logs. The bridge swayed even more and creaked in a new way. She could see the other side of the river. Solid ground was only twenty feet away.

Trying to maintain her balance, she put one foot in front of the other and gripped the rope railing.

A louder creak filled the air. She caught a glimpse of the rushing water down below, dark and cold. The bridge went slack. And then she felt her body slipping backward and down. Her hand flailed, struggling to find something to hold on to.

She grasped only air as her body plunged into the depths of the freezing water.

FOUR

Zane grabbed hold of the rope remnants of the bridge as he drifted downstream. Clarence's body rammed into his and then floated away as the animal struggled to keep its head above water. He saw a flash of Heather's jacket, and then she disappeared beneath the freezing water. His heart squeezed tight, and he waited for her to resurface.

A bullet whizzed past his head. He switched focus to the men—boys, really, no more than teenagers—on the shoreline. The first boy grabbed the gun from the second one, probably not wanting to risk Zane being killed since the orders were for them to be taken in alive.

Zane let go of the piece of tattered bridge as the current pulled him along. There was no more sign of Heather.

Twice, the force of the water pushed him under.

The young men ran along the bank, keeping him in sight. Zane couldn't see Clarence anywhere, but hoped that the mule had managed to reach land—something Zane now needed to do for himself. He swam hard to get to the far bank. That bridge had been the only way across the water for miles. The young men on the shore slowed down as the current carried him along even faster.

Though he couldn't see her, he refused to believe Heather had drowned. She had proved she was a competent athlete.

He knew he had only minutes in the freezing water before hypothermia set in. The current pushed him back toward the closer shore where the pursuers were. He and Heather really needed to get across this river. He rounded a bend. The young men with guns grew smaller then disappeared from view. He felt a rush of relief when he saw Heather up ahead crawling up on a log that had fallen half way across the stream. She had almost reached land, but not on the far shore that would allow them to get back to town. If he followed her, they'd still be trapped on the wrong side of the river. All the same, he was elated to see she had made it out.

He swam through the water, trying to maneuver toward her. She noticed him and worked her way back to the end of the log and held out a hand. She grabbed him by the back of the collar as he drifted by. He angled his torso and braced himself with one of the heavier limbs on the fallen tree as water suctioned around him. She reached out an ice-cold hand and helped him up on the log.

Both of them were soaked and shivering, but at least they'd survived. She rose to her feet and edged her way across the slippery log to dry land. He was right behind her.

He glanced down the shoreline but saw no sign of their pursuers yet. Heather wrapped her arms around her body and waited for him. Water dripped from her long dark hair.

He surveyed the landscape. They'd drifted far enough that it would be a while before their pursuers caught up with them. He knew where he was and where they could go to get warm. "We need to build a fire, but not where we'll be seen easily."

"Where can we go?" Her eyes appeared glazed when she looked at him. Shock was setting in. Hypothermia couldn't be far behind.

He placed his palms on her cheeks, forcing her to make eye contact. "Just stay with me. Do what I say. I got this, okay?"

She nodded.

He sprinted through the trees up toward a rock face until he found an outcropping of rock that would provide shelter on three sides.

"Gather any dry wood you can find," he said.

One of the things he'd pulled off the saddlebags was a waterproof bag containing magnesium fire starter and dryer lint for kindling. As he drew the fire starter out of the plastic bag, he noticed that his whole body trembled.

Heather returned a few minutes later with a pile of sticks. "Everything is pretty wet." Her voice was shaky from the cold and all the color had drained from her face.

They needed to hurry and get this fire built.

"Anything you can find will help." He drew his knife off his belt. "I can split it. The wood on the inside is dry."

"I'll go find more." She turned and dashed toward the trees.

Using one log as a baton and his knife as a hatchet, he split several logs. His vision blurred as water dripped off his hair. He squeezed his eyes shut then opened them.

Dear God, help us stay alive.

He could feel the strength draining from his body and his mind fogging. Heather returned with more wood.

"I've got enough here to start the fire." He pointed at the fire starter. "Do you know how to use that?"

She nodded. "We go camping in California, too, you know."

She knelt down beside him, gathering the kindling into a pile around the dryer lint. She shaved off some magnesium flakes and then slid the scraper across the rod until she made some sparks. Her hands were shaking, too, as she used them to protect the fragile flames. Once the fire consumed the kindling, Zane placed larger pieces of wood on the fire until he could feel the warmth.

He slipped out of his wet coat. "You might want to take yours off. Lay it across those rocks so the fire will dry it out. You'll need to sit close to me…for warmth."

She gave him a momentary stare before stripping her coat and gloves off and scooting beside him.

"All right if I wrap my arms around you?"

She nodded. He took her into an awkward hug. Her body was rigid in his arms, unmoving except for the shivering. Both of them watched the flames as they warmed up and dried out.

"Will they come looking for us?" Her voice sounded very far away and weak.

He lifted his head to look around. Their would-be captors had been tenacious up to this point. There was no reason to think they would just give up now. "Probably." The fire was small, and they were hidden by the rocks, but they couldn't stay here for long without running the risk of being found.

"Who are they?"

Her question fell like a heavy weight on his chest. He took in a breath as the past rushed at him at a hundred miles an hour. This wasn't the first time she'd asked the question. He needed to finally give her an answer. "There's a man who used to live in these mountains. He's a doomsday-conspiracy kind of guy who thinks that the authorities are out to get him. So he lives out in places like this, in the middle of nowhere. He recruits boys and young men who need a father figure, indoctrinates them to be just as wild and lawless as he is. They're his own personal army, committing whatever crimes he plans. This area was his territory for a long time. He left almost seven years ago. He must be back here for some reason."

"How do you know it's him?"

"The way those boys acted. And then I heard them mention Willis's name," he said.

"How do you know all this about him and his boys?" She brushed a strand of wet hair off her neck.

He took a moment to answer. "I used to be one of them when I was a kid. I was just as wild, until I met your father."

The stiffness of her body against his softened a little. She took a moment to ask her next question. "My father helped you get away from this Willis guy?"

He nodded. Seven years ago, Willis had made the mistake of telling Zane he needed to get a job in town to bring in money. It was something Willis demanded of many of his followers whose loyalty he thought was without question. But Willis hadn't known that Zane would bond so deeply with the man who hired him. Stephan's love for God and His creation and unconditional love for Zane had been such a contrast to Willis's harsh world of punishment and rewards.

She seemed to relax even more in his embrace. "Why do they want you—or me, for that matter?"

"I don't know." He had cut all ties with Willis and anyone who knew the man or held similar views.

"Maybe they're looking to punish you because you didn't want to be with them anymore," she said.

"That was years ago. Willis is a little crazy, but he's also very calculating. The law was breathing down his neck when he left here. He wouldn't risk returning just for revenge." Something had drawn Willis back here.

She slipped from his embrace, stood up and moved closer to the fire. "So what do we do?"

"We need to get across that river so we can get to town, contact the authorities," he said. "There's another crossing ten miles down."

Her expression didn't change. She held her hands closer to the fire. "They'll be looking for us there, don't you think?"

"Probably. Willis knows these mountains better than I do." Though he didn't want to scare her, he couldn't lie to her.

"It's never easy, is it?" She crossed her arms over her body. "I just wanted to spread Stephan's ashes, do the right thing." She turned slightly away from him.

He wondered what she was thinking. She must be afraid, yet she hadn't fallen apart, and she hadn't blamed him for the violence she'd been dragged into.

"We're pretty well hidden here. Once we're dried

out, we'll put the fire out and wait until dusk. The darkness will provide us some cover."

She turned back toward him and nodded. Then she sat down beside him again, watching the glow of the fire. He kept thinking that she would cry or get angry with him, but she didn't. Brave woman.

"This fire saved us," she said.

"Yes, it did." He studied her profile as the firelight danced on her pale skin. This was way more than she had bargained for. "I'm sorry. When all this is over and done with, I'll take you back up to that mountain so you can do what you came here to do."

A faint smile crossed her lips and she nodded. But something in her expression suggested that she didn't believe him. Did she think they were going to die out here? "Was it really because of my father that you were able to leave Willis?"

"With Willis you were always scrambling for his approval, trying to accomplish things so he'd pat you on the back. Your father's love was filled with grace. His support gave me the strength I needed to get away from that life."

"I wish I could have known that Stephan." She shook her head, and her voice faltered. "I wish I could have known him at all. If he loved me, why didn't he try to get in touch with me when he was alive? I couldn't have been that hard to track down. His lawyer found me easily enough."

"Maybe he did try once he stopped drinking. Did your mom ever say anything to you about that?"

She shook her head. "Mom died a year ago, so I can't even ask her now."

He stood up beside her and touched her shoulder

lightly, knowing that there were no words that would take away her pain and confusion.

They waited until the light faded. Hunger gnawed at his belly as they headed back toward the river. He'd grabbed protein bars from the saddlebags. Since that was their only food, he didn't want to eat them until they had no calorie reserves left. They might be out here for a long time. He needed to be smart about when they ate their only food.

Behind him, Heather's footsteps stopped. He turned to face her, barely able to make out her features in the fading light.

"Something wrong?"

"Thought I heard something."

He studied the landscape, tuning his ears to the hum of the forest. He understood her jumpiness. He felt it too. Willis taught all his protégés tracking skills, so he had to assume that sooner or later they would encounter one or more of the followers who had been assigned to bring Heather and him in.

As he listened, nothing seemed amiss and nothing sounded human. Still, better safe than sorry.

He turned and headed back down the hill. He heard Heather's footsteps behind him but nothing else. The silence was unnerving as they moved through the forest.

A flood of memories of his time with Willis came back to him with each step he took. He's been barely seventeen when Willis had caught him breaking into his car to sleep. Jordan—Jordie—had only been thirteen when they decided a few months earlier that living on the run was better than foster care. His little brother had been even more impressionable than he had been.

So many of Willis's antiestablishment rants hadn't rang true or lacked a certain logic, but that was easy to overlook when Willis's ragtag community finally gave Zane a place where he felt like he belonged. It was the pats on the back and the way Willis would take the time with him to teach him to shoot, build a lean-to and hunt that had made him want to stay in the wild. The camaraderie with the other boys and men filled a void for him, too. It had been hard to leave that behind, even when he'd known it was the right thing to do. The hardest part had been parting from Jordie, who'd refused to leave with him.

His brother would be twenty now, a man. Jordan had gone with Willis and the others when they left the area, but had he stayed with him all these years?

Zane stuttered in his step. Heather came up close to him. Her shoulder pressed against his as he heard her sharp intake of breath. To the east, the river murmured.

Though he heard nothing amiss, his heart beat a little faster. "You hear something?"

After a moment, she shook her head. "I guess not. I'm just a little nervous."

His warning system was on high alert as well. Now that they were out in the open, he had to assume they were being tracked.

"Stay close," he whispered.

He moved slower, choosing each step with a degree of caution, not wanting a single sound to alert anyone tracking them to their location. Heather seemed to instinctually know that she needed to be quiet. Her steps were almost lighter than air.

A wolf howled somewhere in the distance. Zane's heart hammered out a steady beat. He pushed through trees, seeking more cover. The gray dusk light turned charcoal. Stars glimmered above them, but he could not take the time to notice their beauty. He dared not let himself relax or let his guard down.

"I'm thirsty," whispered Heather as she came up beside him.

She was probably hungry, too.

He just wasn't sure if stopping to eat the protein bars was a good idea right now. "Don't eat the snow. We'll drink from the river."

He followed the sound of the water rushing over stones. He crouched low and chose a sheltered spot where the cottonwoods grew close to the water.

Heather knelt beside the river.

"It's cold. Drink just enough to keep you going. I have food. We'll eat in a while."

He positioned himself beside her and cupped his own hands and placed them in the icy water. After several handfuls, he stood up and tugged on Heather's coat. She rose to her feet and they slipped back into the shelter of the forest.

The canopy of the trees and the encroaching darkness made it hard to see. He heard a yelp that was clearly human off to his side, maybe ten feet away. He grabbed Heather's hand and pulled her to the ground.

Both of them remained still as the footfalls of a human being overwhelmed the other forest sounds. Heavy boots pounded past them.

One guy alone. Zane should be able to take him and get a weapon. Zane leaped to his feet and jumped on the teenager. The young man turned out to be the size of a football player and with the same strength. They wrestled, crashing against the brush. The teenager flipped over on his stomach in an effort to push himself to his feet.

The shouts of the other boys filled the forest. Their position had been given away by the noise of the fight, and reinforcements were closing in.

Zane kept a knee in Football Player's back as he felt along his waistband for a gun. He retrieved a small pistol.

Now the whole forest was full of the noise of their pursuers edging closer. He saw bobbing lights. The mechanical thunder of ATVs coming to life surrounded them.

Heather pulled on his shoulder. "Hurry. They're coming."

She let go of him and turned to head away from the bobbing lights. He stuffed the gun in his waistband and took a step toward her. From the ground where he lay, Football Player grabbed at his ankle. Zane stumbled, nearly falling on his face.

Heather swung around and landed a kick to the kid's shoulder so he let go of Zane's foot. The crashing and breaking of branches alerted them to the closeness of their pursuers. They shot through forest and back up toward a sloping hill. The roar of ATVs pressed on them from all sides. When he glanced over his shoulder, he saw three sets of glowing white headlights. They'd never outrun these machines.

He rerouted toward a cluster of trees. Heather followed him. Once they were deep into the forest, he stopped.

He pointed at a tree. "Climb."

Heather must have realized hiding was their only option. Without a word, she dashed toward the tree and grabbed a low, sturdy branch. She climbed with agility and ease. He ran to a nearby tree and jumped up to grasp one of the lower branches. The ATVs grew louder. Headlights cut a wide swath through the trees. As artificial light filled the forest, he could make out the silhouette of Heather resting her belly on a stout branch and holding on to the smaller limbs of the tree. Evergreen boughs partially hid her, but wouldn't provide enough protection if someone looked her way. He could only hope their pursuers kept their eyes on the ground.

The machines surged by beneath them. He spotted two riders by themselves. A third ATV with a driver and a passenger zoomed by. The ATVs scooted up the hill, the noise of their engines growing faint. The bobbing flashlights told him there were some trackers on foot, as well. These searchers approached at a slower pace, shining their light over the brush and trees. The orange glow of the flashlights landed on the tree where Heather was hiding. Zane tensed. If they were spotted, they'd be shot like coons out of their trees even if it was just to injure them.

In the distance, the ATVs slowed. They must have figured out they'd lost the trail and now they were backtracking. There were three young men with flashlights on foot. One of them lingered beneath the tree where Heather was hiding.

He'd counted seven boys and young men chasing after them in all. As far as he could tell in the dark, none of them were Jordie. Though the passing of time would make it hard to recognize his brother even in daylight. He could only hope that his brother had escaped the control Willis had had on his life.

The lone searcher continued to pace beneath Heather's hiding place, shining the flashlight on nearby trees. Zane could no longer hear the noise of the other two foot soldiers who had split off and disappeared into the forest.

Zane clenched his teeth. All they needed was for this tracker to leave, and they could scramble down and find a new hiding place or even escape.

It sounded like the ATVs were doing circles, trying to pick up the trail. The man shone his light on the tree where Zane hid. The light glared in Zane's face. He'd been spotted. Zane's muscles tensed as the man reached for his gun.

FIVE

Zane jumped down from his hiding place and pounced on the man, knocking the wind out of him. Zane grabbed the flashlight where it had rolled away from the temporarily disabled man. By then, Heather was halfway down the tree. She ran the remaining ten feet to rush to his side.

Between the two other searchers on foot and the ATVs coming back this way, there was only one direction to go. Both of them took off running. Zane led them in an erratic path around the trees, hoping to make them harder to follow.

He caught glimpses of bobbing lights in the forest. They needed to shake these guys before they had any chance of getting back to the river.

He pushed deeper into the forest where the undergrowth was thick. The roar of the ATVs never let up. They skirted around some brush, coming face-to-face with a kid on foot who didn't look to be more than twelve years old. When he saw them, the kid's eyes grew wide with fear. He showed no sign of pulling any kind of a weapon on them.

"I won't tell if you don't," said Zane as he darted off in a different direction with Heather close on his heels.

They sprinted through the darkness of the forest, dodging lights and sounds that seemed to come at them from every direction, feet pounding the ground, breath filling their lungs and coming out in cloudy puffs as the night grew colder.

He dismissed any thought of returning to the river just yet. The river was probably patrolled anyway.

They ran until twenty minutes passed without seeing a light or hearing a human noise. Both of them pressed against tree trunks in an aspen grove, the sounds of their heavy inhales and exhales the only noise around.

They couldn't keep dodging these guys forever. Granted, it looked like Willis had sent the B team, younger men and boys with less high-tech equipment and experience, to track them down, but if Willis was serious about kidnapping Zane and Heather, he'd send the A team or come out himself sooner or later.

Heather pushed off the tree and moved toward him as if to talk to him.

In his peripheral vision, he saw the vapor cloud of someone exhaling by a tree. His heart skipped a beat as he held up his hand, indicating to Heather she needed to stand still.

He watched as the person behind the tree let out another breath from maybe twenty feet away.

Seconds ticked by.

Though her face was covered in shadows, he picked up on the fear in Heather's posture. Both of them stood as still as rocks. His heartbeat drummed in his ears.

Whoever was behind the tree took a single step, feet crunching on snow.

Heather turned her head ever so slightly as if to indicate that she thought they should run. He shook his head. He didn't think they'd been spotted yet, but any noise at all would alert the stranger to their whereabouts.

The stranger took another step. Through the prism of the narrow white and black aspen trunks, Zane discerned the silhouette of a man, standing still for a long time as though he were taking in his surroundings. Probably listening for any noise that might be out of place.

Zane swallowed as his heart raged in his chest and sweat trickled down his back. His mouth was dry.

With the next footstep, the stranger moved away from where he and Heather stood. The footsteps came one after the other before finally fading into the distance.

When the man got far enough away that they could no longer hear him, Heather let out a breath, and her shoulders slumped, but she didn't move until Zane took a step toward her.

She closed the distance between them so she could talk in a whisper. "Who was that?"

"I'm not sure," he said.

Another hunter? Maybe. More likely it was someone in Willis's crew who was out in the woods for some reason other than capturing them. Or someone who was supposed to catch them but who didn't want to get into a wrestling match.

Zane ran his hand over the pistol he'd gotten off the teenager, grateful that he hadn't needed to use it.

"Follow me," he said.

They walked for a distance through the darkness. It was too much of a risk to turn on the flashlight, and the moonlight provided enough light to see the ground. He stopped at the top of a knoll and stared down at the cluster of trees below. He turned the flashlight on and off just to get a glimpse. Something about the arrangement of the underbrush looked unnatural.

Heather followed him down the hill and into the evergreens. Hidden from view from the outside, he saw piles of pine boughs covering some sort of structure. He pulled several of the branches off until he found a small door. The structure was made of heavy duty plastic stretched across PVC pipe and it was not more than four feet high.

"It's like a hobbit house," said Heather.

He poked his head in. A gust of warmth surrounded him. "Actually, it's a little more sinister than that." He pulled out the flashlight and turned it on. As he'd suspected, they'd stumbled on someone's pot farm. "Might as well come in, it's warm inside."

The plants were spaced to allow a single person to get around to tend them. Heather slipped in after him. "Someone has a serious need to support a habit."

"This kind of operation isn't about personal use. Someone is growing this stuff to sell."

And from the look of the empty shelves, much of it already had been sold. He'd received letters from law enforcement telling him to be on the lookout for the pot farms in the high country because it was such a good place to hide an operation. As much time as he spent up here, he was bound to stumble across one sooner or later. He wondered, too, if the stranger they'd encountered in the woods had just left the little hidden farm. Maybe he was part of Willis's group but spent most of his time away from the main base and had no idea about Zane and Heather being hunted by the others. An operation like this required daily attention. From the size of the plants, they'd been up here for a while. With the limited number of people who came up here outside of hunting season, Willis might have been here through the spring and summer.

"I guess they're not likely to get caught this far away from everyone." Heather scooted in behind him and closed the tiny door.

"Right." The more he thought about it, the more certain Zane was that no one besides Willis and his little army would be this far up. The little farm had to be Willis's. Willis had always been against the consumption of drugs and alcohol, but he wasn't above selling it to others to make money. This was a larger crop than Zane would have expected, though. What exactly was Willis up to anyway? What was he trying to finance?

Once hunting season started in a few weeks, Willis ran the risk of being spotted, so it must be something that would happen soon.

Zane shone his flashlight around, spotting a pamphlet that was authored by Willis. Any doubt that this operation was his fell away. Zane noticed a water container. He lifted it and handed it first to Heather. She took several gulps of water as he skirted around the dirt floor to see what else he could find. He came up with a blanket neatly folded and a heavy-duty sleeping bag on a mat.

"There's a little stove here and some canned goods."

He heard Heather's voice but couldn't see her through the foliage.

When he studied the roof, it looked like there was some sort of solar panel set up to keep the place warm. Whoever tended the plants must stay here for extended periods. No doubt he would be back. But hopefully not before Zane and Heather had a chance to take refuge for a little while.

He worked his way over to where Heather had already fired up the little propane stove and was opening a can of beans.

He patted the protein bars in his pocket, grateful he could save them for later. "Let's eat and get out of here. I'm sure someone checks these on a regular basis. The 'farmer' might be the guy we saw a few minutes ago, just out for a brief walk."

Heather poured the beans into the metal tin and placed it on the gas flame.

He felt a sense of urgency. "Maybe we should eat the beans cold."

She cut the flame. "There's only one spoon."

"You first," he said.

She took four quick bites and then handed him the can. He'd finished his third bite when he heard the roar of the ATVs raging down the hill toward them. So much for rest and food. They'd been found again. Time to run.

Bright lights glaring through the clear plastic nearly paralyzed Heather. Zane clicked off the flashlight. She heard him scrambling toward the door. It took her a moment before her brain kicked into gear, and she followed behind him, slipping through the tiny opening and out into the dark night.

The ATVs loomed down the hill toward them, the engine noises sounding like hungry monsters gnashing their teeth. Her limbs felt heavy and muscles cried out with fatigue from having run so much.

Zane grabbed her hand and pulled her toward the shelter of the trees. The ATV noise fell away by half, indicating some of their pursuers must have stopped to examine the greenhouse. She kept her eyes on the back of Zane's head as they fled. They ran until the noise died down to a single ATV and then fell away altogether.

When the silence of the forest surrounded them once again, they ran and rested and ran some more until the sun peeked up over the mountains. Early-morning light washed everything with a warm glow, and she felt her strength returning.

They stopped only briefly to eat the protein bars Zane had gotten from Clarence's saddlebag.

It seemed to her that they'd been running in circles, but she knew Zane was smarter than that, and knew the area well enough to be choosing their direction carefully. He must be trying to figure out a safe way to get down off the mountain, back to the river and back to Fort Madison.

The landscape opened up to flat meadow that was partially covered in snow. She shaded her eyes from the glare. In the distance, she spotted a red and blue object that looked out of place.

She ran toward it. As she drew closer, more colors became evident. It was a backpack. She knelt down.

The backpack was empty. Another hiker who had been robbed maybe?

Zane knelt beside her. He bolted to his feet and glanced around.

Heather stood up, too, studying the partially snowy landscape. She spotted a yellow object attached to the branch of a tree and ran toward it. She pulled the fabric free of the branches, her chest tightening. The fabric was from a man's bandanna.

She glanced up just as Zane disappeared into another part of the forest. Her feet pounded the earth as she followed after him, stepping through patches of crunchy snow and into the trees. The canopy of evergreens cut the light by half as she stepped deeper into the forest. Her breath caught when she glanced down at the ground. Dribbles and several huge circles of dried blood spotted the snow.

Her chest felt like it was in a vice. She tried to tell herself that the blood could be from an animal—but there had been no sign of teeth or claw marks on the belongings they'd spotted. The backpack and bandanna looked like they'd been discarded by human hands.

Zane burst through the trees. His expression was like none she'd ever witnessed before. Eyebrows knit in anguish, his skin the color of rice. Eyes filled with fear. He glanced over his shoulder and then back at her.

"What is it?" She stepped toward where he'd looked.

He grabbed her arm at the elbow. "You don't need to see this."

She pulled away, not able to let go of the idea that she had to know what was going on in these mountains. She darted toward where Zane had come from.

She found the man's body propped up against the

tree. The body had not started to decompose, so he must have been here a short time. The bloodstain on his chest revealed that he had been stabbed.

Light-headed, she whirled away, slamming into Zane's chest. He wrapped his arms around her and pulled her away from the gruesome sight.

Her mind reeled. *Murderers*. She'd been so focused on running for her life that reality hadn't sunk in until she saw the dead man. They were trapped on this mountain with bloodthirsty killers.

She rested for a moment in the security of Zane's arms, trying to calm herself. But her mind raced at a thousand miles an hour. She fought to get a deep breath.

She could barely get the words out. "What happened...there? Did they kill him so they could get his stuff?" She pulled away from him, then paced back and forth gripping her somersaulting stomach. "Do they have so little regard for life?"

He stepped toward her. "Calm down."

"Calm down?" Her words splintered as they spilled from her lips. Her legs felt like were made of rubber. She'd only come up here to spread her father's ashes. How had things gotten to this point where she was fighting to get away from men who acted worse than animals?

He reached out for her.

She darted away, shaking her head. "What is going on here?"

"Heather, please." He stepped toward her.

"You knew these men. You were one of them." Really, if Zane hadn't told her that he used to be under the influence of someone like Willis, she never would have guessed it. Was it really possible a man could change so radically?

"I am nothing like them." Zane's voice was tinged with anger. "Not anymore. And this is way over the top. We never did anything like that when I was with Willis."

"It looks like they are getting more desperate or bloodthirsty, then. What is driving them?" Her voice was barely above a whisper. Her mind clouded as a fear she had never felt before invaded her awareness. She turned nearly a full circle. The killers were out there waiting to attack again, looking for the chance to take her and Zane. But after they used them for whatever they had in mind, would she and Zane die, too?

"Heather, please don't give up." He stepped toward her and cupped his hands on her shoulders. "We need to get back to town so the authorities can come up here and deal with these men."

She nodded slowly. He was right. They could not stop fighting or give in to fear.

Zane took a step back from her. "I'm going to check to see if there's any ID on that man. His family deserves to have closure." His voice was filled with compassion. "There have been no reports of missing hikers that I've seen. He couldn't have been up here for long. The family might not expect him back for weeks. You don't need to come with me. Just stay right here."

She closed her eyes and turned away, unable to get the image of the dead man out of her head. She crossed her arms over her chest and paced in a huge circle, trying to wipe the picture from her brain.

She pushed aside the despair that threatened to pull her into a dark place. She stared up at the blue sky, where snowflakes were drifting down. A memory that had been long buried floated to the surface of her mind. She was outside a cabin with her father, laughing as they caught snowflakes on their tongues. How strange that she hadn't remembered that until now. The memory comforted her at a time when anxiety threatened to rule her.

A rustling to the side of her caught her attention. She turned, expecting to see Zane. A man came at her so suddenly that there was no chance for her to scream or fight. She didn't even have time to register what he looked like before she was knocked to the ground and a hood was put over her head.

Zane put the ID he'd found of the man in his pocket, pausing a moment to say a prayer for the family. His thoughts were interrupted as the engine noise of the ATVs filled the forest.

The pursuers had found them. He needed to get to Heather and fast.

He dare not call out and give away his position. He saw flashes of color and motion through the trees, then he caught a glimpse of a man pointing in his direction. He'd been spotted.

He was able to guess at where Heather had been when a patch of snow revealed her boot print. But where was she now?

Two armed men surged through the trees. Zane slipped behind some brush before they had a chance to get a shot off. He burst up from his hiding place as they drew near. He sprinted, hoping to lose the men in the labyrinth of the forest. The noise behind him increased. More men must have fallen in with the two he'd seen. He had to find a way to shake them so he could circle back and get to Heather.

His heart beat hard in his chest as he ran from one hiding place to the next. The sound of the men yelling commands at each other fell on his ears. They were closing in on him from all sides.

He ran toward higher ground, pushing past a rocky mountainside. When he glanced over his shoulder, he spotted men and ATVs snaking through the trees, converging around him.

Where was Heather? Had she been smart enough to find a hiding place that their pursuers hadn't spotted? It didn't seem likely—these men were carefully trained, and Heather lacked their knowledge of the area. So why hadn't he heard or seen her running, too? He scanned the landscape, not seeing her anywhere.

Three of them men on foot closed in on him, making quick progress up the steep hillside.

Zane dived behind a large boulder and lined up a shot with his pistol. He fired three shots in quick succession. The men gaining ground on him fell flat to the ground to avoid his gunfire.

Zane hurried farther up the hillside before the men had time to recover. If they did want him alive, they'd be cautious about shooting at him, which gave him a slight advantage as long as they were at a distance. But he couldn't let them get close enough to grab him. It was essential that he widen the gap between them, even as his leg muscles strained on the steep incline.

He glanced over his shoulder. The ATVs had slowed, and the men on foot were losing enthusiasm as well. Zane hurried up the remainder of the incline until he reached a high point that allowed him a view of much of the valley below. The ATVs still traversed the countryside but the infantry must have given up for now. The men on the machines would only be able to get so far up the hill before they'd have to get off and walk.

He spotted some ATVs headed away from him. He squinted to make out details. His chest squeezed tight when he recognized Heather's pink gloves, which stood out from her camo outfit. She had a hood over her head.

Heart racing, he jumped from the rock where he'd been perched. He watched the direction the vehicles were headed. Willis must have a camp farther up the mountain than the base Zane remembered. It would take him hours to track them on foot but he had to try.

Aware that the hills were probably still crawling with pursuers trying to earn their stripes, he moved across the terrain on full alert.

The thought of anything bad happening to Heather made him run even faster.

He heard the distant clang of an ATV. He glanced through the trees down the hillside. One machine off by itself, one rider. He could take him and get the transport he needed.

Zane ran out into the open where the ATV rider would see him. The rider turned in an arc and headed toward Zane, kicking up dirt with his wheels. Using himself as bait was risky, but it was the only way to lure the rider and get the machine.

Zane studied the landscape for a good ambush spot and hurried toward it. The noise of the ATV grew louder in his ears as he pressed on toward the high point where he could hide. The trick was to be seen enough so the rider wouldn't give up, but to hide without him knowing it. He was able to slip out of view of the rider.

Though he could not see the machine, he could hear it. The echo off the mountains made it hard to track exactly where his pursuer was. He pushed through to an open area just as rider and vehicle came into view. This was not going as planned. He'd hoped to be hiding and ambush the man. The man twisted the throttle and made a beeline for Zane.

Zane stumbled. The machine sounded like it was on top of him as he struggled to get to his feet. He could hear the engine idling as hands grabbed the back of his coat collar.

This was not a kid. He was dealing with a full-grown man. Zane spun around, but the man was able to land the first blow across his jaw.

With his face stinging from the impact, Zane swung hard with a left then a right, knocking the man on the ground.

He knew this man from seven years ago. His name was John. He'd been just a kid then, like Zane. Now his face looked leathery and weathered, and he was clearly a seasoned fighter. John jumped to his feet and reached out toward Zane.

Zane dodged the intended blow and hit the other man twice in the stomach. His opponent doubled over. Zane ran toward the idling ATV and jumped on, revving it and shifting into gear. He took off with a jerk—but he wasn't quite fast enough to evade John, who managed to grab hold of the back of Zane's shirt.

Zane felt his collar pull tight as he increased speed. Zane shifted into a higher gear, still struggling for breath. The pressure on his neck let up.

He shifted again and headed up the makeshift trail, looking for the ATV tracks that would lead him to the camp. When he glanced over his shoulder, John was just getting to his feet. At least he'd lost that guy, but it didn't mean he was in the clear.

The members of Willis's cult used radios to communicate. It would probably be just a matter of minutes before another pursuer zeroed in on Zane's location. He thought about taking a more roundabout route to where the camp might be, but time was precious if he was going to get Heather out of danger. He could not spare the minutes a detour would cost him.

He sped up. The terrain was more overgrown than he remembered it. This wasn't a part of the mountain where he took hunters, which made it a high probability for Willis's camp. He pushed aside any thought of something bad happening to Heather. Thinking the worst could cripple him mentally. He needed to focus on what needed to be done. He had to assume she had not been harmed and that he'd be able to free her.

He knew, though, that the challenges were growing. Willis had started sending his more experienced and older men. That meant he was upping his game, and it meant he saw Zane as more of a threat than he'd predicted. If Heather was taken to camp, Willis would know to keep her well guarded. Getting her out wouldn't be easy.

He'd cross that bridge when he came to it.

Zane pushed the ATV through the thick undergrowth and across bumpy open areas. He rode until he saw smoke rising off in the distance. That had to be the camp. Reluctantly, he got off the ATV, taking the time to cover it with branches. He would be more likely to avoid detection if he moved in on foot. With God's help, he'd be able to free Heather and come back to the ATV to make a quick escape.

That was the plan anyway. He prayed that everything would fall into place and they both wouldn't end up dead at the hands of Willis's men.

SIX

Heather struggled to take in a deep breath as the fabric of the hood pressed against her face with each intake of air. She couldn't adjust the position of the hood—not with the way her wrists had been bound with rope in front of her. Finally, the jostling on the back of the ATV ceased. The engine clicked off and the rider dismounted.

She shivered involuntarily, listening to the noise around her. She heard footsteps close by and whispering farther away, a conversation that sounded urgent even though it was hushed.

Then she heard the distinct noise of a 12-gauge shotgun being ratcheted back and forth, the lethal cartridge sliding into the chamber.

Her back stiffened and her breath caught like a bubble in her throat. For a long moment, all she heard was the pulsing of her own heartbeat. She squeezed her eyes shut.

Dear God, if they are going to shoot me, let it happen quickly. Don't draw this thing out.

The prayer caught her by surprise. She hadn't prayed to God with such intensity since she was a little girl, on the day her mother had loaded her into the car and pulled out of the gravel driveway, leaving behind Stephan and their life as a family forever. The memory had been buried all these years. But now the image of her father standing in the driveway as she looked out the back window burned through her mind. That had been a sort of death, too.

Several footsteps crunched through the snow, jerking her out of the emotions and images of the past.

"What are you doing?" said a male voice off to her side. His voice was filled with accusation.

She turned her head in the direction of the voice, wondering if he was talking to her.

"I was just having some fun. What good is she without the guy anyway?" said the second voice.

"We *will* catch Zane." The first voice sounded as though his teeth were gritted. "Now put the shotgun away. She'll be useful to us anyway."

Heather let out a gust of air. She'd be spared…for now. Though the word *useful* sent chills down her spine. She'd seen how violent these men and boys could be. What did they have in store for her?

The conversation between the two men was clear enough that she was able to pick up pieces of the exchange. She learned that Zane was still out there and that Heather had been blindfolded from the start so she would have no idea where the camp was located. The older-sounding man who had stayed her execution seemed to be in charge. Was this the man Zane had told her about?

The camp fell silent again. She suspected the two men had wandered away. She could hear other sounds, muffled whispers and even laughter and the crackle of a campfire some distance from her.

Footsteps approached her. She sensed someone close just before the hood was yanked from her head. She'd guess that the man in front of her was maybe twenty years of age, though it was hard to tell because all these men clearly spent most of their life out battling the elements.

He leaned close to her, and she bristled. He was in desperate need of a shower. His hair was past his shoulders, and his beard hit his chest. She couldn't distinguish much more about his features because of the profuse amount of facial hair.

"Get off of there," he said. The voice was the same as the man who had stayed her execution.

Dismounting the ATV was a bit of a balancing challenge with her arms tied in front of her. The man held out a hand and steadied her by cupping her elbow. The gesture seemed out of character for a man who appeared so uncivilized.

She scanned the area without turning her neck so he wouldn't realize she was taking in her surroundings. Why risk getting the hood put back on her head? Three tents placed close together stood not too far from a campfire. She could make out the shadowed figures of men as they stood back from the flames. One of the men stepped closer to the fire, revealing a sneering face.

Her chest clamped tight. Though she could only see one man overtly leering at her, she could feel eyes on her, taking her apart.

Had it been God's mercy to spare her life or was she

about to face a violence she might not ever forget? The man with the long hair pointed toward the center tent.

"Go in there." He lifted his chin at one of the men loitering around the fire. "Get some grub for her."

At least they were going to feed her. Maybe that was a good sign. Though her stomach was clenched so tight she doubted she'd be able to keep any food down. She stepped into the tent.

"Sit down," the man with the long hair commanded.

She settled down on an animal skin. Several other animal skins, a sleeping bag and a crossbow populated the rest of the space. The man with the long hair never took his eyes off her, which only fed her anxious thoughts.

She swallowed, trying to produce some moisture in her mouth.

The man grinned at her. "Relax, you're okay for now." His voice seemed genuine, not menacing.

A younger man poked his head in the tent, holding a piece of wood that contained piles of food. "Here, sir."

The long-haired man took the makeshift plate. He sat it beside Heather, then used a knife to cut Heather's hands free.

"Eat up," he said.

She stared down at the food, which looked to be some kind of cooked red meat. She didn't see a fork. She lifted the first morsel and put in in her mouth. The meat was surprisingly tender and almost sweet tasting.

The long-haired man switched his knife from one hand to the other. The silver of the blade picked up glints of light. His actions made it clear that if she tried to escape, he wouldn't hesitate to use the knife.

"You like it?" He pointed at the meat with his knife.

She nodded. As famished as she was, she would have eaten almost anything, but the meat genuinely was good.

"It's elk," he said. "We hunt it year-round. That's part of the privilege of living up here. We're not beholden to the government's restrictive hunting regulations."

She made a tactical choice not to respond to the ideology that drove his statement. "I've never tasted elk before." Even as she spoke, an unexpected memory floated back into her mind. Her father had prepared a similar meal for her. She could see the rough-hewn logs of the cabin where they'd lived and smell the wood burning in the fireplace. The memories all seemed faint and far away, but real all the same.

Maybe that was why her father had wanted her to come back here. Being in these mountains brought images of her childhood to the surface that her mother's bitterness had buried. She hadn't even realized the memories were there. "I've had deer meat. My father used to prepare it for me."

She took several more bites of the meat. The longhaired man never took his eyes off her.

She lowered her head and looked away. "I'm sorry. Guess I'm eating kind of fast. I'm just really hungry."

The man waved her rudeness away with his hand. "Eat up. There's plenty." He leaned back on his elbows and continued to watch her.

She stopped chewing the meat and studied the man in front of her. His expression was hard to read with the thick beard. His eyes were cold, but he had not been cruel or menacing to her in any way. Was that just as act? What kind of game was he playing anyway? Was he the one who killed the man they'd found in the forest?

The long-haired man sat back up. He stared off to the side and resumed playing with his knife. "So why did you come up here with Zane?"

It seemed a strange question to ask. "Why do you want to know?" The way he said Zane's name, as though he were spitting it out of his mouth, made her think there was some kind of history between the two men.

The man shrugged. "In order to find out."

She concluded that the less he knew about her, the better. "Are you Willis?" A chill ran down her back when she said the name. Though it was hard to judge the man's age, she'd assumed Willis would be older.

The man threw back his head and laughed. "You have no idea." He rose to his feet, grabbed the crossbow and slipped out of the tent.

After a few minutes passed, she placed the wooden plate to one side and peered out of the tent. He wouldn't have left her untied unless he knew there was no way for her to escape. All the same, she had to assess her chances. She counted five men milling around the fire and suspected there might be one or two more in the other tents. Everyone she could see carried a knife or gun on their belts.

She checked her own jeans for the pocketknife she'd used to cut Zane free, but it was nowhere to be found. She must have dropped it in the panic to get away.

She continued to watch the camp. The long-haired man barked orders at the others, and they scattered into the trees. Then he stalked back toward her tent. Heather slipped inside and put the plate back on her lap.

The man stuck his head into the tent. "Get some rest. I'll be back for you in a few hours."

Her mind raced as dark images seemed to assault her at every turn. What did he have planned? Whatever these men had in mind, it sounded like their plan wouldn't work without Zane. The long-haired man had probably ordered the others to go capture Zane.

She was pretty sure she was too anxious to sleep despite having been up for more than twenty-four hours. All the same, she laid her head down on the animal skin and closed her eyes. The fog of sleep overtook her slowly as her thoughts tumbled one over the other…

"Get up."

Someone shook her shoulder. Her eyes fluttered open. How long had she been asleep?

The long-haired man loomed above her. "Time to go, sweetheart."

Through the open tent door, she saw the sky was still light. She'd slept for a few hours at least.

He stepped back to let her through the tent flap. "Hurry it up."

She crawled out and got up on her feet. She thought to bolt for the forest, but his hand clamped around her arm so quickly she didn't have time. He pointed toward a cluster of trees. "Over there," he ordered several young men. "Get out of sight. It needs to look low security."

One of the young men stopped. "What are you doing with her?"

"She's bait for the real prize," said the long-haired man.

The answer sent chills through Heather, but she

didn't argue or protest. She simply followed the man, obeying when he indicated she needed to sit on the ground.

He gave her no opportunity for escape, tying her wrists together again before shouting toward the tents, "Tyler, bring me more rope."

A moment later, a teenager emerged from the shadows and dropped rope at the man's feet.

"Scoot up against that tree," he said.

"Zane isn't stupid. He won't fall for this." Her voice wavered with fear as she struggled to take in a deep breath.

The man ran a strand of rope around Heather and the tree. "The one thing I know about Zane is that his overdeveloped need to rescue the innocent will always trump his common sense."

So he did know Zane.

He stood up and peered off into the distance, frowning before returning his focus to her. "To answer your earlier question. No, my dear, I am not Willis. I'm Jordan. My friends call me Jordie." He leaned a little closer to her, brown eyes flashing with intensity. "You may call me Jordan."

Heather watched the dark trees, knowing that men were lying in wait to grab Zane and then…what, kill her?

"Making some kind of plan, are you?" Jordan leaned close to her. He pulled a scarf off his neck and reached to put it around her eyes.

She jerked her head away.

He grabbed her chin and squeezed it between his fingers. "Don't you dare resist me."

His voice struck a note of fear inside her. Clearly he was a man capable of violence.

The rope around her wrists had very little give. Her shoulders pressed against the tree trunk, not allowing for much movement there either. Though she could see only a few men milling around the camp, busy with their own tasks and seemingly paying little attention to her and Jordan, she had to assume she was being watched. There was little to no chance she would be able to escape on her own.

Jordan was wrong, though. Zane was smart. He wouldn't walk into a trap no matter how much responsibility he felt for her life.

As she listened to the sounds of the forest all around her, she prayed that Zane would be able to come up with a plan that would save them both rather than trying to rescue her and having them both end up dead.

Zane spotted the smoke rising up from a campfire above the trees just as the sky started to turn gray. He was certain it came from Willis's camp. This part of the mountains was remote and rugged. Most hunters didn't even come up this way. Willis could run his crazy operation completely undetected.

Darting from tree to tree, Zane approached the camp until the tents came into view. No one was gathered around the fire. Suspicious. He saw shadows and movement inside one of the tents.

He crawled a little closer. Heather was tied to a tree away from the camp. He breathed a sigh of relief that she was still alive. No guard stood close to her. This had to be a trap. Otherwise, they would have posted at least one guard close to her.

He studied the landscape, open areas and thick forest. Shooters were probably positioned at strategic high points. No doubt other men perched behind trees waiting for the chance to jump him. If he simply blundered into camp, they would both be prisoners.

He needed to create some sort of diversion. Something that would give him a few minutes—just a few, precious minutes—where he could swoop in and cut Heather loose.

He moved in a little closer, crouching low and using the brush for cover. He doubted Willis was close. The man tended to give orders from a safe distance. Zane watched the camp for a long time. Movement inside the tent stopped. A light went out.

Time was on his side. The men who'd been put on watch would grow weary of waiting for him to show up. They'd become distracted and less attentive.

From his vantage point, he could watch Heather. It pained him to see her tied up. She was probably afraid and maybe even cold. Had she been given anything to eat? Water? A place to rest? How much had she already had to endure just because she'd been in the wrong place at the wrong time?

It wasn't just that he felt responsible for what she was going through. He cared about her. The thought of any harm coming to her made it hard for him to breath.

He would break her free or die trying.

He waited and watched as the sky grew even darker. No one came back toward the dying fire, though he detected sounds deeper in the woods that were probably caused by humans. He spotted a propane can used to power a cookstove.

Now he saw his opportunity for a distraction. Nothing like a fire to set men into a panic. He moved past the back of the tent where he would guess the men slept. Even the cracking of his knees as he crept along made him cringe. He stopped and took in a breath.

Inside the tent, he heard the rustling of a sleeping bag. Zane held still for a long moment until the man quieted again. He reached for the propane and worked his way back toward the fire but stayed hidden in the shadows while he tore fabric from his flannel shirt and saturated it with propane. He wrapped the fabric around a stick and shoved it toward the fire. The fire crackled and flamed up as his torch caught on fire.

He had only seconds to act. He poured the remaining propane on the fire. It flared. He ran toward the tent and touched his torch to it and then to the second tent, as well. He tossed the torch in the direction of the third tent and then yelled, "Fire!" They'd be able to put the fire out quickly. He didn't want anyone to be harmed, only panicked and distracted. He dived into the shadows.

It took only seconds for the men in the tent to exit and start shouting for help. Zane slipped farther back into the shadows and made his way toward Heather, pulling his knife from the sheath.

He listened as the ruckus grew louder. Timing was everything. He waited only feet away from Heather for the men watching her to emerge from the trees and race toward the fire.

Three men appeared at intervals and dashed toward the fire. Was that all of them? He couldn't be sure—but he also knew he couldn't wait any longer. The distraction would only work for a short time.

Zane hurried toward Heather and cut her free. She

pulled the blindfold off her eyes. Without a word, they both jumped to their feet and headed into the trees. The crashing behind them told him the men had figured out they'd been hoodwinked.

He grabbed Heather's hand and pulled, indicating that they needed to change direction. They were running in a predictable pattern, which made them too easy to track. She followed as he led. They charged through the forest, circling around to the backside of the camp. Staying close to the camp was risky but it was a move the pursuers wouldn't figure out right away.

The noise of their pursuers grew dimmer and more spread out. Heather and Zane skirted close to the smoldering tent where only one boy stomped on the flames and then sprinkled a canteen of water on it.

Zane's heart pounded against his ribs. Heather's heavy intake of breath told him she was on high alert, as well. He slipped behind a pile of elk and deer bones. Heather pressed in close to him.

He heard the baying of a dog. He tensed. The dog would be able to track them back to the camp faster than people would. He tugged on Heather's sleeve and tilted his head. She nodded in understanding.

They ran in the opposite direction the men had gone until they were some distance from the light of the camp. The barking of the dog grew louder and more intense as he sprinted. Heather's footsteps sounded behind him.

The dog sounded like he was on their heels. When he peered over his shoulder, he saw the men.

Heather caught up with him. Their feet pounded the bare earth. The baying of the dog grew more distant and then more off to the side. For some reason, the dog had lost their scent—or had chosen to chase another one instead.

The breaking of branches in front of him caused him to stop short. He held a protective hand out toward Heather. A doe appeared through the trees. She stopped short when she saw Zane and Heather. Her tail flicked several times before she bounded off in a different direction.

Zane released a heavy breath. The sound of the dog had grown even dimmer. Maybe there was other wildlife around that had distracted the dog. They had only a precious few minutes to escape before the dog refocused and picked up their scent again.

Zane tried to picture the layout of the terrain in this area. Seven years was a long time. But some things didn't change. The river was still downhill. That much he knew, and it was still their best bet for getting out of here alive.

He turned a half circle and took off running. More crashing noises landed on his ears. More deer probably disturbed by the fire and the smoke it had created.

He spotted the silhouette of a man running from tree to tree. Zane stopped short and drew his gun out from his waistband. His gaze darted around. Where had the man disappeared to?

He detected movement behind one of the trees.

"Step out. I've got my sights on you," said Zane.

The man stepped out from behind the evergreen. Zane could barely make out any features beyond the covering of a beard and long hair.

The baying of the dog grew louder again. He'd found the trail again and was close.

The man held his hands up. "Go ahead. Shoot me."

Zane felt as though he'd been punched in the gut. The gun dropped to his side. He knew that voice.

Jordan, after all these years.

SEVEN

Heather watched in stunned silence as Jordan pulled his gun out and held it on Zane. She dared not run. Zane wasn't moving at all. He lowered his head and stared at the ground. Jordan's teeth curled back from his lip. The intensity in his eyes suggested he would pull the trigger if Zane gave him the slightest excuse.

What in the world was going on? Zane had blown their chance to get away.

The baying of the dog pressed on her ears. Other pursuers emerged through the trees.

"Restrain them," said Jordan.

Zane lifted his head at the sound of Jordan's voice. She thought she saw pain in his expression. The two men must have some kind of history. Clearly, Zane thought being captured was better than injuring Jordan so they could get away.

The other men drew close. Heather held out her hands to be restrained without putting up a fight. What was the use? They were outnumbered and outgunned. If they were going to escape, it would have to happen later—provided either she or Zane could come up with a plan.

Zane waited until the men stepped away from them. He leaned toward her and whispered. "I'll get us out of this."

"You could have gotten us out of this a minute ago." She spoke looking straight ahead, not wanting to draw their captors' attention. "Whose side are you on?" She snuck a glance at him.

Zane's face turned beet red and his jaw hardened.

Jordan waved his gun. "You two, stop talking."

They walked back through the woods in silence, both of them with their hands tied behind their backs. When they returned to the camp, the debris from the burned tents had already been gathered into a pile and stacked some distance from the undamaged tents.

Jordan indicated that Heather and Zane should be taken to the tent with the animal skins. Heather settled back where she'd sat previously.

Zane stared at the ground. "I meant it when I said I'd get us both out of here."

She shook her head, still stunned by his actions.

"I'm not one of them. You have to believe me," he said.

"But you used to be one of them. And clearly you still feel some loyalty to them, or at least to that animal, Jordan."

Zane continued to stare at the ground. "He's…he's not an animal." When he lifted his head his eyes were glazed. "He's my little brother."

The shock nearly knocked her over. Her throat went tight as guilt washed through her. "I am so sorry. I had no idea."

Zane shook his head as wrinkles formed on his forehead. "I got out. He didn't. I tried. I really tried to convince him not to stay with Willis." He looked off to the side as though some memory was playing through his mind.

A teenage boy stuck his head through the open flap of the tent. He set down a plate of food and a container of water before reaching inside and cutting the rope around Zane's hands. "Just you get to eat. Jordan says."

A chill ran down Heather's back. Of course they didn't need to feed her anymore. Her *usefulness* had expired.

As soon as the boy had left, Zane leaped across the tent and grabbed Heather's wrists to untie her. She felt a tug as he struggled to get the ropes loose.

"Wish they hadn't taken my knife," he said.

Jordan stuck his head in. "Always quick to act." He lifted the gun he held and aimed it at Heather. "And ready to rescue anyone who is in distress."

Heather cringed when the laser sight of the gun skittered across her chest. Jordan smirked at her fear before he let the gun fall to his side.

Jordan tilted his head toward the plate of food. "Eat up. Willis wants you in good spirits when he sees you."

Zane settled back down and took a bite of food.

"How many years has it been, little brother?"

Jordan jumped across the expanse of the tent and shoved the gun under Zane's chin. "Don't call me that."

Zane gently pushed his brother away and shook his head. "That is who you will always be to me." His voice was filled with compassion, which only seemed to make Jordan angrier.

"Shut up." Jordan shoved the gun in its holster, then moved across the tent and rolled up the sleeping bag.

The tent must belong to Jordan. He seemed to be preparing to not stay in it.

Heather eyed the gun. If her hands were free she was almost close enough to grab it. When she looked over at Zane, he was focused on Jordan's face and didn't seem to even notice the gun.

"You're looking a little ragged, Jordie. How long has it been since you've been to Fort Madison or anywhere civilized?" Zane's voice remained soft, without malice.

Jordan continued to pack up and avoid eye contact with his brother. "I know how to take care of myself." He spun around to face his older brother. "Only my friends call me Jordie."

"I didn't betray you. I don't know what lies Willis told you, but the truth is that I tried to find you for years."

Jordan continued to shove his belongings into a bag. Something in the jerky stop and start of his movements suggested Zane's words had an effect on him.

"Jordan, you're my little brother. We're blood." Zane's comment made Jordan twitch his head. Zane leaned closer to his brother. "Don't you remember after we got away from that home? I had your back and you had mine."

Jordan didn't respond. Instead, he became more frantic in his packing.

"We had some good times. Sleeping beneath the stars. Eating squirrel meat. You remember that?"

Jordan swung around and put his face very close to Zane's. "I know what you're trying to do."

"I'm not trying to trick you or get away." Zane tilted his head as his voice faltered. "I only want my brother back."

"Go ahead and try to grab my gun. I know you were thinking about it." Jordan's voice held a note of challenge.

"I wouldn't do that to you, Jordan. Not to my brother." Zane never broke off eye contact.

Watching the two men face-to-face was a study in contrasts. The younger was bitter, angry and wild. The older was filled with compassion and calm, showing love for his brother. Heather didn't know their whole story. What had happened to their biological parents that had cast them out into the world with just each other? She could not begin to imagine, but both of them had chosen different substitute fathers and it had made all the difference in the world.

Their gazes held for a long moment. Zane was not going to grab the gun even though he'd been given the opportunity. She only hoped his choice wouldn't cost them their lives.

Jordan broke off eye contact. "My brother died seven years ago."

Zane seemed to collapse in on himself. His shoulders slumped.

Jordan spoke without looking at his brother. "Eat the food and drink some water and don't think about escaping or untying her. I've got a guard posted outside." He flipped open the tent flap and crawled outside with his stuff.

The look of devastation on Zane's face was like an arrow through Heather's heart. She wanted to comfort him, but there was nothing she could say. She shook her head as her own eyes filled with tears.

"I had hoped that he wasn't too far gone." He lifted his head and looked at her. He scooted toward her and touched her cheek where a tear rolled down. "Thank you for caring." His eyes filled with warmth.

She felt a tug on her own heart as any doubt about Zane's true character washed away. He was a man of integrity and compassion.

"I never had a sibling. I can't begin to imagine…"

He lifted the container. "Do you want some water?"

She nodded.

He held the container to her lips and tilted it. The cool liquid felt good going down her parched throat.

He leaned toward her, placing the container on the ground. His lips brushed over hers, the moment of contact so fleeting that if the scent of his skin didn't linger in the air, she might have thought she'd imagined it.

Her heart pounded as affection reflected back through his eyes. "I meant what I said. I'll get us out of here."

She understood now that even though he was determined to get them both away from Willis and his men, the one thing Zane would not do was betray or harm his brother. For reasons she could not fathom, Zane still held out hope for Jordan. She prayed that hope would not get them killed.

Shouts of panic burst up from outside the tent, followed by gunfire. Footsteps pounded around the camp, mingled with the sounds of more upheaval and more yelling. Someone shouted something about a bear.

"Now is our chance," said Zane.

Zane grabbed Heather's wrists and tried to untie the knots of the rope that bound her. Jordan had taken all the knives and tools they could have used to cut her free. He searched the tent, coming up with a piece of metal. It would have to do. He sawed it across the ropes.

Outside, the gunfire grew farther away.

He finished freeing her. "Stay put." Using the tent flap as cover he peered outside, scanning the grounds for a moment before he ducked back in. "The guard isn't there anymore. He must have gone after the bear, too."

He slipped outside and stopped directly in front of the tent. The gunshots were spread apart and far away, and she thought she recognized the distinctive *zing* of a long-range rifle. Zane had given her a quick lesson about guns and rifles before they'd left Fort Madison.

Finally Zane moved away from the tent opening and signaled for her to come outside.

Her hand touched the dirt outside the tent as she crawled through. She lifted her head. No sign of Jordan or any of the other men. Zane tapped her shoulder and pointed toward a cluster of trees. Now she saw the plaid pattern of a flannel shirt nearly camouflaged by the evergreen boughs. Some men were still in the camp, still watching. The tracking dog remained in the middle of the camp, tied up and barking wildly. A boy emerged from the trees, untied the dog and pulled him back toward the cover of the forest, probably planning to use the dog to track the bear.

One of the men sprinted through the camp. Heather pressed closer to the tent, but the man didn't notice them. She didn't see Jordan anywhere.

Zane headed around the backside of the tent and she fell in behind him. There was no clear trail to follow. Zane seemed to know where he was going as he raced through the forest. The gunshots behind them died away.

They ran some distance until Zane stopped and

abruptly led them in a different direction. She had to trust that he knew where they were going. Her own navigation skills would only get them lost.

After they had sprinted for some time longer over rough terrain, Zane halted. He took a moment to catch his breath before he said anything. "There's an ATV around here. I covered it with pine boughs." He paced in one direction and then the other.

"Maybe we shouldn't waste time trying to find it," she said. Her gaze darted everywhere. She expected to see or hear Willis's men at any second.

"I can get you down to the river and across that other bridge much faster if we have it. It's a straight shot back to Fort Madison from there. Then I can come back up and try to extract Jordan."

Jordan clearly had no interest in leaving the group, but she understood why Zane wouldn't give up on his brother. So Zane's plan was to get her to safety and then put himself back in the line of fire, all for a little brother who has just stabbed him in the heart.

"I'll help you find it." For Zane, for the love he showed a brother, she would risk the loss of time in looking for the ATV.

Zane studied the silhouette of the mountain in the distance as though that would help him pinpoint the location of the vehicle.

"This way." He took off again running with intensity. She hurried behind him just as the distant baying of the dog landed on her eardrums. Now they were being tracked again. The past two days had already shown that these men were not going to give up easily. Willis must have some kind of sick psychological hold on them to make them so relentless and determined.

Heather pushed her legs to run faster. Her life depended on it. She did not see the unusual formation of pine boughs until they were only a few yards away from it. At a distance, no one would guess an ATV was hidden underneath.

Zane threw pine boughs to one side with a frantic strength and speed. She stepped in and helped uncover the one thing that gave them a chance against the men who were after them.

From time to time, the dog's persistent baying and barking erupted in the forest, a noise that made her chest tight.

Zane jumped on the ATV and started it. She got on behind him. He pushed the vehicle to its maximum speed as they bumped over the rough terrain. Twice they caught air. She held on tight, pressing her face against his shoulder.

Snow started to fall out of the sky again. Lazy, dizzy flakes twirling in the sky at first, but then the wind picked up and the snow seemed to come at them sideways. She huddled even closer to Zane, knowing that he was getting the brunt of the wind. They both were dressed for cold weather but she had lost her hat somewhere along the way. She pulled the hood of her jacket up over her head. Then she noticed Zane had no gloves. Steering the ATV in the cold and snow without them had to be miserable.

She tapped on his shoulder.

He brought the ATV to an idle. Snow stabbed her skin like a thousand tiny swords. She pulled her gloves off and draped them over his shoulder.

"They might be a little small."

He took the gloves and buttoned the top button on his coat. "Thanks. Pink is my color."

She managed to laugh, appreciating that he found humor despite the tension and fear hounding them.

Still, it didn't take long for apprehension to return while they sat there, unmoving. She shivered. The temperature had dropped at least ten degrees since they had taken off on the ATV.

Zane revved the engine, and she huddled in close to him, shielding her face as much as possible.

"Put your hands underneath my coat at my sides to keep them warm," he shouted over his shoulder.

The gesture, though practical, felt a little awkward to her. She slipped her hands beneath his coat, feeling his body heat as she rested them against the warm flannel of his shirt. Gradually, though, she felt herself relax. So much had changed since the previous night when he'd wrapped his arms around her at the fire to keep her warm. She knew Zane in a deeper way now. She saw him for who he really was—a good man trying to do the right thing.

Zane took off again. The terrain became even more treacherous as Zane angled the ATV downhill. She lifted her head to see over his shoulder. She couldn't see any sign of the river and wondered how far they still were.

The ATV slid sideways. Heather wrapped her arms tighter around Zane. He righted the vehicle but brought it to a stop shortly after coasting toward a cluster of trees.

"It's too slick." He craned his neck and spoke over his shoulder. "We need to wait this storm out."

She jumped off the back and stared down the mountain. Going on foot in the storm wouldn't be a good plan either.

Zane leaned close to look at the gauges on the ATV. "We have enough gas." Then he glanced up the mountain, a reminder that they were still being hunted even if they didn't see or hear their pursuers. He tapped the handlebars. "We can cover so much more ground with this." He tore off the gloves she'd given him and handed them back to her. "I only need them while I'm driving."

He grabbed a pine bough and placed it over the ATV. She gathered loose branches and helped him conceal the four-wheeler from view.

The wind and the cold had intensified even more by the time he grabbed her hand and led her to the shelter of some trees that formed a natural lean-to.

The overhang of branches made it seem darker as they huddled together for warmth.

She wanted to ask him how far it was to the river, but somehow she knew the answer would only make her feel more discouraged. Instead, she rested her head against his shoulder. The fatigue of having run so far on so little food and sleep, of having been so close to death overtook her. The tears slipped silently down her cheeks.

Doubt clouded her mind. Were they even going to get off this mountain and back to Fort Madison?

EIGHT

Zane stared out at the snow and listened to the wind whirling around and making the tree branches creak. Heather seemed to melt into his shoulder. He sensed that her mind had drifted a million miles from this cold fortress.

When she reached her hand up to swipe at a tear on her cheek, he knew she was falling apart. He couldn't blame her. He'd seen grown men break down and cry after days of being in the elements, and none of those men had had their lives threatened or had to flee like she had.

The one thing he didn't want was for her to give up hope. He knew his own strengths and capabilities and he was certain he would be able to take her across that river. And then he would get his brother away from Willis once and for all.

He'd seen Jordan start to soften even in the little bit of interaction they'd had. He had to believe he could get his brother back, mind, body and soul.

He returned his attention to Heather. He had to keep her spirits up or that would sink them faster than the cold or the men who were after them. "What are you thinking about?"

She took a moment to answer. "I was just thinking that if I was back in California right now, I would have just finished teaching my Pilates class. Then I might be getting ready to go for a swim or take my dog out for a run in the warm evening."

"Warmth. That sounds nice." He turned toward her. "Heather, I'm so sorry. I know this is way more than you bargained for. It's way more than *anyone* could have bargained for."

"I know you didn't intend for it to happen." She stared out at the falling snow. "It's just a lot to deal with. I don't see how we're going to get out of here."

"We'll make it." He wrapped his arm around her and squeezed her shoulder. He liked how she seemed to melt against him. When he'd kissed her earlier it had been impulsive. Not that he hadn't enjoyed it. But they were from different worlds. If they ever got back to those worlds, she would sell the business he loved and go back to the California sunshine she loved. She rested her head on his shoulder. Gradually, she relaxed even more. Her deep breathing told him that she'd fallen asleep. He kept watch and held still, not wanting to wake her.

The snow continued to fall as the sun sank lower in the sky. He had some tough choices to make. If he waited until nighttime, the headlights on the ATV would make them an easy target for anyone tracking them. If they hiked out on foot, they'd be fighting the storm and the clock.

The prudent thing to do would be to head out on the ATV before sunset. There was a risk of them wreck-

ing in the adverse conditions and terrain, but it was a
risk he was willing to take. The ATV would get them
to safety so much faster.

He closed his own eyes, keeping an ear tuned to his
surroundings. When he'd rested for what seemed like
twenty minutes, he squeezed Heather's shoulder. "We
need to get moving."

Her eyes popped open and fear penetrated her voice.
"Did they find us?"

"No, we're fine. But we can't stay here any longer."

She nodded and jumped to her feet. Together they
uncovered the ATV.

He fired up the machine and got on. She swung her
leg over but then pointed at something over his shoulder. "What's that?"

He turned to look in the direction of her pointing. At
first he couldn't see anything among the evergreens. He
squinted. The snowfall made it hard to discern, but it
looked like a plume of smoke rising up from the trees.

"Most likely a campfire," he said.

She leaned toward him so she could speak into his
ear above the *parump parump* noise of the ATV engine. "Do you think it's them?"

Possible, but it could be hunters out scouting, too.
Someone who would be in a position to help them. "We
gotta find out," he said.

The ATV lurched forward and sped down the mountain. Twice they slid sideways. Heather held on and
didn't even cry out. He glanced at the rising vapor of
smoke. Hope stirred in his heart.

He stopped the ATV some distance from where the
camp was. "I don't want them to hear us coming. Just

in case." It didn't make sense for their pursuers to build a fire…unless they were setting another trap.

Heather dismounted. "Chances are it's not them, right? Why would they make camp? They're probably beating the bushes looking for us."

He cupped her shoulder. "Just what I was thinking. But let's not take any chances."

They moved with stealth through the trees as though they were a well-trained unit. Heather kept up with him, remained quiet and seemed to instinctually know when to push forward and when to remain put.

Zane lifted his head and sniffed at the scent of burning wood that hung in the air as they drew closer. He darted toward another tree.

He heard voices, a conversation on low volume. Two men, maybe. He pushed through the undergrowth to get a glimpse of them. The crackling fire was the first thing to come into view. Zane lowered a branch for a better view.

He'd been right—it was two men. They looked to be in their forties. He'd never seen either one of them before. Zane breathed a sigh of relief. These were not Willis's men. The men would have a brief exchange and then stare at the fire for a long time. Both of them wore hunter attire that looked brand new, not the tattered outerwear that characterized Willis's men. Two horses were tethered not too far from the fire.

Zane stepped into the clearing, holding up his hands in a surrender gesture. "Don't mean to bother you gentlemen. But we need your help getting back to Fort Madison."

He noticed that one of the men's eyes were round with fear. Of him? Did he look that threatening?

"I'm not here to hurt you. I'm a guide for Big Sky Outfitters."

"You ran into some difficulty, huh?" said the second man. His voice sounded stiff and unnatural.

Both men seemed nervous, much more so than he'd expect since they outnumbered him and were armed.

The men's guns were propped off to one side by a tree. Zane wondered if the men were poaching and feared getting caught.

"I don't want to make any trouble. I'm not the game warden." Zane held his palms toward the men in a surrender gesture. "We just need some help."

The first man kept angling his eyes off to the side but not moving his head. Zane felt the hairs on the back of his neck rise as he searched where the man seemed to be looking. He half expected to see a dead animal or a carcass. All he saw was bare ground.

"Who's *we* anyway?" said the second hunter.

Zane glanced over his shoulder. For some reason, Heather hadn't followed him into the clearing. Now he was on high alert. He took several steps back and saw a flash of movement in the trees.

This was an ambush, a trap. The second hunter looked directly at him and mouthed the word *run*.

A shot was fired and the hunter who had warned him slipped off the log he'd been sitting on and fell over, blood flowing from his shoulder. The first hunter dived toward where their guns were. But now there was only one gun there instead of two. Maybe Heather had taken the other one.

The hunters must have been told to act natural so Zane's guard would be down while Willis's men waited with their firearms trained on them for the right moment to capture him.

The second hunter didn't make it to his gun before he cried out in pain and gripped his stomach, scrambling toward the cover of the trees.

Zane dived for cover as the forest lit up like firecrackers from all the gunfire.

The gun battle stopped for a moment, and he heard an exchange of panicked whispering. He slipped farther into the trees.

To his side he heard voices, though he could not see anyone.

"Be careful, we don't want to kill him."

"Where did she go anyway? I don't see her anywhere."

Zane wondered that, too. Where *had* Heather gone?

Heart racing, Heather held on to the rifle she'd grabbed. Gunfire seemed to be coming from every direction. She backed away through the trees. A head popped up from behind a bush. She recognized him from the camp as one of Willis's men.

The man sneered at her as he stepped out toward her. His hand reached for his pistol.

She hit the man with the butt of the rifle, and he collapsed to the ground. She ran away from where the loudest gunfire was. By the time she stopped to catch her breath and rest her back against a tree, she was wheezing in air.

She'd never hit a man before in her life, but she couldn't bring herself to regret her actions. He would've taken her captive at gunpoint if she hadn't. Another volley of gunshots assaulted her ears. She cringed.

Hold it together, Heather. Think straight.

She stared up at the clouds drifting by while she held the rifle in her hand. It didn't look like the ones Zane had instructed her about before they left Fort Madison. Then she realized it wasn't a rifle at all. It was a shotgun. She'd seen one, even—once, long ago.

The gunfire died down. Had Willis's men succeeded in capturing Zane? There was only one way to find out.

Zane wouldn't leave her behind, so she knew she had to go back for him.

She circled back around toward the camp, pushing past her fear with each footstep.

She slowed as she drew near to the remnants of the fire. The air still smelled of wood smoke and cordite. The only noise she heard was the horses' frantic whinnying and the jangle of the metal on their bridles.

She dropped to the ground and worked her way to where she had a clear view of the camp. Her breath caught.

One of the hunters lay dead beside the smoldering fire.

Her stomach did a somersault and she tasted bile. She looked away. Finally, after several deep breaths, she steeled herself to take in the rest of the camp.

She detected no movement and heard nothing that sounded human. Rising to her feet, she ran through the center of the camp, past the dead man. A search of the edges of the area revealed that Zane and the others must have gone. All the tracks she could see led in the same direction. It didn't look like Zane had been able to escape. That had to mean that he was their captive again.

She ran back to where the horses were. Still clearly agitated, the horses jerked their heads up and down.

Her hands were shaking as she reached toward the first horse to untie him. She could cover a lot more ground with some transportation.

Once he was loose, the horse reared up. She stepped back, letting go of the reins. The animal galloped away, crashing through the forest.

Her heart was still racing from nearly having been trampled. She made soothing sounds as she stepped toward the second horse. She stroked the animal's neck and mane. She spotted a saddle not too far away. By the time she swung the saddle over his back and secured it around his belly, the animal had calmed down.

She shoved the shotgun into the leather holder attached to the saddle and untied her ride. She put her foot in the stirrup and got on, determined to find Zane—whatever it took, whatever it cost. They were in this together and they would get out of this together.

NINE

As he rushed away from the camp, Zane heard the frantic voices and movement but still didn't see anyone. Crawling commando style, he sneaked through the underbrush. He was pretty sure the hunter by the fire was dead. While the second one had rushed out of sight, Zane suspected he had been fatally injured, too. The hunters had probably planned to be up here for days or even a week. Family members would not be alarmed for some time. That meant there was no hope of the authorities showing up anytime soon.

He said a prayer for the dead men and their families.

The smart thing to do would be to try to make it back to the ATV and hope that Heather had the same plan.

He rushed from tree to tree, still hearing the occasional breaking twig. The snow had let up some but the cold still stung his face. When he got to where the ATV should have been, he saw that it had been stolen. There was a chance that Heather had gotten to it first, but he feared the worst. And the worst thing he could imagine was that Heather had been taken hostage again.

Maybe she'd been smart enough to grab a shotgun when the opportunity had presented itself. He'd spent some time showing her how a few different guns worked before they left town. A little instruction, though, was not the same as years of experience, and he hadn't told her anything about shotguns.

Several gunshots sounded behind him. His heart squeezed tight. He took off running toward where the gunfire had come from, slowing down and seeking cover as he drew close. He spotted a trail of fresh blood on the new-fallen snow. His heart squeezed tight. He wanted to call out Heather's name.

Instead, he backed up against the tree, listening and watching. No more disturbances. The men could be lying in wait, using Heather as bait once again. Or Heather could be hurt and bleeding.

He traced the blood trail with his eyes. His heart beat out an erratic rhythm. He heard more gunfire some distance from him and to the north. Maybe this was his chance. He had to know. Even if it was bad. Even if it showed him that he'd lost Heather just when she seemed to trust him.

He followed the blood trail into the quiet of the woods. He found the prone body of the second hunter. He checked for a pulse, but knew in his heart that he wouldn't find one. The man was dead, shot through the stomach and a second time through the arm. Zane closed his eyes and said a prayer.

He found the man's rifle a few feet from him. He still needed to locate Heather. He ran north toward where he'd heard the gunshots.

One of the horses that had been tied up at the hunters' camp galloped past him. Clearly agitated, the animal was kicking up snow and snorting, its hooves pounding the earth.

Once it was out of sight, Zane scanned the horizon and all the open areas, not seeing any movement. The silence bothered him. If he heard gunshots, it meant they were still after Heather, which meant she was still alive and running.

He jogged toward the last place he'd heard the gunshots, into the thick of the forest. He slowed, aware that a trap might have been set for him. A sense of helplessness descended on him like a shroud. He had to believe she was still alive. He wouldn't give up hope.

Maybe she was the one who had taken the ATV. He doubted she could navigate to the river crossing on her own, but she could at least get away fast.

Zane turned a half circle. A sudden stinging pain in his hand caused him to drop the rifle. Then his whole arm went numb. His stared down at his hand. It dripped with blood. He'd been shot. He felt lightheaded as he fought not to give in to the shock that pummeled his body.

He heard footsteps behind him and then voices.

"I told you it would work. I'm a good shot," said a young-sounding voice. "Willis just said bring him in alive." The voice sounded triumphant. "It's okay if he's hurt, don't you think?"

These were not men. They were boys barely in their teens. He swung around with the intent of knocking them to the ground with his good hand. No need to harm someone so young. All he needed to do was get away.

He lifted his arm to swing it, but the shock to his body from the wound slowed his movements. The boy he was aiming for had time to step back while his cohort dropped a hood over Zane's head. He swayed slightly from the blood loss.

"Come on, let's take him to Willis."

"Aren't we supposed to call in and wait for orders?"

"Casey took the radio, dude. Let's just take him up to Willis. We got him. We should get the credit."

As he listened to conversation, Zane could feel himself growing more and more light-headed. He needed to stop the bleeding in his hand before he passed out.

He heard the distinctive racking of a 12-gauge shotgun and then Heather's voice behind him, clear and strong. "I don't think anybody is going anywhere today, boys. Don't even think about reaching for your gun. Drop it on the ground right now, then take five steps back."

He heard a thud and footsteps.

"You've got ten seconds to disappear before I start shooting."

More footsteps. This time even more frantic.

Heather pulled the hood off Zane. He tried to focus on her beautiful face. Her gaze fell to his hand and the pool of blood on the ground. She pulled her scarf off and handed it to him. "Until we can get you a real bandage."

He wrapped the scarf around his bleeding hand. The bullet had gone through the fleshy area between his thumb and finger. "Where are the others?"

She tilted her head downhill. "I diverted them away from you and then circled back around to find you."

"Did you take the ATV?"

She shook her head. "I took one of the horses. Come on, we've got to get out of this clearing." She grabbed his good arm above the elbow. "Are you going to be okay?"

He nodded but wasn't so sure it was the truth. He was having a hard time focusing and his stomach churned.

She grabbed the handgun the kid had surrendered and handed it to him. "It'll be easier to carry than that rifle."

She held on to him above the elbow and led him toward the trees. "We better hurry. I'm sure it's just a matter of time before they are able to tell the others our position."

"Those two don't have a radio, but I am sure they can find someone who does." Zane quickened his pace, though he still felt dizzy. "How did you know how to handle a 12 gauge? I never showed you."

Heather stuttered in her step. "I have a vague memory of my father showing me. It came back to me when I picked up the shotgun. I was too young to hold a gun but he explained things to me."

"Strange how memory works," he said.

Her gaze flashed toward him for just a moment. "Yes, I'm starting to wonder if it's why my father wanted me to come back here…so the memories would surface."

"If so, some of the memories might be ones you're better off without. I'm not sure Stephan was exercising sound judgment showing a five-year-old how to use a shotgun." He wondered what Stephan had been thinking, too, when the old man had written out his will. Though, in his defense, Stephan couldn't have foreseen the nightmare the two of them had been thrown into.

"Actually it was more of a safety lecture, and then he locked the gun back up," she said.

Heather glanced over her shoulder and then jogged toward a cluster of evergreens until the horse from the camp came into view. Heather untethered the horse from a branch.

She handed him the reins. "I don't know the way."

Zane mounted the horse struggling a little to do it one handed. He reached down his good hand for Heather.

She swung up behind him, wrapping her arms around him.

He led the horse out into the open and kicked the beast into a canter. He felt Heather's warmth as she held on and pressed close to him. The hand that had been shot was useless. He had to control the animal with only his good hand while he rested the other on his leg.

The light-headedness cleared, and he didn't feel like he might throw up anymore.

The trail before him was easy enough to navigate. He leaned closer to the horse's neck and spurred the animal to go faster. Heather leaned forward as well. They seemed to be functioning as a single unit, each of them knowing what to do without saying anything.

The horse kicked up snow and dirt as it traversed the flatter part of the landscape. The animal slowed once the trail became more winding. Horses weren't as sure-footed as mules, but on this kind of terrain, it was better transport than an ATV.

Zane's mind turned to the horse's owners—the hunters who now lay dead in the forest. They'd been up in the high country without a guide, so they must be local men. Zane might have even seen them before, at the grocery store or the post office. And now they were gone. The damage Willis could do was astounding. Zane vowed that when he got down off this mountain, he'd find the hunters' families and speak to them himself. It was the least he could do.

Willis was usually careful to keep a low profile. Killing was unlike him. And now with three dead men to account for, Willis must be planning something big for him to risk the consequences of being found out. But what could he possibly be after that could be that important? And what did any of it have to do with Zane?

He stared down the series of switchbacks on the trail. A fire had burned out most of the trees on this part of the mountain, providing him with a clear view of much of the trail.

Men were moving up the trail far enough away that they looked like bugs. All of them were dressed in camouflage or earth tones. Most likely Willis's men had gotten the message and were headed back up the trail.

Zane brought the horse to a halt. "Dismount. We need to find a different way down this part of the mountain to get to the river."

Zane swung off the horse and hurried into the thick of the forest with Heather at his heels.

The men were moving at a rapid pace up the mountain, six of them in all. At best, they had a five-minute head start over their pursuers. Not good.

TEN

Even as they sprinted through the trees, Heather felt a heaviness descend. Were they ever going to get out of these mountains? "Is there another way to get to the river?" she asked between deep breaths. Zane quickened his pace and she struggled to follow. "They're watching our access points to it too closely."

"I've been thinking the same thing," Zane agreed. "There *is* another way to get out of here. We won't end up in Fort Madison, though. We'll have a long hike after that to get to civilization."

He stopped and dropped the reins. "We're going to have to let the horse go. It's not a route he can traverse."

Her spirits sank even lower. The horse had seemed like an answer to prayer. "What about the 12 gauge?"

"Carry it if you want, but I think it will slow you down."

After thinking for a moment, Zane mustered up a half smile for her and said, "The horse might work as a diversion." Zane coaxed the horse until it was turned around and then slapped its flank. The animal took off running, making a beeline for the trail. Zane took her gloved hand. "This way."

Her calves strained as they climbed a steep incline away from the trail. Down below, the shouts of the men filled the forest. They must have spotted the horse.

Their voices struck a note of fear inside of her. They were outnumbered and outgunned. Were they ever going to get away or would they be hunted to the point where exhaustion and hunger forced them to surrender?

As though he sensed her losing hope, he squeezed her hand. "Let's put some distance between us and them then we can rest."

The noise of the pursuers faded when they worked their way through the thick trees. They walked for what seemed like hours before Zane let go of her hand. "I think we lost them. We can build a small fire. Find an area where the trees and brush provide a degree of cover." He reached inside his jacket. "There's the fire-starter kit. I'm going to go find something for us to eat."

She took the pouch and headed toward the thicker part of the forest. Zane pulled the pistol out of his waistband and disappeared into the grove of trees. She worried that they weren't far enough away and that a gunshot would alert the men to their position, but she reminded herself that Zane knew what he was doing. She needed to do her part and not question his choices.

She walked a short distance until she found a small open area in the thick of the trees. She couldn't see anything through the brush, so she kept her ears tuned to the sounds around her while she knelt after gathering twigs and several logs.

She opened Zane's waterproof container, which held the fire starter. She felt paper beneath the container.

Zane had inadvertently given her two photographs that he must always keep in his inside pocket. One was of a much younger Zane with another boy who was maybe twelve years old. They were sitting in front of a Christmas tree. She stared at the photo for a long moment before she figured out the younger boy must be Jordan.

She examined the second photograph, Zane with an older man. The older man had his arm around Zane as they stood outside by an evergreen, both of them holding rifles. She had never seen a picture of her father and her memories of him were still vague, blurry. But the resemblance was impossible to ignore. The eyes that looked back at her were her eyes. The photos were undamaged from when they'd fallen in the river.

A faint gunshot somewhere in the distance brought her back to the present moment. She stuffed the photos into the waterproof container and set to building a fire. She dug through the pouch for the dryer lint. Flames consumed the lint and then the twigs. She placed her hands close to the heat and then gathered some sticks that were close by.

She heard a rustling in the trees and looked up to see Zane holding a dead rabbit. "Dinner."

Her stomach growled. She would have turned her nose up at wild rabbit in the past, but now she would eat anything and be grateful.

Zane skinned the animal with a pocketknife he must have snatched from somewhere since his bigger knife had been taken.

Finding the two photographs helped her see him in a different light. They were pictures of the two people who meant the most to him. It was very telling that he seemed to carry them with him everywhere he went.

"Something on your mind?" Zane caught her staring.

"No, nothing." She looked away as heat rose up on her cheeks. She remembered what Zane said about not letting the fire get too big and only placed another log on in when it threatened to die down.

She glanced back up at him. A faint smile graced his face. When she had first met him, she'd thought he was some kind of wild man with his long hair and beard. She had only assumed that her father was the same way if they got along so well. Zane was way more complicated than that. Did that mean that her father had been too?

"I was just thinking about my…my dad."

He stuck the rabbit on a sharp stick he'd fashioned and placed it close to the fire. "Your dad?"

It felt strange to even call him that. "Tell me something about him that would surprise me."

Zane rotated the stick. "He liked poetry."

"Poetry?"

"Not moon, spoon, June stuff either. Sometimes in the evening he'd read out loud around the fire while we settled down. He always started off with a psalm. They were his favorite, but he liked Robert Frost, too."

She'd read Robert Frost as a teenager. "That does surprise me." But it was a good surprise. Well, mostly good. The news made her feel closer to the father she barely remembered but sad at the same time for all that she had missed. "My mother said he used to steal the grocery money so he could spend it on liquor."

"That is not the man I knew. I wish you could believe that."

"It's just hard to let go of all the ugly things my

mother said about him, the stories she told that made me hate him."

She didn't think her mother had been lying. Stephan had been a drinker. It had probably been the smart, safe choice for them to leave him. But after they'd gone… was there a chance he really had changed? She was starting to believe that maybe such a transformation was possible. If Zane could have changed so dramatically just by being under Stephan's influence, maybe her father could have changed, too. Jordan represented what Zane would have become if he hadn't gotten away from Willis.

Confusion whirled through her like a hurricane. She hadn't had much time to think about her father since Willis's men had come after them.

Zane lifted the now blackened rabbit from the fire. "I think this is about ready to serve." He laid it on a flat stone he'd brought with him. "My hand still isn't working real well. Would you carve?" He handed her the pocketknife. "I'll hold it in place."

She flicked open the knife and cut into the meat. She drew her hand back when she touched the smoldering flesh.

"Careful, it's kind of hot," Zane said.

"I got that. That's what fire does. I just wasn't thinking." Her own stupidity made her shake her head. She offered Zane a quick glance. Amusement danced in his eyes, too.

"We all have our space cadet moments," he said.

The sparkle in his eyes. The warmth of his voice. The way she felt close to him. She could get used to those things about Zane.

She cut off a chunk of meat. The two of them ate

in silence. She hadn't realized how hungry she was until the first bite of food made her mouth water and her empty stomach cry out. The meat was stringy and charred but it was better than any lobster she had had off the pier.

After they both had eaten all the meat she'd cut away, Zane pointed to the carcass. "There's still meat on the bones if you want more."

She patted her stomach. "I think I'm full." She warmed her hands over the tiny fire.

Zane finished the rest of the meat and tossed the bones. He stared at the sky. "We better get going."

They put out the fire and stepped out into the open. The sun was low in the sky as they headed up the steep incline.

How long would it be before Willis and his men figured they'd given up on getting out by way of the river?

"How many men and boys are with Willis?" Heather asked.

"The number is hard to figure out. When I was with him, there were a number of people who lived in town who helped him and sympathized with his crazy beliefs, and then there were the true believers who stayed with him in the wild."

"How many of those were there?"

Zane stopped walking, tilted his head toward the sky, probably to mentally count. "Maybe thirty men and boys back then. I doubt the number has changed much. He always finds his share of new boys, but not everyone sticks around. Some—like me—leave by choice. Others get arrested for a variety of crimes, or recognized as runaways and brought to the authorities."

Her chest squeezed tight. They'd seen at least twenty

men and boys. "Are they scattered all over the high country?"

"Willis liked to have several camps. He figured that made us stronger. If the law came down on one camp, he wouldn't lose all his men at once." He walked for several more steps. "I doubt he has changed his strategy."

They pushed on through the night until darkness descended, slowing their progress.

Zane pressed close to Heather. "I know it's hard to see, but I think we should keep going."

She picked up on the urgency in his voice. "Did Willis always camp in the same place?"

"He moved around, but he had some favorite hideouts."

She wondered if they were close to one of those hideouts but was afraid to ask. Her heart was already beating fast enough and every cell in her body was on high alert. If she had learned anything in the last two days of running, it was that she should never let her guard down.

They walked in silence with the stars twinkling above them. Her own breathing and the pounding of their footsteps created a strange harmony. They separated slightly, but she could still tell where he was by the sound of his boots padding across the hard earth.

Her foot gave way beneath her. She stumbled then fell, rolling several feet. Darkness surrounded her.

"Zane?" Her heartbeat drummed past her ears. Every second he didn't answer, panic embedded deeper into her. "Zane?"

Clouds rolled by above her and she reached out to climb up the incline she'd tumbled down.

She heard a voice above her.

"There you are," Zane said. The voice drifted down to her, though she couldn't even make out his silhouette.

She let out a heavy breath. His voice was a comfort in the darkness.

"It's just so dark. I lost you in an instant," he said. "Are you hurt?"

"I don't think so. I didn't fall that far." She was beginning to wonder how prudent it was to travel by night without any light. "If you could give me your hand?"

No response.

"Zane?"

She scrambled up the rocky incline, feeling for solid ground. Instinct told her not to cry out again. She'd probably given away their position by crying out in the first place.

Instead, she crouched and listened. It took a few minutes for her to parse through the sounds that were just a part of the forest to hear something that might have been a grunt and one man punching another.

She crawled closer, waiting and listening, while her heart pummeled her rib cage.

This time the sound of flesh hitting flesh was more distinct. Still on all fours, she made her way toward the sound. Her knee jammed against some rocks, causing several to roll. She froze, fearing the noise had given her away.

Light flashed in her peripheral vision. Before she could turn toward the light source, clawlike hands dug into her shoulders, flipped her around and landed a blow to her jaw. Pain radiated through her whole face and down her neck. Her eyes watered.

She rolled onto her belly and struggled to get to her feet. In the darkness, hands grabbed at the hem of her coat. She thrashed, seeking to get away from her invisible assailant even as he grabbed her arm. She punched the air, hoping to hit something. Finally her hand connected with flesh. A voice grunted in protest and the grip on her arm loosened.

She turned and ran, stumbling over the rocks and veering away from where she'd fallen. Getting an idea, she slowed her steps. Maybe she could cause her pursuer to fall in the same way she had.

She kicked some rocks, making noise on purpose. Light flashed again. She saw the silhouette of a man just as he took a step toward her.

Her heart pounded. Adrenaline coursed through her body. She planted her feet, waiting, listening to the rapidly approaching footsteps. When it sounded like the man was close enough to grab her, she slid to one side as quietly as possible.

Rocks crashed against each other. The man screamed. She moved to get away from the incline, but she'd waited too long. A hand reached up and grabbed her ankle, pulling her down. She twisted around and landed on her butt. The impact sent vibrations of pain up her spine.

She kicked with the leg that was still free but only connected with air. The man pulled her down even more. She flipped over on her stomach, clawing at the rocky surface to get leverage.

A light blazed off to the side. This time it remained on and another man approached her. His foot pressed on her hand.

She wasn't about to cry out in pain.

"Let's quit this dog and pony show." The voice was Jordan's. He shouted down at the other assailant. "Get up. We've wasted too much time." Jordan pulled Heather to her feet and yanked her hands behind her.

The venom she heard in his voice sent shivers down her back.

Jordan shouted at the man who had fallen down the incline. "Crawl up out of there and let's get moving." Jordan pressed Heather's hands together and wrapped rope around them.

He pushed on Heather's back. "March, double time."

He switched on his flashlight and used it to point. "That way." He held his gun up so she could see it. "Trot and don't try anything."

As she took a step, Heather tried to calm herself with a deep breath. Was he marching her into the woods to shoot her or was she still *useful*?

"Did you catch Zane, too?" She purged her voice of the fear that had invaded every cell of her body. Was this the end for her?

Jordan didn't say anything.

Heather stopped and turned sideways.

He lifted his gun. "Keep going. Toward those trees."

His voice gave nothing away.

If this was the end for her, she had to let Jordan know how much Zane cared about his brother. "He keeps a picture of you two together when you were kids."

Jordan's hand clamped on her shoulder, and he spun her around. His face was close enough to hers that she could see the whites of his eyes even though he held the flashlight at an angle. "I know what you are trying to do. You're lying to me so you can try to break me."

She held his gaze despite th[...] [...]
through her for her own life. "No, [...]
what I am trying to do. I'm telling y[...]

An emotion flickered across his fa[...]
curtains seemed to come down over h[...]
giving them that glazed look of the brain[...] ...My
brother left me."

"He left *Willis*, not you."

That little moment of vulnerability she'd witnessed
gave her hope. Maybe she wouldn't live to see it, but
Zane might get his brother back.

Jordan's features hardened. Whatever door had been
opened had slammed shut. "Turn around and march toward those trees. I can't believe how much time we've
wasted."

That was the second mention of wasted time. Whatever it was they had planned, it must have become
more urgent.

Heather made her way toward the trees wondering
if she had only minutes to live.

ELEVEN

Zane's head hurt where he'd been hit with the butt of a gun and his hand ached from the gunshot wound. He'd fought hard against the three other men who ambushed him. But in the end, he'd lost. One of the men continued to hold a gun on Zane, even though Zane's hands were bound.

Zane had no idea what had happened to Heather. They'd gotten separated in the fight and darkness.

The second man watched from a distance, a sneer on his face. All of the men were older, better equipped and better trained than the teenagers and young men he and Heather had first encountered.

Static sounded on the second man's radio. He pressed a button and turned away, talking in low tones. All Zane could pick up on was a lot of "yes sir, no sir" remarks.

When he got off the radio, he signaled for the third man who Zane recognized as John, the man he'd stolen the ATV from. They put their heads together, and then the John picked something off the ground and stalked toward Zane. Once he was close enough, Zane could see that the man held a hood.

He wasn't leaving without a fight. Zane put his head down and charged toward John, who held the hood, knocking him down. The man with the gun grabbed him from behind and hit him once again in the head. Zane buckled to his knees as black dots filled his vision.

The man with the gun leaned over and picked up the hood, placing it over Zane's throbbing head.

"You just never quit fighting, do you?" said the man with the gun. "You don't need to see where you're going, pal."

He was led some distance through the trees. He had no idea where they were headed other than they were pointed north. The wind gusted around him. He felt a tap on his shoulder.

"Get on the ATV," said John.

Zane estimated that they traveled over steadily rising terrain for at least twenty minutes before they stopped, and his captors commanded him to dismount. He was led along another path. He smelled a dampness that indicated they were near a cave.

A hand was placed on top of his head, and he ducked down. He was commanded to sit, and he obeyed. Fading footsteps indicated someone had left the area, but he sensed that someone else was still in the cave with him.

The warmth from a fire covered his face and chest. He sat on a thick animal fur. He heard the grunting of someone repositioning himself. The fire crackled.

Zane had a pretty good idea who was in the room with him. Willis liked to play psychological games. The silence was meant to intimidate him. As a young man, he might have fallen victim to the games and tricks Willis used, but no more. He could wait out the master manipulator if need be.

With the hood still on his head, Zane closed his eyes and prayed. More than anything, he hoped that Heather was okay.

Willis was the first to break the silence. "Been a long time, Zane."

Zane did not respond. He just kept praying.

"Pull his hood off," Willis barked.

A hand grabbed the hood and yanked. The guard stepped back and pressed against the cave wall, still holding the hood. It took a moment for Zane's eyes to adjust to the dim light. He spotted another guard at the entrance of the cave.

His eyes traveled around, assessing the possibility for escape. He let his eyes wander for a long time, knowing the man wouldn't appreciate being ignored. If he could get the man to lose his temper, he might slip and release some information that Zane could use. But finally his eyes turned to his old mentor.

Willis had white hair in a buzz cut. His clean-shaven face revealed high cheekbones. Though his skin was leathery from time spent outdoors, his slim physique made him appear much younger than his fifty or so years. As always, he was in top athletic shape.

Willis lifted his chin. "Heard the old man died." His voice took on a mocking tone. "Too bad."

The remark was meant to sting, to put Zane on the defensive about the man who had meant so much to him. Though his heart ached at the mention of Stephan's death, Zane gave nothing away in his expression.

"I suppose you're wondering what all this cat-and-mouse stuff has been about." Willis flicked away debris on his shirtsleeve.

"You never play a game just to play a game."

"True." Willis rose to his feet and stared down at Zane. Nothing Willis did was an accident. The change in position was meant to dominate Zane. "It seems we need your expertise."

Zane was sure the expertise referenced was not his ability as an outfitter. Willis knew this mountain better than anyone.

"The man who trained you to build thermite bombs has to serve a lengthy prison sentence," Willis said.

A bomb. One of Willis's plans had always been robbing banks using explosives—usually on commission to acquire an item someone wanted. An enemy to any authority other than his own, Willis enjoyed making the bank employees and customers feel threatened and exposed by breaking down the security they took for granted, and the money he made from acquiring the item for his own customer helped keep his ragtag group in supplies.

Zane had been in training to help with that goal when he left the group. Thermite bombs were designed to melt metal at high temperatures. Willis must have either been hired or gotten wind of a low-security bank that had something of value in it. A thermite bomb would melt a vault door. "You know I won't build something that destructive."

The robberies took place after-hours, and the instructions were always to disable any security guards rather than kill—Willis knew better than to provoke the kind of manhunt that killing indiscriminately would cause—but there was still a chance of people getting seriously hurt. It had happened before.

Willis shook his head. "How did I know that would be your response?" He lifted his chin toward the guard by the door, who immediately left the cave.

A moment later, the guard returned with Heather in tow. Zane's chest went tight. She had a gag in her mouth, and her eyes held a haunted quality. Rage rose up inside of him. If they had hurt her...

Willis continued to talk as though he didn't even see Heather. "Now we have gone to some trouble to gather all the materials for you, and you *will* comply."

Willis didn't have to say "or else" to get his message across. If Zane didn't build the bomb, Heather would die and probably be tortured first.

"What did you do to her?"

"Relax. We just made her run a little. You know hurting women is not my thing." Willis's tone remained casual, as though they were two men exchanging fishing stories.

Willis lifted his chin toward the guard, who picked Heather up and dragged her to the cave entrance. The look of fear in Heather's eyes as she gave Zane a backward glance cut him to the bone.

Willis leaned close to Zane's ear. "I trust you'll want to get started right away."

Zane resisted the urge to hurt Willis. Rage coursed through him like hot lava, but he kept his expression neutral as Willis straightened.

"Take him to where he needs to be." Willis turned his back.

The second guard sprang into action. Resolve formed inside Zane. He wasn't going to build the bomb, but he had to find a way to escape and get Heather free, too.

As they walked out of the cave and through forested areas, Zane could pick out several camouflaged tents. Was Heather in one of those? He had to find out where they were keeping her.

Whatever it took, he was going to get Heather and himself out of this compound. And he would do everything in his power to prevent the attack Willis had planned.

The guard pulled Heather through the brush until he came to a hole similar to the one she'd fallen into days ago.

"I'll undo your hands. You lower yourself down by that rope." The young man pointed toward a mud-soaked climber's rope.

A weariness had set into Heather's bones. Though the guard looked to be barely out of his teens, she knew trying to escape would be an act of futility. If he didn't catch her, one of the other men she saw wandering around would. Her hands gripped the rope, and she slid down to the bottom of the pit. A layer of straw covered the mud floor. The guard threw a dirty backpack down to her, pulled up the rope and covered the hole with a lid woven from sticks and tree boughs. A little moonlight filtered through the tiny holes.

Heather collapsed on the straw and opened the backpack, which contained a canteen, jerky and dried fruit. She ate the fruit and had a sip of water. She rose and wandered around the deep pit. It was a good twenty feet to the top, and there was no place on the slick muddy walls to get a grip. She took her boot off and used it as a trowel to try to dig a foothold in the wall. Her hands became muddy from the effort, but eventually she made some progress. She stood back to catch her breath.

By the time she had started on the second foothold, the sky had grown darker. Voices and footsteps alerted her to someone approaching. She dived back down on the straw, slipping her foot without the boot under her leg and hiding the boot under the backpack. The lid to the hole was drawn back. She shielded her eyes as a flashlight beam shone in her face. Her heartbeat kicked into high gear. If they saw the holes, she'd be dead.

The man shining the light on her appeared in silhouette. Finally he pulled back, taking the light off her and then placing the cover on the hole again. How many times in the night would they check on her? She waited until she heard fading footsteps before jumping up. She felt along the wall to where she'd been digging. After some time, she was muddy and out of breath, but the second foothold was in place.

Loud rock music played in the distance. She heard voices shouting and guns being shot.

She shoved her foot that still had a boot on it in the first foothold and placed her hand in the second hole in order to dig the third one. Her bare foot grew cold as she reached up and dug into the muddy wall. The task would take forever. She had to keep jumping down to rest from the strain on her muscles.

Approaching footsteps made her resume her position on the ground by the backpack. The lid slid back and a rope came down.

"Climb up. We need you," a disembodied voice said.

She hurried to put her boot on. "Can you give me a

second? I was sleeping." She wiped her muddy hands on the backpack, rose to her feet and gripped the rope. "Okay, I'm ready." She tried to climb, but her arms felt weak. "Can you help me a little?"

Even her body had its limits. Two days of running with little food and sleep was taking a toll.

She felt a tug on the rope as she held on and was pulled up. She reached out for solid ground, climbed to the surface and let go of the rope. A hand gripped the back of her shirt and lifted her up.

Off in the distance, a huge fire had been built. Men danced around, shooting guns and playing loud music. She saw the glow of lanterns in several tents.

The man behind her pushed on her upper back. "Get moving."

They walked away from the camp into the darkness of the forest. Her heart seized up. Was this man going to shoot her?

She slowed down. He punched her shoulder blade. "Where are we going?"

He didn't answer.

Her chest squeezed even tighter.

She took several more steps deeper into the forest.

"Stop here." His voice was devoid of emotion.

Heather swallowed to try to produce some moisture in her mouth. She couldn't get a deep breath.

"Put your hands behind your back." He poked her with the hard barrel of a gun.

She did as he said and the man wrapped rope around her hands and jerked it tight.

"Don't try anything." The man stepped out in front of her, got down on all fours and proceeded to pat the ground.

Her heart raged against her rib cage. It felt like her chest had been wrapped with a tight bandage. What was going on here?

The man swung open a door on the forest floor. Light flooded out.

He turned to face her. "Go down those stairs."

She took a step toward what looked like some kind of underground bunker. She placed her foot on the first wooden step.

"Don't even think about running. I have a gun pointed at you," said the man.

She stepped down the remainder of the stairs. The door above her closed. Glancing around, she saw that the bunker had concrete walls lined with stacks of food, cots and a machine that was probably a generator. A guard stood in a corner. Zane sat at a table, pieces of metal, wire and containers in front of him. The hand that had been shot was wrapped in a fresh bandage.

A look of shock filled Zane's features when he saw her.

She must be a muddy mess. "I'm okay. They didn't hurt me."

The guard stalked toward her. "Shut up." He grabbed her shirt at the shoulder and dragged her toward a chair.

"Don't treat her that way." Zane lurched toward her, but was stopped by the chain around his foot.

The guard pushed her down into the chair and then took his position back against the wall.

She raised her head to meet Zane's gaze.

"No talking," said the guard as his hand brushed over the gun holstered on his waist.

Zane raised his eyebrows and attempted a smile as if to lift her spirits. The gesture in such dire circumstances warmed her heart. She lifted her chin, trying to give him a positive message back.

Between them was a large wooden box holding a revolver. The guard remained in the corner, his hand hovering over his own gun.

The only sound in the room was a clock ticking away the seconds.

Zane stared at her, and she kept her gaze on Zane. She saw compassion in his eyes. The clock kept ticking. The room felt unusually warm. Sweat poured past her temples. She fixated on the gun in the box.

Clearly someone was playing some sort of sick psychological game. She pulled her gaze away from the gun and stared at Zane. Looking into his eyes was the only thing that made her feel safe.

A door scraped open to the side of her. She turned her head. No one stepped out. Minutes passed. More game playing. Trying to increase her fear.

She turned again to look at Zane. He shook his head and shrugged his shoulders, a gesture that was meant to reassure her, but she saw the fear behind his eyes.

She heard footsteps and the door opened farther. Finally, the lean older man with a short buzz cut she'd seen earlier in the cave stepped into the concrete room. He crossed his arms over his muscular chest. His smile sent chills down Heather's spine. His eyes were an icy blue. When she had first seen him, the arrogance and the air of authority he gave off told her the man must be Willis.

He signaled to the guard, who walked across the room, picked up the revolver and spun the cylinder around before locking it in place. He put the gun back down on the table.

"It seems Mr. Scofield here thinks it's okay to try to trick me." Willis shifted his weight and crossed his arms over his chest. "By hiding some of the chemicals needed to make this bomb work." Willis took a few steps toward Zane, combat boots pounding on the concrete. "There is always a price to pay for betrayal."

A long moment of tense silence was followed by the tapping of footsteps. Someone else was coming into the room. The door creaked open even wider and Jordan entered.

He stepped toward Heather. Her whole body stiffened. She glanced at Zane, who had gone completely white.

Jordan looked over at Willis, who gave him a nod. Then Jordan picked up the gun on the table and pressed it against her temple. The room seemed to be spinning. She tried to focus on Zane. Her vision blurred. She couldn't tell what he was trying to communicate with his expression. Her breath caught in her throat.

Jordan pulled the hammer back and placed his finger against the trigger. She squeezed her eyes shut and the trigger clicked.

Nothing happened.

Her whole body was shaking as her eyes blinked back open.

Jordan pulled the gun away from her head, turning slightly toward Willis.

Heather glanced toward Willis, who nodded. "Again," he said.

"No, please." She looked over at Zane, expecting to see rage for what was happening to her. Instead, he offered her a small shake of her head. He was trying to tell her something. How could she feel reassurance with a gun pointed toward her head?

Jordan placed the gun on her temple again. She gulped in air as tears streamed down her face. Was she going to die here? She lifted her head, locking onto Zane's gaze. Now she saw the warmth and compassion she'd searched for. His eyes seemed to be almost pleading with her.

It must be tearing him up to know that his brother was this brainwashed.

Again Jordan pulled the hammer back. A long moment passed before he placed his finger against the trigger.

Heather bit her lower lip and held her breath. The trigger clicked. She cringed, expecting a blast and then darkness.

She opened her eyes to the concrete room and took in a sharp breath. Zane was still there staring at her, trying to communicate something with his eyes.

It felt as though an elephant was sitting on her chest.

Willis's voice pelted her. "That's probably enough for now. I'm sure Mr. Scofield finally sees the error of his ways."

The guard lifted Heather off the chair. Her knees buckled, and she struggled to stand up. Her legs were as limp as cooked noodles.

The guard half dragged, half carried her to the door. He knocked on the door with his gun. The door swung open, metal hinges creaking. Another guard peered down.

"Take her back." The guard pushed Heather toward the stairs. It took all her strength to walk up them.

The second guard grabbed her shoulder and pulled

her up. She took a few steps and fell on the ground. Her knees pressed into the snowy earth. She was still shaking from the emotional torture she'd endured.

"Get up."

She stared at the ground. "Please give me just a moment." She tried to get to her feet but collapsed.

"Fine, I'll take you to medical." The guard lifted her up and roughly carried her to a tent. He dropped her on the tent floor. "Get in there and wait."

With her hands still tied behind her back, she scooted inside the tent. Through the open tent door, she could see the guard pacing outside.

The revelry by the fire had died down, though she still heard occasional shouts and gunfire. Willis's army was finally settling down for the night.

A man poked his head inside the tent. He studied Heather for a moment and then crawled inside. He carried a backpack with him that had a red cross on it.

"Anything broken?"

She shook her head.

He unzipped a pocket on the backpack and pulled a flashlight out. "I need to check your eyes."

She recoiled.

"I'm not here to hurt you in any way. That is somebody else's job."

He turned the light up on the lantern that sat in the middle of the tent. Heather thought she detected a hint of compassion in his voice. Something she had witnessed in none of Willis's other followers.

"Are you a doctor?"

"Combat medic. Iraq. Three tours."

He shone the light in both her eyes. The man seemed

almost normal. "Why are you here with Willis?" she asked.

"I have PTSD that led to episodes of violence. I don't fit into polite society anymore. When everyone I knew turned their back on me, Willis took me in."

"My name is Heather."

He stopped rummaging through his bag and met her gaze. "I'm Nathan. You look pretty shook up. Do you want a sedative?"

The last thing she needed was to be sedated. "No."

"Then I'll just recommend that you be sent back to wherever they're keeping you."

She leaned toward him, wishing she could make a connection with him by touching his arm, but her hands were bound behind her. "Please, I need your help."

He pulled away. "Forget it, lady. I never want to get on the wrong side of Willis. The guy gives me three squares a day, and all I have to do is stitch men up when they bleed." His raised his voice as though he wanted whoever was listening outside to hear. Then he leaned closer to Heather. "I'm bugging out. Willis is planning on robbing the bank in Fort Madison. He got word that some rich guy just put a bunch of valuables in the safety deposit boxes. The other guys are acting like it's totally normal, just another day on the job. I didn't know they were like that when I joined up. I can't be a party to the things they're willing to do."

"Can you go down and warn the bank?"

"I've got my own legal troubles that keep me out of town. I'll take my chances living on my own in the wilderness."

Before she could react, Nathan moved toward the door of the tent and shouted, "She's ready to go."

He dug into his pocket and threw an object by her hands before leaving the tent.

She scooted on her bottom a little to grab the object. Her hand wrapped around cold metal. Nathan had thrown her a pocketknife. A guard stuck his head into the tent. She gripped the knife in her fist to hide it.

"Let's get moving," said the guard.

She worked her way toward the tent door while he stood outside waiting. Strength had returned to her legs. She gripped the pocketknife, hoping the guard wouldn't notice. He pushed her in a different direction than the pit she'd been left in before.

The guard pointed toward a small shed. "Nathan thought you would do a little better aboveground." He opened the door.

She stepped inside the dark space and slipped down to the floor. She was exhausted, and the trauma of having a gun to her head had taken its toll on her body, but she needed to find a way to escape and to get Zane free, as well.

She flipped the knife around in her hand until she could open it and saw away at the rope that bound her. As she worked, she tried to come up with a plan. She had a better feel for the layout of the camp. The place where they were keeping Zane was away from everything else. That might help in being able to secure his freedom unnoticed.

Time was of the essence. The cover of darkness was one of the only things working in her favor right now. She sawed on the rope and prayed that she and Zane could get out of here alive.

TWELVE

"You get an hour to sleep." Jordan didn't make eye contact when he approached where Zane was working.

Zane couldn't bring himself to look at his brother either. Was Jordan so far gone that he was indifferent to the cruel torture he'd put Heather through?

Zane knew Willis's games, and he'd seen that the gun didn't have even one bullet in it. Willis needed Heather alive for now to use as leverage until the bomb was complete. The stunt had been to scare her, not to actually hurt her. He had tried to communicate that to her without much success.

Jordan tossed a key on the table so Zane could undo his shackles. Zane knelt down and stuck the key in the slot. He knew without looking that Jordan had a gun trained on him. The betrayal hurt.

This was his little brother. They'd stood holding hands at their parents' funeral, shivered together in the dark and cold when they'd run away from foster care, protected and taken care of each other. But now his brother had become someone he didn't know at all.

Zane placed the key on the table and Jordan leaned to get it.

He couldn't give up. Jordan was blood. As repulsed as he was by what Jordan had done to Heather, he had to believe that the Jordan he loved was still inside that body and mind.

"There's a cot over there in the corner," said Jordan.

Zane's muscles were stiff from leaning over the worktable for so long. He'd built the bomb as slowly as possible. Twice Willis had ordered the guard to hit him for being too slow. He'd delayed as much as he could. He tried to come up with a way that would make the bomb look like it would work, but not be operational. But Willis knew enough about bomb building to catch him in that. Hiding the chemicals had been a last-ditch effort to create a bomb that wouldn't work.

Zane glanced up to where he was sure a camera was. He had no doubt that Willis was watching them. The underground bunker had only been a dream seven years ago. Willis must have been here since the spring to have time to build something like this.

Feeling defeated, Zane collapsed onto the cot. He knew if he spoke the microphones would pick it up. How could he reach Jordan?

Jordan pulled a chair across the floor. The scraping noise of metal on concrete made Zane cringe. Jordan sat in the chair. Still holding the gun, he crossed his arms.

Zane stared at him, hoping to force him to make eye contact.

Jordan glanced from side to side, deliberately not looking at Zane.

The room was especially warm. Zane took off his flannel shirt. His gaze fell to the tattoo on his arm, the one that said "Brothers are Forever." Jordan had the same tattoo. Zane crossed his arms and tapped the tattoo over and over.

It was hard to read emotion in Jordan through the thick hair and beard. Zane wasn't sure whether or not Jordan even noticed, but he didn't stop trying. He just kept tapping the tattoo. If Willis or one of the guards were watching, they probably wouldn't understand what he was doing.

Zane thought he saw some sort of emotion flicker across Jordan's face.

Jordan shifted in his chair, pointed the gun toward the floor and stared down the barrel. "Why don't you get some sleep?"

Jordan's back was to the camera. If he wanted to show some sign he got what Zane was doing, he could.

Jordan finally made eye contact. What Zane saw in Jordan's eyes was glacial.

A deep sadness sank in as he realized how lost his brother was. "What did Willis promise you? Some kind of promotion?"

Jordan looked to the side as if seeing some faraway scene through the wall. "Get some sleep. We need to get that bomb built."

Zane lay down and flipped over on the cot so he faced the wall. He closed his eyes but knew he wouldn't be able to sleep.

A moment later, he heard Jordan get up from his chair and stomp across the floor. He tapped on the trapdoor. It swung open on creaking hinges. Jordan shouted up at the other guard. "Hey, can you take over? I'm beat."

"Sure, man." Zane heard more stomping and the

door closing. The guard grunted as he sat down in the chair.

Zane made deep breathing noises so the guard would think he was sleeping. His mind was racing too fast for him to even close his eyes.

As soon as the bomb was finished, both he and Heather would be killed. They only had a few hours to live unless he came up with a way to escape.

Heather tore the cut rope off her wrists. The shed was small, maybe four foot square, made from one of those kits you could buy at a home-improvement store. She pushed on the door. It opened. That meant that there was probably a guard close by. She eased the door open just a bit and poked her head out. The large central bonfire still smoldered, but the men who had gathered around it earlier were gone. She heard snoring, but could see no movement anywhere. No sign of someone pacing with a rifle. She slipped outside, crouching and listening, waiting for her eyes to adjust to the light. She couldn't assume she'd just be able to walk through the camp. It might have been a trap to leave the shed unlocked. She had a fleeting moment of wondering if it *had* been locked and Nathan had come by and unlocked it when no one was looking.

As she was able to discern objects in the dark, she saw the source of the snoring—a man propped against a tree with a rifle resting across his lap. She skirted away from the guard.

Voices alerted her to two men walking by. She flattened herself against the ground, not even daring to breathe as their footsteps pounded past her. She could easily navigate to the bunker where Zane was by going through the camp, but there was risk of being seen.

She opted to head toward the forest, circle around the edge of the camp and try to find the bunker that way. She hurried through the trees running in the general direction of the bunker. But after a few steps, she stopped, confused. Had the bunker been this way? Or another way instead? There was nothing distinctive about the part of the forest where the bunker was. She could end up wandering around here until daylight, and then her opportunity to get Zane and escape the camp would be gone.

She feared, too, that the guard might wake up to check on her. Then the camp would go on full alert. She had to hurry.

Heather scurried as fast as she dared until she had a view of the camp. Several men sat by a smaller campfire talking in low tones and cleaning their rifles. Their backs were to her. Now she saw the trail that led to the bunker. She'd have to sneak past the men, coming close enough to be detected if she wasn't careful.

As she crouched by a bush, she watched. The men seemed engaged in their conversation. None of them lifted their heads or looked around.

She rose and sprinted for the cover of the next bush.

There was an eruption of loud noises at the other end of the camp. Adrenaline shot through her system. The men at the fire jumped to their feet and ran in the direction of the noise. She pressed low to the ground as they rushed by her.

Once they were out of earshot, she headed toward the trail running through the trees. She stayed to the side of it—she'd be too visible if she walked along the path—but kept the trail in sight. More men dashed by on the trail. Some sort of alarm had been sounded. Had they checked the shed and found out she was gone or was there some other disruption?

She hurried into the forest again. The eruption of voices increased and more men ran through the camp. The trail ended. Her gaze darted around. Panic threatened to make her shut down. Nothing looked familiar. Where was that trapdoor? She ran in one direction and then the other, remembering that a guard had been posted outside the door. She didn't see anyone. Had he already left to deal with the disruption on the other side of the camp? It didn't seem like a guard would abandon such an important post when there were plenty of other men to deal with the disturbance.

The noise on the other side of the camp grew louder. They were coming this way. She sprinted through the forest, frantic to find the trapdoor. Finally, she spotted trees that looked vaguely familiar. She ran back and forth in a zigzag pattern until her foot touched metal. She got down on her knees and brushed the tree boughs away. If there was still a guard inside, he would hear the door creak as it opened. She found a log, flipped open the door and stood back waiting for the guard to stick his head out.

She raised the log. Footsteps came her way.

The noise of the mob of men reached her ears. They were getting closer. They must be looking for her. The guard's footsteps sounded on the stairs. Sweat trickled down her back as she waited. She would only get one shot at this. His head emerged and she swung at him just before he turned and would have seen her. The guard crumpled to the ground. She pushed him aside and rushed down the stairs.

Zane leaped up from a cot as soon as he saw her. He ran across the room and grabbed his coat.

She felt suddenly dizzy when she entered the room as images of the torture she'd endured bombarded her.

Zane grabbed her arm. "You did good. Let's go."

White dots filled her field of vision.

"I'm sorry for what happened here. But I promise you were safe the whole time. There were no bullets in the gun." He squeezed her arm above the elbow and brushed his hand tenderly over her cheek.

He instinctually seemed to know how the room affected her. The comfort of being near him again made some of the panic recede. The spots cleared from her eyes, and she was able to follow him when he pulled her toward the open trapdoor. Once outside, she saw torches in the distance down the trail, men growing closer. They must be searching for her. They'd probably figured out she'd come to rescue Zane.

Zane pulled her toward the trees just as several men stepped into the clearing. They ran haphazardly through the forest. Branches brushed her head. She jumped over logs that seemed to loom up toward her in the dark. She kept her eyes on Zane's back as she gulped in air and willed her legs to move faster, be stronger. *Run, run, go.*

Zane darted even farther ahead of her. She heard a crackling and swooshing sound. Zane groaning. She caught up with him to find that Zane hung in a net suspended from the air. Willis's men must have set traps all over the forest.

She could hear the men approaching. She only had

seconds to free him. She pulled the pocketknife out. The torches shone through the trees as the shout of the men pounded on her ears.

She had to stretch her arms to reach the netting that held Zane captive.

"Heather, there's not enough time. Run. At least that way one of us will be free. They'll have no leverage against me to force me to finish the bomb if they don't have you."

She glanced over her shoulder. The men were breathing down her neck. But she wasn't ready to give up. "I can get you out." She reached up to cut a strand of the netting.

The noise of the pursuers pressed on her from all sides.

Zane's voice intensified. "Go."

She could hear the men as they pushed their way through the trees, drawing near.

She cut another strand of the netting. The men were within yards of finding them. Her face was very close to Zane's.

"Go," he whispered.

He was right. "I'll come back for you. I'll get you out."

"I know you will."

She dashed off into the darkness, praying to God she would be able to keep her promise to Zane.

THIRTEEN

Zane listened to Heather's retreating footsteps. The men came into the clearing. Jordan was with them.

"Spread out," Jordan said. "We need to find the girl."

The men ran in several different directions, leaving Jordan and one other man to get Zane out of the net. It tore Zane up inside to think of Heather out there alone in the cold night.

Zane tried to keep his tone light, still hoping to reach Jordan. "I forgot about all the traps, little brother."

Jordan didn't respond. Instead, he walked to where the release was for the netting and pulled it.

The impact of hitting the ground sent waves of pain through Zane's back. The other man tore the netting off Zane while he kept a gun pointed at him.

"This will have to be reset," said Jordan.

"I can get that done," said the second man.

Jordan pulled out his own gun, which had a light on it. He pointed it at Zane. "Let's get moving. You have a bomb to finish."

The image of his brother pointing a gun at him nearly broke Zane's heart. "Oh, Jordie," he said, shaking his head. His brother was the only blood he had. How had it gotten to this point?

In the limited light, he couldn't read his brother's response to his heartfelt cry. He thought he saw Jordan's shoulders slump, but was that just wishful thinking?

Jordan led him back to the bunker, then disappeared through the side door without even a backward glance. This time, the guard didn't shackle Zane to the wall. He stared at the nearly complete bomb in front of him before sliding down the wall and sitting. At least for now they had no way of making him finish the bomb.

A moment later, Willis and Jordan burst through the side door.

Willis crossed his arms and stood with his feet shoulder width apart. Jordan took up the same stance.

"I think it's time you complete your job," Willis ordered, jerking his chin up.

"I'm not building your bomb. I'm not participating in whatever destruction you have in mind."

Willis signaled the guard with a head nod. The guard marched across the concrete and pulled Zane to his feet. Zane braced to be hit or tortured or whatever they had in mind. He didn't care what they did to him.

The guard hit Zane in the back with the rifle. His knees buckled, and he grabbed the table for support. He offered Willis a glance that had steel in it.

"Kill me if you want. I'm not finishing that bomb." Zane spoke through gritted teeth.

The look of stone-cold indifference on Jordan's face hurt worse than the blow to his back.

Willis stared at Zane for a long moment before pulling his radio off his belt and saying something into it. A moment later, the trapdoor opened and another guard appeared.

Willis's blue eyes seemed to turn even icier under the cold fluorescent light. He kept his gaze on Zane while he spoke to the guards. "It seems Mr. Scofield here is not properly motivated to complete his job. What can we do about that?"

A long heavy silence descended in the room like a shroud.

Jordan crossed his arms and lifted his chin.

"What we need to accomplish here is so important for the future of our country, don't you agree, Jordan?"

Jordan nodded.

Willis continued, still not taking his eyes off Zane. "You've been my right-hand man for almost a year now, haven't you?"

Again Jordan nodded, though his gaze darted from one of the guards to the other and his forehead wrinkled. He didn't seem to know where this was going. That made two of them.

Willis walked over to the table where the gun they had used on Heather still lay. He opened the cylinder and pulled a bullet out of his pocket, put it in and spun the cylinder. He stared at the gun. "Yes, what Mr. Scofield needs is the proper motivation."

Zane straightened and placed his hands on his hips as a show of defiance toward Willis. Fine, Willis could play Russian roulette with him if he wanted to. He didn't care if he died; he wasn't going to have it on his conscience that a bomb he'd built was used in a crime to terrorize people and steal their prized possessions. He wouldn't be able to live with himself anyway.

Willis signaled both the guards. They moved in and

grabbed Jordan, forcing him to sit in the same chair Heather had sat in.

Jordan protested. The look in his eyes was wild.

Zane had seen that look when Jordan had been unfairly punished for something another kid had done in the boys' home they'd been placed in.

The two guards secured Jordan to the chair while he struggled to break free. The cry that came out of Jordan's mouth sounded almost childlike.

Watching Jordan resist made Zane feel like his own heart was being torn out. Willis had never cared about people. His own twisted goals meant more to him. Zane had figured that out once he was no longer under Willis's influence. But Jordan was clearly figuring that out for the first time. It had to be a harsh shock that Willis, the man Jordan looked up to and admired, saw him as expendable.

Once Jordan was restrained, Willis walked over to him. His boots pounded on the concrete. He raised the gun and pointed it at Jordan's temple, still staring straight at Zane.

"Do you feel properly motivated now?"

Zane could not tear his eyes away from Jordan. He was breathing through his teeth and sweat glistened on his forehead. The look of utter defeat in Jordan's eyes spoke volumes.

Zane stared down at the bomb components and then back up at Willis as he held the gun to Jordan's head. His brother might die, just when he'd started to see Jordan's loyalty cracking. This final act of betrayal may finally help Jordan see Willis for the selfish egomaniac he was, but it might be too late.

"Get to work," said Willis. He pulled the hammer back on the revolver.

If this bomb got built, a robbery would happen. Even if no one was hurt or killed in the robbery itself, Willis might end up using the money from the robbery and the pot farm to finance more destruction and even death.

"What exactly are you planning on doing with this?"

"Quit stalling." Willis shifted his weight and jammed the gun barrel against Jordan's temple.

Zane glanced at his brother, who looked like he'd completely fallen apart.

He couldn't let Jordan die. He'd have to find another way to stop the snowballing of this violence.

As he picked up the container that held the chemicals to create the bomb, he prayed that Heather had escaped and found a way back into camp. He would do everything he could to get out of here to prevent the disaster Willis had in mind, but he needed her help. The only way out of this was if they worked together. All his hope for a good outcome hung on that.

Heather entered the camp just as sunlight peeked through the trees. This time she had no problem finding the bunker. With all the chaos in chasing her and Zane, the branches to cover the entrance hadn't been replaced. Even better, a guard had not been put back on the trapdoor. It was not a safe way to enter the bunker though. They'd hear the door opening and have too much time to prepare as she came down the stairs. And there was probably at least one guard inside.

She remembered the side door where Willis had come from. Maybe there was a separate entrance.

She had to act fast. Men were still out looking for

her. She'd managed to throw them off the trail and double back, but it would be only a matter of time before they tracked her down.

She scanned the area around the trapdoor and looked up toward where Willis's cave was. Maybe there was a passageway between the cave and the bunker. That might be why Willis came through the side door.

After glancing over her shoulder, she hurried up toward the cave. No guard stood outside the entrance. She slipped inside, prepared to fight if she had to. A man slept in the corner with his back to her.

She tiptoed deeper into the cave. Light shone from one of the openings. Her chest squeezed tight. All of this might be a waste of precious time. The sleeping man started to roll over. She dashed toward the lit tunnel.

She hurried through the cool dampness of the cave. Battery-operated lights revealed the path she needed to take. As she rounded a corner in the tunnel, voices echoed. Whatever she was stepping into, it would be dangerous. Nathan was the only member of Willis's army who had not shown blind loyalty to Willis and he was probably gone by now.

The cold stone of the cave turned into wood. She stepped into an area filled with shelving that contained food, cleaning supplies, blankets, first-aid kits and boxes of bullets. The supplies someone might need to survive long-term.

The voices grew louder and more distinct as the distortion from the echo in the cave faded. Now she could discern Willis's voice.

She had no gun, no weapon at all but her pocket-knife. She couldn't just enter the bunker. She stared at the shelves of food and supplies. She remembered from high school chemistry class that if she put sugar and the potassium nitrate from the cold packs in the first-aid kit together, she could create a smoke bomb. Maybe that would be enough of a distraction for her to get Zane out. She worked to gather the items and a container to hold them. She grabbed a box of matches.

The voices in the room next to her quieted. She tensed, fearing Willis would come stomping through at any moment. Her heartbeat drummed in her ears as her hands trembled. Once her smoke bomb was assembled, she eased toward the door. Silence seemed to press on her from all sides. What exactly was going on in that bunker?

She'd have only a moment to take in the scene before smoke from her bomb filled the room. She lit the matches that served as a fuse and held the bomb until it began to smoke.

Another voice floated into the room. "Please stop doing this to him. Doesn't his loyalty mean anything to you?" That was Zane's voice.

"Get back behind the table." Willis sounded nervous.

Zane must be making his move. Now was the moment. She pushed open the door and tossed the smoke bomb as she entered the room. Zane had come out from behind the table where the other bomb was being built.

She caught a flash of Jordan tied to a chair, his head hanging, hair covering his face. Was he dead? Willis turned to see her, a gun in his hand, just as the room filled with smoke. A gunshot reverberated through the concrete room. Zane found her hand in the smoke. She pulled him toward where she thought the door was.

Her hand touched solid wall. She reached for the door. Her fingers scraped over what felt like metal hinges. She lunged toward a break in the concrete. The smoke followed them into the supply room but dissipated enough that she could see where they were.

She pulled him through the room.

He stopped. "We have to get Jordan."

Willis kicked open the door and aimed the gun at Heather as the smoke cleared.

There was no time to go back now. She took off running, knowing that Zane would be right behind her. In the narrow enclosed storage room, the noise of the gunshot made her ears ring. The bullet must have pierced the food supplies because flour poured out of a bag above her and spilled onto the floor.

She hurried up to the cave, where the guard was now wide awake. Though he appeared surprised to see Heather, he lunged at her, reaching for her neck. Zane came up from behind and landed a blow to the guard's jaw just as he grabbed Heather.

The guard pounced on Zane and tackled him to the ground. Zane rolled across the cave floor, coming dangerously close to the fire. He managed to get on top of the guard and land several debilitating blows to the man's face and chest. Eventually the guard seemed to lose his will to fight. Zane got off him, breathing heavy and ready to jump into the battle again.

Flames shot up around the hem of Zane's coat.

Heather pointed. "Fire!"

Zane glanced down.

Though he still looked disoriented, the guard picked up a stick by the fire and raised it to whack Zane on the head. Heather charged toward the man from the side.

The move caught the man off guard. He stumbled sideways.

Zane ripped his coat off and stomped on the flames. The man recovered enough to lunge toward Zane with the stick still in his hand.

Heather jumped on his back and bit into his shoulder. The man yowled and tried to shake her off. Zane landed a blow to the man's stomach that doubled him over. Heather slipped off the guard's back.

"Come on, we don't have much time." Zane hurried toward the cave entrance.

Willis appeared at the other entrance.

They dashed out of the cave. Men rushed toward them from down below. Willis must have radioed ahead.

Panic flooded through Heather's awareness. "We can't go down there."

Zane headed up the mountain. A rifle shot bounced off a nearby rock. Heather froze. She could feel herself shutting down as her vision blurred. This was all too much. Zane turned and grabbed her hand.

"We've made it this far. Don't give up."

His voice was enough for her to shake the paralysis. They pushed up the mountain and over the other side. Wind rushed around her as they stood on the summit. Down below, several men were still snaking up the path toward them.

Zane rested his hand on her shoulder. "It looks like they're giving up."

She glanced down. The men had slowed their pace.

"The real danger will be at the bottom of the mountain on the other side. They can get around to there with their ATVs faster than we can get down. They'll be waiting to ambush us."

She tensed. "When will this stop?"

"We are witnesses, Heather. Willis is not going to let us out of the high country alive."

Her stomach tightened into a knot.

He grabbed her at the elbows and pulled her toward him. The look in his eyes intensified. "I know you want to give up. But hold on. Can you do that for me?"

She nodded, but felt as though her knees would buckle.

He drew her into his arms. "You're smart and strong. You got me out of that bunker. We can do this."

His arms enveloped her. She melted into the warmth of his embrace breathing in the scent of his skin. "I just don't see how."

He held her close. "There is more at stake than just you and me. A bank robbery is going to happen—they have the explosives to make it happen. I couldn't let Jordan die. I had to assemble the bomb."

She relished the strength she got from being held by him. "I know you did everything to prevent it, but I wish the bomb wasn't finished."

"It may be finished, but it won't work without this magnesium ribbon." Zane pulled what looked like a piece of metal out of his pocket.

"That will make him hunt us all the harder." Her voice faltered.

"This isn't just about us. I don't know what exactly Willis has planned, but we have to stop him," Zane said.

He was right. She'd seen firsthand that Willis was evil. "I have it on good authority that Willis is going to rob the safety deposit boxes in Fort Madison. Apparently, a rich man around here has recently put items of value in there."

Zane smoothed over his beard. "Makes sense. He likes to target low-security, rural banks like Fort Madison." He touched her elbow. "Let's keep moving."

Fear permeated every cell of Heather's body as she stared down the steep incline knowing that they were probably walking into an ambush and that they had no choice.

FOURTEEN

Zane worked his way down the steep mountainside with a heavy heart. He'd left his brother behind, even though Jordan might be in a different place now that Willis had betrayed him so horribly. Maybe now he'd be ready to leave Willis.

Heather stumbled on a rock as she ran beside him. He grabbed her arm at the elbow. He had to think of Heather. She'd risked her own life to save his. He wiped his mind clean of the pain thinking about his brother brought up. "You all right?"

She gave him a raised eyebrow look. "Just peachy."

He smiled despite their dire situation. "I appreciate the positive outlook."

He stared down the mountain. They could see most of the valley from this vantage point. Though he didn't see any men or ATVs yet, he knew it was just a matter of time.

"Is there some way we can avoid them?"

He picked up on the fear in her voice and wanted to say something comforting, but he couldn't lie to her. "The descent is treacherous, and there are only a few places where we would come out into the valley. I'm sure they will post guards at each of them."

She let out a breath and shook her head. "Are we anywhere close to getting out the way we had planned?"

He shook his head. "At this point, it would be faster to try to get out by the river."

He watched as she climbed. Her focus was on the rough terrain as she slanted her feet sideways to keep from slipping. Her long dark hair was still pulled back in a single braid. She'd been so brave and strong thus far. And this wasn't even her fight.

He gripped a rock and worked his way down, as well. What could he say to her that he hadn't already said? Holding her close had renewed his own strength and resolve. He wondered if she had felt the same way.

As they made their descent, he kept watch for signs that Willis was assembling forces below. He caught a glimpse of ATVs moving through the trees. He had to assume they were walking into a firefight.

Heather's feet slipped, and when she fell, she remained seated. He came up beside her and cupped his hand on her shoulder. The look on her face was of complete exhaustion.

"Rest a moment," he said.

She pulled her glove off and patted his hand. The warmth of her touch seeped through his skin.

She stared at the sky. "I know these men are dangerous. I know they need to be stopped."

She must be trying to find some inner resolve to keep going. He sat beside her, resting his elbows on his thighs.

She leaned against his shoulder.

"I wish there was an easy way out of this," he said.

He studied the valley below and the possible trails to get to the base of the mountain.

She covered his knee with her hand. "Me too."

"Your father used to tell me that the harder something was, the more worthwhile it would be in the end. That there was value in the struggle."

She caught him in her dark eyed gaze. "Sometimes I feel like when I look at you, I get a glimpse of my father. If he hadn't come into your life, you would have been like Jordan...so lost."

Sadness washed through Zane all over again and he hung his head. "I tried to get him out when I left. I really did." Maybe since Willis had used Jordan in such a horrible way, his brother might still be reached. He had to hold on to that hope.

She leaned closer and touched his back. "I didn't mean to upset you. I only meant to say you're such a good man, it must mean my father was, too, at the end of his life."

He turned to face her. Her brown eyes held a spark in the early-morning light. He felt drawn to her.

He rested his hand on her cheek, leaned in and kissed her. She responded. Her lips were like silk as he deepened the kiss.

He pulled back first, tracing the edges of her face with his fingers. Her expression brightened beneath his touch.

He wanted to stay in that moment forever, but down below, he heard the sounds of ATVs and caught a flash of color and movement.

"They're already getting into place," she said. Dread tainted her words as the special moment between them gave way to reality.

They might not be able to avoid Willis's men altogether, but he could increase the odds that they would be able to escape. "We can come out where the ATVs can't go. Then we're just dealing with men on foot." He stood up and mentally scoped out the path they would take.

He hurried down the steep hillside, slipping a little. Heather was right behind him. She crashed against his back several times until they were in thick brush and could hold on to the trees for balance.

A rifle shot zinged over their head. Both of them ducked.

Zane studied the surrounding hills until he saw the glint of glass reflecting the sun. Willis had put a sniper in place. Anytime they were in the open, they'd be easy to pick off. Both he and Heather were targets now. Willis didn't need Zane alive anymore. He just needed the magnesium strip, and the men could take that off Zane's dead body. He thought to simply toss it away, but decided it might buy them leverage if they were caught.

"Every time the terrain opens up, stay low and move slow." The camo they both wore would give them a degree of cover, but a really good sniper knew what to look for. "Put your gloves in your pockets. They make you too easy to see."

They worked their way down the steep mountainside until they came to an open area covered with rocks. The camo wouldn't do them any good here.

"Move as fast as you can and stay as close to the brush as you can get," he said.

"Why not just go into the brush?"

"Too thick. Too treacherous." The tangled junipers and other brush would be impossible to navigate through.

Heather took the lead, dashing across the rocks, choosing the larger ones for cover. The first shot hit a stone right in front of Zane. His heart skipped a beat but he kept running.

Heather was within ten yards of cover when another rifle shot sliced through the air. She went down.

His heart seized up as he hurried toward her, expecting to see a pool of blood seeping out from beneath her. Another shot came close to his head. He couldn't get to her without being a target himself. He dived behind a large rock and poked his head around it. She still wasn't moving.

"Heather." His voice cracked.

She turned her head to face him. "I'm all right. Just lost my courage."

Relief spread through him. For a moment, he'd seen his life without her, how empty it would be.

She offered him a faint smile before rising and bolting for the cover of the trees. He looked across the landscape to where the sniper was positioned. Then Zane jumped to his feet and made a mad dash for the cover of the trees.

The sniper probably had the best spotting equipment money could buy. He might even have a spotter helping him. Even if he couldn't get a clean shot off, he would be able to track them down the mountain.

Though he kept his pessimism to himself, he wasn't real hopeful about their chances of making it to the bottom alive.

* * *

Heather was out of breath as she pushed her way through the thick brush.

Zane came up behind her, placing his palm on her back. "Wait." He studied the area in front of him. "We're almost to the base of the mountain. Let's go horizontal until we can find a good place to exit."

She knew he was looking for potential ambushes. The more treacherous the path they came out on, the less likely it was that they would be caught.

Zane stopped and crouched low, peering through the trees. The brush was so thick she could only see a few feet in front of her. She pressed close to him and listened. Branches creaked in the wind. A crow cawed from a distant tree.

She didn't hear or see anything that suggested Willis's men were lying in wait. If they were there, would they eventually grow nervous and impatient and start to talk? Or would they remain hidden and silent, weapons drawn, watching for any movement?

Zane signaled for her to keep moving. He made an abrupt turn and headed toward the base of the mountain, running in a serpentine pattern to stay in the cover of the brush.

She could see the base of the mountain and the forest beyond. Zane came to where the brush ended and crouched. He must have studied every tree, trying to discern movement.

Finally, he signaled for her to step out. She followed behind him. Her gaze darted everywhere. It felt like an elephant was sitting on her chest as her ears tuned into all the sounds around her.

She tried to take in a deep breath. As the landscape

leveled off and opened up, Zane broke into a trot. She ran beside him, still expecting to be attacked. Every once in a while, he'd stop and study the landscape and look at the sky.

Her hands grew cold. She slipped her gloves on while she kept running.

She watched the trees for any sign of movement or flash of color. Still nothing. It didn't seem possible that they had outwitted Willis's men. But gradually the fear of getting caught was overwhelmed by other concerns. She was exhausted and hungry. And it was cold enough that she could see her breath. Zane ran shoving his bare hands into his pockets from time to time.

She stopped and pulled her gloves off. "Here, we'll take turns."

He put the gloves on. They ran through the day. Gradually the terrain started to look familiar. She recognized the mountain peak, the place where she was supposed to spread her father's ashes. The slim wooden box still pressed against her rib cage.

Clouds covered the sun. "Let's build a small fire and get warmed up," said Zane.

They gathered tinder and wood and chose a place where the trees surrounded them so the fire wouldn't be easy to spot.

She made a seat of dry evergreen boughs, sat and crossed her arms, mesmerized by the flames. Her legs ached from having run for days. And her empty stomach growled.

Zane found a plastic pop container that a hunter must have dropped or littered on purpose. He cut off the top, washed it with snow and then melted snow in it so they had something to drink. They passed the container back and forth, both of them staring at the fire.

"Why haven't they come for us?"

Zane scooted close to her. "We may have outwitted them. He might have only put a few men at the base of the mountain. My guess is that Willis positioned his men at all the points we might use for escape. That means his forces are spread pretty thin. Maybe two or three guys at each post."

"So if we try to cross the river at that other bridge to get back to Fort Madison, he'll probably have men waiting for us there?" She shivered, not from the cold but from the possibility of another battle.

"We have to cross the river. From where we are at now, it's the fastest way out."

She knew he was right.

Zane rubbed his beard with his hand. "Here's what I think we should do. They're expecting us to try to cross at one of the bridges. So I say we make a raft and just float down into Fort Madison."

Make a raft? Was he light-headed from exhaustion? "The only tool we have is my pocketknife."

"I know. And we'll have to come up with something to lash the poles together. If we can't make something seaworthy, we won't do it. But it's an option we need to consider."

Despair sank into her bones. Had it come to this unrealistic idea? She let out a heavy breath. "It just seems time and energy consuming. Aren't you wilderness guys always weighing energy expenditure against results and outcomes?"

"And you know this because—" There was a note of amusement in his voice.

"The survival shows on Discovery Channel."

Zane laughed. "Okay, so maybe my head isn't working right due to a lack of food. What do you suggest?"

She stared at the fire. Her stomach growled. "We need sleep and food and weapons."

"Stopping to rest is out of the question. Willis's men have the only weapons and food nearby. Are you saying we should ambush them?"

The thought made her stomach squeeze tight. "Some of the guys with him are just boys. They might have food on them and weapons for sure. If we get the chance, we should try."

Zane raised his head, brushing both hands over his beard. "Willis used to leave stashes of food and sometimes weapons buried or high up in the trees in case we were ever attacked. They'd be marked in a unique way. I forgot all about that."

Now she felt like they were getting somewhere. "So what were the markings like?"

"Something from nature, but out of place all the same. Roots braided together and hung on a tree or a ring of dried leaves. He might still be doing that."

A tree branch cracked not too far from them. Both of their backs straightened as they lifted their heads. Zane rose to his feet and kicked snow on the tiny fire. "Could be nothing but let's not take any chances."

She stood up, studying the trees section by section. Her heart drummed past her ears. "What if it's someone we could overpower?"

He tugged on her sleeve. Another noise—this one more distinctly human, a grunt—made them both take off running.

As they ran, she could hear the man or men behind

her charging toward them. Her tired leg muscles burned with pain. Still, she kept up with Zane as they jumped over fallen timber and angled through narrow spaces between the trees.

The pursuer never closed in on them but remained close enough that stopping and hiding wasn't an option.

She could feel herself slowing down and weakening. Zane decreased his pace, as well. One of the men was almost on top of them. They'd come this far and gotten this close; she wasn't about to give up. Both of them sped up to put more distance between them and the man or men chasing them.

When they could no longer hear their pursuer, Zane dived behind a log and flattened out. She scooted close to him. Her breathing sounded unbelievably loud.

She heard the footsteps of their pursuer as he ran through the trees past the log. Was it really just one guy out by himself? It seemed like Willis always sent the men and boys out in pairs.

"He might come back," Zane said. "We should try to take him. Grab a rock and climb a tree. Hurry."

With some effort she found a tree whose boughs would shield her from sight. Zane chose a tree not too far from her and climbed up. The minutes ticked by. She heard noise off to the side deeper in the trees. Maybe their pursuer had gotten sidetracked.

She heard a different man approaching, walking much slower. Heather took in a breath and prepared to be the attacker instead of the attacked.

FIFTEEN

Zane held the rock, ready to drop it. A tremendous crashing and breaking of branches coming from a different direction alerted him. An elk moved into his field of vision. Even from this angle, the animal was huge and magnificent. Its hooves pounded the earth as it thundered across the terrain. When it left the clearing, the area seemed even more silent.

A moment later, a teenage boy holding a bow stepped through the forest. One of Willis's followers, no doubt, hunting out of season. There were other things taking place besides chasing down Heather and Zane. The men relied heavily on the wild game they hunted. Zane realized even if the kid did come near the tree, he couldn't drop the rock on him.

These boys and young men were not truly evil, though they had been taught to do evil things just to stay alive or avoid Willis's wrath. They were lost just like he had been. Just like Jordan was.

He watched as the kid moved stealthily through the trees and decided that ambushing him would be pointless. The bow wouldn't be much of a weapon anyway. If they were going to face Willis's men at the river, they needed a gun. The bow hunter disappeared into the thick of the forest.

Once he was sure the bow hunter was gone, he dropped his rock on the ground. "Let's head toward the river. That kid was chasing down the elk, not us. If we do get a chance to jump one of them who has a gun and not kill him, we should take it."

Heather climbed down, dropping the last five feet to the ground. They hurried through the trees for at least half an hour. A smell filled the forest. Zane recognized that coppery taste in his mouth. They were getting close to a fresh game kill.

Heather put her hand over her nose. "What is that odor? Is it…a body?"

He picked up on the fear in her voice. "Yes, but it's not human." Zane made his way through the trees until he came to where the elk carcass lay. The bow hunter had worked fast. The animal was already dressed out and the hunter was gone. The teenager was on foot with no means of transporting the fresh meat before it spoiled. That meant he must have radioed for more men to come this way to pick it up.

The bow hunter had probably already moved on to try to get more game before the day was over.

"Let's get out of here." Zane tugged on Heather's sleeve. He heard noises to the side of him. He crouched behind some brush and Heather pressed in beside him.

Three young men wearing backpacks ran past them. One of them stopped to check his compass. "It's around here somewhere. Hurry."

These men were not after Heather and Zane. They were the cleanup crew for the elk. Less experienced and probably not fully trained to fight. He turned to-

ward Heather. They could probably take one of the boys
and get a weapon with no one being hurt. She nodded,
showing she understood.

They leaped to their feet and fell in behind where the
teenagers had just run. He could see that at least two
of them had guns. They needed to wait for the chance
when one of them was far enough away from the others to be vulnerable.

The boys' rapid pace slowed as they seemed to have
lost their sense of direction. One of them checked the
compass again. "I think we've gone too far. Let's split
up. A hundred paces in different directions. Holler
when you find it."

Zane dipped behind some brush, splitting off from
Heather so they could come at the kid approaching
their direction from either side.

Once he was in the cover of the trees, the kid slowed
down and walked more aimlessly.

Zane caught a flash of movement through the trees
that told him where Heather was. The kid stopped,
placed his pistol on the ground and leaned over to tie
his tennis shoe.

Heather ran ahead, bursting through the trees. She
grabbed the gun and pointed it at the kid. "I don't want
to hurt you."

The kid held up his hands. "My friends will be coming back this way."

Zane stepped into the clearing after her just as the
kid whistled—probably some sort of signal for the
other two. "We don't want to kill anyone today. That
was never the plan."

A moment later, the other two young men appeared

on the opposite end of the clearing. One of them raised a rifle and pointed it in their direction.

Heather kept the gun steadily pointed at the first boy even as she said, "I really don't want to have to shoot anyone today."

Zane raised his hands in surrender. "We just need the gun."

The young man aimed the rifle at Zane and then at Heather. But his hands weren't steady, and those were not the eyes of a killer. He was afraid. That didn't mean he wouldn't impulsively pull the trigger though, which made him just as dangerous.

"We really need to get out of here." Tension threaded through Heather's words.

Zane called out, "If you'll just let us back off…" He turned his head sideways and spoke to Heather in a low voice. "Take a step back."

Heather continued to look down the sight as she backed up.

Zane pointed. "Your elk is off that way about thirty paces. If you don't get to it quickly it will spoil, and then you'll be in trouble."

The kid still twitched between aiming the gun at Zane and at Heather. The second young man only had a knife. Just as they slipped back into the trees, the second kid pulled out a radio and spoke into it. Great. Now that they'd been located, Willis's whole army would descend on them.

Both of them rushed through the thick forest. Zane directed their route toward the river.

Heather stopped, speaking in between breaths. "You should take the gun, since you're the better shot."

She met his gaze momentarily. There was a weightiness in her stare. "I couldn't shoot that kid. It was a total bluff."

"I know." The last thing he wanted to see was one of those boys die. Looking at them was like looking in a mirror at himself seven years ago. Willis was the bad guy here. All these kids deserved some kind of chance at a normal life and maybe a father figure who didn't attach conditions to his affection or make them fear his wrath.

They ran out into open, flat country, the sound of the river growing more prominent. Within minutes, they heard ATVs roaring across the landscape, becoming louder and closer.

The river came into view, a welcome sight. They hurried downhill to the steep, brush-populated bank.

"Let's get down there. It's a little narrow, but it gives us some cover."

Heather held out a hand for balance as she descended. The roar of the water filled his ears when he climbed down behind her. The path between the steep bank and the river was extremely narrow. They held on to the brush and balanced on a ledge no more than a few inches wide.

The dark, foaming water rushed over rocks and pushed debris downstream at a rapid pace. He'd already experienced the freezing chill of the river once and had no desire to live through that again.

Heather slipped and her toe dipped into the water. He caught her elbow.

"I'm all right," she said.

This close to the river the temperature dropped several degrees. They worked their way along the narrow bank. Though the sounds of the ATVs indicated that they were still not in the clear, the pattern of noise and the way it grew louder and then fell away indicated that the searchers were still cutting a wide swath to find them.

If they were found out, they would be like fish in a barrel. Although he was sure that Willis had ordered the men to retrieve the missing bomb component, the men wouldn't be foolish enough to shoot in such a way that Zane fell in the river and floated away with it.

They made progress inch by inch on the narrow pathway. The wind picked up a bit and his hands turned colder and stiff since he couldn't put them in his pockets for warmth. He needed to use them to balance. The shoreline opened up into rocky beach that allowed them to walk without risk of falling into the river.

The beach curved around. Zane slowed his pace. Up ahead he could see that several men were camped out where access to the river was easy. He and Heather were shielded from view by a rock formation.

"What do we do now?"

"We have to get back up on the bank and circle around them."

They started their ascent just as the sky turned a dusky gray. Once he was back on level land, Zane lay flat in the short grass and watched the men. There were three of them and they'd built a fire. Every ten minutes or so, one of them picked up a rifle and paced out a big circle. They must have been positioned here for some time. Their posture and lack of attention to their surroundings suggested boredom rather than vigilance. But Zane knew that all that apathy would switch to violence if they saw Heather or him.

Heather stayed close to Zane. Zane pointed at the

trees and then crawled commando style toward them. Several times, he glanced in the direction of the men to make sure no alarm bells had gone off for them.

Once they reached cover, they got to their feet and sprinted away from the river. A shout to the side of them told him they'd been spotted. Once the alarm was sounded, the forest seemed to come alive with pursuers. The ATVs were on top of them within minutes.

He and Heather ran as fast as they dared, forced to go through a part of the forest that had been burned by fire. They wouldn't find much cover in this part of the forest and the camo did them no good. The noise of men on the move seemed to surround them. Had they come all this way only to lose?

He'd run until he had no breath left. He was pretty sure Heather would do the same. He heard the barking of a dog, and it was like a blow to his gut. This was not going well. He prayed even as he sprinted and skirted around another burned tree.

God, please help us.

The noise of the pursuers seemed to surround them on three sides. Zane made a beeline toward where the forest had been unaffected by the fire. Though he was relieved to reach an area where the evergreens hid them from view, they weren't safe yet. They kept running. Zane wasn't sure how they were going to get away. He felt the fatigue in his own body. These men had had time to rest and refuel. He and Heather had not.

All the same, they kept a steady pace through the evergreens.

Jordan stepped into the clearing in front of them.

Both of them stopped.

Jordan had a gun in his holster but it wasn't drawn.

"Come with me, I can get you out of here."

Zane's throat went dry. Was his brother telling the truth or was this a trap?

Heather could feel her cheeks flush and her heart race at the sight of the man who had held a gun to her head. Clearly, this was a setup. She turned on her heel to run away.

Zane caught her by the elbow. "I think he's telling the truth. A lot happened back at that bunker."

The baying of the dog grew louder and closer.

"We don't have much time," said Jordan.

Heather couldn't shake her confusion. Jordan still looked wild eyed.

"This way." Jordan took off running.

Zane pulled Heather along even as she wrestled with uncertainty. Zane was Jordan's brother. Maybe he saw something she couldn't see. All she knew of Jordan was his violence and his loyalty to Willis at all costs.

The dog was so loud it sounded like it was at their heels. The forest grew denser. The trees were close enough together that it slowed their progress. Heather glanced over her shoulder. She could still hear the dog but not see it.

Jordan patted Zane on the shoulder and pointed. "Go on up ahead. I'll catch up with you."

They hurried through the thick grove of barren aspen trees.

Heather jogged as she spoke. "How do we know he's not leading us into a trap?"

Zane pushed through the trees staring straight ahead. "Things happened. I think Jordan's becoming disillusioned with Willis."

Was Zane seeing that in his brother because it was true or because it was what he so desperately wanted?

The barking of the dog grew farther away. Jordan must have pointed the searchers in a different direction. A few minutes passed and Jordan came running through the trees. "I've thrown them off for now. Come this way."

Jordan led them through the forest.

Heather felt a tightness in her chest. Where was Jordan taking them? He must know that Zane had the bomb component. If that was all he wanted, he could just shoot them. As far gone as Jordan had seemed, maybe even *he* couldn't shoot his brother. Could that small piece of humanity be left inside of him?

Her anxious thoughts tumbled one over the other. Finally, she planted her feet. "Where are you taking us?"

Jordan turned toward her. She thought she saw a flare of anger in his eyes. "We've only got a few minutes before that dog picks up the trail again. We need to keep moving."

Zane squeezed her hand and then took off running. She chose to follow even as she battled uncertainty. The grove of aspens ended, and they stepped toward a rocky incline. Jordan climbed with ease up the incline. Heather held out a hand and gripped a jagged rock. Jordan hadn't asked for Zane's gun. Maybe he did intend to help them.

A chill ran down her spine when she thought of the gun pressed against her temple and the coldness she'd seen in Jordan's eyes. She wanted to believe they weren't being set up. All the same, fear made it hard for her to keep going.

The rocky area leveled off. She glanced down below,

where she saw several men and the dog headed up the same winding trail they were on.

"They're gaining on us."

Jordan and Zane's response was to walk faster. Heather fought to keep up on the narrow trail. The brush was thick enough down below that she could only see their pursuers in quick flashes, which meant the pursuers wouldn't have a clear view of them either.

The barking of the dog intensified.

"They're getting too close," she shouted up ahead.

Jordan turned and lurched toward Heather. She took a step back as her heart pounded against her rib cage. He grabbed her at the elbows, sending shock waves of fear through her. Zane came toward them.

In his usual gruff manner, Jordan pulled Heather toward him and then pushed her in Zane's direction. "Take her and hide up there behind those rocks. Hurry."

Zane gathered her into his arms, but her panic levels were still high from having been manhandled by Jordan.

Zane whispered in her ear, "It's going to be okay."

She wasn't so sure about that. A man didn't change years of ingrained thinking in a few days.

They slipped behind the rocks, shoulders pressed close together, just as their pursuers arrived.

She could catch only bits and pieces of what Jordan said to the group of searchers, but it sounded like he was rerouting them and suggesting they go in a different direction because of what he had seen.

One of the men in the group seemed to protest Jordan's order.

Jordan raised his voice to shouting level. "What I say goes."

The dog continued to bark excitedly.

Zane leaned close to her as the wind buffeted around them. His hand slipped into hers. She had no idea what Jordan was up to, but she knew she could trust the man who crouched beside her. They waited for a long moment as the barking of the dog faded.

Jordan popped his head around the rock. "Come on, hurry."

Why did Jordan insist that they simply follow him blindly? Why couldn't he explain what he had in mind, where he was taking them?

Fear gripped her heart.

Jordan led them up another incline without saying anything more. He stopped midway down the other side of the mountain and looked around.

Heather turned nervously from one side and then to the other, half expecting armed men to emerge through the trees.

Jordan walked over to a distinctive white rock and then counted out ten paces before dropping to his knees. He turned and looked at Zane. "Give me a hand here."

Jordan started to clear away rocks and debris from a flat area. Zane knelt beside his brother and began to help. So did Heather. Gradually a steel plate came into view.

Jordan pulled a knife off his belt, flicked it open and used it to twist a dial on the steel plate. Jordan pushed the plate open and pulled out a bag. He tossed what looked like packets of food toward Heather and Zane. "Take this GPS." He threw a small velvet bag in their direction. "There are coordinates programmed into it that will take you the high point on the mountain range above the river. You'll find a stash of paragliding equipment there. Flying over that river is the only way you can avoid Willis."

Jordan closed the lid to the steel box and screwed it shut. All of them worked again to cover it with leaves and dirt. Once they were finished, they stood. Jordan patted his brother on the shoulder. "I need to get out of here before I'm missed."

Zane leaned toward his brother as though to give him a hug. Jordan stepped away, turned and disappeared down the trail.

Heather let out a breath, not sure what to think or believe.

Zane opened the bag with the GPS device and then studied the mountain. "We'd better get moving. We have about half a day's hike ahead of us."

"Do you think he's telling the truth?"

"We don't have a lot of choice here, Heather." A tone of defensiveness colored Zane's words. He skirted past her and took off walking.

She startled when she heard a rustling in the forest.

Zane came up beside her, drawing a protective arm across her back and cupping her shoulder. "Wild animal, maybe. Just keep moving."

They continued on the trail at a little quicker pace, running single file on the narrow path. Suddenly, two men jumped out on the path in front of them. Each held a gun.

They turned to run in the other direction.

Two more armed men stepped out onto the trail, blocking their path of escape.

Behind those two men stood Willis. "Well, well, well…what have we here?"

SIXTEEN

Zane could not believe what he was seeing. The emotional devastation nearly made him drop to his knees. They'd been surrounded—as if Willis had known their location all along. Had his brother betrayed him? At the core of his being, he didn't want to believe that was true.

Willis rubbed his buzz cut and stroked his clean-shaven jaw. "I think you have something I need."

Zane's thoughts felt muddled. He couldn't let go of what Jordan had done. Was it really possible? But he knew he had to push those feelings aside to focus on the danger of their situation. Once Willis got the magnesium strip, both he and Heather would be shot.

One of the men holding a rifle leaned close to Willis. "You want me to search him?"

Willis waved his hand. "I am sure Mr. Scofield will give me what I want of his own free will."

Willis could just shoot them both and search his lifeless body for the component. With Willis, though, everything was about domination and control. And right now he wanted Zane to surrender the strip and admit he was beaten.

The back of Heather's hand brushed his, then she slanted her gaze down the mountainside.

"You win, Willis." Zane shot her a quick look and then reached inside his jacket as though to pull something out.

With all eyes—and guns—pointed at Zane, Heather leaped off the trail and down into the thick trees. Zane followed. A few seconds passed before the gunfire started. The abundance of narrow lodgepole pine provided them with a degree of cover, though the mountainside was so steep they were practically sliding down. Would the men follow them into the treacherous terrain or run on the trail and try to meet up with them at the bottom?

His guess was that Willis would split his forces. Two down the steep mountainside and two on the trail.

The hillside became so steep that both he and Heather sat down and slid rather than trying to run, braking with their hands to keep from going too fast. A gunshot broke up the dirt close to his feet. When he glanced over his shoulder, he saw movement through the trees.

They continued to slide until the trail came back into view. Both of them jumped to their feet and started running. He heard shouting behind them. Another gunshot ricocheted off a tree close to Heather. She grabbed his arm. Her eyes were filled with fear. He patted her upper arm trying to reassure her. "Just keep going."

Their feet pounded the trail as they struggled to move faster.

The trail lengthened out into a long straightaway. The men were only twenty yards behind them. He and Heather headed back into the thick of the woods. The mountainside was not as steep here, but it was still way more treacherous than the trail.

Heather's foot caught beneath a root. She fell forward. Zane reached out and caught her, but the fall had cost them precious seconds. One of the men stepped out, aiming his gun at them.

He and Heather turned to head up the mountain into thick cover of the forest, but the second man stepped through the trees aiming his gun at them, as well.

The second man said, "Put your hands in the air. You best be heading down to the trail."

Both Zane and Heather complied. Zane's heart still raced from exertion and adrenaline. He fought off the impending sense that they were defeated and without hope. There had to be a way out. There had to be a way to stop Willis.

One of the men walked a few paces away and spoke into a radio. The man who was left to guard them looked like he was fairly young, maybe in his early twenties. His beard was splotchy and his eyes darted around nervously. His white eyebrows contrasted with his red hair.

"Can I put my hands down?" Heather said. "I'm getting tired."

The redheaded man nodded. "Just don't try anything."

Heather let her arms fall. Zane did the same. The man on the radio stopped talking and turned to face them again, aiming the gun at Zane. The redhead had his gun on Heather.

They waited for what seemed like an eternity. And then footsteps sounded on the trail above them.

From behind, they heard applause. And then Willis's voice. "A valiant effort. I taught you well, Zane. Just like I taught your brother."

The last comment was intended to cut through Zane's heart. The possibility that his brother had betrayed him weakened him even more.

"Both of you turn around and face me."

They turned slowly. Rage boiled to the surface when he saw the smirk on Willis's face, but Zane held it in check. Any sort of outburst could be deadly.

Willis held out his hand. "So, I think you have something I want."

Zane didn't move. His mind reeled, struggling to find a solution, but with three guns trained on them at close range, there was no way out that he could see.

Willis shook his head and made a tsking noise. "Not going to give it up, huh?"

Willis signaled the older of the two men, who opened his revolver and emptied it of all the bullets but one. He then dived and grabbed Heather by the hair, pushing her to the ground. She cried out when her knees impacted with the hard packed dirt of the trail. The man raised the gun to the back of Heather's head.

Zane's heart lurched. "I'll give it to you."

They were going to die anyway. Heather didn't need to go through the torture of roulette again.

"Very good," said Willis.

"It's in my inside pocket. I'll have to unzip it."

"I'm waiting," said Willis.

Zane reached inside his coat. He had a thought that he could just pull the strip out and toss it down the mountain. But once the strip was gone, he and Heather were dead. And there was too much risk the men would still be able find it.

His fingers grazed over the GPS device Jordan had led them to. Willis had not asked for the device. Did that mean he didn't know about it? Maybe Zane would die here today, but he refused to believe that his brother had betrayed him. Maybe Willis had been tracking them for some time and Jordan had had nothing to do with it.

He reluctantly handed over the component to Willis. Willis didn't even make eye contact as he walked away and barked orders at the two men. "I have a schedule to keep. We need to be in town by tomorrow morning." He put the component in his pocket. "I have no more need for these two. Do away with them." He cupped the shoulder of the redheaded man. "Earn your stripes."

Willis trotted down the trail, rounded a curve and disappeared.

Both men looked at each other. The older one only had one bullet in his gun, and the younger one didn't look like he could kill a rabbit.

"Turn around and get on the ground by your girlfriend," said the older man. Heather lifted her head to look at Zane.

This could not be the end for them. There had to be a way out. The older man opened the cylinder of his revolver to reload it, reaching into his pocket for the bullets.

Zane stepped as though he were going to move toward Heather but instead lunged at the redheaded man, punching him in his face and stomach. Zane grabbed the man's gun and turned it on the older man.

"You'd have to close the cylinder before you could fire, and with only one bullet, you'd have no way of knowing if it's the next one in the chamber."

The man held up his hands.

"Drop the gun."

He complied.

Heather hurried to pick up the discarded gun. She held out her hand. "Give me the other bullets."

The man dug into his jeans' pockets and slammed them into Heather's hand.

"Both of you on your knees, facing away from me."

"What are you going to do to us?" Fear permeated the redhead's voice.

Zane leaned close and said, "I'm not the animal Willis is." He knocked both men on the side of the head with the butt of the gun.

"Are they going to be okay?"

"They'll wake up shortly. And then I'm sure they'll come after us and bring reinforcements." He took the radio off the man and tossed it down the mountain. "You heard Willis. He's planning on hitting that bank in the morning."

He took off running up the trail.

"Where are we going?" She was out of breath as she spoke and jogged at the same time.

He turned to face her and patted the pocket where the GPS device was. "Willis didn't know about this. He didn't try to take it away from me."

"You think Jordan was telling us the truth. That he didn't set us up to be ambushed."

"It's the only shot we have. We've got to stop Willis from detonating that bomb."

Heather's forehead wrinkled. "What if we get to the place where the paragliders are supposed to be and they're not there? We will have wasted all our time on a fantasy."

His mind had been mulling over everything that had happened since Willis was able to find them so easily on the trail. Maybe Jordan had chosen to help his brother but still intended to stay with Willis. That possibility broke his heart. Was his mind so brainwashed that he'd stay loyal to Willis no matter what?

Zane shook his head. "This is our only option. We have to hope that Jordan was telling the truth."

Zane turned on his heel and ran, knowing that Heather would follow. He knew approximately where the high point on the mountain was that Jordan had referenced. They'd have to dip down into a valley and then climb up to the summit, a four-or five-hour hike if they kept up a good pace.

He glanced over his shoulder and slowed a little allowing Heather to catch up. The trail widened so they could run side by side. He could see only trees above him—very little light sneaked through this late in the day. Down below, he could still see some of Willis's men who had been part of the hunt. They weren't coming after him and Heather for the moment—but that would change as soon as the two men he'd knocked out woke up and shared the news that their would-be victims had turned the tables and escaped. Zane feared that someone would be waiting to jump them at the top of the trail as well.

After they'd rounded several curves and the men were no longer in sight, he stopped and pointed up through the forest. "We can't stay on this trail. They'll start looking for us here soon. There might even be men at the top."

She rested her hands on her hips, breathing heavily from the exertion of running. Both of them stared at the evergreens and steep hill that intersected with the winding trail.

"The trees will at least hide us from view," he said.

They pushed through the steep terrain, gripping the trees and brush to make it up.

He sat down to catch his breath and Heather sat beside him.

"We're almost to the top. If men were signaled that we were headed this way, they'll be looking for us but expecting us to come out on the trailhead."

Heather nodded.

"You might want to put those bullets in your gun now," Zane suggested.

She pulled the bullets from her pocket and clicked open the cylinder, placing the rounds in one by one. She clicked it back in place and put the gun in her pocket with the safety on.

They pushed silently through the trees until they had a view of the ridgeline. Zane surveyed the trees and the brush for any movement.

He crawled a little farther up, still watching. They used the shelter of the trees, walking parallel to the trail. His heart pounded out a wild rhythm as he braced for an attack.

The trees thinned, and they stepped out into the open. The wind was more intense without the shelter of the trees. They were on what was nothing more than a game trail. For the moment, they seemed to be alone.

Zane pointed out the route they needed to take. "We'll dip down into that valley and then climb up to the summit there."

Heather let out a heavy breath. "That's a long way."

It would be dark by the time they made it...*if* they

made it. "Once we get up to the summit, we'll be able to see the river on the other side.

"Let's eat the food Jordan gave us and then we'll have to run as much as we can." He glanced around again, still not seeing any signs of Willis's men.

They settled in with their backs against a fallen log. The only noise was the sound of their chewing.

"I hope you're right about Jordan," Heather said. "Not just so we can have a chance of getting into town, but because he's your brother." She placed her hand on his.

Zane squeezed his eyes shut. Willis had influenced Jordan at a very impressionable age. That sort of brainwashing didn't get erased instantly. "I hope I'm right, too. We'd better shove off. We've got a lot of ground to cover." He rose to his feet and turned to face Heather. "This wasn't your battle to fight. All this violence is because of me and my past. But you stuck with me without complaining." He touched his hand to her cheek.

Heather placed her hand over his. "I wouldn't have it any other way. I know now that my father must have been an extraordinary man—because you are. You must have learned it from him, just like Jordan learned violence from Willis."

He thought he saw the glow of affection in her eyes. Could there be something between them? Maybe if they got out of here alive and their lives calmed down. "It does matter who your fatherly influence is."

"My father's faith must have been deep because yours is. Makes me wish I had that kind of faith."

"How do you know you don't? Maybe it's just never been tested," Zane said.

A light came into her eyes and she nodded. "You

might be right. I know I've never prayed before like I have since all of this started."

They were both aware of the peril and risk they faced. There was still a chance Jordan had lied to them. They might not get off this mountain alive. Maybe that was what compelled them to speak so honestly.

He brushed his hand over her forehead and down her cheek. "We'd better get moving."

They stepped out onto the ridgeline and headed down into the valley at a steady jog.

Within minutes, men emerged through the trees, coming at them from both sides and at a high rate of speed—two men from the east and one from the west.

Zane and Heather ran faster through the snow-laden valley as the men closed in on them. Heather pressed close to him as he pumped his legs, willing them to go faster.

One of the men raised a gun to shoot at them. Zane grabbed hold of Heather and plummeted to the ground as the bullet whizzed over their heads. The snow was cold on his bare hands. He rose to his feet and helped Heather up.

They headed toward the shelter of the trees just as the men converged on them. They pushed through the trees with the men twenty yards behind them.

Zane studied the trees, looking for the markers that indicated traps had been set. He saw the subtle indicators that only expert eyes would notice. Notches in a tree, a piece of faded fabric tied to a branch. Maybe the old traps were still here and maybe these men didn't know about the older traps.

He ran in the direction he thought a net might be. The men were within forty feet of them.

He wrapped an arm around Heather and pulled her close when she nearly stepped on the trigger for the net. The men closed in on them. One of them raised his gun. Zane dashed out of the line of fire, hoping the men would follow him. Their pursuers ran through the clearing…and two of them were drawn up into the net, leaving them hanging upside down.

Heather came out of the shadows where she'd been hiding. She and Zane sprinted through the trees. Hopefully the third man would be delayed getting the other two out of the net.

They kept moving as evening came on, stopping only to catch their breath or eat a handful of snow while nibbling the jerky Jordan had given them.

The temperature dropped as they made their way up the mountain.

"Don't eat any more snow," Zane instructed at one point. "It will drop your core body temperature." They didn't have time to build a fire and melt some snow. They'd have to go without water.

The climb up the mountain became steeper and more treacherous, slowing their progress. Zane lifted his head. The summit was in sight. He only hoped they were doing the right thing, that Jordan hadn't deceived them and sent them on a wild goose chase. If he had, there would be no way to stop Willis—or for him and Heather to survive.

He prayed he'd made the right choice.

SEVENTEEN

Heather's arm muscles strained as she pulled herself up over a boulder. Their progress slowed to a crawl as they worked their way around rock formations and trudged up steep inclines.

In the dimming evening light, she could see the three men moving along behind them. They were far enough away that they looked like large bugs inching along.

She treaded up a steep incline, choosing where she put her foot carefully. A few rocks rolled down the mountain, banging against each other. Her throat was dry and she longed for a drink of water.

She hoped they hadn't gone on a fool's errand. Zane had a blind spot where his brother was concerned. He so desperately wanted to see Jordan's life turn around.

They came to a wide, sheer cliff face.

Zane put his hands on his hips and took in a breath. "We don't have time to go around this. We'll have to climb it using hand and footholds."

They had no ropes or equipment. The wall was maybe twenty feet high. A fall would probably not kill them, but it could severely injure them. She'd climbed faces like this before, but always with a harness and ropes.

"I'll go first. Follow me," he said.

Heather put her gloves in her pocket so she could grip the rock more easily. Zane worked his way up, moving sideways to find a firm hold. She put her foot into a crevice and reached for the first handhold. The rock was cold to the touch.

Zane was near the top when his foot slipped.

Her breath caught as she held on and watched helplessly. He dangled for a moment before securing another foothold. He pushed himself up and over the top.

Heather worked her way sideways and then up. In the waning light, it was hard to see the holds. She felt around until her fingers found a bump to grip. Zane reached down to pull her up.

His arms wrapped around her, and he drew her close. Her hand rested on his chest as she caught her breath from the exertion. His heart beat beneath her palm. She felt herself relaxing in his embrace, wanting to linger.

He held her a moment longer. "We should probably keep going."

She didn't pull free of his embrace. "Yes, I suppose."

She tilted her head. His finger traced the outline of her jaw and then his lips covered hers. His touch made her feel like she was melting. His strong arms held her as he kissed her more deeply.

He lifted his head but still rested his hand on her cheek. She reached up and pulled a strand of his hair off his forehead, wishing the moment could last forever. She felt light-headed, dizzy even.

Slowly, they separated from each other and came

back to reality. Willis's men were still making their way up the mountain. Willis himself was on his way to blow up a bank. They couldn't stay here forever.

Zane pushed himself to his feet and held out a hand to her. He glanced down the mountain, as well.

"We're not that far from the summit. Let's try to pick up the pace." He touched her face, leaned in and kissed her forehead.

Still a bit wobbly from the first kiss, she nodded. He took off at a jog. She fell in beside him. Her whole body ached from the running they'd done. She longed for water and sleep and warmth. Somehow, though, she found herself realizing that where she really wanted to be was with Zane in whatever conditions. As long as he was by her side, she could endure anything. The top of the mountain came into view. Zane slowed and pulled out the GPS device. He turned a half circle then looked down at the device again.

Down below was the river, and beyond that, the lights of Fort Madison twinkled. The sight renewed her hope. Even after they got across the river, it would be a long hard run through the night to get to town. But still, if Jordan had been telling them the truth about the paragliders, they might make it in time to stop Willis.

She saw no lights or fires along this part of the river that indicated any of Willis's men were waiting for them. That, too, lifted her spirits.

Zane continued to walk around and check their GPS position.

The men were closing in on them from down below. If Jordan had lied, they'd be trapped.

Zane disappeared into the trees. Heather held her

breath and followed, finding Zane on the ground, pushing tree boughs and rocks out of the way.

Heather hurried over and dropped on her knees to help him. All she felt beneath her fingers was dirt.

Zane turned slightly. "Maybe we're just off by a bit."

Tension coiled around Heather's torso. Not just over the fear that Jordan had set them up and that the realization would break Zane's heart, but also at the idea that they were losing precious time while the men who wanted them dead were closing in on them.

Zane picked up a rock and started to tap the ground, listening for a metallic sound. The pounding sounded like a funeral dirge to Heather.

She hit the ground with a rock, too. Though she felt hope slipping away, for Zane's sake, she wouldn't give up either.

And then she heard a metallic echo and joy burst through her. "Here."

Zack shifted toward her, working quickly to clear away the dirt and leaves. The lid creaked when he opened it up, and he pulled out two huge canvas bundles.

"We're going to have to lay them out and attach the harnesses. I'll get started. You go check and see where those men are."

She sprinted out from the shelter of the trees and ran along the ridgeline. The men were jogging up the trail. At the pace they were going, she and Zane had five or maybe ten minutes before they were here. She ran back to where Zane had assembled one of the paragliders and gave her report. He nodded, but kept his focus on the gear in front of him.

"They come together fast," he said. "Help me with the second one."

The paraglider was a nylon wing attached to a harness.

Zane's face was red from exertion. "You ever done anything like this before?"

She nodded. "Once when I was a teenager."

"Go to that high point, get a running start, wait for the wind to lift your parachute. When you come to the edge, take off. The wind will lift you up." He pointed to two strings that came out of either side of the wing. "You steer with these." He picked up one of the paragliders. "Grab yours. I'll help you lay out the parachute."

They hurried out to the high point on the summit where the wind was more intense. Willis's men had just reached the top and were headed in their direction. Her heart raced. Zane saw them, too.

"Let me get you strapped in. Remember, no hesitation once your parachute is up. Take off right away." He kissed her. "I'll fight these guys off and then follow after you if I can. If I don't make it, the way into town will be clear. You need to get down there and warn them."

The thought of losing Zane sent a wave of panic through her but she nodded. This was what had to be done. Once she was strapped into the harness, she grabbed the controls and took in a breath.

"Let me get your leg straps." Zane leaned over and buckled her in. He glanced over his shoulder. The men were within a hundred yards. "Get going."

Zane took several shots at the trio of men. One of them fell to the ground, but the other two kept coming.

She willed herself to look away, shifted focus to the steep incline and took off running, gaining speed. She could see the edge of the cliff. The two men took shots at Zane who scrambled for cover and fired back. In the hurry to get airborne, she'd set her gun down and forgotten it.

Her feet disconnected with the earth. The wind caught the parachute and jerked her skyward. When she glanced backward, she saw that Zane was in a hand-to-hand battle with one of the men.

A current caught her parachute and she drifted even higher. She could see the river down below. Her heart raced at the thought of falling in the freezing water. The weight of the paraglider would drown her. She had to get across.

The wind pushed her down. She steered toward the narrowest part of the river as she lost altitude. She was low enough that she could see the black, cold rapids of the river.

Her feet skimmed the water as she dipped even lower. But she was nearly across. She only needed a little more momentum to reach the other side.

Please God. Help me.

A gust of wind pushed her the remaining distance, landing her on the rocky shore. She unclipped herself from the harness and turned back around, searching the sky for Zane's paraglider.

He had to make it. He just had to.

She tilted her head, gaze darting everywhere. No sign of Zane.

Every minute was precious. How long should she wait before she gave up on Zane and made the final trek into town on her own?

* * *

Zane landed a blow to the last man standing. The other two had been put out of commission with gunshot wounds. He'd managed to get the gun away from the third man. This man, though, fought like a trained fighter, the Bruce Lee of the mountains. Zane could feel himself tiring.

He was grateful that Heather had been able to take off. Even if he died up here, at least she would survive—and there was still a chance they could prevent that bomb from being used.

Bruce slammed a fist into Zane's jaw, and his vision filled with white dots. Zane fought to maintain focus, to not give in to the pain. Bruce came at him again. Zane blocked the shot aimed at his head and punched the other man hard in the stomach so he doubled over. Then Zane landed a blow to his opponent's back, which sent Bruce to his knees. That wouldn't be enough to keep him down long enough for Zane to strap himself into the harness, though. Zane pulled his pistol out and hit the man on the side of the head so he collapsed on his belly.

Zane sprinted up toward where he'd left the paraglider and strapped in. One of the other men—seriously but not fatally wounded from Zane's gunshots—struggled to his feet.

Zane had only precious seconds. When the wind lifted his parachute, he ran down the hill even as the man closed in on him. His feet came to the edge of the cliff. The man reached out to grab him just as his feet separated from the earth. A gunshot broke through the silence of the forest. When he looked up, he saw a small tear in the wing.

Down below, he could see the bright lime and hot
pink of Heather's paraglider. She'd made it. He saw no
sign of her and wondered if she had chosen to head into
town on her own when he'd been delayed. The choice
would have been a prudent one.

The wind fluttered the nylon fabric of his parachute.
He worked the levers to maintain altitude, hoping to
catch another gust of wind. If he dipped down too soon
he'd land in the cold water or be forced to land on the
wrong side of the river.

He continued to study the landscape below, hoping
to catch a glimpse of Heather. Except for those pink
gloves, she was dressed head to toe in camo, so it would
be easy enough for her to blend into her surroundings.

He shifted his weight to one side, steering to land
close to where Heather had. A current lifted him up
and then slammed him down even lower. Steering became a challenge as one wing remained lower than
the other despite his shifting to balance his weight
evenly. He angled his head to examine the parachute.
The wind had torn the gash from the bullet, making
the tear even larger.

He dropped altitude as he drifted over the river. The
mumbling roar of the dark cold waves pressed on his
ears. He lifted his feet to avoid getting them wet. The
shore was twenty feet away. One side of the wing remained higher than the other as he prepared to land.
His feet touched the rocky shore but then he was lifted
up again. Momentum forced him to run for some distance before he could stop and click out of his harness.

He turned in a full circle, still hoping to see Heather.
He called her name, softly at first and then louder. Half
a dozen crows fluttered in the trees and took flight,

but Heather didn't answer him. He had to assume that she'd taken off down the trail…or that a squad of Willis's men had been warned by their attackers from the top of the mountain via radio, and Heather had been taken captive or worse.

With no way to know where she was, or if she was even still alive, there was nothing he could do to search for her. And there was still the bank to be protected. The lights of Fort Madison shone down below over several hills and forested areas. He'd have to run all night if he had any hope of getting to town before Willis and his men did. Because of where he'd crossed at the river, he'd be coming into the east side of town instead of the west where the sheriff's office was.

He said a prayer that Heather was all right and on the same path as he was, then he took off jogging.

He'd paced off several miles and rounded a curve when he saw motion up ahead. Heather's porcelain skin shone in the moonlight. He called out to her, and she stopped and turned.

She ran toward him, wrapping her arms around his neck and drawing him close. Her voice filled with exuberance. "I thought you didn't make it." She pulled back to gaze into his eyes.

"'Course I made it." The affection in her voice and the warmth in her eyes made him wish they could stay in the moment forever, but that wasn't possible. "We need to keep moving. We don't have much time."

She nodded. Her arms fell away from his shoulders. She brushed her hand over his cheek, then whirled around and took off running. He fell in behind her. They ran through the night, slowing down from time to time but never stopping.

He was dizzy with fatigue but he pushed himself to keep going.

The sun peeked up over the horizon when they were a few miles from the edge of town.

Zane turned his head as a noise to the east of him caught his attention. ATVs headed in their direction. Heather stuttered in her step.

Of course the pursuers at the top of the mountain had sent word that he and Heather had made it across the river.

Zane scanned the landscape looking for possibilities for escape as the ATVs and armed men bore down on them.

EIGHTEEN

A tightness suctioned around Heather's chest when she saw the lights of the ATVs rapidly approaching. She and Zane were so close to town, so close to being able to stop Willis and his path of destruction.

Zane tugged on her arm and pointed at a cluster of trees that led them off the path.

It was the only choice they had. One of the ATVs switched on a huge searchlight just as they dived into the thick of the forest. With the trees so close together, the men would be forced to search for them on foot.

Zane pulled her deeper into the brush. They were moving away from town instead of toward it, losing ground. How long would they be delayed? Would they be able to get away at all?

The ATVs' engine noise stopped abruptly. That meant the men were at the edge of the forest.

Heather heard a barked command and then a searchlight flooded through the trees. They'd be spotted if they kept running. There were no tall trees to hide in either.

Both of them hurried toward separate hiding places.

Heather slipped in under the thick boughs of a juniper and Zane disappeared behind a bush.

Heather's breath caught as a charge of panic skittered across her nerves.

The bush did not completely hide Zane. She could see his feet.

The voice of the men grew louder and more intense. The searchlight swept the forest floor.

There was no way she could signal Zane without giving herself away. She held her breath.

Zane must have done a final check because he pulled his feet out of view just as the searchers stepped into the clearing.

From her vantage point with her cheek pressed against the ground, Heather caught only glimpses of the men and heard only pieces of their conversation. A pair split off and headed into a different part of the forest. One of those men held the searchlight.

The other two walked in circles close to them, returning twice to where she and Zane were hidden. Her throat went tight with fear.

The men were right next to her, talking in hushed tones. She could see their worn-out combat boots.

She prayed that they wouldn't look too closely under the brush and trees.

"They've got to be hiding. No one runs that fast."

She dared not move or even breathe. The men were so close she could reach out and touch their feet.

"Look around. They've got to be here somewhere." A flashlight clicked on above her.

The light swept over her, but the man did not spot her.

She heard noises from where Zane had hidden.

"There's one of them," the pursuer shouted as he ran away from her. The other followed.

Zane had created a diversion to save her. She hoped he would be able to get away.

Once the men left the area, she slipped out from underneath the juniper and ran toward another bush for cover. She could hear the men shouting at each other, getting farther away from her but closer to Zane.

Please, God, don't let him get caught.

Their voices died away.

She ran from one bush to another, making her way back toward the path they'd been on.

"Heather."

A whisper rose up from off to the side of her. Zane lifted his head above the bush and then ducked back down.

She listened for a moment, not hearing any of the men. She darted toward where Zane was hiding.

He touched her arm lightly. "We have to hurry. I'm sure they will backtrack like I did in a few minutes."

Zane sprinted toward the trail just as the voices rose up behind them.

The men had left their ATVs at the edge of the forest but there were no keys to allow Heather and Zane to take one. They'd have to keep running. Zane hurried down the hill toward town, sticking to the thick brush where the ATVs would have a hard time following.

They ran hard and fast as the sun rose up over the horizon. Behind them, they could hear the ATVs revving up.

It was a struggle to keep moving, but Heather reminded herself that her life depended on it. The lights of the town still looked so far away.

Both of them alerted to noise off to the side, someone coming through the brush at a high rate of speed. They kept running until a braying noise filled the air.

Both of them stopped short as Clarence stepped through the brush. He must have made it across the river after the bridge collapsed. The animal raised and lowered his head, sniggering, then lifted his muzzle and showed his teeth. He looked a little beat up with some scratches on his neck and legs. The mule was thinner but he'd clearly found enough to eat to survive for the past few days.

Heather shook her head as relief spread through her. "I think I love that guy."

Clarence tromped toward them. He still had his bridle, though the saddle must have come loose. But it shouldn't be a problem to ride him bareback, and they'd be able to get into town that much faster.

Zane cupped his hands so Heather could use them as a stirrup to get on Clarence's back. Once she was settled and had the reins in her hands, she angled her foot and held out her hand so Zane could get on behind her.

He pressed in close to her, his breath warming her neck. She spurred Clarence into a trot. As the path evened out, Clarence increased his speed to a gallop.

She could see the edge of town up ahead and hear the ATVs buzzing behind them. They'd be safe once they got into town around people. Clarence trotted past the private residences on the edge of town. Main Street was mostly empty at this early hour.

They dismounted Clarence and headed up the street toward the sheriff's office. The pursuers on the ATVs rolled onto Main Street, as well.

The bank probably wasn't open yet. They didn't

know if the plan was to wait until the bank opened or hit it before. Zane had told her that Willis usually robbed banks when they were closed—but perhaps the delay in getting the bomb ready this time meant that the time frame had changed. There was no way to know for sure.

Fort Madison was a small town of a few hundred people; mostly it was a place for outfitters and fly-fishing guides to meet their clients. No businesses were open at this hour.

Heather felt a tightening in her chest as they turned on the side street where the sheriff's office was.

Zane held a hand out, signaling her to halt. He crouched low and approached the office. All the shades were drawn. He signaled her to follow him around to the other side. Both the sheriff's cars were parked out back.

Zane crouched beneath a window and tried to see under the pulled blind.

Heather glanced around, spotting two parked ATVs.

Zane whispered in her ear. "There's only a sheriff and a deputy for law enforcement for the whole county. It looks like Willis's men might be holding them hostage so they can't respond to the robbery."

Heather's spirits sank. "There's no time to get them free, is there?" It was up to them to stop the madness.

Zane nodded. "We've gotta get down to that bank and fast."

Resolve settled in her belly like a heavy rock as she fought to find the strength and courage to engage in one more battle.

The back door to the sheriff's office burst open. She recognized one of Willis's men, who sprinted toward them as they took off running. Zane led her through alleys and backstreets. She doubted their pursuer would call attention to himself on this quiet morning by shooting at them.

Zane pulled her into the lobby of an abandoned hotel as the man ran past. He pressed against the wall and peered out the dusty window.

"He's coming back," said Zane. He pulled her toward the high check-in counter just as the door creaked open. Footsteps pounded on the wooden floor.

Heather breathed in dust. She pressed her nostrils together to suppress a sneeze. Her heart raced. Zane's back stiffened. The footsteps continued to pound around the lobby, then they heard the squeak of footsteps on the stairs. The noise stopped all together.

Heather held her nose tight. Her eyes watered. The footsteps stomped back toward them. The man came around the counter.

Zane leaped to his feet and charged at the man. The two men punched each other. Zane was backed up to a wall.

Heather searched the area for something to use as a weapon. She picked up a metal pipe and slammed it against the assailant's shoulder. The man turned and lunged at her.

Zane spun him around and hit him hard enough across the jaw that the man fell to the floor.

They ran toward the front of the hotel. Halfway through the revolving door, Zane turned around and swung back into the lobby.

"Men out there, too," he said.

The man on the hotel floor was incapacitated but conscious. Zane hurried past him up the stairs. Heather followed, not sure what Zane had in mind, but he knew this town better than she did.

He led her through the dusty upstairs hallway toward a back room, where he swung open a window. "Climb down." Zane ran over to the door and clicked the lock, probably to keep the man downstairs from getting to them.

Heather stuck her head out the window. There was no fire escape, only a metal trellis. Her heart squeezed tight as she stared at the ground below.

"It's just a matter of minutes before they come around to the back of the hotel," said Zane.

She nodded and slipped out the window. Though it didn't look overly strong, it was only two stories.

The man from downstairs was slamming his body against the locked door, trying to break it down.

She shoved her leg through the window and positioned her foot on the trellis. It creaked as she climbed down it. Zane slipped out of the window before she reached the bottom. He started to climb down. One of the bolts that held the trellis to the brick wall of the hotel broke loose and clattered to the pavement down below.

Heather jumped the remaining feet to the concrete just as the trellis swung away from the wall it was fastened to. More bolts pulled loose and fell out as Zane climbed down.

Heather took in a sharp breath. Men rushed around the side of the hotel. The same men who had been chasing them in the forest. Zane still had fifteen feet to go before he could jump. Another bolt disconnected as the metal trellis swayed.

"Run," Zane shouted at her while he kept descending.

She took off just as Zane jumped the remaining distance to the ground. He dashed after her, with their pursuers hot on their heels.

She had no idea where the bank was. She worked her way back to Main Street, glancing over her shoulder to see if she could spot Zane. No one was there.

She reached Main Street and scanned the dark shops, not seeing the bank. She ran in what she assumed was the direction of the bank, the way they'd been going before.

Zane joined her from a side street. He sprinted in front of her, racing past a garage with dark windows. She saw the bank up ahead, a newer building with a large parking lot.

None of Willis's men stood outside to block their way, so Zane and Heather rushed toward the bank entrance. The bank had large glass doors. Inside a man in a suit ran by in a hurry. She could see a bank teller whose face was stricken with fear and a security guard lying on the floor.

Zane reached out for the door handle. It was locked.

Heather couldn't see any of Willis's men inside. Yet it was clear they'd been there and had disabled the security guard and locked the building.

Zane pounded on the glass, trying to get the bank teller's attention. She continued to stare at the fallen bank guard.

He took a step back. "Maybe there's an employees-only entrance that's open."

Her heartbeat thudded in her ears. "Willis's men must be in there even if we can't see them."

Everything seemed to be moving in slow motion. Even Zane's response felt delayed. "I know that."

The men who had been chasing them entered the parking lot but remained at the edge of the pavement.

A stillness seemed to fall on them like a heavy blanket. Heather heard a percussive boom followed by an echo. Glass shattered around her as she felt herself being lifted up and thrown back by a hot, forceful wind.

NINETEEN

Zane felt his body turning in space. The heat and light of the explosion surrounded him. He couldn't tell up from down until his back hit the hard pavement of the parking lot. He slid for several feet. He registered pain in his back. Glass showered down on him and he lifted his arm over his face to shield himself. He couldn't hear anything, though he saw men running inside the bank and knew that alarms must be going off. But no one would answer the alarms. The sheriff was being held captive. There was no other law in Fort Madison. Even the volunteer fire department would be slow in arriving. He had to find a way to keep Willis from getting away with this.

The thermite bomb wouldn't have caused such an explosion. Willis must have had an additional bomb designed to do damage and maybe even hurt people. He glanced across the street. With the bomb primed to do that much damage, the bomber wouldn't have wanted to set it off manually, so it must have been remotely detonated. Was the triggerman hovering close by?

Zane scanned the area for anyone looking suspicious, but instead spotted Heather laying on her back and not moving. He pushed himself to his feet, stared at his bloody palms then he ran toward her prone body. He turned her over. She opened her eyes and said something to him, but he couldn't hear it.

He shook his head, still trying to orient himself. The men who had been in the parking lot ran into the bank through the broken glass of the doors. He saw then that the steel vault had been blown completely open as the men drilled the safety deposit boxes and emptied the contents. They seemed to be selective in the boxes they chose, consulting the man in the suit who was being held at gunpoint.

He didn't see Willis anywhere. He must be waiting outside of town for the loot to be brought to him.

He helped Heather to her feet. Glass cascaded off her clothes and hair. She had a gash across her forehead. He knew that she continued to shout at him from the way her mouth moved, but it felt like he had cotton balls in his ears.

Two of the men came out of the bank, each holding a small duffel. One of the men was Jordan. Jordan jumped in a Jeep and took off out of the parking lot, not even noticing Zane and Heather.

Zane could not process what he was seeing. What was Jordan doing?

Heather continued to shout at him and point at a place outside of town toward the foothills. Her expression was frantic. She placed her face very close to his and mouthed the words again as she gripped his upper arm.

Finally, his ears cleared out. Her voice seemed to echo and sound far away at the same time.

"I saw a helicopter land over there. It's the direction Jordan is driving."

It stung to hear Jordan's name. Why had Jordan helped them just to participate in the robbery in the end? Had Jordan simply tried to save his brother while his loyalty remained with Willis? Zane collected his thoughts and pushed down the confusion that threatened to overtake him. "That must be Willis's escape plan to get out of here with the loot."

"We need to get over there and stop them."

The robbers had already disappeared, probably headed back up to the high country or some new hiding place before they could get caught. Maybe Willis had set up some sort of rendezvous point.

Zane glanced around. They needed a car, and fast. There were several parked in the corner of the lot that remained undamaged by the blast. Zane ran into the bank, his boots treading over broken glass.

The bank teller was on the phone touching her hands to her face and talking rapidly. The man in the suit who must be the bank manager was bent over the security guard.

Zane stepped over the debris. The room still hadn't cleared of the dust. "Are those your cars out there? I need keys. I can catch the guy who did this."

The bank manager pulled keys from his pocket and tossed them to Zane. "It's the silver Honda." He stared down at the prone security guard, his voice filled with concern. "The ambulance has to drive all the way from Badger. It will take an hour." He shook his head. "Why didn't Sheriff Smith come?"

Zane didn't have time to answer the man's questions. "Can I have his gun?"

Hopefully the volunteer fire department would get here faster to help.

The bank manager was so dazed he wasn't even questioning who Zane was. He pulled the gun from the unconscious security guard's holster and slid it across the floor. Zane picked up the gun.

Zane stepped over the broken glass and out into the early-morning sun. Heather waited for him. He handed her the gun. "I saw you didn't have yours." He pointed toward the car. "Over there."

They both ran to the car. He unlocked it, and she got into the passenger side. He knew the road that would take them up to where the helicopter had landed. He shifted into Reverse and hit the accelerator, burning rubber as he left the parking lot and zoomed out onto the two lane road.

Heather gripped the armrest. Zane pushed the car to go faster up the country road. Anxiety encroached on his thoughts. He didn't want to have a showdown with his brother. But he might not have a choice.

They rounded a curve. He could see the bright red of the helicopter in the brush up ahead. He slowed the car and pulled off to the side. "Best if we approach on foot. You stay back."

"You might need my help," she said.

They didn't have time to argue. He clicked open the door. "Use your best judgment." They'd been through enough that he knew she'd be smart about what she did. She knew when to take a risk and when to refrain. And there was no one he trusted more at his back.

Zane bent over and hurried along the road. Heather followed but at a distance. The helicopter came into view again. He dived to the ground and watched. Only one man paced beside the chopper, someone he didn't recognize. He must be the pilot.

The Jeep was parked to one side, but Jordan and Willis were nowhere in sight. What was going on here?

Zane craned his neck and noticed that Heather was no longer behind him. She must have slipped into the brush to have a different vantage point. Zane moved in a little closer. Now was his chance to take the pilot out while Jordan and Willis weren't around.

As soon as the pilot turned his back, Zane pulled the gun and sprinted. He hit the pilot on the side of the head. Zane caught him and laid him on the ground. He saw Heather now on the other side of the chopper, hiding in the grass. The two bags from the bank were already loaded on the chopper.

He scanned the foothills. Jordan and Willis had left to go get something—maybe more loot, such as the profits from the marijuana sales or some other theft they'd committed.

Heather continued to hide in the brush. Zane crouched by the chopper and scanned the hills all around him.

Cold metal touched the back of his head.

Willis's voice cut him to the core. "I don't think you're going anywhere today."

Heather watched in horror as Willis put a gun to Zane's head. Jordan stood behind Willis, holding a metal box that was covered in dirt.

"The pilot is out," said Jordan.

"I see that. Revive him." Willis kept his gun on Zane's head as he reached down, pulled Zane's gun out of his waistband and tossed it aside.

Heather's heart pounded against her rib cage as she gripped the gun. She wasn't that good a shot. If she missed, Willis would shoot Zane right away. She needed to be closer.

Jordan disappeared inside the chopper and then poked his head out and walked over to the pilot. What was Jordan up to? Was he really just going to let Willis shoot Zane after he'd helped get them safe across the river? She could only guess that a split loyalty had driven Jordan's choices. The younger brother had probably never imagined it coming down to this.

She had to act quickly. She moved in closer trying to line up a better shot.

Jordan worked to revive the helicopter pilot by slapping his cheeks.

"March away from the chopper over to those trees," Willis commanded Zane. "All of this could have been yours if you had stuck with me. Now your brother gets the lion's share."

Jordan stopped and looked up, but then returned to reviving the pilot.

Heather scrambled out and lifted the gun. She stood on her feet, aimed the sights toward Willis and pulled the trigger.

Willis stopped short and spun around. She didn't know if she'd hit him or not. He raised his handgun at Heather. Jordan jumped up, placing himself between Heather and Willis. Willis either didn't notice or didn't care as he pulled the trigger. Jordan crumpled to the ground.

Heather screamed.

She dived down to help Jordan as another shot was fired. Jordan opened his eyes and smiled at her. She reached up to his neck where she still felt a pulse, but blood seeped out of his side onto the ground.

When she looked up, Zane had taken advantage of Willis's momentary distraction to jump him from behind. Willis's gun was in the brush and the two men wrestled in hand-to-hand combat.

Zane was going to have to deal with Willis without her help. She kept her focus on Jordan, who needed medical attention fast. She said his name several times before he focused on her.

"You've been hit," she said.

Jordan gripped her arm as he struggled to get the words out. "I was going to stop him. I was the only one who could. Just had to wait for the right moment. So sorry it had to go this far. Never had the chance. Willis must have sensed something."

So that had been the plan.

"I'm going to get you to a hospital." She laid him down gently on the ground.

"Sorry for what I did to you." Jordan's voice was weak as he turned his head to one side and closed his eyes.

Heather ran over to the parked Jeep. The keys were still in the ignition. She fired up the engine and drove it to where Jordan lay prone and bleeding out.

The helicopter pilot had just started to stir. She remembered what the bank manager had said about an ambulance having to come from far away. Jordan didn't have that kind of time.

She ran over to the pilot, hoping and praying that he had no loyalty to Willis, that he was just hired help. He was blinking rapidly and rubbing the side of his head, but he didn't seem hostile, just looked up at her with a puzzled expression when she approached.

"You have to take me and this man to the hospital in Badger."

"That's not what I was hired to do."

She gripped his collar and drew him close to her face. "Your orders have changed. Help me lift this man on that chopper." She spoke in a tone that meant business, hoping that would keep the pilot from arguing.

The pilot threw up his hands. "I don't care as long as I get paid."

Jordan moaned as they lifted him into the backseat. Heather crawled in beside him to keep pressure on his wound.

The blades of the chopper sliced through the air as the pilot fired up the engine. She couldn't see Zane or Willis anywhere. Their hand-to-hand battle must have taken them into the trees.

The helicopter lifted off. She wrapped her arms around Jordan and whispered in his ear, "It's going to be all right."

"Zane?"

"He's going to be okay, too. You did good."

As she searched the ground down below and saw nothing, she prayed she was telling the truth on both counts.

TWENTY

Zane could feel years of pent-up rage smoldering and growing hotter as he lifted his hand to hit Willis across the jaw. Willis blocked his punch. Willis had extensive martial arts training, and though he was older than Zane, his skill level was much higher. Not to mention Zane was exhausted after hard days of being chased through the mountains with limited supplies and little rest.

Zane spent way more time dodging blows than he did delivering them as Willis backed him into the high brush.

He could hear the helicopter taking off. He'd caught a glimpse of Heather and the pilot loading Jordan into the backseat. Jordan had stepped between Heather and Willis's bullet. Why he'd played along with Willis's schemes to this point was anyone's guess, but it was clear now where his loyalty lay. He prayed his brother would be all right.

For Jordan and for all the young men who'd been led astray, he wanted Willis to go to jail. Willis swung his leg for a high kick. Zane ducked out of the way as rage boiled over inside him. He lifted his hand to land a blow, but Willis reached up to block it. He switched to the other arm and then double punched Willis. The sudden move caused Willis to take a few steps back.

Zane charged toward him and knocked him to the ground. They rolled until Willis was on top. Willis hit Zane twice across the jaw, first with one fist and then with the other. The blows left Zane stunned and unable to focus. Willis got to his feet and dashed off through the brush.

Zane shook off the dizziness and bolted to his feet. When he came out from the brush, Willis was perched in the Jeep, turning the key in the ignition. The Jeep was backed up and then Willis shifted, lurching forward and then gaining speed on the dirt road to rumble past Zane.

Zane ran to catch up with it, pushing his tired legs to go faster. He jumped in the back of the Jeep. Willis shot over his shoulder without looking. He must have had a gun in the car. The bullet hit the metal sides of the car. The car swerved and Zane was nearly thrown out. He plunged to his knees and inched toward the driver's seat.

Willis placed the pistol on his shoulder again while he kept his eyes on the road. Zane flattened himself as another shot reverberated through the air.

Willis pulled out onto the main road and increased his speed. Zane struggled to get upright as the wind rushed around him. Willis jerked the wheel back and forth in an attempt to throw Zane out.

Zane held on and crawled toward Willis, who held the gun in one hand and drove with the other. That left him without any hand free to protect himself from attack. Zane wrapped his arm around Willis's neck, so

Willis's chin was in the crook of Zane's elbow. Zane squeezed.

Willis slowed down but lifted the gun.

Zane released Willis from the neck lock and lunged for the gun. His hand wrapped around it as the car veered into the other lane and down a bank. The Jeep rolled, landing upside down. Zane was thrown free and impacted with the hard ground as he stared up at the bed of the Jeep. Metal creaked all around him.

Zane flipped over to his stomach and crawled out from underneath the Jeep, grateful that the roll bars had kept him from being crushed. Willis was not in the driver's seat. Zane pushed himself into a sitting position and looked around. Willis was running away up the ditch, favoring one foot. He worked his way up the bank and stuck his thumb out for a ride.

This man was not going to get away, not on Zane's watch. Zane pushed himself to his feet, groaning from the bruising his legs and arms had taken in the crash. All the same, he ran hard to catch up with Willis as a car drew nearer on the road and started to slow down.

Willis ran a little ways down the road. The car came to a stop. Willis reached for the passenger-side door. Zane pumped his legs even harder. Willis got into the car. It rolled into motion just as Zane grabbed the passenger-side door handle and yanked it open.

The driver shouted in protest.

"Go, this man is a lunatic," Willis said as he reached to click his seat belt in place.

Zane grabbed Willis and pulled him out of the car as the surprised driver hit the brakes. Willis rolled down the bank and Zane lunged after him as the images of his brother and the other young men flashed before his eyes. He landed enough blows to Willis's face and stomach to debilitate him.

Zane was out of breath as he stood over Willis, who drew his legs up toward his stomach and struggled for air.

"Is there something I can do?" the driver of the car, a fortysomething man, shouted from the road.

"This is the man who needs to be arrested...not me," Zane called back. "He just robbed the bank and is trying to make a getaway."

The light of understanding came into the man's eyes and he nodded.

"Do you have a cell phone? Please call the sheriff. This man needs to be taken into custody." He doubted the sheriff was still being held hostage.

"Yes, I do." The driver returned to his car.

Zane stood over Willis, ready to subdue him if he decided to fight back or run. He heard sirens in the distance.

Willis caught his breath but remained on the ground with his legs drawn up to his stomach. "Maybe you won this round. But I wasn't at the bank. Your brother was. He'll be the one going to jail...if he makes it."

Zane felt as though a sword had been stabbed through his gut. What would happen to Jordan was still uncertain. He only hoped that Heather had been able to get him medical help fast enough.

Heather sat on the hard plastic chairs of the hospital waiting room. Jordan had been wheeled in for emergency surgery as soon as the chopper had landed. That was over an hour ago. She'd talked to the police in Badger but they didn't know where Zane was.

Her chest felt like it was in a vise being squeezed tighter and tighter. Jordan had risked his life to save hers. She wasn't sure what she would do if he didn't make it. It would tear Zane to pieces, too. Her heart squeezed even tighter. If Zane had made it himself. What if Willis hurt or killed Zane and then got away? She could not bear the idea of the loss and the injustice of it all.

A nurse in scrubs came out into the waiting room. "You're the woman who came in with Jordan Scofield."

Heather jumped to her feet. "Yes."

"His next of kin is not here?"

Heather shook her head. "Um... I'm hoping he'll be here soon."

"I guess I can tell you. Jordan came through the surgery. We were able to stop the bleeding and remove the bullet. He should be waking up shortly."

Heather nodded, not sure what to say.

"As soon as his next of kin gets here, please let us know." The nurse turned on her heels and disappeared around a corner.

Heather sank back down into her seat, feeling numb. Though the news about Jordan had lifted her spirits, anxiety plagued her thoughts. What would she do if Zane didn't make it? She'd thought she'd be on a plane back to California by now, leaving Montana behind her, but that wasn't an option anymore. So much had changed.

Even with all the danger, there was something special about the high country of Montana and something even more special about Zane. She wasn't that crazy about getting on the plane anymore.

She stared up at the television that was on in the

waiting room. A local news story flashed on the screen. She saw a Jeep overturned in a road—Willis's Jeep.

Her heart racing she hurried over to the receptionist. "How do you turn the sound up on that TV?"

The receptionist lifted the remote and pointed it. The sound of the local newscaster filled the room. There were shots of the sheriff's car and Willis being led away in handcuffs, but none of Zane. The female newscaster signed out. "Reporting for KBLK in Fort Madison, this is Elizabeth Tan Creti."

Her spirits sank. What had happened to Zane?

She felt a hand on her shoulder.

"I always was a little bit camera shy."

The sound of Zane's voice filled her with exhilaration. She fell against his chest and he wrapped his arms around her. She took in a breath and relaxed for the first time since she'd gotten on the chopper. Zane had made it.

"Jordan?"

She pulled back and looked up into his eyes glowing with affection. "He's just waking up from the surgery. We can go see him in a bit."

Zane nodded. She reached up and lightly touched the scratch on his face.

"Took quite a bit to get Willis under control."

"But you did it."

He brushed a strand of hair out of her eyes. "We did it."

The word *we* echoed through her brain. They made a pretty good team. She felt pulled in two directions. Her whole life was in California.

The nurse came around the corner. "Jordan is awake. You can see him." She glanced at Zane. "You must be the next of kin. Brother, right? I see the resemblance. He's in room 212."

Zane nodded. He grabbed Heather's hand. "I want you to come with me."

The walk down the long hospital corridor seemed to take forever as they made their way to Jordan's room. What kind of future lay ahead for Jordan? Clearly his loyalty was no longer with Willis, but he had been under the other man's control for so long. Getting free of that kind of brainwashing would take time and hard work.

The two of them stood outside room 212. Heather took in a breath and prayed for a healed relationship between the brothers and clarity on why she was so conflicted about going back to California.

TWENTY-ONE

Heather and Zane stood on the summit where her father had wanted his ashes spread. The landscape took Heather's breath away. From this vantage point, she had almost a 360-degree view of the area. She could see Fort Madison off in the distance and the river winding its way through the valley.

"I see why my father loved this spot," she said.

Zane had kept his word and helped her fulfill her father's last wish, a week later than planned.

Zane stepped closer to her. "He told me he came up here to pray. He said you could see all of God's creation for miles."

Zane had made a sacrifice to take her up here so quickly. Jordan was still in the hospital. He was going to be okay physically. While he would be held accountable for the crimes he had committed over the past several years, the sheriff seemed to think Jordan would receive a light sentence in exchange for testifying against Willis.

Heather walked over to Clarence and pulled the thin wooden box out of his saddlebag. "I suppose I should do what I came to Montana to do in the first place."

The words weighed heavy in the air. So much had happened since the day they'd taken off for the high country. All the assumptions she had made about Zane had been wrong. Everything she thought she knew about her father had been turned upside down.

Zane came and stood beside her. "Did you make your plane reservations for going home?"

"I thought I'd wait. I still have to meet with Dennis Havre."

His tone darkened to bit. "Right, to sell Big Sky Outfitters."

That had been her plan all along—to sell and then get back on an airplane, never to see Montana again. "Yes." She felt a tugging at her heart. What had seemed like the right thing to do a week and a half ago now turned her stomach in knots.

Zane ran his fingers through his hair and shifted his weight from side to side. "I don't have the money to buy Big Sky Outfitters, but maybe we could work out some kind of payment plan? I care more about protecting the legacy of your father's reputation than Dennis does. That has to mean something."

She saw the pain in Zane's eyes. "Of course it does." She had come to respect what he did for a living and to love the high country. She stared down at the box then clicked it open. Her breath caught. There were no ashes inside.

Zane stepped toward her.

Inside the box was a stack of letters addressed to her. She recognized her mother's handwriting where she had written "return to sender."

Tears warmed the corners of her eyes. "He *did* try to have contact with me."

"Whatever your mother's reasons for not wanting you to know him, I want you to understand that he was a changed man by the time he came into my life."

"I know that now because of who you are. Without my father's influence you would have been like one of those young men who chose to believe Willis's lies."

He kissed her forehead. "I'm going to miss you, Heather. Please consider my offer to let me buy Big Sky Outfitters over time."

She gazed at the man in front of her as the mountain breeze whirled around her and the expanse of God's creation was laid out before her. She knew then that she loved him, and loved this place. "I have a better idea. What if we ran it together? Do you think you could teach me how to be a guide?"

He let out a breath as the corners of his mouth turned up and light came into his eyes. "You've already proved to me you have the mettle to survive under the most traumatic of circumstances. I'd be proud to take you on. But I'd like to be more than just business partners."

She tilted her head.

"I'd like you to be my wife." His fingers touched her temple and trailed across her cheeks. The face looking at her was full of love.

Her own heart burst with joy and she knew what her answer was. "Yes, Zane Scofield. I will marry you."

He wrapped an arm around her waist and drew her close. They stared out at the natural beauty that spread out before them. Trees, rivers and mountains, everything her father had loved.

"Do you suppose my father wanted you to guide me to this spot because he thought we might hit it off?"

"I wouldn't put it past him." Zane kissed the top of her head. "He was smart that way."

She stared down at the letters, knowing that she would get to know the man who had brought she and Zane together even better by reading what he had written her.

Heather tilted her head and looked into the eyes of the man she wanted to spend the rest of her life with. He leaned in and kissed her.

* * * * *

WE HOPE YOU ENJOYED
THIS BOOK FROM

LOVE INSPIRED SUSPENSE
INSPIRATIONAL ROMANCE

Courage. Danger. Faith.

Find strength and determination in stories
of faith and love in the face of danger.

6 NEW BOOKS AVAILABLE EVERY MONTH!

SPECIAL EXCERPT FROM

LOVE INSPIRED SUSPENSE
INSPIRATIONAL ROMANCE

A K-9 officer and a forensics specialist must work together to solve a murder and stay alive.

Read on for a sneak preview of
Scene of the Crime *by Sharon Dunn,*
the next book in the True Blue K-9 Unit: Brooklyn series
available September 2020 from Love Inspired Suspense.

Brooklyn K-9 Unit Officer Jackson Davison caught movement out of the corner of his eye: a face in the trees fading out of view. His heart beat a little faster. Was someone watching him? The hairs on the back of Jackson's neck stood at attention as a light breeze brushed his face. Even as he studied the foliage, he felt the weight of a gaze on him. The sound of Smokey's barking brought his mission back into focus.

When he caught up with his partner, the dog was sitting. The signal that he'd found something. "Good boy." Jackson tossed out the toy he carried on his belt for Smokey to play with, his reward for doing his job. The dog whipped the toy back and forth in his mouth.

"Drop," Jackson said. He picked up the toy and patted Smokey on the head. "Sit. Stay."

The body, partially covered by branches, was clothed in neutral colors and would not be easy to spot unless you were looking for it.

He keyed his radio. "Officer Davison here. I've got a body in Prospect Park. Male Caucasian under the age of forty, about two hundred yards in, just southwest of the Brooklyn Botanic Garden."

Dispatch responded, "Ten-four. Help is on the way."

He studied the trees just in time to catch the face again, barely visible, like a fading mist. He was being watched. "Did you see something?" Jackson shouted. "Did you call this in?"

The person turned and ran, disappearing into the thick brush.

Jackson took off in the direction the runner had gone. As his feet pounded the hard earth, another thought occurred to him. Was this the person who had shot the man in the chest? Sometimes criminals hung around to witness the police response to their handiwork.

His attention was drawn to a garbage can just as an object hit the back of his head with intense force. Pain radiated from the base of his skull. He crumpled to the ground and his world went black.

Don't miss
Scene of the Crime *by Sharon Dunn,*
available wherever Love Inspired Suspense books
and ebooks are sold.

LoveInspired.com

*While investigating a series of deaths in the Sonoran
Desert, Border Patrol agent Sam Cross comes face-to-
face with Jolene Nighthawk, the woman he once loved
beyond all reason. Now, as the two join forces to get
justice for the voiceless, old sparks reignite even as
someone wants to make sure their reunion is cut short...*

*Keep reading for a sneak peek at
Carol Ericson's* Buried Secrets...

He grabbed his weapon and his wallet and marched out to his rental
car. When did Border Patrol ever stop working? Especially when an
agent didn't have anything better to do.

He pulled out of the motel parking lot and headed toward the
highway. His headlights glimmered on the wet asphalt, but on either
side of him, the dark desert lurked, keeping its secrets—just like a
woman.

Grunting, he hit the steering wheel with the heel of his hand and
cranked up the radio. Two days back, and the desert had already
weaved its spell on him. He'd come to appreciate its mystical,
magical aura when he lived here, but the memory had receded when
he moved to San Diego. When he left Paradiso, he'd tried to put all
those feelings aside—and failed.

When he saw the mile marker winking at him from the side of
the road, he grabbed his cell phone and squinted at the directions. He
should be seeing the entrance to an access road in about two miles.
A few minutes later, he spotted the gap and turned into it, his tires
kicking up sand and gravel.

His rental protested by shaking and jerking on the unpaved
stretch of road. He gripped the wheel to steady it. "Hold on, baby."

A pair of headlights appeared in the distance, and he blinked. Did mirages show up at night? Who the hell would be out here?

His heart thumped against his chest. Someone up to no good.

As his car approached the vehicle—a truck by the look of it—he slowed to a crawl. The road couldn't accommodate the two of them passing each other. One of them would have to back into the sand, and a truck, probably with four-wheel drive, could do that a lot better than he could in this midsize with its four cylinders.

The truck jerked to a stop and started backing up at an angle. The driver recognized what Sam had already deduced. The truck would have to be the one to make way, but if this dude thought he'd be heading out of here free, clear and anonymous, he didn't realize he'd run headlong into a Border Patrol agent—uniformed or not.

Sam threw his car into Park and left the engine running as he scrambled from the front seat. The driver of the truck revved his engine. Did the guy think he was going to run him over? Take him out in the dead of night?

Sam flipped open his wallet to his ID and badge and rested his other hand on his weapon as he stalked up to the driver's side of the truck.

Holding his badge in front of him and rapping on the hood of the vehicle, he approached the window. "Border Patrol. What's your business out here?"

The window buzzed down, and a pair of luminous dark eyes caught him in their gaze. "Sam? Sam Cross?"

Sam gulped and his heart beat even faster than before as the beam of his flashlight played over the high cheekbones and full lips of the woman he'd loved beyond all reason.

Don't miss
Buried Secrets *by Carol Ericson,*
available September 2020 wherever
Harlequin Intrigue books and ebooks are sold.

Harlequin.com

Love Harlequin romance?

DISCOVER.

Be the first to find out about promotions, news and exclusive content!

f Facebook.com/HarlequinBooks

t Twitter.com/HarlequinBooks

◎ Instagram.com/HarlequinBooks

P Pinterest.com/HarlequinBooks

ReaderService.com

EXPLORE.

Sign up for the Harlequin e-newsletter and download a free book from any series at **TryHarlequin.com**

CONNECT.

Join our Harlequin community to share your thoughts and connect with other romance readers!
Facebook.com/groups/HarlequinConnection

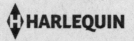

HSOCIAL2020